AN ASTOUNDING MIRACLE.
TWO VICIOUS MURDERS.
A SECRET THAT COULD
CHANGE THE WORLD...

THE
ROSARY
CHRONICLES
BEGIN.

# Closer to God...

Anatoly turned and saw the uniformed guard approaching.

*"Può aiutame?"* he asked, trying to look like a confused tourist.

The guard stayed put, tucked his chin into his chest, and glared. Anatoly pointed to the top of the fence.

*"Che cos'è?"* the guard asked.

The guard's eyes were lifted upward like a martyr's when Anatoly plunged the knife into him. He unbuttoned the man's uniform jacket as he eased the dying man to the roof.

Dressed in his victim's clothes, he would be able to use a more direct way into the Apostolic Palace than he'd originally planned. All he needed now was a place to change and hide the body.

*Some things,* Anatoly thought, *worked out perfectly.*

It boded well for his mission.

# THE THIRD
# REVELATION

✤ The Rosary Chronicles ✤

## RALPH McINERNY

JOVE BOOKS, NEW YORK

**THE BERKLEY PUBLISHING GROUP**
**Published by the Penguin Group**
**Penguin Group (USA) Inc.**
**375 Hudson Street, New York, New York 10014, USA**
Penguin Group (Canada), 90 Eglinton Avenue East, Suite 700, Toronto, Ontario M4P 2Y3, Canada
(a division of Pearson Penguin Canada Inc.)
Penguin Books Ltd., 80 Strand, London WC2R 0RL, England
Penguin Group Ireland, 25 St. Stephen's Green, Dublin 2, Ireland (a division of Penguin Books Ltd.)
Penguin Group (Australia), 250 Camberwell Road, Camberwell, Victoria 3124, Australia
(a division of Pearson Australia Group Pty. Ltd.)
Penguin Books India Pvt. Ltd., 11 Community Centre, Panchsheel Park, New Delhi—110 017, India
Penguin Group (NZ), 67 Apollo Drive, Rosedale, North Shore 0632, New Zealand
(a division of Pearson New Zealand Ltd.)
Penguin Books (South Africa) (Pty.) Ltd., 24 Sturdee Avenue, Rosebank, Johannesburg 2196,
South Africa

Penguin Books Ltd., Registered Offices: 80 Strand, London WC2R 0RL, England

This is a work of fiction. Names, characters, places, and incidents either are the product of the author's imagination or are used fictitiously, and any resemblance to actual persons, living or dead, business establishments, events, or locales is entirely coincidental. The publisher does not have any control over and does not assume any responsibility for author or third-party websites or their content.

THE THIRD REVELATION

A Jove Book / published by arrangement with the author and Tekno Books

PRINTING HISTORY
Jove mass-market edition /March 2009

Copyright © 2009 by Tekno Books.
Cover design by Richard Hasselberger.
Cover image of the Vatican copyright © Wilfried Krecichwost.
Stepback image of Text courtesy of Réunion des musées Nationaux / Art Resource, NY; image of
Couple copyright © Tom Brakefield; image of Antique Dagger copyright © C Squared Studios.
Interior text design by Laura K. Corless.

ISBN: 978-0-515-14592-2

JOVE®
Jove Books are published by The Berkley Publishing Group,
a division of Penguin Group (USA) Inc.,
375 Hudson Street, New York, New York 10014.
JOVE® is a registered trademark of Penguin Group (USA) Inc.
The "J" design is a trademark of Penguin Group (USA) Inc.

PRINTED IN THE UNITED STATES OF AMERICA

10  9  8  7  6  5  4  3  2  1

*In homage to*
*Robert Hugh Benson*

Wherefore we love thee, wherefore we sing to thee,
    We, all we, through the length of our days,
The praise of the lips and the hearts of us bring to thee,
    Thee, oh maiden, most worthy of praise;
For lips and hearts they belong to thee,
    Who to us are as dew to grass and tree.
For the fallen rise and the stricken spring to thee,
    Thee May-hope of our darkened ways!

—GERARD MANLEY HOPKINS, "AD MARIAM"

# PROLOGUE

"Is it you, or must we wait for another?"

He slipped his knife into the knapsack of the girl ahead of him as the line approached the security check at the entrance to Saint Peter's Basilica. She wore her hair in a crew cut, and her shapeless T-shirt could not conceal the ripe body within. Anatoly was counting on the distraction of her breasts to keep the guards' attention off of him.

It worked.

The girl was smiled through the checkpoint without a search of her bag, and Anatoly, too, was waved through, though without a smile. He walked up behind her. She turned in alarm when he opened her knapsack.

"Security," he said, in a reassuring manner. He plucked the knife from the knapsack. "I'll take that."

"Where did that thing come from?" she asked.

"You are free to go," he told her. "Thank you for your cooperation," he said, putting the knife safely back in his pocket.

She walked off, clearly confused.

She was no longer his problem.

He swam through the sea of people, stood in another line, and finally rose to the roof. He hurried along the front of the basilica, behind and below the great statues that looked out on the square and at Rome beyond. When he reached the archway that linked the basilica and the Apostolic Palace, he stopped. A steel fence, the width of the bridgelike top of the archway, barred his way. The rods were two inches in diameter and rose to speared tips.

He looked across at the palace and then at his watch. He must get there within the hour. Everything depended on it.

There was a voice behind him.

*"Signore!"*

He turned.

A uniformed guard. Anatoly beckoned him.

*"Può aiutame?"* Anatoly asked, trying to look like a confused tourist asking for help.

The guard stayed put, tucked his chin into his chest, and glared. Anatoly pointed upward to the top of the fence.

Slowly, the guard came toward him.

*"Che cos'è?"* the guard asked.

The guard's eyes were lifted upward like a martyr's when Anatoly plunged the knife into him. He unbuttoned the guard's uniform jacket as he eased the dying man to the roof, taking his weapon.

By dressing in his victim's clothes, he would now be able to use a more direct way into the Apostolic Palace than he'd originally planned.

All he needed now was a place to change and hide the body.

*Some things,* Anatoly thought, *worked out perfectly.*

It boded well for his mission.

❖

*Would nothing go well today?* Cardinal Maguire thought as he walked onto the roof of the Vatican Library. He glanced at the nearby villa, which was his penthouse home as prefect, then walked to the patio where potted lemon trees and a vast array of flowers and greenery created a living reminder of his native county. He sat, closed his eyes, then opened them in annoyance. He had fled here from another interminable conversation with the Russian ambassador.

Fled, but not before putting both his diplomacy and his charity to the test. The ambassador had persisted, talking on and on.

Maguire had sighed and had said again with as much diplomatic patience as he could muster, "Your Excellency, I am not authorized to accede to your request."

The Russian's flat Slavic face was expressionless, but his recessed eyes seemed to be reading the cardinal's lips rather than listening to what he said.

"Meaning, of course, that what I seek is in the archives, Excellency," the ambassador responded.

They traded titles almost ironically, more a sign of distrust than of respect. "I have not said that," the cardinal replied.

"I can infer as much from your silence. Imagine what mischief such information could cause in the wrong hands."

"There is no danger of that." Especially if the Russian did not manage to get into the archives.

"Ah, you live in the next world, not in this one." The diplomat did not mean it as a compliment.

"Not today, although eventually, I hope to." The line of the cardinal's lips widened and something like dimples appeared on his cheeks.

"Who can authorize you to respond to my request?" The Russian would not listen. Or perhaps he was not used to taking no for an answer.

"The secretary of state," the cardinal offered.

"He sent me to you."

Cardinal Maguire smiled. Ah yes. Such was the Roman way.

"And you send me back to him," the Russian went on, aggrieved.

"Perhaps a private audience with the Holy Father," Maguire suggested.

Silence.

That should have ended the conversation. It was one they'd had twice before, with the same outcome. But this time Chekovsky seemed rooted to his chair. On the previous occasion, the cardinal prefect had turned the ambassador over to Brendan Crowe. The young priest from Maguire's home county had been trained in moral theology. He thus could manage to deceive without actually deceiving.

Why did this Russian have such a fixation with the reports on the long-ago attempted assassination of John Paul II? That pope had died a natural death after a protracted and debilitating illness. The papacy had changed hands in an ordered manner, with appropriate pomp and ceremony. Years earlier, the USSR had given way to Russia. For both their people, it was a different world.

He wondered what the Russian needed. Reassurance that all the bodies had been buried? Of course the KGB had been behind the Turk Ali Agca's attempt on the life of the pope. John Paul's memo on his conversation with his would-be assassin when he visited him in his prison cell made that clear enough. But at this late date, the government that had sponsored the attack was gone, lost in the rush of politics and time. But still the Russian pressed on. What, Maguire wondered, did he think was in those documents?

And why was he so desperate to lay his hands on them?

❖

"Did Agca ever mention accomplices?" Father Crowe asked when Maguire had had him fetched from his office.

"Why do you want to know?"

"Because Agca is still alive. What he said to the pope he could say to anyone. But if he has spoken to others . . ."

"Have you ever looked at the materials?"

Crowe seemed to find the question surprising. But where is there an archivist who is not curious? The CIA and British intelligence had provided the Vatican with their lengthy reports on the assassination attempt. Once, Maguire had found such materials intriguing, but his experience with Chekovsky made the whole matter loathsome.

"So there were others?" Crowe asked.

Maguire displayed his palms. "I am sick to death of the matter."

And so he was. He left Father Crowe and slowly climbed to his rooftop garden, his Garden of Eden. Well, Dante had located it on the top of Mount Purgatory. Relaxed in his chair, he closed his eyes again and this time found the peace he craved. Soon, he sat there napping, surrounded by his greenery.

❖

With the guard's pistol on his hip, and the guard's uniform making him anonymous, Anatoly stood in the Bernini Colonnade as if on duty. He waited for his moment. When the young Swiss Guard stood alone at the door while his companion was occupied answering the questions of a little band of tourists, Anatoly strode toward the entrance, saluted the guard, and continued inside. He projected the flat, calm look of a man doing his usual, boring business, just like the Swiss Guard he passed. His whole back seemed to have become one of those disks that pick up signals from satellites far out in space. But the guard had not even returned his salute, and simply waved him on into the building. Anatoly marched steadily on, reviewing in his head the plan of the palace he had memorized.

He was inside. And he knew just where to go.

Up a staircase worthy of a czar, along a corridor whose walls were lined with Flemish tapestries, he made his way to the office of the Vatican's secretary of state. In the reception area, at a desk that seemed miniature in the huge salon, sat a young priest plinking away at the keyboard of a computer. He looked up at Anatoly, his gaze inquiring, but not wary.

Odd how a uniform chased away thoughts that this was an intrusion.

Which it wasn't.

It was something far more dangerous.

"I have been ordered to check the cardinal's office," Anatoly said.

The priest started to rise.

"Don't trouble yourself," Anatoly said. "It is most likely a nuisance call. This will only take a minute."

It took three minutes.

The Vatican secretary of state sat in his desk chair, resplendent in his cardinal's robes. The chair was turned so that the light from an open window fell on the breviary he was reading. He might have been a painting by Goya—except for the modern leather desk chair. His lips moved in prayer. Like Hamlet before his praying uncle, Anatoly hesitated.

The chair turned and the secretary of state looked up at him. Again, the uniform seemed to be a perfect disguise.

"Yes?"

*The pistol or the knife?* He hesitated just a fraction of a second too long. Hesitation. That was bad.

Doubt appeared in the cardinal's eyes.

*Time to act,* Anatoly thought.

"I've been asked to check your office for possible security violations."

The cardinal sighed, waved permission, and returned his attention to his book.

Anatoly circled the desk, gripped the back of the chair, and pushed it rapidly to the window.

How frail the old man was.

Even as the startled prelate began to struggle in Anatoly's arms, Anatoly lifted him easily from the chair. He ignored the cardinal's outraged glare and threw him out the window. The cardinal was too startled even to scream as he fluttered through the air and formed a broken scarlet flower on the pavement below.

"Where is the cardinal?" the priest from the outer office asked Anatoly upon entering the room.

Anatoly turned to look at the man. "He stepped out."

"Stepped out? That's not possible. I was sitting at my desk. He never went past me." The confused priest looked around the office for his superior.

"Truly, he left the building. But come close, I have something interesting I'd like you to see." Anatoly beckoned the priest to the window. The man, still uncertain, came up beside him. Anatoly pointed down at the pavement. Just as the priest stiffened in horror at what he beheld, Anatoly grabbed his cassock and lifted. A moment later, the priest joined his superior on the pavement below.

Now, Anatoly had to move swiftly.

In an armoire in the corner, he found a plain black cassock and a little round box of Roman collars. The cassock was short, so he rolled up his trousers. He decided against taking the pistol with him. Instead, he hung the uniform and the weapon in the armoire and hurried away, looking at his watch.

*Ahead of schedule,* he thought, and smiled.

⁂

There was no peace to be found in the roof garden today, Maguire thought, even though Chekovsky did not react angrily as he had the time Cardinal Maguire had turned the ambassador over to Brendan Crowe.

"Father Crowe knows as much as I do, Excellency," Maguire had said before leaving the ambassador.

"Or as little," Chekovsky muttered. The Russian's little

eyes seemed to be imagining how a certain cardinal would look in a Treblinka cell. He shuddered with outrage but controlled it. "Thank you, Your Excellency," he said finally.

Maguire left the area. He knew he could trust Crowe to get rid of the Russian.

Chekovsky watched Maguire leave, then turned to Crowe. He studied the younger man for a long minute. Brendan could feel the sting of his anger in the glance.

"Are things ever stolen from the archives, Father?"

It was a strange line of questioning. But Brendan was too well disciplined to let that thought show on his face. He could answer a thousand such questions without ever once letting unnecessary information, or a lie, cross his lips. "Would we admit it if that ever did happen?" he asked.

"I suppose bribery could be effective even here."

"I wouldn't advise it."

"What would you advise?"

"Let sleeping dogs lie."

"We say much the same thing in Russia."

"I know." Crowe rattled off the phrase in Russian. The ambassador's eyes lit up. He studied Crowe closely.

"Is it you, or must we wait for another?"

"Another devil quoting Scripture?"

The Russian gave a slow smile. "You know your New Testament better than that."

"*Are* you waiting for someone?"

The ambassador's flat face became expressionless again. He stood. "I am wasting your time, Father."

Crowe escorted Chekovsky to the elevator. When it arrived, an odd-looking priest emerged from it and hurried past them. Brendan saw the Russian safely into the elevator and out of this level of the building. As the elevator doors closed on the Russian ambassador, Crowe turned around to look for the strange priest. He hadn't recognized him, which was unusual. But there was no sign of the man.

At his desk, Brendan returned to the task that had been interrupted when Maguire fetched him, but he found it hard to concentrate. He sat back, wishing for peace, envying Maguire his little aerie on the roof. Maguire usually found the solace he needed there.

Just as he thought he had his concentration back, a very tall Swiss Guard suddenly burst into the office. The young man's usually cool and calm expression was distraught.

"May I help?" Brendan asked.

"An assassin is loose!"

"What?"

"I tell you, someone is on a rampage. The secretary of state and his assistant have been murdered. I would advise you to leave at once and seek a place of safety."

And then he was gone.

Crowe was on his feet. And then he was running to the stairway that led to the roof.

When he came through the door and onto the roof, he stopped and looked around. For a moment the peacefulness of the place reassured him. And then he saw Maguire, sitting in a chair on the patio he had turned into a garden. He approached his superior cautiously.

"Your Excellency? We need to seek shelter. I've just been told a killer is on the loose."

It seemed a shame to wake the cardinal, but the situation was urgent. He placed his hand on Maguire's shoulder, ready to shake him into consciousness. And then he saw the knife buried in the cardinal's chest.

No blood was visible, revealing its presence only as a damp spot on the red robes.

But the pall of death was unmistakable.

Brendan's first thought was a priestly one. He murmured the formula of absolution over the body of Cardinal Maguire.

Only when he had finished did he take a careful look at the scene. A briefcase lay on its side on the floor by the body, its contents spilled across beautiful tiles. Then he heard the slam of the stairway door.

The killer?

He ran toward the sound, not at all sure what he would do if he found someone. But the stairway door was locked.

He could hear footsteps thundering down the stairs.

He ran across the rooftop to his superior's dead body as he punched numbers on his cell phone.

❖ PART I ❖

# CHAPTER ONE

### ✢ I ✢

**"I'll want to talk to him first."**

When former CIA agent Vincent Traeger arrived in Rome, he avoided both the consulate and the embassy, located on the Via Veneto, and went directly to a restaurant in Trastevere. He was unhappy to be here at all, unhappy to have his peaceful retirement interrupted, and very unhappy about what had brought him here.

He'd been instructed to make contact with the Vatican representative at the restaurant. One of the agency's top field agents for decades, Traeger was used to clandestine meets, but he still hated going in without knowing his target. No name for the Holy See's rep had been given him. Still, it was the function, not the person, that was important. Traeger took an outside table. After a moment, he began slapping a rolled up copy of *Le Figaro* against his leg as he studied the street. A minute later, a man took the other chair at his table.

"*Ça va?*"

"*Comme vous voulez.*"

"Ah, you speak French."

"As little as possible."

"I noticed your newspaper."

Traeger looked directly at the man. Of middle size, hair shot with gray, a meaty nose.

The man made a little sibilant noise, then asked, "What is left when 'Ciao' has a vowel movement?"

"CIA."

The man nodded. "I have a table reserved inside."

"Do you have a name?"

In answer, the stranger who'd approached Traeger took out his wallet and opened it enough to show his Vatican City identity card.

"Llano?"

"Rodriguez. Llano was my mother's name."

They went inside to a table in a secluded corner.

"It is good of your government to lend us your services," Rodriguez said.

Traeger shrugged. Only a handful in Washington knew he was here. But then only a handful knew who he was. He'd spent most of his adult life in deep undercover.

"So, Mr. Rodriguez, what do we do now?" he asked the Vatican rep.

"We find a cunning killer," Rodriguez said softly. "And we stop him."

"And what have you done so far?"

"What we could," the man replied.

And so they discussed the four brutal murders in Vatican City: two cardinals, a priest, and a basilica guard.

"Why isn't the Vatican in an uproar?" Traeger had spent enough time in the Holy See to know that four murders there, and in a single day, would have brought the Vatican to its knees. And media flocking to its gates.

"Only the news about the murder of the guard has been made public," Rodriguez replied. "We've ascribed the other deaths to natural causes and spaced out the funerals."

"I caught some coverage of the secretary of state's funeral. Quite a send-off, the full state ceremony," Traeger said.

"Yes. There is much to be said for a great pontifical funeral. It can cover even a murder with obscuring clouds of incense. Cardinal Maguire was said to have died quietly of heart failure, which was true enough in its way—his heart failed instantly when someone plunged a knife into it. His body was sent home to Ennis for burial. The secretary of state's young

assistant received quieter obsequies a few days later that elic-
ited little curiosity. The basilica guard was declared to be the
victim of a demented tourist—a common enough form of
street crime. The police are seeking him."

"Do you really believe this is the work of some fanatic?"
Traeger asked.

"It is possible. If only one had been killed, perhaps that
might even be true. The secretary of state was a lightning rod,
drawing on himself all the anger of malcontents who would
not want to criticize the Holy Father directly. And the guard's
death was incidental, merely a way to gain entrance to areas
within the Vatican that are off-limits to the public. But the
other deaths make this into something far more sinister."

"Was there only one killer?"

"Certainly only one who participated in these killings. He
killed the guard and stripped him of his uniform. That got him
past the Swiss Guards into the papal palace. He threw the secretary of state out a window and did the same to his assistant, a
young priest. There he left the guard's uniform in an armoire
from which he took a collar and cassock. He was wearing those
when he showed up at the Vatican Library."

"He seems to have known his way around the Holy City
quite well."

"Indeed. Too well. The only living person who saw him is
a priest who worked for the head of the Vatican Library and
Archives."

"For Cardinal Maguire." Traeger considered the sequence
of crimes. Except for the living witness, they were fast, well-
executed, and deadly. Worthy of Traeger himself. But the witness was a mistake.

"They were both from County Clare, the cardinal and Crowe.
I'm told they were close."

"I'll want to talk to him first," Traeger said.

Rodriguez looked away, rubbed the tip of his nose, and again
made that little sibilant noise. "He is not being cooperative."

"Oh?"

"He was at first, but answering the same questions over and
over again has tried his patience."

"I see. I need to know something. You've clearly dug into
this investigation. You're following up on all the leads. Why
did you ask for me?"

This was the important question. Traeger hadn't come all this way to get a crime report. What lay behind these killings? Why did the Vatican think Traeger could help?

Rodriguez took a deep breath. "The Russian ambassador seems somehow linked to what has happened. He had been importuning Cardinal Maguire to release some materials from the Vatican Archives to his government."

"I take it he is asking after my old acquaintance Ali Agca?"

Rodriguez smiled grimly. "Yes. Incessantly."

"That explains what I'm doing here. I worked cleanup on that one. You were sent my report on the assassination attempt, were you not?"

"And the British report."

"Killing four people would not be a good way to get hold of that material."

Rodriguez shrugged.

"Are there other possible explanations than the reports on the attempted assassination? That was a long time ago. Very old news."

"We suspect that these killings may be connected with something even longer ago than the attempt on John Paul's life."

Traeger waited.

"What do you know of Fatima?" Rodriguez asked.

"She was the daughter of the Prophet Mohammed," Traeger said.

Rodriguez smiled. "Wrong Fatima. Think Portugal."

"Nineteen seventeen?" Traeger said, surprised.

Rodriguez was impressed. "Your memory must be a hard drive. Yes, when the Blessed Virgin appeared to three peasant children."

"Are you sure? That seems unlikely. And it isn't my area of expertise."

Rodriguez shrugged. "What little evidence we have seems to point there."

Traeger waited for more information, but the silence stretched between them. Rodriguez did not elaborate.

And Traeger did not pursue it. That possibility would not justify his being involved.

So, silence still hanging between them, both men ate. Traeger relished his soup, his pasta, and his veal, and the hovering waiter kept the wine flowing.

"You are paying for this, aren't you?" Rodriguez smiled when he said it, but that didn't mean he wasn't serious. "The CIA's expense accounts are legendary."

Traeger sighed and got out a charge card with his cover identity on it.

"Just remember, the next one is on you."

⚜

Traeger had spent a lot of time in Rome. He spoke the language. He'd done extensive work with the Vatican at the height of the Cold War and during the Soviet Union's collapse, back in the late seventies and eighties. He was the official author of the agency's secret report on the attempted assassination of Pope John Paul II. He was essentially the CIA's man in Rome, so he had led the team that conducted the investigation into the shooting. And he hadn't liked what he'd turned up. The Russians, as represented by the KGB, had their hands all over that plot, in Traeger's opinion.

Traeger's digging led him to believe that Zilo Vassilev, the Bulgarian military attaché in Rome, had masterminded it. Among the connecting threads that made Agca's assassination attempt unlikely to be a lone-gunman attack was the fact that Agca's shooting of the pope was not his first political assassination. Agca had already killed for political reasons. On February 1, 1979, Agca murdered Abdi Ipekci, editor of a moderate newspaper called *Milliyet* in Istanbul. Agca was then working under the orders of a group called the Grey Wolves, a radical terrorist organization seeking to destabilize Turkey.

Though only Agca was present when the trigger was pulled, the op had the strong scent of state-sponsored terror. Traeger had figured back then that the Russians were worried about what a popular and dynamic pope from Poland and his apparent intention to unravel the Communist Party might do or say. It turned out that they had good reason to worry.

But that was all long ago, in the past. The USSR had imploded, democracy blossomed in the satellite states, and Pope John Paul II lived into old age despite the assassination attempt and died of natural causes. Traeger had left the agency two years ago. These days he gave his full attention to the computer consultant business that had always been his cover, and spent his free time—a novel concept in his world—keeping in shape by playing lots of tennis and golf. After all, he'd just hit fifty when he retired from the CIA. He looked forward to many years of normal living.

Everyone around Traeger had noticed the change.

"You are traveling less," Bea, his secretary, said when he asked her to set up the tickets to Italy. "Is this trip business or pleasure?"

"Both," he said, hoping this would be true.

Bea had been with Traeger longer than it would have been polite to mention. He had often wondered how much she knew of his undercover work for the government. Of course he didn't ask her what she thought.

If she knew anything about his shadow life, it was their little secret.

Where, Traeger wondered, did such devoted women come from?

In the Washington, D.C., area, there is a notorious surplus of women. They arrive fresh and young and ambitious, but the unfavorable ratio of men to women keeps most of them single. Bea was perilously close to fifty, but she must have dismissed all thoughts of marriage years ago. A shame. But then he himself was a monk. Many agents become serial monogamists in D.C.'s happy hunting ground, but Traeger had recoiled at the thought of placing the heavy burden of his work on the innocent shoulders of a spouse. But lately . . . Traeger shook the thought away.

"Traveling less, but enjoying it more," Traeger had said to Bea. He let the impression that he was off to Rome for a lark stand. She sighed.

"It's the one city I long to see."

A bizarre thought popped into Traeger's mind. *Ask her to come along.* The thought seemed more of a joke than a real possibility. Already his mind was full of the task ahead.

He had been approached through the usual channels. Dortmund asked him to lunch in an out-of-the-way place in Alexandria. The agency man's crew cut was now snow white, his eyes full of secrets. Dortmund had been Traeger's chief until he retired.

"Do you read the papers?" Dortmund asked.

"The Vatican guard's murder?"

Dortmund rewarded him with a smile. Almost from the beginning they had been able to read one another's minds. "The Vatican murders."

"Murders?"

Traeger got the real story then; how two cardinals and a priest went down as well as the basilica guard. It was clear that Dortmund sensed a connection to the Ali Agca affair and the attempted assassination of a pope. Neither of them had been satisfied with the report Traeger had written. But neither had they seen enough of a link to justify military action against the real instigators of the plot.

"There must be something else we can pin this to. We know that there's someone else behind it."

"Ali Agca insisted he was working alone," Traeger said.

"Bah."

"I know, I know. The whole mess has to go back to the Russians." But the young Traeger had been unable to do anything but fume.

Dortmund had not needed to spell out his current suspicions to Traeger over lunch in Alexandria. Half a dozen disaffected agents were loose in the world. The Russian president had been in the KGB, but not all his former colleagues had been so upwardly mobile. How could they wean themselves from the intrigue and violence that had always defined their lives? And there would be smoldering resentment at the way their empire had melted away. Dortmund was fearful that one of them was involved in the killings in the Vatican. At that Alexandria luncheon with Traeger, he'd said he wanted his own man in Rome now. Both to help the Vatican put a stop to the trouble and put a lid on the news.

Traeger agreed to go.

※

But the connection between today's murders and yesterday's assassination attempt was fragile indeed. The only reason the Vatican had to regard these recent murders as connected with the assassination attempt on John Paul II was the repeated demands of the Russian ambassador that all documents concerning the Ali Agca affair be turned over to his government.

※

Traeger learned about this small piece of the puzzle from Rodriguez in the restaurant in Trastevere.

"He had visited Maguire that very day," Rodriguez said. "Not an hour before the murder."

"Would the Russians have known of the rooftop villa?"

"Of course. It's no secret. Maguire was proud of the place and liked to show it to people."

"Are you sure the Russian ambassador left the library?"

"Father Crowe put him on the elevator. That was when Crowe got a glimpse of the assassin. The killer came out of the elevator when the doors opened."

"As I said, I'll want to talk to Crowe first."

Rodriguez leaned forward and dropped his voice. "The killer moved fast and freely." A pause. "He might have gotten to the pope."

Traeger nodded.

"Of course security has been increased exponentially," Rodriguez said.

"After the horse has been stolen," Traeger observed.

"What?" Rodriguez did not know the saying.

Traeger spelled it out for him.

"Ah. No doubt you will want to speak to the head of the guard."

"After Crowe. Why did you mention Fatima?"

"The third secret."

"Ah."

The Blessed Virgin Mary had warned at Fatima that the pope would be assassinated. Had She been proved wrong?

"John Paul II always credited Mary with saving his life," Rodriguez said, and the two men fell silent.


❖ II ❖

"It stopped being a game long ago."

Father Brendan Crowe accompanied the body of Cardinal Maguire back to Ireland for burial—a Mass in the cathedral at Ennis with half the bishops in the country crowded into the sanctuary, the primate down from Armagh officiating. Old classmates, former mentors from Maynooth, and cousins galore treated him with that chummy deference the Irish excel at.

"You'll be going back, Brendan?" they would ask.

He was going back. He said it as if pronouncing sentence on himself, but the truth was Ireland seemed foreign to him, prosperous even here in the western counties. How young he had been when they sent him off to study in Rome; what an eternity ago that seemed.

"A dreadful business, Brendan," the primate said in a low voice. He was the only mourner who knew how Maguire had died.

"We have here no lasting city, Your Eminence," he said. The unctuous words were out before he could stop them.

A bow of the head. "No, indeed. At least you do not. When do you return to Rome?"

Did the cardinal imagine for Brendan a clerical future like that of the man they were burying?

"Almost immediately."

"Is your mother still with us?"

"Gone to God, Your Eminence." How trippingly on the tongue such phrases came. Both his parents were dead, and he felt no inclination to linger with his cousins.

"You must keep me informed." Again, the primate's voice had lowered.

Brendan had said he would, and the following day he boarded an Aer Lingus flight to Rome, wondering what he was flying back to. Father John Burke came to Fiumicino to meet his plane, and on the drive into the city Crowe told the younger priest of Maguire's funeral. John Burke, like the mourners in Ennis, thought Maguire had died of natural causes. At the Domus Sanctae Marthae, Burke insisted on carrying Crowe's bag, and they rose in the silent elevator.

"You must be exhausted, Brendan."

"Sit down, sit down. I brought some Jameson's."

He poured them each a dollop and sat back in his chair. It came almost as a surprise to realize how tired he was.

"Did he have a history of heart failure, Brendan?"

Crowe looked at young Father John Burke when he asked the question. John had Irish ancestors, of course, but to Crowe he seemed a generic American. Most of the Irish in the world lived anywhere but in Ireland, but it was difficult for Crowe to think of them as the genuine article.

"He was killed, John."

"What?"

"Stabbed in the chest."

Burke reacted as to a macabre joke, studying Crowe's face.

"But *L'Osservatore Romano* said . . ." He stopped. "My God."

"There were four murders in all that day."

"I don't believe it!"

"Well, it's not an article of faith. Simply a fact."

Crowe felt that he was corrupting youth by divulging this, but there was something faintly distasteful as well as attractive in the American priest's naïveté. Burke was young, but he had been in Rome long enough for disillusion to set in. All those days in Ireland Crowe had been suppressing these terrible facts. Now that he had raised the subject with John Burke, he could hardly just dismiss it. He told his young friend almost all he knew.

"But what is being done?"

"What would you suggest?"

"I simply do not understand why, or how, such things can be kept secret."

"Perhaps they won't be. After all, I'm telling you."

⁂

Crowe made no mention of the talk he'd had with Traeger before he had left for Ireland. That clerical jurist's training stood him in good stead once again when John asked what was being done. An investigation, secret, needless to say, was in the works. And Crowe couldn't wait until it started. He figured that most of the history of the modern world had gone on in secret. If the attempt on the life of a pope had not called forth the real explanation of what had happened back then, it was doubtful that these recent murders would.

"Were you here in the Vatican then?" Traeger had asked him when the attempt on Pope John Paul II came up in their first conversation about the recent rash of murders.

"No. I was a student." How old did Traeger think he was?

"Where?"

"In Rome."

"Ah. Now about the strange priest who came out of the elevator when you saw the Russian ambassador off. How did Chekovsky act when he saw him?"

"I don't think he noticed him."

"What nationality was he?"

"Chekovsky?"

Traeger never smiled. Just waited.

"He wasn't a Turk."

"Why do you say that?"

"That was a later judgment, of course. At the time, he was just a strange priest."

"In the sense that you didn't know him?"

"That, too."

"I suppose what you sensed was that he wasn't a priest at all."

"Perhaps," Crowe conceded.

"You had never seen him before?"

"I said he was a stranger."

Traeger seemed about to correct this, but he let it go. He pointed out that the killer's actions, which had been minutely tracked and timed, indicated that the Vatican was not strange to him.

"The question is, who is the mole?" Traeger mused.

"The mole?"

"His accomplice. Someone in the Vatican must have briefed him. He knew where to go, and he knew his victims would be where they were."

Not precisely true, Traeger's assumption. Any basic travel guidebook sold on the streets of Rome would give a map of the Vatican and its palaces. Anyone might have learned of the layout of the Vatican without an accomplice. It was the fact that his victims had been where they were when he came that justified Traeger's little leap of logic.

"The personnel records here are not terribly informative."

"I've never seen them," Traeger said. "How did you come to work in the Vatican?"

"Cardinal Maguire asked for me."

"You were both from County Clare."

"Yes."

"Had you known him before coming to Rome?"

"No. I was living in the Irish College when he visited there, as he often did."

"Where is that?"

"Near Saint John Lateran."

"Isn't that where Tony Blair stayed when he came to Rome?"

"In one of the cottages on the grounds," Crowe said. "There are several."

Traeger took some papers from a briefcase, then leaned the case against his chair. "Let us go over your colleagues here in the library."

It was an uncomfortable exercise. As Traeger said the names and asked the questions, Brendan wondered if it was possible that any of these priests or laymen had aided the killer. Then he imagined them being interrogated by Traeger about himself. And he remembered Chekovsky's question. *Is it you, or must we wait for another?* He should have told Traeger of that, but he hadn't. Why? In the hope that these questions would end, that interest would die. That Traeger would fly off to another assignment. But Brendan knew that that would not happen anytime soon.

⁂

Traeger's interrogations resumed the day after Brendan returned to Rome.

"We must construct the face of the strange priest," Traeger said.

The method Traeger used on the first attempt was crude. He had a dozen sheets of paper on which portions of a face were drawn. The portions were put together in various ways. Each time, Traeger watched Brendan for any sign of recognition. The face they ended with looked only very vaguely like the strange priest who had come out of the elevator. The face they later constructed by means of the more sophisticated program on Traeger's laptop wasn't much closer.

"Weren't there any fingerprints?" Brendan asked. "On the knife, on the gun found in the armoire, on the windowsill?"

"Oh yes," Traeger said.

"Well?"

"The cooperation we would need to check them has not been forthcoming."

"Russia?" Brendan asked. "Are they stonewalling?" An image of Chekovsky flickered in his memory.

"Yes." From his brusque tone it was clear that Traeger preferred to ask the questions. What a strange task was his. Brendan was almost curious about what led a man into this line of work. Why would a man want to be a secret agent? Traeger was obviously intelligent, and educated. Well read, too. He had known that Somerset Maugham had written a spy novel.

Finally Brendan couldn't stand it any longer. "Why did you become a spy?" he asked.

"Things were simpler then," Traeger said after a long pause. "It was a game played by gentlemen."

"And now?"

"It stopped being a game long ago."

✛

It did not help, as Brendan had half hoped it would, to tell John Burke some of this. When the younger priest began to connect the recent murders to the Fatima apparitions, Brendan suggested they have a beer in the basement bar of the Domus. In the States there are Civil War buffs; in Ireland, those who brood over the Troubles. But interest in Fatima knew no national boundaries. There was Guinness in cans, which Brendan regarded as an abomination. Better Nastro Azzurro, he said, than that.

"My sister is in town," John said. "I'll be seeing her tomorrow. I've told you about Ignatius Hannan."

Crowe smiled. "I want to hear more about your plutocrat countryman."

✛ III ✛

"It's a bit like the Pentagon."

*Is there a more beautiful spot on earth?* Laura Burke asked herself just before she walked out of the courtyard of the Hotel Columbus on the Via della Conciliazione into Roman traffic.

A car zipping along the street running parallel to the Via della Conciliazione nearly flattened her when she stepped off the curb.

*And are there crazier drivers anywhere else in the world?* She felt a powerful and uncharacteristic impulse to give a digital salute to the car. However good it might feel, it wouldn't do a bit of good. And it *would* have been out of character. She and Ray had been sitting in the courtyard of the hotel, near the fountain, reading the *Herald Tribune*, when she looked at her watch and got to her feet.

"I'd better get going, Ray."

"Sure you don't want me to come along?"

She put her hand on Ray's shoulder. "Better not."

He thought about it, then nodded. "Don't forget to ask him."

It took a moment before she understood.

"The paintings," he said.

"Of course."

The noise and traffic on the Via della Conciliazione, and the heat, came as a shocking contrast to the cool and secluded peace of the hotel courtyard from which she had just come. There were taxis, tourist buses, hundreds of pedestrians flowing to and from Saint Peter's Square. Pilgrims come from the four corners of the earth to visit the churches and pray, to feel closer to God here where the Vicar of Christ on earth dwelt in the little city-state familiar to television viewers throughout the world.

She headed toward the piazza that was embraced by the massive Bernini Arcade and the enormous size of the basilica, its massive dome seeming to lift her off her feet, causing her to stop. Jostled by the eager pilgrims, Laura suddenly felt like a hypocrite among them. She had just left her lover at the hotel and was now hurrying to meet her brother, Father John Burke, for lunch at the Domus Sanctae Marthae where he lived, inside the Vatican walls. What would John, a Catholic priest from tip to toe, think of the life she was leading if he knew of it?

No need to wonder. In thoughtful moments she would pass the same judgment on herself.

Calling it love didn't seem to help.

But it had changed her world. For a long, long time, work had been the focus of her life.

Ignatius Hannan, her boss, was a billionaire computer maven. Hannan's net worth could scarcely be calculated, even by one of the computers on which his fortune was based. Laura was called Hannan's "administrative assistant." It was a dream job, as long as you liked late hours, incredible pressure, impossible demands, and being on call 24-7. But she'd always believed it was worth a certain amount of suffering to work for a true genius.

Ray Sinclair, Hannan's right-hand man, had been important to Laura first as a colleague, then as a lover. It didn't change the job. But it changed Laura.

Hannan hadn't even given the growing relationship between

his two closest associates a passing thought. He had other interests. Bigger interests. And neither she nor Ray could get him to think of anything else.

Hannan had dropped out of Boston College in his sophomore year. Already his electronic wizardry and Midas touch had manifested themselves. By the time he was in his midtwenties he had hired Ray, his former classmate, to oversee operations, lest he be robbed by his employees. Hannan himself was more than a match for his competitors. Laura managed his day, made sure his plane was ready at the Manchester airport in New Hampshire so that they could take off at an hour's notice, was in effect his factotum. The pace of the business had seemed to spin the three of them out of reach of the religion in which they had been raised.

Now, in his early thirties, rich beyond the dreams of avarice, Ignatius Hannan had got religion again. He'd returned to the Catholicism of his youth, but this time with an almost obsessive focus. He had become what his enemies called a "ferocious Catholic." He even wanted to change the name of the company from Empedocles to Sedes Sapientiae.

The board had balked.

"What's it mean?" they'd asked Hannan.

"Seat of Wisdom."

Blank looks were rampant around the table. The businessmen in the room hadn't a clue what the words meant, much less why Hannan wanted to use them.

Laura said, "It's one of the titles of the Blessed Virgin Mary."

The members of the board observed a moment of stunned silence. Then they all began talking at once. After the general hubbub had died down, the voice of reason finally got a word in.

Ray said, "Nate, it would cause no end of problems." He began to outline them, from the loss of name recognition to the expense of a campaign to establish the new image, to the difficulty of changing everything in the company from logos to stationery. Long before Ray was through, Hannan put up his hand.

"All right, all right."

He gave up the idea of a name change. He settled for having a replica of the grotto at Lourdes erected behind the administration building.

Ray had once said that Nate was a eunuch for the kingdom of mammon's sake, his ascetic, frantically paced life carrying him from one financial triumph to another. He seemed completely unaware that there were such things as women in the world.

"An occupational hazard," Laura said.

"Oh, I don't know," Ray said. They'd been lovers for two years by then.

At the time, she and Ray had been enjoying a rare respite from the demands of their positions, off to Vermont to see the autumn leaves. They stopped at a small inn for dinner and then decided to stay. Ray went to the desk, and it was only when they went upstairs that she realized he had not taken a separate room for her.

"Okay?" They stood at the door of the room, and suddenly she felt the inevitability of what they were doing. It was as if they had to prove that they were flesh and blood, unlike Hannan. They both knew all the reasons why this should not be happening, but the rules and prohibitions seemed faded and remote, dead as autumn leaves. She took the key and opened the door and they went in.

And so it had started. Perhaps at the beginning she had imagined that it was all a prelude to marriage, but the stolen moments seemed all there was likely to be. What made it acceptable was that the two of them agonized about it, apologizing to one another, the whole affair the better because they felt so bad about it. But mainly neither of them gave any sustained thought to the nature of their relationship. Times together were oases of stolen peace.

The twinkle in his eye now made it clear that, unlike Hannan, he was no ascetic.

"No time for that. I've got too much on my plate to even think about it," Laura went on. "You know, sometimes I feel we're both married to Nate."

"Hey, I'm not that kind of fella."

"You know what I mean."

He knew what she meant. They were, each in their different ways, footnotes to the life of Ignatius Hannan, at his beck and call. They were paid astronomical salaries for the privilege. And it was a privilege. There was something predestined about Nate's success, and the rising tide of his fortune lifted all boats, and none higher than theirs. Nate seemed unaware of their relationship.

"You make me feel guilty," he had said to Laura.

"It's a woman's role."

"No, I mean it. This is no life for a woman."

This was after he returned to the religion of his fathers and decided that business was no career for a woman.

"Read Chesterton. *What's Wrong With the World*," he urged.

"What is?"

"Read the book."

"Are you firing me?"

He looked surprised. "I couldn't get along without you."

"I'll bet you say that to all the girls you can't get along without."

It was as if he had to process a joke in order to recognize it as one. "You're the exception to the rule."

❖

Laura emerged from the colonnade in front of the Libreria Ancora and dashed across the road to the square. The heat was relentless, and the square was a maze of wooden barriers to direct the passage of pilgrims. She looked up at the window from which the Holy Father gave his Angelus address on Sundays at noon, that remote figure in white the symbol of all the moral values she seemed to be flouting.

She hurried to the shade of the Bernini Arcade and followed the great curved walkway bordered by enormous pillars to the point where she could leave it and enter by the gate to the left of the basilica. John had been ordained in Saint Peter's three years before, and Laura had come with her parents for the occasion. As if he had fulfilled his purpose in life, his son a priest, her father died a month after their return to the States. Her mother went into swift decline and was now in a nursing home in a Boston suburb. Nate assumed the expense.

"Think of it as a fringe benefit."

She could have kissed him. John would have insisted on sharing the expense with her, and he couldn't afford it. His Vatican salary was a pittance. He had room and board, but even so. She told Nate how grateful John would be.

"Have him say a Mass for me."

Nate liked the thought that her brother was a priest. Well, she liked it, too, as if it were a kind of insurance policy. That was when she told Nate that her brother could be of help in his grand new project. He'd agreed and sent her off to Rome. She was surprised and unequivocally delighted when Ray said he would accompany her.

"Have you told Nate?"

"He insists on it." He rubbed the tip of his nose. "I told him I wanted to obtain a plenary indulgence."

"You're awful."

"Count on it."

Raised a Catholic herself, Laura had long since felt the ties that bound her to her faith loosening, then slipping away entirely from her daily life. She did not feel as distant from her lost faith as Ray apparently did. Still, the thought of having days with him in Rome was exciting.

Remorse for another fall from grace could wait.

And she wouldn't embarrass her brother with news of her relationship with Ray. Which is why she was coming to this meeting alone.

She approached the gate and received a snappy salute from the Swiss Guard. She told him that she was having lunch at the Domus Sanctae Marthae with Father John Burke. A glance at a list and it was the open sesame. One of the guards walked with her until he could point to the clerical residence in which her brother lived. And then she saw John standing in front of the building, on the lookout for her. He recognized her and she ran to him, throwing her arms around him. In half a minute he stepped back.

"Mustn't give scandal."

"Oh John." Laura laughed at the thought.

"It's a bad idea for a priest to be seen in the arms of a beautiful woman," John said. "Even if she is his sister."

She hooked her arm in his. "Better?" she teased.

"Much better. I'm so glad you're here. Come inside. I can't wait to show you this place."

⸎

When they entered the building, they were on a balcony that overlooked the main floor, which was reached by twin curved staircases to their left and right. Just below was the desk of the concierge. The exterior of the building had not called attention to itself, the better to fit in with its surroundings. From the front entrance one looked across the cobbled street to the vast bulk of San Pietro, a side view seldom seen by tourists. To the left was a little park in which a fountain whispered. Just up the street was a row of gas pumps where official vehicles were fueled. One caught a glimpse of the Vatican Observatory. The building that housed the Pontifical Academies, where John worked, was reached by circling the basilica, climbing a surprisingly steep hill—but after all, the Vatican was one of the seven hills of Rome—going through another park, and there it was.

The Domus Sanctae Marthae had been built by John Paul II as a residence for priests and prelates who work in the Vatican as well as a residence for visiting bishops, far more convenient than the Casa del Clero near the Piazza Navona or one of the hotels. Of course American bishops also had the Villa Stritch. Most of the tables in the dining room were already occupied, and from them came the buzz of conversation. Laura was surprised at the number of bishops.

"And archbishops," John added, leading her to an unoccupied table. "It's a bit like the Pentagon, filled with generals without armies. These men are titular heads of dioceses that are now *in partibus infidelium*. Obsolete, that is."

Food was brought by nuns: pasta, bread. Bottles of white and red wine were already on the table. But first came soup in a large, shallow bowl, ladled out by a cheerful little nun. John told her in Italian that this was his sister. A radiant smile of acknowledgment followed.

"So what do you have, John, a room, an apartment, what?"

"Two rooms, and a bath."

"And you can walk to your office?"

"Yes. Thank God." When he had lived at the Villa Stritch, which was outside the city, and had to drive back and forth through notorious Roman traffic, John had seriously wondered if he wanted to keep his assignment. Of course it was regarded as a plum—almost any Vatican assignment was—the unstated implication being that a man was then on a path that would lead to the episcopacy. But the ordeal by traffic that began and ended his day had cast a pall over his work. He'd thought of it as a penance, a spiritual test. And he wasn't sure he could endure it indefinitely. With the move to the Domus, his life had been enormously simplified and something like serenity settled over him.

"Of course I miss the company at the Villa. It's nice to speak English when you're off duty."

"You don't here?"

"Nope. Italian, mostly, but also German, French, sometimes Latin. Even Polish. It's like the UN." He sat back as the nun removed his bowl. "But what a delightful surprise that you're here."

"One of the perks of my job."

"Instant vacations?"

"Oh, this isn't a vacation. I've come to pick your brain. Hope it's big enough."

"Oh ha." John had gone off to California to study at Thomas Aquinas College in Santa Paula, famous for its great books curriculum topped by theology. It was said that graduates of the college had to marry one another in order to be certain they had an intellectual peer. And many, like John, went on to the priesthood or religious life.

"Seriously," she said.

He refilled her glass with white wine, and his own with red. "The Spanish have a saying. The worst red wine is better than the best white wine." He added, "This isn't the best." It was a *vino da tavola*. "Not that I'm a wine snob. You're not kidding? You came all this way to ask me a question?"

She tasted her wine and found it good. "More than one."

"I don't understand. Couldn't you just search the Internet or ask a local authority?"

"Of course, but my boss likes to go an extra mile. Or, in this case, a few thousand extra miles. To understand it, you'd have to meet Ignatius Hannan."

"And then?"

"You'd understand. Great entrepreneurs are dreamers, romantics. They act on impulse. Later, when they've made their pile, some of them write books describing what they've done as a rational plan, carefully executed. But it's all about gut instinct. Hannan's got it and I don't question it. Twenty-four hours ago I didn't know I'd be here."

"And you got a ticket?"

How to tell him that she and Ray had been sent off in the larger of the company's Learjets? It all sounded impossibly indulgent and luxurious. Because it was. The real coup for Laura had been getting a room at the Hotel Columbus. "The trip was easy," she said.

"How long will you stay?"

"We could fly back tomorrow morning."

"We?"

*Oops*. What John didn't know wouldn't weigh on his spirit. She sipped her wine and said, with a smile, "The company pilot and I."

That was stupid. As if mentioning the colleague with whom she was traveling would immediately suggest something else. And, in this case, the truth of the matter. Sitting there with John in this clerical setting, with his cassock and Roman collar, still looking as young as a seminarian, she was almost filled with panic at the thought that he might learn that she was having an affair with Ray. She wondered if she could bring herself to go to confession. One didn't go to confession to one's brother, of course. In fact, she hadn't been to confession for years. The practice had stopped, unable to compete with the pace of her life. When she stopped going to confession, it seemed that her faith had just slipped away, like sand in a glass. And so it had been with Ray.

"Matthew Arnold," Ray had said. " 'Dover Beach.' "

"Delaware?"

He winced at her feigned illiteracy and began to recite the lines in which Arnold had described the loss of faith as a "melancholy, long, withdrawing roar / Retreating, to the breath / Of the night-wind, down the vast edges drear / And naked shingles of the world."

"Arnold knew that the faith was dying, but he also knew that he and the world would miss it."

"Do you?"

"Of course."

Ray's matter-of-fact assumption that Christianity, which had defined Western culture for two millennia, was dying seemed so odd here in the dining room of the Domus Sanctae Marthae, where she was sitting with her brother the priest, who would doubtless have smiled at such agnosticism. Possibly while recognizing its pervasiveness. The Vatican had to know what it was facing in the modern world.

She leaned toward him.

"John, do you ever wonder if all this," she waved her hand at the room they sat in, and by inference taking in the whole grand and glorious enclave that was Vatican City, "is obsolete?"

"This?" He looked around. "Why, it's hardly twenty years

old. You do realize that this is where the cardinals stayed during the conclave that elected Benedict? If I had lived here then I would have had to give up my rooms to a cardinal until the conclave was over."

She could have hugged him for not understanding. That was the best answer to her question. She found that she wanted her younger brother to go on believing, to say his Mass, recite his breviary, oblivious to the growing indifference out in the world to all his life represented.

The other tables had begun to empty before they were half through with their meal, and priests and bishops began to leave.

"Back to work?"

He smiled. "First, a siesta. It's an Italian necessity."

After they finished eating, they went down a flight to the bar for coffee. She was almost shocked when John lit a cigarette. She shook her head when he offered her one, trying not to show her horror. America might be turning its back on the Catholic faith, but new commandments took the place of the old, chief among them "Thou shalt not smoke."

"So what's the question?" He blew a series of perfect smoke rings. "Do you know that joke of Henny Youngman's? A man says to his lawyer, 'Can I ask you two questions?' and the lawyer says, 'Certainly, what's the second one?' "

"I'll get to the questions soon enough. First, I have to tell you a bit about the recent transformation in Ignatius Hannan."

"Do you call him Ignatius?"

"Nate."

"Sounds like a hillbilly."

"Far from it. He's a genius. An entrepreneur. And he has become very religious."

"What was he?"

"He was born and raised Catholic, of course. He became caught up with building his business and, well, he was just too busy, I guess. A year ago, one night when he was unable to sleep, he turned on the television to EWTN and listened to Mother Angelica. Do you know her?"

"I know who she is."

"She was talking about devotion to the Blessed Virgin. Fatima. She urged her listeners to say the rosary every day. The next morning he asked me to buy him a rosary. That was the beginning."

"Don't tell me he wants a papal audience."

"Could you arrange one?"

He made a face. "Is that why you've come?"

"No. Not at all. It was an afterthought. Though it would be an important day in Nate's life if he could meet the pope. But back to Nate's conversion. He began to watch EWTN regularly and was struck by the works of art that were featured in the transitions from one program to the next."

John said nothing.

"A couple of days ago he asked me to get him a list of the best and most famous paintings depicting the mysteries of the rosary. He was particularly interested in the Annunciation, the Visitation, the Nativity, the Presentation, and the finding of the Child Jesus in the temple."

"The joyful mysteries," John said.

"Yes. I told him it was out of my area of expertise but that my brother was a priest in the Vatican with a fine education in sacred art. He told me to hop in the plane and come see you."

"Just like that?" John said.

"Just like that. And here I am. And I'm asking you."

John listened to this account, put out his cigarette, and said, "And what will he do when he has the list?"

"Knowing Nate, he'll buy them."

John's laughter brought home to Laura that it was incredibly naive to think her boss, however incredibly rich and well connected he was, could just walk into wherever the paintings were and make an offer.

"Can you give me such a list?" Laura said.

"You're serious."

"I'm not. Nate Hannan is."

He shrugged. "I'm not the one to do it, but I can have it done. I'll ask Brendan Crowe."

"Who is he?"

"An Irish priest who works in the Vatican Archives. He lives here."

"How long would it take to put together such a list?"

"That depends. I think I won't tell him why you want the list. He might drag his feet if he knew what it was for."

"I understand."

"I'll ask your question. I'll call you when I get the list."

"Thanks, John."

"How many pushy sisters do I have?"

Laura couldn't resist. She got up and went to hug her brother again, dropping a kiss on the top of his head.

He blushed like a six-year-old caught with his hand in the cookie jar.

"Laura . . ."

"It's just so good to see you."

"You better get going."

"Thanks, John."

And so they parted.

Later, Laura would wonder what she would have done then if she had known the ripple effect such a simple question would have on the people she loved, and on the Church itself.

❖

On her way back to the hotel, Laura went through the basilica, telling herself it was a shortcut. Once inside the enormous church she found herself wandering about like any other tourist. And then she noticed the confessionals. The priest sat behind a little Dutch door and penitents knelt on either side. His head was tipped toward the person confessing. Above his little box was a sign indicating the languages in which he heard confessions. It seemed odd to think of sins as Spanish or Italian or English.

Laura lingered in fascination, imagining what it would be like to wait her turn, to kneel there, and when the grill was opened, to pour out the sins of her life. The thought exercised a powerful attraction. Confession, absolution, pardon, and peace. But what was the point? She would have to have a firm purpose of amendment.

She would have to change her sinful ways.

She had no intention of doing so today.

She went slowly down the nave and out the great doors, across the piazza, to the Hotel Columbus and Ray Sinclair.

❖ IV ❖

To pray is to put oneself in the presence of God.

Heather Adams had known Laura when they were students at Boston College. Not well, but better than she knew most of her fellow students.

"Nebraska?" Laura had sounded as if Heather had come from the farside of the moon.

"Red Cloud, Nebraska. It's where Willa Cather grew up." Then she added, "The novelist."

"So why did you come to Boston?"

"I wanted to come east. Willa Cather came to Pittsburgh. The city, not the university."

"Heather, I haven't the faintest idea who Willa Cather is."

Heather told her, even though it was clear that Laura had little interest in fiction. Heather herself was a math major and not a great reader, but she had read all of Willa Cather, first as a matter of local pride and then because *Death Comes for the Archbishop* had been the beginning of what she supposed was her secret life. *Shadows on the Rock* was even more important to her. Those novels had brought her eventually to Catholicism, and it was a puzzle to her that Willa Cather herself had not made the same journey. Mathematics is abstract, but life is concrete, and Heather wasn't the first mathematician who had found that the ethereal world of quantity opened her to something that changed her view of the concrete. Once she had thought that Pascal was simply a computer program; now she had a special devotion to the saintly mathematician.

She was not yet a Catholic when she left Boston College— her timid overtures to a Jesuit on the subject had not been encouraged—to pursue her MBA in New Haven. The Yale drinking song had spoken to her almost as directly as the novels of Willa Cather. "God have mercy on such as we, damned from here to eternity, bah, bah, bah." The plangent lyrics had the impact of a hymn. When she made up her mind to take instruction in Catholicism and had gone off campus to a city parish in Manchester, she felt like an imposter among the working-class parishioners. Not that they paid any attention to her as she stood and knelt and sat and looked around her and realized that Catholicism was all about the Mass. Others in her pew had to push past her into the aisle at Communion time, and she longed to go forward with them but knew that wouldn't be right.

The pastor's name was Krucek. He was in his sixties and was very matter-of-fact when she showed up at the rectory and told him she wanted to become a Catholic.

"What are you now?"

"Protestant, I guess."

"Don't you know?"

"I was raised a Lutheran."

He was silent for a moment when she told him she was a graduate student at Yale. "What do you know about the Church?"

"That I want to receive Holy Communion."

He gave her books to read, he met with her for half an hour every week for several months, and then said he would give her conditional baptism.

"Conditional?"

"Chances are you're already validly baptized." He quoted the creed to her. One baptism, for the forgiveness of sins.

She made her First Communion at a weekday Mass, seven thirty in the morning at Saint Cyril's, but only she and Father Krucek knew that it was her first. From then on, she went to Mass every day, sometimes on campus, usually at Saint Cyril's. After she got her degree, she wrote to Laura and asked if there were any openings at Empedocles. There had been a write-up about Laura in the Boston College alumni magazine. Heather was asked down for an interview, she and Laura had a pleasant reunion, and she was offered a job in purchasing.

That had been three years ago. However good it was to see Laura again, and however much Heather knew she owed her friend for her job, they just didn't click the way they had in college. For one thing, Laura's life was lived in a blur these days, always at the beck and call of Mr. Hannan, off on trips with no forewarning, busy, busy, busy. How could she call her soul her own?

"When do you have time to think, Laura?"

"I'm not paid to think."

"Ha."

She had thought that now that she was a Catholic, they would have that in common, too, but Laura did not find it an exciting subject. Except to brighten up and say, "My brother is a priest, you know. In Rome."

Heather decided that what now chiefly interested her was not easy to talk about, nor was that necessary. What do you say about prayer?

How odd it was that such a simple word, one she had known all her life, turned out to hide things of which she had never dreamt before. One Christmas vacation, she had read through all the volumes of Churchill's account of World War II and had been particularly struck by a surprising locution in his instructions. "Pray do this, or pray do that." The French would have said *je vous en prie*, the Italians, *prego*. The English equivalent had all but dropped from usage, which is what made Churchill so different; praying now meant asking for something, the way she had prayed she would get the job with Empedocles. Had she thought of it as an answer to a prayer?

Now she began to read Teresa of Avila, first the autobiography. And second, too. When she finished it, she immediately read it again. The saint seemed to speak directly to her across the intervening centuries. From that point on, she was more happy than sorry that she and Laura had not again become close. Oh, it wasn't the gossip that flew around about Laura and Ray Sinclair. There was no protection against what people might say. God knows what they thought of her. She had become reconciled to the fact that her enthusiasms were not shared by others.

⚜

The house she had bought was isolated, on a country road, surrounded by woods that seemed to offer protection as well as seclusion. When she came home from work and turned into her driveway, she could feel her spirits lift. It was the first house she had ever owned, and it was furnished like every other house, more or less. The difference was in the lower level, which the previous owner had used as a home office. Carpeted, freshly painted, it had become her oratory. Reading about hermits and consecrated virgins as well as the Carthusians, Heather had in effect founded her own religious order. There was a prie-dieu, an altar with a portrait of Teresa of Avila flanking the crucifix. After a swift supper, she descended to her oratory and her real life.

To pray is to put oneself in the presence of God. Since we are all already there, in His presence, that sounds easy, but the realization of it took quiet, an inner silence, waiting. She had no expectation of mystical experiences—reading Teresa had informed her of the danger of such expectations. All she wanted was to realize that simple statement. To be in the presence of God. Saying the rosary helped put her there. She had come to love the rosary, its repetitious prayer, each decade devoted to some great event in the story of salvation. It had surprised her when she came upon Mr. Hannan on his knees in the grotto behind the main building, saying the rosary.

It seemed that some things connected all the faithful.

# CHAPTER TWO

## ❖ I ❖

### The third secret of Fatima

The Confraternity of Pius IX was formed in the late 1960s by half a dozen disenchanted priests, a sede vacantist or two, men certain the present occupant of the Chair of Peter was an imposter and the post legally empty; a variation on this, several were men convinced that Vatican II had been a heretical council, contradicting what had been Catholic teaching for centuries. They occupied a villa overlooking the Grande Raccordo Anulare where it intersects with the road to Leonardo da Vinci airport and Fiumicino, and they formed a religious community of sorts, bound together by their several discontents, dreaming of the restoration of orthodoxy and vindication of their accusations. They were under the leadership of Bishop Frederick Catena, Federigo, in the familiar democracy of the confraternity.

Catena had been ordained for the diocese of Peoria forty-two years ago and had come to Rome for the Council as the secretary of his bishop. He had never been home since. Other members of the confraternity focused their discontent on what they considered doctrinal aberrations in the Church. At the center of Federigo's own discontent were the apparitions at Fatima, Portugal. Some years before his attendance at sessions of the Council, as a seminarian, he had made a pilgrimage to the shrine, traveling by train to Lyon and then through Spain to Portugal. On his knees, he had traversed the great square to the spot where the Blessed Virgin had appeared to three peasant children. It had been his devotion to Mary that had carried Federigo safely through temptations against his vocation, periods of dryness and moments of gladness, too. From the time of his visit to Fatima he had said the rosary, all fifteen decades, every day. He read everything he could lay his hands on that concerned the apparitions and their significance. And he had become obsessed with the so-called secret of Fatima.

This secret had been written out for the Holy Father by Sister Lucia, one of the seers who had survived and become a nun, and it was sent to Rome, with the understanding that it would be read and made public in 1960. But the year 1960 came and went, and no statement on the secret emanated from the Vatican. Federigo was appalled. This was direct defiance of the wishes of the Blessed Virgin Mary.

His bishop had been trained in canon law and was rightly famous for the building program he fostered in his diocese. New parishes were created, churches built, parish schools opened. The bishop went off to Rome with the conviction that America had a thing or two to teach the universal church about renewal, the aggiornamento called for by good Pope John XXIII. They crossed the Atlantic on the *Statendam*, and on the journey Federigo spoke to the bishop about Fatima.

"You must press for the revelation of the third secret, Your Excellency."

"What were the first two?" Bishop Spelling seemed amused.

Father Catena told him. The bishop nodded. Prayer, the need for punishment, the threat of hell for the unrepentant. "Sound doctrine," he observed. "Not what I would think of as a secret, Father."

If the journey had been longer, Father Catena would have begun a novena for the enlightenment of his bishop. That night he did not go to bed but knelt on the floor of his cabin and prayed that the Blessed Virgin would stir the heart of Bishop Spelling and cause him to rise up in the Council and demand that the third secret of Fatima be revealed. He fell asleep on his knees, and it seemed a special grace, but his prayer was not answered. Bishop Spelling became impatient whenever his secretary got on the subject of Fatima. In Rome, Catena began one novena after another, certain his prayers would be answered. Then even his silence seemed to annoy the bishop. After the second session, before the bishop went back to Peoria, he had a long talk with Father Catena.

"I want you to stay in Rome and study."

Catena bowed submissively.

"Canon law would not be your cup of tea, I think. Theology?"

"Philosophy."

"Good, good. I was thinking of the Dominicans. The Angelicum."

"Yes, Your Excellency."

It was difficult to think of an assignment to study in Rome as exile, but he knew his bishop wanted to get rid of him.

⚜

With the advent of the Internet, he came into contact with even more kindred souls who were appalled and astonished by the Vatican's refusal to dedicate Russia to the Immaculate Heart of Mary, one of the requests that had been made at Fatima. For Catena, it was the refusal to divulge the third secret that held center stage. Speculation as to what it contained was rife. A missionary in Taiwan whom Catena had met at the Council, where Father Leone had been in the entourage of the lone cardinal from China, advanced the theory that the reason the secret was kept secret was that it contained the Blessed Virgin's negative estimate of the Council. There was also Jean-Jacques Trepanier, a firebrand in New Hampshire whose Fatima magazine enjoyed wide circulation but whose intemperate attacks on the Curia had brought him under a cloud. Catena became acquainted with various *episcopi vagantes*, men who had been ordained bishops illicitly but validly by other wandering bishops. When Catena decided against returning home to Peoria, he severed relations with his bishop and was himself ordained a bishop by a Melchite who had fallen out of favor with other members of his rite. The elevation made him the clear choice for superior when the community was formed and took possession of the villa overlooking the Grande Raccordo Anulare, the gift of a disenchanted Argentine who spent half her year in Fatima.

A website now disseminated the views of the confraternity

worldwide, while contributions from sympathetic souls put the community on a secure financial footing. A newsletter carried the various discontents of members of the confraternity to the four corners of the world, eliciting a gratifying response. Now they seemed to be in competition with Trepanier for the allegiance of alienated Catholics. When John Paul II had been elected, hope had risen that a pope whose Marian motto was *Totus tuus* would be sure to divulge the third secret. The pope, like his predecessor, went to Fatima and met with Sister Lucia, but that was all. Well, not quite. The canonization process for little Francisco and Jacinta had progressed. Nonetheless, Federigo's personal confidence that John Paul II was their man was dashed when the famous *Ratzinger Report*, an interview with the prefect of the Congregation for the Doctrine of the Faith conducted by Vittorio Messori, appeared in 1985. The cardinal was asked if he himself had read the third secret. He had. And why had it not been made public in 1960? The reply, that it might have seemed sensational, convinced Federigo that a cover-up was involved. A month later, Brendan Crowe, an Irish priest who was an avid reader of the confraternity's website, came to the villa and expressed interest in the community there.

"You are a student, Father?"

"Yes, Bishop."

"You are from Ireland?"

"County Clare."

A thought formed full-blown in the mind of Federigo that could only be regarded as divine inspiration. He told Crowe that he could be a member of the confraternity, but only in petto.

"I want you to continue your studies, and conceal your judgment of the path the Church is on. You will study history at the Gregorianum. Your goal is to be assigned to the Vatican Archives."

There was no need to spell out his mission to Crowe. The third secret was in the Vatican Archives. Only an insider could hope to gain access to the explosive document.

"You must live as if the confraternity does not exist."

"I understand."

"We will communicate only by e-mail."

Father Crowe rose after he had knelt and kissed Federigo's ring. Now, or at least eventually, there was hope that the truth would come out, the Blessed Virgin would be vindicated, and the post-conciliar Church would be revealed for the heterodox body it had become.

Crowe had been a disappointment. He seemed to have taken on the Vatican reluctance to make the third secret public. But Crowe's revelation by e-mail of what had really happened to the secretary of state and Cardinal Maguire seemed to corroborate all the confraternity's judgments on what the Church had become in these last days.

A den of evil.

✣ II ✣

"You could be next."

Traeger had Brendan Crowe take him up on the roof so he could see where Cardinal Maguire had been killed. The scene when they came through the door suggested those one sometimes saw from hotel rooms in Manhattan, the rooftops of lower buildings turned into patios and gardens. Traeger sat where Maguire had sat, thinking of the knife that had been sunk in the cardinal's chest. Rodriguez had spoken with awe of what had happened to Maguire.

"He could be considered a martyr, you know."

Traeger had said nothing.

"Depending on the killer's motive," Rodriguez added with apparent reluctance.

That had brought it back to ground familiar to Traeger.

"You won't need me," Crowe said now, turning to go.

"Wait. Please sit down."

Crowe was cagey, and Traeger hadn't understood why before. In the meantime, he had discovered the priest's apparent connection with the Confraternity of Pius IX. Crowe sat down, reluctantly.

"There's nothing more I can tell you that I haven't told you a dozen times."

"Oh, there's always more, Monsignor."

No reaction.

"I've been told that Cardinal Maguire should be considered a martyr."

"Who said that?"

"Do you think so?"

"That's the point of cardinal red, you know. Expressing a willingness to shed one's blood for the faith."

"You could be next."

Crowe was startled. "What do you mean?"

"Think about it. You saw the killer. And he saw you."

Crowe thought about it, and apparently his vulnerability had never occurred to him before. "The Russian ambassador saw him, too."

"He has people to look after him. And what the killer was after is here, not at the Russian embassy."

"The report on the attempted assassination of John Paul II?"

"That has been the assumption."

"It was Chekovsky who wanted it."

"Maybe he decided to get it the old-fashioned way, just take it."

"Well, he failed," Crowe said with a trace of pride.

"Maybe our assumption is wrong. What else could he have been after?"

Traeger watched Crowe shift in his chair. "The archives are filled with valuable things."

"Valuable enough to kill for?"

"Apparently."

"Like the third secret of Fatima?"

"That's already been made public."

"I'd like to see it."

Crowe shook his head. "I can't show you that."

"Are you sure it's still down there?"

"Of course it's still there."

Traeger steepled his hands, his fingertips touching. He brought them under his chin. "It's missing."

"How could you know that?"

"Call it a guess."

Traeger was sure Crowe knew the third secret was missing.

❧

The night before, Carlos Rodriguez had taken Traeger through the empty Vatican Library to the archives where a spidery little priest named Remi Pouvoir awaited them. Carlos showed the priest the authorization from the Congregation for the Doctrine of the Faith, which Pouvoir read slowly as if he were memorizing it. Finally he nodded, turned, and led them downstairs. They came into a vast temperature-controlled area with aisle after aisle of shelving on which archival boxes stretched into the distance. Pouvoir led them through the maze, seeming to know in advance exactly where the desired file was located. He stopped. A sunken light over his head seemed to illumine him. The priest's thin hand went up, his finger sought and found a looping ring on the bottom of the archival box, and he pulled it out. Then, hugging it, he led them to a table, placed the box on it, and stepped back.

Rodriguez was looking at the gray cardboard box with awe. Here was the secret written out by Sister Lucia, meant for the eyes of the pope alone. The three of them had stood there as if they expected the box to open itself. Traeger stepped forward and lifted the top of the box.

It was empty.

"Empty!" Rodriguez was beside Traeger, and his voice betrayed the shock and more that he felt. Where was the message from the Blessed Virgin?

Pouvoir remained in the attitude he had struck after placing the box on the table and stepping back. His eyes were cast down. It occurred to Traeger that the priest must have known the box was empty when he put it on the table. He had lifted it from the shelf, hugged it to him, brought it to the table. Surely he would have known the difference between an empty box and a full one?

Rodriguez, over his first shock, demanded to see the record of those who had examined the contents of the box. Pouvoir nodded, approving of the demand. He closed the box, returned it to the shelf, and then led them back the way they had come. He produced a ledger in which were entered by dates the requests for archival items. He found what he was looking for. Under 2000. The name beside the entry was Cardinal Maguire.

They didn't speak until later, after they had left the strangely unperturbed Pouvoir, exited the building, and gone across the vast, now empty piazza to a bar on the Via della Conciliazione. Rodriguez had walked in silence, still shaken by what they had found—or hadn't found. He ordered brandy and drank half of it. Then he began to talk.

"The third secret was revealed in the year two thousand, when Ratzinger was prefect of the Congregation for the Doctrine of the Faith."

"Perhaps he didn't return it."

"That's what we're going to find out."

"Just drop in on Pope Benedict and put the question to him?"

But Rodriguez was in no mood for levity. What he meant was that first thing in the morning they would go to the Congregation for the Doctrine of the Faith. Most of those who had worked for Ratzinger were still in place there: Di Noia, Brown, others.

"Meanwhile, we get drunk," Traeger suggested.

He didn't mean that, of course. In his present mood, Rodriguez could have drunk a quart of brandy without much effect. But they did have several drinks while Rodriguez talked, just talked—he had to talk. After a time, he subsided, and then, out of the silence, he said, "So the murders weren't in vain. That's what he was after."

❖

Traeger didn't realize at first that Eugenio Piacere was a cardinal. Like Joseph Ratzinger before him, he eschewed the cardinalatial robes while in the office, arriving in a simple black cassock with a beret pulled low on his head. When he took it off, he might have been displaying his high-domed bald head. He received them with a small smile, bowing them into his office, closing the door, and indicating where they could sit. He himself went to a brocade armchair that seemed too large for him.

"Your message was alarming," he said softly, looking from Rodriguez to Traeger. Rodriguez slumped in his chair.

"You didn't know?" he asked.

"I didn't know." The smile had been replaced by an expression of sadness. "Sometimes I wonder if the Blessed Virgin knew what trouble she would cause by telling those things to Sister Lucia."

Traeger said, "But wasn't the third secret made public?"

"It was. The hope was that that would stop all the wild speculating about its contents. Of course, withholding it for so long had inflamed curiosity. The strangest ideas became current as to what the secret said. Finally, the Holy Father—Cardinal Ratzinger as he then was—decided the time had come to put an end to all that. So the secret was published and he wrote a magnificent commentary." The wistful smile was briefly back. "And immediately we were accused of deception. It was said that there must be more that was being withheld."

Traeger looked at him. "And there wasn't?"

"Everything was made public."

"Who would have stolen it?" Traeger asked.

Piacere's hands opened as if he were saying Mass. "It would be rash of me to speculate."

"We have to speculate, Your Eminence," Rodriguez said. That was when Traeger first realized that this mild little priest with the aura of holiness about him was a prince of the Church.

"I will leave speculation to you," Piacere said sweetly. "What disappointment the thief must be feeling."

He went on then, developing the thoughts Cardinal Ratzinger had put into the document accompanying the revelation of the third secret in 2000. The essence of Christian doctrine had been revealed in its completeness at the time of the apostles. Since then of course there had been what Cardinal Newman called the development of doctrine, drawing out the implications of that original deposit of faith. But no development could be authentic that did not conform with the original revelation.

"We learn more and more of what we cannot understand, not in this life." Piacere twisted the ring on his right hand, as if he feared it would slip off.

Of course there were private revelations, some of which received official Church approval, but in their case, too, the test of authenticity was their agreement with the faith that had been entrusted to the Church.

"Private revelations have good and bad effects," Piacere murmured. "Many useful devotions are the results of such apparitions. The bad effect is a passion to know what lies ahead, to have prophecies. There are those who seem almost to long for the end of the world. Of course, the apparitions at Fatima are a great blessing to the Church. Paul VI went there, as did John Paul II. But the heart of the Fatima message is as old as the Church itself. Prayer, repentance, fasting. The secret is that there is no secret."

"But the assassination attempt?" Traeger said.

"Yes, yes. There is that."

By the time they left Piacere, Traeger had thought that, if he ever got religion, he would want Piacere there at his deathbed.

❖

And so, that afternoon, talking with Crowe on the rooftop of the Vatican Library, Traeger had known of the missing third secret. And he could not rid himself of the thought that Crowe, too, knew of it. What he did not know, despite Rodriguez's remark the night before, was whether those murders in the Vatican were connected with the missing third secret.

"Be careful," he said to Crowe, when they had gone downstairs and were standing outside the monsignor's office.

"I'm always careful."

"Good."

He would reserve for their next meeting what he had learned of Crowe's connection with the Confraternity of Pius IX.

❖ III ❖

The engine room of the bark of Peter

Brendan Crowe waited half an hour after Traeger had left him, the door of his office open. Anyone passing by would have seen him busy at his desk, this day a day like any other. Finally, he rose, shut the door and locked it, and stood very still, taking deep breaths. He had been shaken on that dreadful day when an assassin had roamed the Vatican; he had been deeply moved when he discovered the body of his chief on the roof above. But now, for the first time, he sensed the truth of Traeger's warning. He had seen the assassin. If the man were apprehended alive, it would be Brendan Crowe's task to say, "That is the man." But far more than his personal safety concerned him. The double life he had been living for years now threatened to become one life.

"Now."

That had been the single word in the message from Catena. He had received it the day before, in a cybercafé on the Via Boezio, using the AOL address he held in the name of John Burke. Burke was only the latest of several names he had used to provide a buffer between himself and the e-mail address that connected him with the Confraternity of Pius IX. It had all seemed a game.

Not all priests who were assigned to Rome became disenchanted with the all-too-human aspects of Church governance. When John Henry Newman had been named cardinal, he asked and received permission not to come to the Eternal City to receive the red hat. It was better, the Englishman had confided to friends, not to get too close to the engine room of the bark of Peter. Brendan Crowe was one of the disenchanted.

It had begun while he was still a student, shocked by the heterodoxy of professors teaching in the very shadow of the Vatican. The time came when he wondered if it was he rather than they who were out of line. Surely the wild theories were known by the Curia, by the Holy Father. Vatican II was interpreted in ways that called into question the hierarchical nature of the Church. Now, it was alleged, we are the People of God, not a monarchical bureaucracy deriving from the age of Constantine. The gap between clergy and laity must be closed, as well as that between men and women in the Church. Celibacy, they were assured, would soon be a thing of the past, a reminder of the Church's failure to understand fully the incarnational character of the faith. Crowe had appealed to old Father Donohue, a fellow Irishman, who taught Church history and was clearly out of sympathy with his more radical colleagues.

"Of course it's madness," Donohue said. He had produced a bottle of Irish whiskey and poured half an ounce for Brendan.

"You're not having any, Father?"

"I have to keep my wits about me. Such as they are."

Donohue developed a theme he had already discussed in his lectures. In the long history of the Church, the period after an ecumenical council was often a time of turmoil. This was particularly true in recent times. Take Vatican I. He went on about Dollinger and Lord Acton and the scourge of modernism, the Old Catholics who broke from Rome. The long view of history seemed to provide all the consolation Father Donohue needed: this too will pass. It had not been enough for Brendan Crowe.

The teaching going on in the pontifical universities in Rome after the Council suggested that a coup had taken place. It was as if the Reformers of the sixteenth century had been offered professorial chairs in Rome to spread their doctrine. From there it had been a small step to think that a palace coup had taken place in the Vatican itself and that hostile forces were in charge, bringing about the demise of the Church.

Brendan Crowe had resisted this upsetting interpretation of what was going on in the Church. Who was he to stand in judgment of men far wiser than he, more educated, in positions of responsibility? Perhaps the differences were not as deep as he thought. For years after the Council, as he worked in one of the more obscure dicasteries of the Vatican, disputes about such matters had seemed to him just an exchange of personal opinions, both sides of any issue occupying positions suggestive of authority. And then in 1985, twenty years after the Council closed, at the second extraordinary synod held in Rome, the synod following on the famous *Ratzinger Report*, the assembled bishops had acknowledged that there was a false spirit of the Council abroad in the Church. This was contrasted with the true spirit, and the marks of each were enumerated and stated. Crowe had known the great relief that what hitherto had seemed merely his opinions were now identified as the true spirit of the Council. Now at last would come clarity and unity, a dying away of the surly undertone of dissent.

But nothing changed. The report of the synod was filed away with all the previous post-conciliar clarifications to be ignored by all those Crowe now saw as his adversaries. The time seemed to have come to follow the example of Donohue, get out of Rome and back to Ireland and comparative sanity. Oh, for a little rural parish in County Clare where he could be sustained by the solid faith and piety of his people. Two things intervened.

The first was the then Bishop Maguire's stay at the Irish College where Brendan roomed. The prelate had just been created cardinal and had come to Rome for the ceremony. One afternoon, when Brendan was pacing the graveled walks of the college ground, while most of the residents were taking their postprandial nap, a voice called. It was Maguire, sitting on a bench.

"You are pensive, Father."

"My thoughts are not Pascalian, I'm afraid."

Maguire had liked that, and he had recognized the west country accent. He patted the bench beside him and Brendan sat.

Two Irishmen in a foreign land, two clerics from County

Clare with a fund of common memories and all of Holy Ireland
sustaining them—there was immediate rapport. Brendan had
described the work he did in the Vatican but mentioned his intention of returning home. Maguire sighed.

"I won't be going back."

He told Brendan of his appointment as head of the Vatican
Library and Archives. Before they rose, he had asked Brendan
to come there as his assistant.

"I'll want someone whose Italian I can easily understand."

Brendan had asked for and received a day to think on it.
And then he had gone to Catena.

He had made the appointment before Maguire had made his
offer, with the intention of telling Catena he was returning to
Ireland. But things were more complicated when he kept the
appointment. If he accepted Maguire's offer, he must sever all
connections, however informal and clandestine, with the Confraternity of Pius IX.

"It is the answer to a prayer, Father," Catena had said.

Neither man had said it in so many words, but the implication was clear. Brendan Crowe would become the confraternity's man in the archives. No need to mention that the third
secret was stored there.

"I couldn't do that."

"Couldn't work for the good of the Church? Surely you
don't imagine that I am asking you to be subversive. The subversives are already there."

Catena was a persuasive man and, Crowe had to admit, it
was flattering to be recruited by both Maguire and Catena.
Even so, Crowe's agreement had been tacit. Over the intervening years, he had kept in touch with Catena, but had never been
asked to do anything that could have been construed as disloyal
to Cardinal Maguire. Sometimes he almost persuaded himself
that he was keeping a watch on Catena and the confraternity.
And then had come the awful day when an assassin had roamed
the halls, had found the villa on the rooftop of the library, and
had plunged a knife into the breast of Cardinal Maguire.

❧

He had found the third secret of Fatima on the bedside table in
Maguire's villa, just lying there where the cardinal must have
placed it after reading it, perhaps while in bed. If the assassin

had had time, he could have found the folder and been off with it. Crowe knew why Maguire had been perusing the secret. After the publication of it in 2000, a steady stream of letters came that claimed that parts of the secret had been suppressed. Maguire had said he would put an end to that once and for all. In the greatest of secrecy, Crowe had removed the secret and brought it to his chief. And now, here it was.

Of course he should return it to the archives. He himself felt no impulse to open the folder to see if the complainers had a case. His motives when he put the secret into his briefcase were obscure to himself, then and later. It was as if he were removing the documents from harm's way when he took them back to his room in the Domus Sanctae Marthae. He remembered Chekovsky's enigmatic question—Is it you, or must we wait for another?—and Traeger's suggestion that there was a mole in the Vatican. He had feared that Traeger meant him. It was the thought of little Remi Pouvoir, flitting among the rows and rows of archived materials, that decided him. And he had another idea, a wild idea, prompted by Burke's account of the eccentric billionaire for whom his sister worked.

✤ IV ✤

"He is a self-made Croesus."

John Burke's rooms were on the same floor in the Domus as Brendan Crowe's, and the two priests had formed a friendship, the younger looking to the older for counsel, Crowe fascinated by the eager zeal of the younger man. Burke had taken Crowe to the building that housed the Pontifical Academies and showed him around, and Crowe in turn had acquainted Burke with the inner sanctum of the Vatican Library and the publicly accessible parts of the archives. In their conversations, the range of Crowe's knowledge impressed the younger priest—patristics, philosophy, the manuscripts in the Vatican Library, even an effortless authority about the art works in the museum. It was this last that prompted Father Burke to seek the older priest's help in compiling the list Laura had asked for.

But before he could broach the subject, Crowe had made the

dreadful revelation that four recent deaths in the Vatican had been murders. After that, it was difficult to get back to the wishes of Ignatius Hannan.

"The mysteries of the rosary?" Crowe said.

"The best artistic depictions of them."

"There is scarcely unanimity on that."

"Well, the best in your opinion, then."

"I could mention two or three for each mystery."

"I can't thank you enough," John said, as if Crowe had agreed.

"What is the purpose of the list?"

In answer, Burke told his friend more about the eccentric billionaire for whom his sister worked in New Hampshire.

"I suppose he wants reproductions of them?"

"He could scarcely obtain the originals, Brendan."

Burke himself had been devoting months to gathering archival materials for the use of the commission looking into the canonization of Pope Pius IX, who had begun his papacy as a liberal and then, appalled by political upheaval and revolution, reversed his field. He had fled the Vatican for Gaeta, joining the list of popes who had suffered from secular forces. Burke possessed an Irish eloquence that made dramatic his account of Napoleon's kidnapping the pope of the day and bringing him to Notre Dame to crown him emperor.

"In the event, Napoleon put the crown on his own head. Poor Pius."

"Pius?"

"Paul V. After the fiasco in Russia, he offered protection and asylum to members of Napoleon's family. A truly Christian gesture. There are those who think that Napoleon's defeat in Russia was punishment for his treatment of the pope."

Full of his subject, Burke had then gone on about Paul Claudel's trilogy of plays.

❖

From time to time, the two priests went out for dinner to Ambrogio's in the Borgo Pio, absenting themselves from felicity awhile, in Brendan's phrase—or not his phrase: his conversation was a florilegium of quotations—taking an outside table in clement weather. And that is what they did this evening.

"Tell me more about your sister's employer, John."

"I think I've already told you all I know. He is a billion-aire."

Brendan's eyebrows lifted. "Is that hyperbole?"

"Apparently not."

"He inherited the money?"

"Far from it. He is a self-made Croesus. Electronics."

"Hanson?"

"Hannan. Ignatius Hannan."

"Irish?"

"Apparently."

"Ah, an apparent Irishman." Brendan was filling his pipe. "And a pious man though rich?"

"That is quite recent. He was too busy to practice his faith for years but suddenly it all returned. Pietistic might be a better term." He told Brendan of the replica of the grotto at Lourdes that Hannan had put up on the grounds of his company.

"Ah."

"I suppose it would be difficult to have something built that would resemble Fatima."

Crowe said nothing, puffing on his pipe, looking at passersby. "La Salette might interest him."

Burke looked blank.

*"Celle qui pleure?"*

He shook his head. Crowe sat forward and began to talk of the apparitions at La Salette, also in the nineteenth century. Did Burke know Leon Bloy? A shame that he did not; he must read him. The writer was a great champion of La Salette because the messages were such an indictment of abuses in the Church. "Now don't tell me that the name Jacques Maritain means nothing to you."

"Of course I know Maritain."

"Bloy's godchild, as was his wife, Raissa. Maritain wrote a book on La Salette but was advised not to publish it."

"Why?"

"He consulted the pope." Crowe's eyebrows rose as if in explanation.

⁂

On the day before she was to return to America, Laura invited John to tea at her hotel, and he brought Brendan along. To his delight, his sister and the learned Irishman got along, each immediately at ease with the other.

"I didn't think Americans drank tea."

"Haven't you heard of the Boston Tea Party?" Laura taunted.

"I was thinking of that. You dumped the tea overboard."

They talked of her employer's interest in paintings depicting the joyful mysteries of the rosary. Brendan drew a folded sheet of paper from the sleeve of his cassock.

"This is what I came up with."

Laura was delighted.

"Nate will find a way of thanking you," she promised.

&#9753;

John Burke took Bloy's *The Woman Who Was Poor* on vacation to Maiori on the Amalfi Coast and tried unsuccessfully to enjoy it. When he checked his e-mail there was a long message from Laura. Could he come to the States and see Ignatius Hannan in order to discuss an exciting new project? He replied asking why they couldn't consult by e-mail or telephone. "He wants to make you an offer you can't resist." That was nonsense, of course, but the prospect of a visit to the States was attractive. He put it to his superior, saying a bit about Hannan. Bishop Sanchez Sorrondo stirred in his chair. That the academies could use the financial support of the American billionaire seemed to be his thought.

"By all means, go."

It was not a flattering thought that his absence would mean so little. He telephoned Laura and said he would come. "I'll look into flights and let you know."

"Nate will send a plane for you."

"Good Lord, no."

A moment of silence. "As you wish. Would it be possible to bring your friend Father Crowe?"

"I doubt he could come."

"Ask him."

Apparently working for Ignatius Hannan had convinced her that all wishes could be realized.

To his surprise, Crowe agreed.

"I've always wanted to discover America."

"You already have."

A blank look.

"Saint Brendan's voyage."

John Burke telephoned Laura with the good news. He also changed his mind about the company jet, and one morning the two priests flew off from Ciampino in unimaginable luxury.

❖ V ❖

### "Why are you following me?"

Traeger had first suspected that he was being tailed on the Via Veneto. Several times he had become aware of the swarthy little fellow who seemed to keep about thirty yards between them. When Traeger stopped at a newsstand and ignored the girly pictures on display, the little man took a chair at an outdoor café and began to tie his shoelace. Traeger went on and it became clear that the man was staying with him. The only way to handle this was to become the pursuer rather than the pursued.

He stepped into a bar and headed immediately for the men's room. As he had hoped, there was a door leading outside. He went into the alley, then doubled back, crossed the street, and waited. The man appeared in the door of the bar, then darted inside again. Traeger waited. In a few minutes, the man emerged from the side street, looked up and down, and then gave up. He hailed a cab and Traeger got another. The man got out at the Piazza Cavour. Traeger hopped out of his cab, a miniature camera in his palm. He got two good shots, got back in his cab, and took off.

Three days later Traeger went through the bar of the Caffe Greco into the warren of little rooms beyond; the walls were crowded with engravings of Rome as it once had been, mementoes of the English literati who had frequented the place. Keats had died in a house abutting the Spanish Steps only fifty meters from the café.

A waiter in formal dress studied Traeger as if to decide if he were someone worthy of his obsequiousness. Traeger went past him into one of the smaller inner rooms. At a table for two under a framed account of Lord Byron was the man he had come to see. Traeger sat across from him. The man looked up from his newspaper as if to protest.

*"Buon giorno, Antonio."*

"You have mistaken me for someone else," the man answered in Italian.

"Why have you been following me?"

The waiter came and stood beside the table, haughtily avoiding Traeger's eyes.

*"Un caffe, per favore,"* Traeger told him.

The waiter went away, and Anatoly folded his paper, crossed his legs, and lit a cigarette. He blew out the match and put it into a tray on the table. "I like these ashtrays." They were saucerlike, white with an orange band, and had, at the bottom, obscured by ashes, "Caffe Greco" in orange letters.

"You could buy it," Traeger suggested.

"I've already stolen one."

Traeger nodded. The man was a creature of habit. Once Traeger had become aware that he was being tailed, he reversed the process. Every day at midmorning Anatoly came to the Caffe Greco and spent forty-five minutes over his Arabic newspaper. Traeger considered his prey, then reached out and turned the paper over. "Istanbul?"

Anatoly took the paper and put it on his lap. "Why did you call me Antonio?"

"It's the Italian equivalent of Anatoly. I looked you up." Bea had taken the request to Dortmund, who still had access to the data banks at Langley. Bea had been with Traeger longer than it would have been polite to mention. She knew of his undercover work for the government, but they didn't talk about it. It was as if his shadow life was their little secret.

Anatoly sat in silence for half a minute. "Who are you?"

"We were enemies once."

"Ah." The eyes narrowed.

"I wrote the agency report on Ali Agca."

"A pathetic man."

"Aren't we all?"

A hint of a smile. "Things are not as they were."

"Well, one of your guys ended up as premier."

"Putin!" He made it sound like spitting. "A traitor."

"It's a different world. Maybe soon Russia will be admitted to NATO."

There was almost camaraderie between them. Traeger sensed that Anatoly felt somewhat as he himself did. Decades after fierce battles are fought, survivors of the two sides can get together and enjoy a strange intimacy with others whom they once had done their best to kill. Traeger remembered a reunion of German soldiers he had once stumbled upon at Montecassino years ago. They were with veterans of the Polish outfit that had finally routed them from the monastery, and no one would have known they had once been enemies. It is much the way with old spies, if he and Anatoly were any test.

"I'm retired," Traeger said, when Anatoly finally put the question.

"And you are in Rome just on holiday?"

"Aren't you?"

"Exile would describe it better."

Traeger laughed. He was reminded of Dortmund grousing about old enemies becoming alleged friends. In retrospect, the Cold War had the look of a golden age, when black was black and white was white. The dissolution of the USSR must have seemed like the end of the world to those who had risked their lives for it.

"I have interviewed Chekovsky," Traeger said. Of course Anatoly would know that. It was when he had left the Russian embassy that Traeger had first become aware that he had acquired a shadow. Anatoly's face was expressionless. "An adaptable man."

Anatoly looked at his watch, then hailed the waiter. "I want a drink. Will you join me?"

Traeger joined him. At one o'clock they left and walked a few blocks to the Otello where they had an outside table, under the grape arbor.

"Why are you following me?" Anatoly asked, stirring his pasta with a fork.

"That was my question to you. And you began following me first."

"What is your connection with the Vatican?"

❖

That, of course, was the question Chekovsky had put to him when he visited the Russian ambassador.

"I am a computer consultant," Traeger said. "The library and archives need a new system."

Rodriguez had provided Traeger with the requisite identification when he went to interview the Russian ambassador. Chekovsky was affable and uninformative.

"It was a mere coincidence that I had an appointment that day with the archivist," the ambassador said.

"Father Crowe?"

Chekovsky's nose wrinkled. "I had come to know Cardinal Maguire."

"Did you see him that day?"

Chekovsky ran a hand over the sleeve of his coat. "Briefly."

"You were at the elevator with Father Crowe when a strange priest emerged."

Chekofsky thought about it. "I don't remember."

"We think he was the assassin."

Chekovsky sat forward. "Some people who were trained for a certain task cannot unlearn it."

"Do you have anyone in mind?"

Chekovsky sat back. "Unfortunately, there are dozens."

"Mr. Ambassador, I have advised that the materials you requested from Cardinal Maguire be turned over to you."

Chekovsky almost managed to conceal his delight. "Loose ends."

No doubt Chekovsky was concerned that if those reports on Ali Agca got into the wrong hands they would embarrass the new Russia, not least because of Putin's past.

Father Crowe had objected to the suggestion, adding, "In any case, I do not have the authority."

Rodriguez was working on that. How Byzantine were the workings of the Vatican. Elsewhere, such caution would have been attributed to the desire to retain deniability for something done.

Anatoly posed a more serious problem. Could Father Crowe identify Anatoly as the strange priest who had emerged from the elevator when he was saying good-bye to Chekovsky?

# CHAPTER THREE

❖ I ❖

## "I said a novena."

In high school Ignatius Hannan had already been a consultant on beta programs for software companies and was always surprised when his suggestions met with such enthusiastic responses, since they all seemed so obvious to him. One day a large car pulled up in front of the Hannan home and Nate answered the doorbell. The visitor was in his thirties and wore jeans, a T-shirt with Mickey Mouse on it, and sandals. Nate looked past him at the luxury automobile at the curb.

"Is your father in?"

"He's at work."

The visitor fished a card from his pocket and handed it to Nate. "Tell him it's about beta programs."

"He doesn't know a thing about them."

The visitor scratched his beard. "Doesn't Ignatius Hannan live here?"

"That's me."

The visitor looked at the sixteen-year-old for a moment, then grinned. "You?"

"Yes."

"Can we talk?"

His name was Leopardi and his company was Elektra. "How old would you say I am?"

Nate thought about it. "I don't know."

"It doesn't matter. I wasn't much older than you when I was hired by Bill Gates. An insufferable man, but a genius. I began to wonder why I was making him rich and went out on my own."

He told Nate that young though he was, he was Elektra's best consultant. The upshot was that Leopardi offered him a summer job.

"Where?"

"I'm just outside of Boston."

"I'd have to ask my parents."

"Of course."

His parents couldn't believe it. Leopardi came back that night, still dressed as before, and Nate's father was sure the man was some kind of nut. He said as much.

"I suppose I am." He mentioned what Nate would earn for his summer's work. It was more than his father earned.

It wasn't the money that interested Nate, but Leopardi's description of what he was working on. "This is all confidential, of course."

"I don't understand a word of it," Nate's father said.

In response to his father's request, Leopardi took the tablet from Mrs. Hannan and dashed off what he was offering Nate. Handshakes all around and then he was gone.

"It's all a bunch of bull," Mr. Hannan said.

"Look at that car," Mrs. Hannan said, awe in her voice.

"He probably stole it."

The next morning, a weekday, his mother took him off to Mass and told him to thank God for what was happening. Nate had been an altar boy when he was younger but quit when there began to be altar girls. His parents lamented the changes that were taking place in the Mass, in everything.

"It's all falling apart," his father grumbled.

That summer he went to work for Leopardi, staying with an aunt who lived closer to the building that housed Elektra. After the first meeting with several others who dressed as informally as Leopardi, Nate got a pat on the back. "You're like Christ among the elders in the temple." That seemed sacrilegious to Nate.

A program he designed that summer still earned him royalties, although he had soon fallen out with Leopardi. He designed a web page and incorporated, with his father president, his mother vice president, himself CEO. For the next several years, consultant fees poured in.

At his parents' insistence, he enrolled at Boston College, where he was bored with classes and aloof from his classmates, all of whom were a year or two older and seemed to do nothing but drink and talk dirty about girls. The name for the company he would form came to him in a philosophy course. Empedocles. He just liked the sound of the name; what the philosopher had taught was quaint—four elements, fire, air, earth, and water, plus love and strife to keep them active. He stopped going to classes and then dropped out.

"You've got to make a living," his father objected.

"I am making a living."

The fact was that he was now supporting his parents.

"But what if it doesn't last?"

"What does?"

The question seemed prophetic. Half a year later, his father, who had been arguing with the television set, stood up, looked around with a surprised expression, and then crashed to the floor. His death aged Nate's mother overnight. She spent much of her day in church and became worried about the fate of her husband. Her mission in life became his release from Purgatory.

It was wireless access to the Internet that became Nate's obsession. He developed the hardware, he lobbied cable companies, he rented space on a communications satellite, and for a time it looked as if, like many others, he would suffer from being ahead of the wave. He was overextended, deep in debt, so worried he actually told his mother about it, and then, when disaster seemed to loom, the heavens opened and he was swept to the top of the industry. His mother was not surprised.

"I said a novena."

"Well, it worked."

"Of course it worked."

That was about all Nate did—work—even more so after his mother contracted Alzheimer's and he placed her in a luxury nursing home. His religious faith might have been one of the memories she lost. There was no big crisis. He always supposed that if he sat down and thought it through it would make complete sense to him. He had no doubts. He just stopped thinking about it, or doing it, always in a whirl now that Empedocles was generating money in astronomical amounts. He hired Ray Sinclair—they had been altar boys together and Ray was vegetating in the personnel office of Boston College. Laura Burke showed up in response to an ad.

"Where did you go to school?" Hannan asked.

"Boston College."

"Another one? What was your major?"

"Philosophy."

"Come on."

"Ask me a question."

"Who was Empedocles?"

She rattled it off. It was the only philosophical answer he could have judged.

"The town is now called Agrigento."

She was right. He looked it up. And he noticed the name of the harbor. Porto Empedocle.

"What experience do you have?"

"None."

"Good." He liked her manner, he liked her mind, and he liked her honesty. He hired her. As with Ray, it was one of the smartest moves he ever made.

"Is everyone here Catholic?"

He thought about it. "I never took a poll."

How high is up? With Ray and Laura, Empedocles found new roofs to go through. On his thirtieth birthday Nate thought of what he was worth—a guess; who really knew?—and the number he came up with frightened him. He had a sleepless night. He turned on the television and there was a nun talking away, looking at him as if she knew all about him. He had been about to change channels when she started to talk about the Blessed Virgin. She sounded like his mother. He was fascinated. He watched the channel, EWTN, for hours. He turned it off when sun shone in his windows. He called Laura and told her he wasn't coming in.

"You're kidding. I've got you booked solid all day."

"Reschedule everything."

A pause. "Are you sick?"

"No. Nothing like that. I just want a day off."

"You are sick."

He visited his mother, not just popping in, staying a minute, and fleeing, as he had before, but sitting with her and wishing they could have a real talk. But there was no chance of that. Her lunch came and he helped her with it. The shrunken little woman with the bewildered expression seemed a metaphor of the fragility of life. What did it profit a man if he gained the whole world and suffered the loss of his soul? He hadn't had a thought like that in years. Suddenly his wealth seemed a curse.

He leaned toward his mother and whispered in her ear. "I'll be a good boy."

He tried to imagine she understood him. Did he understand himself? He whispered again. "I'll go to Mass." And then he added, "I'll go to confession."

The next morning, he went to Mass and watched people going to confession. The boxes he remembered had been replaced by reconciliation rooms in which penitents sat facing the priest and chatting about their sins. When they emerged their expression was not the one he remembered wearing when he came out of the confessional. He remembered the way his parents had griped about what was happening to the Catholic Church. How could you come back to something that wasn't there anymore?

He flew to Birmingham, Alabama, to Mother Angelica's church, and waited in line forty-five minutes before he got into a confessional. What followed was more like it.

"Father, it's been years."

"Very well. Would you like help in examining your conscience?"

"Please."

The priest began with sins against the flesh.

"There's been none of that."

"Good." He went down the list of capital sins, and Nate wanted to accuse himself of them all, but it wasn't until they came to greed that he felt on firm ground. He had been devoting twenty-four hours a day, seven days a week to making money. "I haven't been to Sunday Mass since I don't know when."

"And now you've come to confession."

"I'm going to change."

"I couldn't give you absolution otherwise."

For his penance he was to say the rosary every day for a week. Laura had got one for him, the first day he returned to the office. "Yes, Father."

"Now thank God for the grace of this confession."

When he went into the church and knelt it was with the feeling that scales had fallen from his eyes. He looked at the altar, at the sanctuary light flickering there. God had made him rich, and now he would use his wealth to honor God. And Mary his Blessed Mother.

It was then that he resolved to put the bulk of his fortune into a foundation, the Refuge of Sinners Foundation. Who would run it? He couldn't spare Ray or Laura. He prayed that he would find the right person as director, then flew home.

## ✣ II ✣

### "What do they pay you?"

Ignatius Hannan was wearing jeans, loafers, and a Notre Dame sweatshirt when Laura ushered her brother John and Father Crowe into his office. The loafers were propped on the wastebasket: he sat deep in his chair, his face in his hands, facing the window through which the grotto was visible. A contemplative moment. When he sat up and swung toward them, Laura was almost relieved that he didn't have a rosary in his hands.

"The Roman delegation," she announced.

Immediately, he was on his feet and rounding the desk, and on his face was the great smile he reserved for competitors whose company he intended to buy.

"Welcome to Empedocles!"

Brendan Crowe smiled, although he would have seen the name of the enterprise any number of times during the drive up the private road to the administration building.

"I suppose you would like wine?"

It was midmorning. Laura intervened, offering coffee, mineral water, a soft drink. Coffee it was, and soon they were all seated at the big table in the conference room and Nate was telling his clerical guests about his new dream. Refuge of Sinners.

"A rest home?" Crowe asked. He had the look of someone trying to get used to aliens from another planet.

Hannan looked at him. "It does suggest that, doesn't it? I am open to other names for it."

John asked what the aim was, and Nate was once more in

full flight. Enthusiasm is contagious, but the enthusiasm of Ignatius Hannan was in a league by itself. Laura watched the wariness fade from Crowe's face. John of course was easily won, but it was important that Crowe be sympathetic.

John had faxed ahead the preliminary list of paintings that Crowe had drawn up, including subject, artist, current location.

"No prices?" Nate had asked.

"They're all in museums."

Nate asked, "Don't museums buy their stuff?"

"I suppose."

"Then they'll sell it," Nate said.

Laura wasn't going to argue with him. She had some sense of the lack of realism in Nate's assumption that whatever he wanted was for sale and he could afford to buy it.

"A kind of museum?" Crowe asked.

Nate frowned. "It's what they represent, mysteries of the rosary. I want Refuge of Sinners—assuming we keep that name— to sell devotion to the Blessed Virgin with every marketing technique available. I have several people at work designing a building. What do you think of our present buildings?"

"Very impressive."

" 'Monuments to mediocrity.' Duncan Stroik told me that."

Laura had been there when the young Notre Dame architect made this dismissive judgment. She had feared that Nate would undo the young man's bow tie and drape it over his ears.

"He's right," Nate said now. "I want something different, a building appropriate to the purpose of the foundation."

The luncheon that eventually followed was also dominated by Nate, and the two priests were beginning to show strain. Whether it was ESP or simply belatedly remembered courtesy, Nate suddenly switched gears.

"Father Crowe, tell me what you do?"

He wanted a job description, and he got it, low key, self-deprecatory, but in a tone that conveyed to Nate that he was listening to a man who spoke with authority.

"I liked the list you made out."

"Anyone could have done that."

John protested. He seemed worried that Crowe would be taken on his own self-effacing description. "Father Crowe is second in command in the Vatican Library and head of the archives as well. He will very likely succeed Cardinal Maguire as prefect."

"Good Lord, John," Crowe said.

"It's true."

"What do they pay you?" Nate asked.

Silence fell. Crowe hadn't gotten much opportunity to speak before this, but now he was rendered speechless. He looked at John. John looked at him. In that setting, in the atmosphere of Empedocles where worth and wealth were two names for the same quality, the two men were nonetheless astounded by the directness of the question.

"Don't answer," Nate said, holding up a hand. "Whatever it is, I'll multiply it by as many factors as you wish."

"Nate," Laura pleaded. "Father Crowe is not looking for a job."

"That's why he's the man for the job."

In preliminary conversations, once they knew John was bringing Father Crowe with him, Ray had made the point that the Vatican librarian would doubtless be able to suggest names for the new post of forming and developing Refuge of Sinners. It had never entered Laura's mind that Nate would actually offer the job to Crowe. What wasn't surprising was that he assumed a large enough salary would overcome any reluctance.

"Father Crowe could act as a consultant," John said. "You could do that, couldn't you, Brendan?"

Crowe tried to laugh away this onslaught, he tried being serious, he tried everything, and Laura could see that he was flattered. And weakening. Of course, he couldn't be expected to pull up his roots in the Vatican and relocate to New England, but the role of senior consultant would not entail that.

"You could fly in every other week," Nate said. "You can keep an eye on things here from there. We'll provide state of the art access and make that easy."

Laura was instructed to draw up a memo indicating the current planning on the project. Planning? There had been effusions from Nate, excited and disconnected thoughts that might be considered the elements of what he was proposing to Brendan Crowe. Nate took Crowe out to the see the grotto, and Laura turned to John.

"Did I hear him agree, John?"

"He didn't say no."

"What do you think?"

"I feel I've been witnessing a seduction."

Through the course of the day, it was obvious that Brendan Crowe had an effect on Nate. It did take persuasion to get him away from the idea that he could simply buy up the list of paintings Crowe had prepared.

"But I know I've seen several of these."

"In books."

"On walls."

"Reproductions. Copies."

"They look real enough to me."

"They're real enough. They're just not the originals. Nowadays it's almost impossible to tell the difference."

And so emerged the idea that the new foundation would commission reproductions of the great works of art on Brendan Crowe's list. Crowe assured him that this would entail a healthy expenditure, and the deal was done. Brendan Crowe had already earned his title of chief consultant.

### ❖ III ❖

Hannan liked the little lecture on Thomas Aquinas.

Brendan Crowe felt that he had been taken to the pinnacle of the temple and shown all the good things of the world, good things that could all be his if only he would bend his will to that of Ignatius Hannan. When the exuberant tycoon rose from his knees at the grotto, he turned to the man he hoped he had gotten to join his team and said, "What do you think of it?"

He meant the grotto. Brendan found words to express his admiration for the exact replica. Americans were more amazing than he had thought. Hadn't one of the Rockefellers transported a medieval monastery stone by stone from Europe to New York? Hadn't the London Bridge been brought to Texas?

"It's more accurate than the one at Notre Dame," Hannan said, admiring what he had wrought.

Crowe had no words for that.

"You think I'm crazy, don't you?"

"Why would I think a thing like that?"

"Father, the only sure way to learn that money isn't the answer is to have it. I have it. More than I myself know. Of course my value fluctuates all the time, but it is a rising line. Where does it lead? How much more will be enough?"

Crowe, who for the first time in his life was in a position where he had only to reach out his hand and have things he had never really wanted before, nodded. "Saint Thomas Aquinas says much the same thing."

"Tell me about it. Come, let's walk."

Hannan led the way along a path that would take them to the building in which guests were lodged, while Crowe, feeling at once ridiculous and wise, gave Hannan a sketch of Thomas's discussion of all the things that cannot make us happy, cannot fulfill our desires. Wealth, fame, power, pleasure.

"After the abstract arguments against any of these, or all of them, being the happiness we seek, he adds what you just said. Having them is the best argument against them."

"Because it's God we want."

"That's right."

"And God came to us as a human being and to do that he needed a mother. He came to us through Mary. She's the way we go to him."

Sound doctrine, of course, but Brendan would never have imagined he would hear it preached in such a setting.

Hannan said, "Why do I have money? There's got to be a reason besides just having it. Well, I finally saw the reason and I want to do something about it. That's the point of Refuge of Sinners."

He made it easier, putting it like that. After all, why else was Brendan Crowe a priest if not to lead people to God? Being a priest had become his studies, his work in the Vatican Library, helping Maguire administer the museums, the archives, the library. And of course saying his daily Mass at the Domus, reciting the office each day. If Hannan's life seemed odd to him, what must his own seem to Hannan? He thought of the almost childish pleasure Cardinal Maguire had taken in his rooftop villa, and the garden he had there.

Then of course he thought of what had happened to the cardinal in that redoubt of peace. And he thought of Traeger. He was the man's prey, he was sure of it. And even if he weren't, Traeger's investigation would turn up things about Father Crowe, his connection with Catena, and that would be the end

of his Vatican career. It was fear that had prompted him to
agree to this incredible trip. It meant respite from Traeger's
incessant and unsettling questions. And now he was being
offered permanent refuge. In the Refuge of Sinners.

Cardinal Maguire's little rooftop garden had been transported from Ireland the way Hannan had made a replica of
Lourdes here in New Hampshire. Hannan had been to Lourdes
and to Fatima. Again, Crowe was struck by the power of the
man. No need to make arrangements for flights, bend his
schedule to that of airlines. He had only to call for his private
plane—one of his private planes, as it turned out—and off he
went. What must it be like to be able to act immediately on
any impulse like that? What kind of person would he himself
be in such circumstances?

Most moneyed people were self-indulgent libertines, forming marriages, breaking them up, finally not even bothering to
marry. Nouveaux riches, actors and actresses, athletes. Money
seemed to sweep aside all inhibitions; it certainly swept aside
most obstacles to instant gratification. Gather ye rosebuds
while ye may. Carpe diem. Go for all the gusto you can get.
Had Hannan gone down any of those other paths before he got
religion? Apparently not.

Earlier, when Laura was taking them to Hannan's office,
showing them the Empedocles complex, as she called it—it
sounded vaguely Freudian—Crowe had said, "It's like a religious community."

"And Nate is our abbot."

"What was he like before he returned to the faith?"

"He's always been a monk. He didn't have to change much."

Crowe had sensed Laura's distance from her boss's religious enthusiasms. Nothing overt, no condescension. More like
a wistful envy of his simplicity. What was her own life like, he
wondered. John seemed to assume that Laura was just a lovely
young woman who had been too busy to marry yet, but Crowe
guessed something else when Ray Sinclair was with them. Not
that he would ever bring up the subject with John, of course.

Hannan liked the little lecture on Thomas Aquinas. They
sat on one of the benches that were positioned at intervals
along the path.

"I want you in on this, Father."

"That's very flattering, of course."

"I'll be frank. Maybe there are others who know as much as you. I doubt it, but say there are. You've got the Roman connection."

"Exactly. And that's why your offer is unrealistic."

"I thought we settled that."

"Did we?" He found himself wishing that they had.

"You could be the chief consultant. You don't have to move here. You can get back and forth as often as needed. It won't interfere with your life."

He seemed actually to believe that. He was offering him a kind of instant mobility not even the pope could command. A double life.

But what else had he been living for years? He had been ready to respond to Bishop Catena, had shared the dissident prelate's conviction that things had gone woefully wrong in the Church as a result of the Council. That conviction had weakened under John Paul II, weakened but not gone entirely away. Some of the bishops that had been named! The madder heretics untouched by discipline or even scolding. The long patience of Rome, that was the usual explanation. But under Benedict a new intellectual rigor had been introduced. Crowe had come to think that a quiet revolution was going on. He remembered the hope that had risen at the time of Cardinal Ratzinger's interview with Vittorio Messori, the *Ratzinger Report*. The hopes raised had not been realized. But now Ratzinger was Benedict XVI. It was possible to believe that the decades of tumult were coming to an end. John Paul II had been a tireless cheerleader for the Council through his papacy. Benedict had spoken frankly of wrong turns taken, turns that had to be reversed.

"Why doesn't he just do it then?" Catena had said, his voice heavy with skepticism.

Crowe had sought out a meeting with Catena, to see if the confraternity was changing its attitude toward the papacy under the new regime.

"You can't just reestablish the Latin liturgy overnight."

"Why not?"

"If the people have been confused during these decades, what would a sudden change like that do to them?"

Catena obviously relished the thought of such an upheaval. He seemed to long for an immediate separation of the sheep from the goats.

"And don't forget the trickery about the third secret."

All that had flared up again when Cardinal Bertone published *The Last Seer of Fatima*. In the book he claimed that Sister Lucia agreed that what he and his then boss Cardinal Ratzinger had released in 2000 was all there was to the third secret. But zealots had immediately attacked Bertone for lying to the faithful. Scocci, Trepanier. And of course Catena.

They had met on the parapet of the Castel Sant'Angelo, the huge mausoleum that had been built to contain the remains of the emperor Hadrian. Two millennia had passed and the building still stood, a feature in much of the intervening history of the Eternal City, now a tame station on the tourist rounds. Crowe looked at the stern profile of Catena. He was glaring at the dome of Saint Peter's half a mile off, as if at the camp of the enemy. Crowe was suddenly weary of it all. Had he actually ever thought that this grumpy American knew something the Holy Father didn't?

Catena rehearsed all the familiar complaints. What had been made public could not be the whole secret. It did not connect with the text that had been long known, broken at the point where Lucia had been told to tell the rest only to the Holy Father. "In Portugal, the faith will . . ." Why hadn't the text Ratzinger had made public continued from that point?

"We know why."

What Catena knew, or thought he knew, was that the text had gone on to speak of the travails the faith would know in lands other than Portugal. It would have spoken of the ravages that had been wrought on the Church by Vatican II. That of course had to be suppressed. The prefect of the Congregation for the Doctrine of the Faith was not likely to make public the Blessed Mother's rejection of the Council. That was the key. The status quo had to be protected, no matter the desires of the Mother of God.

"You must have looked at the secret," Catena said. He had turned toward Crowe and studied his face.

"No."

"Surely you could."

"It is under the direct control of the prefect. And the Holy Father."

"Of course."

The beauty of Catena's theory was that everything fit into it.

The memory of that meeting at the Castel Sant'Angelo had come back when he found the documents on Cardinal Maguire's bedside table. It had taken no lengthy inner debate to take them and put them in his briefcase and spirit them out of the library. He had no desire at all to read the documents. His motive was to keep them away from people like Catena. Or Remi Pouvoir. Let the matter be closed, once and for all. That must have been Ratzinger's thought in 2000 when he had made public what he had.

Now Brendan Crowe sat on a bench with Ignatius Hannan in the Empedocles Complex in New Hampshire and the subject came up again.

"What do you think of these people who claim that parts of it were suppressed?" Hannan asked.

"Not much."

"Where is the thing kept?"

"In the Vatican Archives."

"Where you work?"

"Yes." Brendan got out a cigarette and lit it. Hannan watched with fascination.

"I never smoked."

"It's not necessary for salvation."

It took a while, but finally Hannan smiled. "Have you looked at it?"

The secret. "No."

"Could you?"

What would Hannan think if he knew that the document was in Crowe's briefcase in his suite in the guest building?

"Anybody can. It was made public in the year two thousand."

"Let me tell you about a priest named Jean-Jacques Trepanier."

## ❖ IV ❖

### "I thought you wanted money."

Gabriel Faust had a doctorate in art history from the University of Chicago, but his subsequent academic career had been brief. The lure of foundation grants, short-term tasks—cataloguing the holdings of private collectors—and modest dealings in minor art works, bringing buyers and sellers together, had brought him at the age of fifty to the recognition that he had not become what he had set out to be. His beau ideal was Bernard Berenson, whose villa in Florence had become the property of Harvard University. An early fellowship at the Villa I Tatti where the legendary Berenson, long since gathered to his fathers, remained the genius loci had caused Faust to turn his back on campus and classroom and embark on what he had hoped would be the replication of Berenson's career. With thus far unsatisfying results.

What fascinated Faust in Berenson was the fact that his model had fashioned his own job description, managing by shrewdness, vast knowledge, and a touch of larceny to dominate the art world, becoming the all but universally recognized final arbiter on art. It was that little touch of larceny, accounts of questionable dealings that had come under scrutiny only posthumously, that became central to Faust's admiration for Berenson and came to define the character of his own hoped-for career.

The epiphany had come on the night of his fiftieth birthday. He was in Paris on a fellowship from the National Endowment for the Arts. A planned celebration with friends had been postponed when a freakish bout of weather covered Paris with snow and all but extinguished life in the City of Light. In the end, he dined alone, had two bottles of wine, and then trudged back to his apartment where he continued to drink, nursing the feeling that the world was treating him badly. After fifteen years of abstinence he opened the pack of Gauloises Bleues he had bought on the way home and lit up. It was his way of giving a return one-up to the fickle finger of fate.

Any birthday can be the occasion of long thoughts, but to hit the half-century mark makes brooding mandatory. Faust reviewed his career and, in his melancholy mood, found himself concentrating on the defeats and reversals of his life since graduate school. He felt as bank tellers must, condemned to count out the money of others and receive a pittance in recompense. Art auctions were bringing in unprecedented prices. Faust had sat through half a dozen auctions during his stay in Paris and marveled at the amount paintings commanded long after their makers were dead. Great art that had been produced in garrets became a commodity traded for sums of which the artist would not have dared to dream. What irony. It became clearer to him than ever that it was the dealers, the middlemen, who were cleaning up. What had his broad and deep knowledge of Renaissance art brought him except small grants, the occasional commission to write a catalog for an exhibition in some midwestern town, dribs and drabs of income, and a reputation that hovered between anonymity and recognition from those whose recognition meant little? Must he return to academe and the security of a tenured position, frozen in mediocrity?

In search of aesthetic consolation, he began to shuffle through the small reproductions he had bought at Versailles some days before. This brought back his admiration for a Japanese artist, Inagaki, who worked at his easel making an exact copy of an El Greco while tourists wandered past, sometimes stopping to kibitz, then moving on. Faust did not move on. He sat on a windowsill behind the artist and watched him work. All that skill devoted to reproducing the work of others. Surely, the artist had not set out to become what he was. Faust thought of violinists in the metro playing their instruments with consummate skill to indifferent passersby whose thoughts were only on the next train. From time to time, someone would drop coins into the beret the musician had put on the pavement before him. All musicians play the music of others, of course, but surely this haunted fellow had not devoted months and years to mastering his instrument in order to coax a few coins from indifferent subway passengers. But Faust could not put the copyist in the Versailles palace among other instances of dashed hopes. For one thing, the man seemed wholly absorbed in what he was doing, as if this had indeed been what he set himself to do. His copy was as good as the original; in some ways it seemed better. But hadn't Charlie Chaplin entered a Charlie Chaplin look-alike contest and come in third?

Faust finally drifted away, but with the intention of returning to the spot when the museum was closing. He wanted to make the acquaintance of the Japanese copyist. But when he went back, the easel was covered with a cloth and the artist was gone. His surge of disappointment made clear to him that his interest in the man was not a whim. And then, ah destiny, kismet, providence, he saw the artist waiting at the bus stop, smoking a cigarette. Faust hurried toward him as if he were keeping an appointment. He introduced himself. The artist smiled in incomprehension. Faust repeated himself in French.

*"Vous êtes vraiment artiste."*

*"Merci, mais non. Je ne fais que des copies."*

Faust shook his head. *"Une photographe est une copie. Ce que vous faites est quelque chose tout à fait autre."*

"I do speak English." A little bow. "I thought you wanted money."

Not a flattering estimate, but Faust brushed away the remark that had the makings of an unintentional insult. He felt that this was a moment of maximum importance in his life, though he scarcely knew why.

"Gabriel Faust," he said, putting out his hand.

"Inagaki. Miki Inagaki."

"I have a car. Can I take you someplace?"

He hesitated. Then he looked at the crowd waiting at the bus stop. He picked up his paint box and they went off to Faust's car.

Inagaki was staying in a little hotel near Saint Germain des Prés. Faust found a parking place and took the artist off for a drink at Les Deux Magots. They drank sweet vermouth while Faust questioned the artist.

"What do you do with the finished painting?"

"Oh, it is commissioned. I never begin without a commission."

"Is it profitable?"

Inagaki became wary, so Faust reassured his new friend with an account of his own life, the kind of edited curriculum vitae that made all the difference between a successful and unsuccessful grant application. Inagaki would have been forgiven if he thought he was drinking with a university professor on sabbatical.

"If I could afford it, I would give you a commission myself."

Inagaki smiled as at a polite remark.

"What are your fees?"

"That depends."

"I'm afraid there would be a large gap between what I think your work is worth and what I could afford to pay."

"What painting were you thinking of?"

Faust's grant was meant to enable him to study Delacroix, an effort to branch out. Would Inagaki think one of the artist's watercolor sketches of horses too undemanding? Inagaki smiled enigmatically.

Faust had not pressed the matter. Now, on his fiftieth birthday, alone and morose, he thought of Inagaki, he thought of Berenson, he smoked and drank and let the fuzzy idea form. In the morning, he had forgotten all about it, but then he had a terrible headache. The little reproductions from Versailles brought it back. Night thoughts, particularly when fueled by drink, seldom survive the scrutiny of daylight. But this idea was different.

For the rest of his stay in Paris, he had cultivated Inagaki. They became friends of a sort. Several times they went off to a brothel and this seemed to seal some unstated bargain between them. Before he left Paris, Faust had exchanged e-mail addresses with Inagaki. He was almost surprised when the Delacroix arrived. He was about to go to Massachusetts at the invitation of Zelda Lewis, one of his patrons, a woman for whom he had cataloged the paintings her dead husband had collected. He sold her the Delacroix for a large sum but far less than a putative original should bring. He sent half of that to Inagaki, and so they had become partners of a sort. Going to bed with a tipsy Zelda had been almost inadvertent, but once in bed the discrepancy of their ages was forgotten. After some years of abstinence, Zelda proved a voracious lover. Afterward she wept at such infidelity to the memory of her husband. Faust soothed her, and soon there was a second round.

"It will be our secret," he whispered. He might have meant the Delacroix.

# Chapter Four

## ❖ I ❖

**"What are we looking for?"**

Brendan Crowe had disappeared.

When Traeger learned that Father Crowe had not been to his office for two days, his first impulse was to check the rooftop villa to see if Crowe had met the same fate as his boss. The librarian had clearly never thought of himself as in danger until Traeger had mentioned it to him. Now he wished he hadn't. The frightened Crowe seemed to have just vanished.

Rodriguez, fortunately, had been on the job.

"He's gone to America."

"America."

"He and Father John Burke."

"Where in America?"

Rodriguez could only guess. But he was sure it was connected with Father Burke's sister Laura's visit. "Have you ever heard of Empedocles?"

Traeger thought. "There are two possibilities. A pre-Socratic philosopher and a New England electronics firm."

"Laura Burke is the administrative assistant to the founder of Empedocles."

"Ignatius Hannan."

"Do you know him?"

Traeger knew of him, of course, because of his consulting business. And through Zelda Lewis he had learned more of Ignatus Hannan. Bea didn't approve of Zelda.

"She's a customer."

Bea's silence was eloquent. Well, she wasn't that far off. Zelda played the forlorn widow card masterfully, but the memory of her husband Chuck seemed all the protection Traeger needed. During the first year, he had taken his turn with Dortmund, helping Zelda through her bereavement.

"She ought to marry again," Dortmund said, not complaining, just expressing a wish.

"You never did."

"She's still a young woman."

Well, younger than Dortmund. About Traeger's age.

"A home computer?" Bea asked when Zelda called to ask him to come check her system. Not exactly the level on which Traeger worked, but he thought of Chuck. What the hell. Zelda had hired a man to do a catalog of her collection. Most of the paintings she had brought to the marriage with her. Chuck would have collected baseball cards if he collected anything. But it had been a happy marriage, so far as the outside observer could tell. However their tastes and interests diverged, it was pretty clear that the fundamental point of marriage was there. So Traeger had driven off to see Zelda, one more favor to a fallen colleague.

"I don't understand how I'm supposed to access the program," Zelda complained after the teary reminiscences were over.

"What are we looking for?"

"Oh, nothing in particular. I just want to know how to get at things."

"Who set it up for you?" Traeger asked.

"An art historian. The man who did the catalog. Gabriel Faust."

"Didn't he break you in?"

Zelda got flustered. "Break me in?"

"Show you how to use the program."

"I guess I didn't pay close enough attention. I hated to call him." She looked away. "A stranger."

It was an Empedocles program, far more than what was required for the catalogue Faust had put together. Even so, Traeger was sure Zelda's call had just been an excuse. Well, why not? She must lead a lonely life. She showed him her Delacroix and Traeger said the usual things.

"Pretty expensive?"

"I can afford it."

It turned out that it had been her suggestion that Faust use an Empedocles program. She spoke of Ignatius Hannan with awe.

"Do you know him?"

"I own stock, Vincent. I go to the meetings."

So Traeger had found out who Hannan was, beyond the programs and billion dollar company he had fashioned, that is.

Zelda adopted a pious expression. "And I see him at Mass."

"What's he like?"

"Devout." She sounded disappointed.

Devout was the word. Traeger kept checking and found out about the replica of the grotto of Lourdes. He also checked out the Delacroix. The painting Zelda had bought was in a museum in Cincinnati.

"I wonder what the original would cost," he asked Zelda.

"Oh, that is an original."

If Traeger had had time, he would have checked out Gabriel Faust.

⚜

It was Rodriguez who had mentioned the Confraternity of Pius IX.

"What's that?"

"A bunch of crazies. They have a kind of community under a man who calls himself a bishop."

"Isn't he a bishop?"

Rodriguez shrugged. "China is full of bishops."

Traeger needed an explanation of that. In China bishops were ordained for the national church, against the wishes of Rome.

"It's not that they're not genuine bishops. But their status is irregular. Only Rome can appoint bishops."

"And Catena is an irregular bishop?" Traeger said.

The Catholic Church was becoming a very complicated place. During his years in Rome, Traeger had thought of it as a monolith. He must have been aware of the grumbling among traditional Catholics who thought the Church had taken a wrong turn. But what one usually heard about was wild theologians who made media careers out of contradicting whatever came out of Rome.

"Are you saying Crowe is connected with this confraternity?"

Rodriguez seemed to compose his answer in his mind before voicing it. "No. But he had a meeting with Catena at the Castel Sant'Angelo. Out in the open, on a parapet one afternoon. But it had the look of a clandestine meeting."

"What holds the confraternity together?"

Rodriguez wrinkled his nose. "Fatima."

"The secret," Traeger guessed.

"That's right."

No need to develop the thought. The secret was missing and now Crowe was missing, too. Traeger decided to look in at the Domus Sanctae Marthae.

Inside the building, at the desk, he said he wanted to get in touch with John Burke. The man behind the desk seemed delighted to be able to disappoint him.

"He's away."

"When will he be back?"

Thick brows rose above thick glasses. "I'm afraid . . ."

"It's important."

There was the unmuffled sound of high heels on the marble floor as a young woman approached the desk and joined the man with the eyebrows. She spoke to the clerk in Italian. As she answered, she looked at Traeger.

"He's gone to America," she said. "Just a visit."

"Is Father Crowe in?"

She beamed. "They went together."

The man with the eyebrows disapproved of such cordiality and helpfulness and moved away down the long counter.

"You're not a priest," she continued.

"Not yet."

She laughed. It seemed a waste of a good woman, working in a residence filled with clerics, priests, bishops, archbishops.

"I know we've met," he said, looking thoughtful. "It's Donna, isn't it? Donna Quando?"

She dipped her head and turned the nameplate so he couldn't read it anymore.

"Oh is that yours? I thought it was his."

He liked her laugh.

Even apart from the hope that she could tell him things he wanted to know, he found her an attractive woman. Thirty at the most, with thick black hair that set off her olive complexion.

"Who are you?" But there was a chuckle in her voice.

"I only talk over coffee."

She looked at him. She looked at her watch. "I just came back from coffee. I finish at four."

At ten after four she came through the gate, earning a salute from the guard, and marched right up to Traeger.

"Where to?"

"You're the native."

At an outdoor table, she ordered a Cinzano and Traeger asked for a scotch and water, but when that drew a blank with the waiter, he too asked for Cinzano.

"I tasted scotch once," Donna Quando said. "It tasted like iodine."

"I've never tasted iodine."

Their drinks came and he took a sip. "This tastes like mouthwash."

"All right," she said. "Who are you and what are you after?"

"I'm Vincent Traeger."

"I already know that."

"I didn't give you my name."

"Carlos did."

"Rodriguez?"

She nodded. There are questions you just don't ask, and he was not about to ask her if she worked with Rodriguez. And there was apparently no need to explain to Donna what he was doing in Rome.

"Tell me about John Burke."

"There's nothing to tell. He's a marvelous young priest, attached to the pontifical academies. I suppose he'll spend a few more years here and then they'll send him home as a bishop."

"The same with Brendan Crowe?"

"He's older, you know. Older than John Burke. His career is likely to keep him right here. Of course you know what happened to Cardinal Maguire."

"You think Crowe will succeed him?"

"It's possible. He's standing in for Maguire until an appointment is made. Not that he would be created a cardinal, at least not right away. Leonard Boyle was not even a bishop when he died."

Leonard Boyle, who had been prefect of the Vatican Library before Maguire, was an Irish Dominican who had died in office and was buried in the crypt at San Clemente.

"Do you know where all the former prefects are buried?" he asked her.

"Only those who are dead."

"Is being Irish part of the job description?"

"Oh no. Boyle's predecessor was a German."

Donna thought Rodriguez was making quite a jump, linking Brendan Crowe to the Confraternity of Pius IX. "That's a pretty weird outfit, you know. There were actually people who thought Paul VI was an imposter. The real pope spirited away and another put in his place. It turned on earlobes."

"You're kidding."

"The real Paul VI had longer earlobes than the man who took his place." She laughed. "Andre Gide."

He waited.

"*The Caves of the Vatican.* A terrible novel. A terrible author."

"The Vatican Library does seem an odd place for a weirdo."

"Crowe is a quintessential insider. Part of the bureaucracy."

"A mole would have to be plausible."

Had Rodriguez told her of the missing secret of Fatima? It didn't come up.

"The man Father Burke's sister works for wanted a list of paintings of the Blessed Virgin. Crowe put it together. I assume that's the purpose of the visit."

❖

Traeger was trying to put together two motives for the murders in the Vatican. Chekovsky's curious insistence suggested one, the missing Fatima secret, another. The third secret of Fatima and the reports on the attempted assassination of John Paul II were connected, because the secret had predicted an attack on the pope. Even so, Traeger didn't know if there really were two problems and if so which of them was his. His experience with Anatoly the day before left the question up in the air.

So he sat sipping Cinzano with Donna Quando and thought

of Brendan Crowe off in New Hampshire. You might have thought that Crowe was on the run.

## ✣ II ✣

### The number of mosques in Rome had grown.

Cardinal Piacere awoke with the realization that he had been dreaming of the task that faced him today. It was four thirty. Immediately, when his eyes opened, he threw back the covers and swung his old legs over the side of the bed. The marble floor beneath his feet felt sharply cold. He stood, his feet pressed down more firmly against the marble, and the difference of temperature between flesh and stone began to diminish. He stood, palms pressed tightly together, eyes closed, and offered this day to God.

How many trains of thought can the human mind accommodate simultaneously? He entered the routine of another day with little need to think of its stages. He shaved with an electric razor, then three minutes in the shower, the water as cold as he could bear, cleaning his teeth and anchoring his partial, then dressing. Trousers, shirt, Roman collar, and then the black soutane with buttons running from collar to shoe tops. But of course the buttons were ornamental; the cassock had a zipper. When he sank to his knees on his prie-dieu, it was as if his prayers were continuing, not beginning. His hand closed over his breviary.

The *Liturgia Horarum* was the considerably reduced daily prayer of the clergy and religious. In becoming briefer, requiring half the time the *Breviarium Romanum* had taken, the new office had lengthened by providing choices, alternatives. All lovely readings, no doubt, but what is the basis for choosing between an excerpt from the Epistle of John and Augustine's comments on it? Piacere had gone back to the old breviary for a time, but then decided that was an affectation. And it could have formed the basis for one of those pieces of gossip that went under the name of news. Vatican Official Refuses to Accept New Liturgy.

Was it simply nostalgia? After reciting the first two hours of the office, Piacere rose and went down the corridor to the chapel. His five o'clock Mass was the first said there each day. He used the *Novus Ordo* introduced by Paul VI, in Latin, and the Roman canon, and Luigi the sacristan acted as altar boy, bringing the cruets of water and of wine, pouring water over Piacere's fingers at the end of the offertory. The Latin words he murmured meant "Lord, wash away my iniquities and cleanse me of my sins."

Throughout all these familiar daily actions, done with attention and devotion, Piacere's mind was also on today's meeting with the Holy Father.

Once he and Josef might have discussed the epistemological problem involved. How many thoughts can the mind entertain simultaneously? He could imagine the answer. An indefinite number. Once his old friend had said of another that he knows everything. Piacere had chided him for such hyperbole. He was fixed by the kind Teutonic eye and then:

"Does he know animal?"

Piacere lifted his hands.

"In knowing animal he knows both man and beast. Does he know living thing? Then he knows both plants and animals. Does he know substance?"

It was because the man knew being that Josef felt justified in saying that he knew everything.

"But then it's no longer praise. *Ens est primum quod cadit in intellectu humano.* We all know everything."

"Potentially."

They went on to angelic knowledge then, and how it differed from human. Piacere smiled.

Mass said, thanksgiving made, he went to the refectory where he had his breakfast while standing. All over the city, Romans would be standing in bars having their coffee and croissants. Why should he sit down for his? Back in his rooms, he sat, cleared his mind of all competing thoughts, and concentrated on the problem of the day.

Within the past weeks they had lost two cardinals: Rampolla, the secretary of state, and Maguire, the prefect of the Vatican Library. Murdered, both of them, and while at their daily tasks. Incredibly, the deaths had not aroused the suspicion of the corps of newsmen who lolled around the Sala Di Prenza much of the day. Wars, natural disasters, and political upheaval elsewhere had reduced events in the Vatican to the back pages.

Vatican City, within the walls, seemed an island of peace and security, and so in many ways it was. But a pope had been shot in Saint Peter's Square not long ago, and now an assassin had gained access to the Apostolic Palace and killed two cardinals. The guard, too, of course, and Buffoni the young priest who worked in the secretary of state's office. Piacere murmured some prayers for them all. Can a bishop go to heaven? Can a Vatican bureaucrat be saved?

Piacere had preached the Lenten retreat for the Holy Father the year before, and had based his conferences on Saint Augustine's warning to those raised to the episcopate. It was an odd thought, that rising in the ecclesiastical hierarchy increased one's spiritual danger. It was an odder thought that it increased one's physical danger. Or was it? John alone of the apostles had died a natural death, doubtless because the Mother of the Lord had been entrusted to his care. The cardinal red that Piacere would wear when he kept his appointment with the Holy Father signified his willingness to die for the faith. There were long stretches of time when that seemed a quaint thought. But the world was once more a savage place.

Anarchists and assassins there had always been, but the televised collapse of the twin towers in New York had brought home the vulnerability of the world's sole remaining superpower to the attack of dedicated madmen. Mad with religion. The number of mosques in Rome had grown, the vast mosque down the Tiber from the Vatican was only the most obvious instance, a deliberate and hostile move, and there was talk of an eventual caliphate of Rome. The centuries-old war between Christendom and Islam after a long quiescent interval had entered a new phase. No wonder the Russians wanted the reports on the attempted assassination of John Paul II made public. Over the years it had become the common opinion that the USSR and the KGB had been behind that attempt. Piacere and the Holy Father knew it was not quite that simple. But what good would be served by making the truth known?

But it was the absence of the third secret of Fatima from the archives that was on the agenda today.

Who would have taken it, and why?

Piacere had said to Rodriguez that he would not speculate when the head of Vatican security had come to him with the news. And he would not, not aloud. Except to Benedict.

If the document written by Sister Lucia was gone, anything might be substituted for it. And there were those whose single-minded discontent would tempt them to supply the message they were sure had been suppressed when Josef had made public the secret in the year 2000. Forty years after it should have been made public.

There was no point in second-guessing the prudent decision of others to withhold the secret. Josef had tried to mitigate the failure when, in 1985, he had spoken of it to Vittorio Messori. The reporter asked if the cardinal had read the Fatima document.

*"Si, l'ho letto."*

He had read it. So why hadn't it been made public? Speculation about it was everywhere. The reply had been that everything that need be known about the faith was known. Fatima merely recalled the need for conversion. And then he had said, *"Pubblicare il 'terzo segreto' significherebbe anche esporsi al pericolo di utilizzaioni sensazionaliste del contenuto."* To publish the third secret would run the risk of sensational uses of its content.

Further than that, he would not go. But why would the secret lend itself to sensational use?

The reaction to those few remarks had made it clear that they would not suffice. They had waited for the skepticism to subside, but already they had known that nothing short of full disclosure could quiet those who did not hesitate to accuse the Vatican of duplicity. And so in 2000, the full disclosure had been made.

The result had been a little book, beginning with a lengthy introduction by Tarcisio Bertone, then secretary of the Congregation for the Doctrine of the Faith, and ending with then Cardinal Ratzinger's theological commentary. Sandwiched between, *ut ita dicam*, was a letter of John Paul II to Sister Lucia and a sermon preached at Fatima by Cardinal Sodano. In four short pages, written by Sister Lucia on January 3, 1944, the third secret, that is, what had previously been withheld, was published. Those pages were provided in facsimile in the document. The first part of the secret was a vision of hell the three children were given, where poor sinners go; poor sinners must be prayed for in the hope that they would repent and avoid such dreadful punishment. The second part was the key to preventing souls from going to hell and preventing earthly punishment of sin as well.

Worse wars will come if people do not cease offending God. Devotion to the Immaculate Heart of Mary, prayers and penance, but specifically the request that the Holy Father consecrate Russia to Mary, can prevent this. If this is not done, another and worse war will break out during the Pontificate of Pius XI.

So much had been known for many years, World War II had come and devotion to Our Lady of Fatima had spread around the world. But for some, curiosity about what had not been made public became almost an obsession.

And what was the third part of the secret? Piacere consulted the little booklet on his desk.

> *The third part of the secret revealed on July 13, 1917 in the Cova di Lira, Fatima.*
>
> *After the two parts which I have already explained, at the left of Our Lady and a little above, we saw an Angel with a flaming sword in his left hand; flashing, it gave out flames that looked as though they would set the world on fire, but they died out in contact with the splendor that Our Lady radiated towards him from her right hand: pointing to the earth with his right hand, the Angel cried out in a loud voice: "Penance, Penance, Penance!" And we saw in an immense light that is God, something similar to how people appear in a mirror when they pass in front of it a Bishop dressed in White, we had the impression that it was the Holy Father. Other Bishops, Priests, men and women Religious going up a steep mountain, at the top of which there was a Big Cross of rough-hewn trunks as of a cork-tree with the bark; before reaching there the Holy Father passed through a big city half in ruins and half trembling with halting step, afflicted with pain and sorrow, he prayed for the souls of the corpses he met on his way; having reached the top of the mountain, on his knees at the foot of the Cross he was killed by a group of soldiers who fired bullets and arrows at him, and in the same way there died one after another the other Bishops, Priests, men and women religious, and various lay people of different ranks and positions. Beneath the two arms of the Cross there were two Angels each with a crystal aspersorium in hand, in which they gathered the blood of the Martyrs and with it they sprinkled the souls that were making their way to God.*

That was it. A prophecy of persecution of the Church, the killing of pope, bishops, nuns and priests, and laity. Had the assassination attempt on John Paul II been the fulfillment of that prophecy? Well, he survived the attack, and attributed that fact to the intercession of Our Lady of Fatima.

⚜

Piacere had begun his career teaching ascetic theology at the Gregorianum, the university of his Jesuit order, an outgrowth of the Collegio Romano where luminaries of the Counter-Reformation had taught. From it had gone out over the world the Ratio Studiorum, the blueprint for higher education that had formed the Catholic mind in Europe and in the New World. It was as a professor that Piacere had learned that students, facing an examination, had an insatiable curiosity for any information as to what lay ahead. He had provided notes, outlines, sample questions. It was never enough. He should have known from that experience that for those whose minds were fixated on the third secret of Fatima, nothing would suffice to allay their doubts; not even the complete document, as the revelation of 2000 had proved.

And now the document was gone. It was easy to imagine those who had gained possession of it poring over it and finding that what they sought simply was not there. All he had to do was put himself in their shoes. To call them zealots was not enough. They were fanatics. After the initial disappointment would come the supposed explanation. They had come into possession of an altered document, carefully planted in the archives against just such a theft as had occurred. Fatima zealots dismissed the assurances of Sister Lucia herself that the Holy Father had done all that the Blessed Mother had asked of him. In America, the intemperate Trepanier insisted that the dedication of the world to the Immaculate Heart of Mary, with particular reference to Russia, had not been sufficient. Sister Lucia said otherwise. Of course she did. Sister Lucia was being manipulated by Church bureaucrats.

Piacere's advice to the Holy Father would be that they must prepare for the publication of a forged document that would contain the message desired by the zealots.

More seriously, they could not counter it with the original, now that it was gone.

Piacere's eyes lifted to the picture on the wall between the two windows that looked out on the courtyard of his residence building. A Giotto. A copy. But it could be compared with the original. He glanced at his watch, unnecessarily; he was on schedule. He took out his rosary and began to tell the beads.

The Annunciation. The Angel of the Lord declared unto Mary, and she conceived of the Holy Spirit. Here was the first chapter in the history of salvation, Mary's acceptance of her role as the Virgin Mother of God. But he was distracted by the thought of what effect on the faithful the annunciation of a forged third secret of Fatima would have.

The People of God had been put to the test during these decades since the Council; there was no need to deny that. The liturgy made banal, the loss of the common language of the Church, the ritual subjected to the silliest alterations. And confusion about the moral teaching of the Church, the long, sad history of *Humanae Vitae*. When contraception had been proposed as the remedy for marital difficulties, Piacere had been sure that the argument would fall of its own weight. How could the denial of the nature of conjugal union make marriages flourish? But the dissenters had succeeded in subverting the teaching of the Church, and the results were all around, at least in the so-called first world.

What would the confused faithful make of the claim that the Church had deliberately suppressed the judgment of the Blessed Virgin, that the Council itself had been subversive, that the Church had been conquered by her enemies, enemies within the walls who would be made to seem far more menacing than those without?

His phone rang. It was Rodriguez telling him that Brendan Crowe was nowhere to be found. Crowe was to have accompanied him on his visit to the Holy Father.

"You're sure."

"He's gone to the United States."

✣ III ✣

"Is that an invitation?"

In the Sala di Prenza on the Via della Conciliazione, questions were asked about the deaths of Cardinal Rampolla, the secretary of state, and Cardinal Maguire, the prefect of the Vatican Library. Two cardinals in one day. What would a slot machine pay off on that? Neal Admirari asked the question of Pescatore of the *Corriere della Sera* and got a smile. But then Pescatore always smiled when he hadn't heard what was said. Pescatore began waving his hand at the Iberian smoothy who was spokesman for the Vatican. Opus Dei. A medical doctor. What was he doing here? Secret assignment? The press called him Ferdinand the Bull. Pescatore's hand was ignored, but Neal's was not.

He stood. It seemed a sign of respect. But otherwise he might not have been visible to his cameraman. "As a medical doctor, what do you think is the likelihood of two prominent figures expiring on the same day, at the same hour, in the same place?"

"Are they in an airplane?"

Laughter all around. Neal joined in. He could be a good sport. "Say they have offices in the Vatican?" Neil asked.

"And are well into their seventies? Even with the advances of modern medicine, those in their seventies are in the twilight of their lives."

The melodious voice dropped as he spoke, lids half lowered over dark eyes, portrait of a medical man lamenting the limits of his art.

"What were the exact ages of Rampolla and Maguire?"

"Copies of their obituaries are available in the back of the room. Next." He looked brightly about the room in search of other questions not to answer.

Before sitting down again, Neal looked toward the corner. Rorty, his photographer, touched the tips of thumb and index finger. Of course there was no assurance that the footage would be used. Neal wasn't sure he wanted his performance shown on the network news at home.

"That was a good question," Pescatore said to him when the press conference was over. He seemed serious.

Neal shrugged. Pescatore's next remark was more typical, a criticism.

"You might have mentioned young Buffoni, the secretary's secretary."

The description made the priest sound like Jeeves, a gentleman's gentleman. "Did you ever play the slots?"

Pescatore backed away, as if his honor had been questioned. Neal shouted after him, "Take two if you can get them. You don't need three to win."

Pescatore, who had a wife in an apartment on Monti Parioli and a mistress in another in EUR, reacted with alarm. He bowled his way out of the press room, looking back at Neal as if fearful of some further outrage.

"What's with the guinea?" Rorty asked. The cameraman's snobbishness had caused him to overlook Neal's origins.

"A guinea is a shilling more than a pound."

"Shillings are obsolete."

"So is calling Italians guineas."

They parted on the sidewalk outside the building, which was located on the Via della Conciliazione, the thoroughfare now clogged with buses, taxis, other vehicles. The walk swarmed with sweaty tourists. Rorty looked about him with disdain. Rorty would be off to a shower, and then, dressed the part, the means of his livelihood stashed, he would hang around the lobby of the Grand Hotel hoping to be picked up. Someone had told him he looked like George Clooney, and he could usually be found in places where affluent, unspoken-for ladies were looking for diversion. Neal was sure that someone must have meant Clooney in *O Brother, Where Art Thou?*

The Vatican correspondents were an odd group: the Europeans, militant secularists; the Asians, inscrutable; those from the third world pretending innocence and naïveté. Among the so-called first world representatives, there was a preponderance of laicized priests with a chip on their shoulder or lapsed Catholics of various kinds, mostly those whose doctrinal difficulties had emerged from their irregular personal lives. There were also writers from Catholic news services, a few columnists famous in the pages of diocesan papers. Neal Admirari did and did not fit in with this group, a hesitation felt on all sides. Who among them had won so important an honor as the Pulitzer? Alas, that had been years ago, but Neal still lived in the large hope of repeating his feat by coming up with a scoop that would reinvigorate his career. What else did he have? His long-term affair with Lulu van Ackeren had finally run its course and she had married a man five years her junior. Neal had felt betrayed.

"Neal, if I wanted a career as a waiter, I could have taken a job in a restaurant."

"Okay, we'll get married."

"Go to hell."

"I mean it."

"A civil wedding?" she hissed. "Or have you found some priest who will overlook my previous marriage?"

Among the impediments to a sacramental marriage, having a valid previous marriage where the former spouse was still living was a bar to a Church-sanctioned union. He had tried to convince Lulu that it was only a matter of time until she could find a way to get her previous marriage annulled.

"When?" she asked. "A century? Two centuries?"

The cynic he thought he was would long since have made Lulu the wife of his heart by whatever ceremony she chose. Before Lulu, he had been a marauding bee, avid for the nectar of many and various flowers. Serial fornication, or adultery, as the priests might call it; whatever they called it, he knew it was sinful. Periodically, Neal had gone to confession and was dealt a new hand. But he had soon returned to the same game as before. But Lulu had been different. He had loved her exclusively for five years. Only after he realized he was in love with her, that he wanted to marry her, had she mentioned her first marriage.

She tried to load it all on him, but Lulu was Catholic, too. She knew Neal Admirari didn't make up the rules. She accepted those rules herself. It added a zestful dash of tragedy to their affair. The star-crossed lovers, forever prevented from plighting their troth before a minister of God. During all that time Lulu had honed her role, knowing she could count on Neal's adherence to Church law, safe to suggest that she would settle for one of those chapels in Las Vegas. *Casamentos.* He told Lulu it meant casements. The ladder into the pits.

And she had married Martinelli.

Martinelli!

"He's Italian?" Neal asked.

"Only on his parents' side."

"Have you become a widow?"

"For the kingdom of heaven's sake." She had actually gotten an annulment of her first marriage.

Neal had stared at her in disbelief. The big impediment was no more. And she had married Martinelli.

That was the unkindest cut of all. Neal volunteered for the Rome post when his predecessor was arrested for currency speculation and had to be spirited out of the country. Rome was either the end or the new beginning of his career. Pescatore's praise came back to him. Were these simultaneous deaths his ticket out of impending oblivion?

He beat out a fat couple for a free table, ordered a birra alla spina, and called Donna Quando, the contact he had inherited with the job.

"Tell me about Buffoni."

"Is that an invitation?"

"I was thinking of Sabatini's."

"I'll meet you there."

## ✣ IV ✣

### "Better well hung than ill wed."

Gabriel Faust had a dream, a dream that had been considerably scaled down over the years.

Once he would have imagined ending in a villa near Florence, filled with art works, a magnificent library, with scholars from around the world coming to him for consultation. I Tatti as it had been, that is, and himself the Bernard Berenson of the day. But many things had conspired to alter the dream.

What had happened to Europe? What had happened to Italy? What had happened to Florence? He had read the inflammatory trilogy by Oriana Fallaci, the famous Florentine journalist's enraged indictment of the Italian government's capitulation to the demands of the Muslims who had poured into the country and were now intent on redefining it as a caliphate. Their contemptuous desecration of the baptistery in Florence seemed a sign of things to come. It was appalling. And he could accept for himself Fallaci's self-description—a Catholic atheist. No, Italy was no longer the land of his dreams. Not Florence. Not even Sicily. Sardinia, perhaps, or Corsica? But either would have been a poor second best. And now he had come to

Corfu and had to erase one more island as the possible candidate for the land of his dreams.

Where can one hide in the modern world? That had become the question that haunted him. Possible answers to the question had to be dismissed one by one, but he could not entirely abandon his dream. Somewhere his Shangri-la must still be awaiting him.

The problem, however, was not so much location as his personal status. However much, in the privacy of his own mind, he rehearsed the role of art mentor to the Western world—his wealth an incidental accompaniment perhaps, but wealth indeed, if not beyond the dreams of avarice, certainly exceeding the limits of immoderate appetite—an arctic honesty came over him. The role eluded him because he did not fit the role.

A corner had been turned when he entered into alliance with the incredible Inagaki; one that had made him the agent of the talented Japanese, not to say his pimp. Faust no longer sought the modest commissions that had kept him afloat. He no longer bothered applying for grants—the getting of them was child's play but being awarded them left him treading financial water. None of his research projects had come anywhere near the vast promise he had expressed in understated form in order to receive the pittance that seemed only to provide more time for witnessing the dying of his dream. His last major grant had been from the NEA when he had failed to emerge from Renaissance into modern art, classifying Delacroix as modern. His last commission had been the cataloguing of the impressive if modest collection that Zelda Lewis had inherited and added to in a small way. It was her purchase of the bogus Delacroix that had been Gabriel Faust's Rubicon. In the cold light of wakeful early morning, or when too drunk to kid himself, he knew he had entered the world of art fraud. Inagaki was indefatigable and incurious about the commissions Faust got him. But then the Japanese, who could paint anything at least as well as the original he copied, exhibited no curiosity as to the way Faust marketed his wares. Inagaki could always plausibly claim not to know that Faust sold his copies as originals. Those who bought and marketed the copies were no more deluded about what they were than Faust himself. He had entered a network of crooks, and he was one of them.

It was in a hotel in Corfu, where Faust had planned to stay just overnight, that, in the morning, he let the ship go on to Greece without him. His midday breakfast was a cup of thick, strong coffee and a local pastry. From the window of his hotel dining room he looked out at the sea that had known a thousand shipwrecks and still rolled on in blithe indifference to the hopes and dreams of men. It seemed particularly disdainful of the dreams of Gabriel Faust, sliding into the shore and curling back on itself. He had arrived at a moment of sober truth. It was there, in the all-but-deserted dining room, that he heard, though he was on the wrong coast for the allusion, the thin, seductive siren call of Zelda Lewis.

He remembered her home, he remembered her collection, he remembered the warmth with which they had sinned together. His thoughts began to travel along unfamiliar lines. Was Zelda Lewis the destiny toward which he had been headed all along?

He waited for the thought to depress him, but the more he entertained it, the more gently attractive it became. Her estate, her wealth, could be his equivalent of Robert Louis Stevenson's South Pacific final resting place. Home is the sailor, home from the sea, and the hunter home from the hill. He put through a call to Zelda, collect.

It was morning in New Hampshire and Zelda took the call while still abed. Her softly seductive voice seemed to emerge from the world of dreams. Where was he calling from?

"Corfu."

"You needn't be nasty."

He located it for her and her tone altered, as if she were sitting up in bed and propping the pillows behind her. She had never been to Corfu.

"I'm not sure I've ever heard of it before."

"It's still largely unspoiled," he lied. "Prince Philip, the queen's consort, was born here. You would love it."

"Is that an invitation?" Whatever is received is received according to the mode of the receiver, in this case the telephone receiver.

"You mustn't raise my hopes, Zelda."

"Darling, are you serious? Would you like me to join you there?"

"You must have a hundred better things to do."

"How long do you plan to stay?"

"That's up to the doctor."

"The doctor! What's wrong?"

"Physically, nothing. But he insists that I need complete rest for an indefinite period. I will not bore you with the story of how hard I've been working."

"And you're alone?"

"Zelda, I'm always alone."

"Oh, that sounds so sad," she cried and, after a moment, added, "I know exactly how you feel."

"Come then, and we'll be lonely together."

She came, arriving three days later, taking a flight from Rome to Brindisi, and then coming by boat to Corfu. She could have flown in but couldn't face the prospect.

"It looked like a hang glider."

"Better well hung than ill wed."

She took him in her arms. "You say the most unusual things of any man I've ever known. That's a quotation, isn't it?"

"Kierkegaard," he said, keeping it simple. "You look marvelous."

And she did. While he waited for her, he had steeled himself for disappointment, remembering the discrepancy in their ages. It had been over a year since he had seen her last, but she looked younger than he felt. She had stepped back to examine him.

"You don't look at all ill."

"You make me feel that I lured you here under false pretenses."

They took a cab to the hotel where he had reserved a room for her, on the floor above his. She tried to conceal her surprise.

"This way, we can be lonely together," he explained.

"Let's just be together, shall we?"

He canceled her room and they spent the next three hours in bed. Afterward, from where they lay, they had a marvelous view of the sea. In the harbor to the left, the boat she had come on lay anchored. She said dreamily, "And to think that on the flight over I wondered if it was wise for me to do this."

"It's certainly not otherwise."

But she wanted to be serious. It seemed a moment when her Catholic conscience would go to work and fill her with remorse for the good time they had just had. That wasn't it at all.

"Why are you lonely, Gabriel? Why am I lonely? We're so

good for one another." And she brought her body against his. He couldn't agree more.

The next day, they rented a car and drove to a small inn that overlooked an impossibly blue body of water with an island on which an impossibly white chapel with a blue tile roof stood.

"Corfu is a painting," she cried.

He was about to say he would paint the scene for her. He hadn't held a brush in years. In any case, she had taken out her digital camera. After the chapel, she took his picture. Later he took hers. One could not get photographs of middle-aged nudes developed, of course.

"Not that you need development, my dear."

It might have been flattery, but he was feeling the unfamiliar attractions of honesty. Up to a point, of course. The point of the exercise was to make their union permanent. And she was beautiful, earthy and beautiful. He would marry her, if it came to that. In the end, it was she who proposed to him. Her conscience had kicked in, and the idea seemed to be that they were on their honeymoon, anticipating the joys of marriage, but they could make it all right.

"Why have you never married?"

"I've been asking myself the same thing."

All the priests on Corfu were Orthodox, which would have been all right with him. It turned out that it wasn't all right with the Orthodox priests, nor with Zelda.

"We must do it right."

They did it right in Rome, in Santa Susanna, the celebrant a jovial Paulist who regarded rules as subject to interpretation. Gabriel described himself as Catholic, thinking of Oriana Fallaci. When they went to bed in the Hilton it was as man and wife.

"Where will we live?"

"I let the lease on my apartment in Paris go." And so he had, years ago.

"Where are your things?"

"In storage." The phrase conveyed much more than met the case.

"I am going to take you home with me," she said triumphantly. "My trophy husband."

They flew home first-class and on the flight whispered like lovers, sipping drinks, ignoring the awful movies.

"Now it won't matter that I never mastered that program you used."

"Explain."

She explained. She told him of Vincent Traeger, a colleague of her husband's. "My first husband," she added, poking him in the ribs.

"Colleague?"

"Chuck was in the CIA. I told you that."

If she had, he had forgotten it.

"He loved the Delacroix you got for me."

### ❖ V ❖

Brendan Crowe had disappointed him.

Catena spotted Harris exit from the main house into the colonnade and darted into the enclosed garden, tiptoed on the crunchy gravel, and stopped at a coconut palm. He put his hand against it and held his breath. He could hear nothing, but then his hearing was bad. He prayed that Harris would walk along the colonnade, reenter the building, and be on his way. Of course. It was nonsense to think the man was pursuing him.

"Bishop Catena," said a voice behind him.

He all but levitated. He turned around. It was only young Quinn.

"What do you want?" Catena was angry at being relieved that it was only Quinn.

"I printed these out for you." Quinn passed a sheaf of pages, printouts of e-mails.

Catena took them, thanked Quinn, wanted to apologize to the young man for his impatience, but most of all wanted to get away before Harris caught him. Perhaps they were all pessimists, but Harris brought gloomy foreboding to a new level.

Before he himself went inside again he looked back, and through the shrubbery and gaudy flowers he could see the massive Harris standing motionless, eyes closed, before the statue of Our Lady. Catena struck his breast. Mea culpa. He should not assume that Harris was always at his worst.

❖

During the final weeks of Pentecost—there was no nonsense about Ordinary Time at the Confraternity of Pius IX—Catena felt the thrill he had always felt when hearing the prophetic passages chosen for the Gospel readings during that time. The end of the world. The signs by which it would be known. And yet the exact hour can never be known. Not even the angels know that. But God vouchsafed signs to his people, and read them we must, as best we can. Bishop Catena knew that throughout the history of the world, men, and women, had been sure they were living in the end times. The first generation of Christians seemed to think that they would be the only generation, that the end of time and the coming again of Christ were imminent. There were scoundrels who took that to weaken the authority of Scripture and tradition. Surely all it meant was that every age was nearer to the end times. "It is later now than when we first believed," Paul said. And so it is. For all that, Catena had the mounting certainty that something big, very big, was about to happen.

It had begun with the scythe that had moved through the Vatican, an assassin cutting down two cardinals with the ease of an instrument of God. Of course that didn't justify what the man had done, murder was murder, but God can turn even evil to good effect.

Brendan Crowe had disappointed him there. Catena admitted that to himself, not wanting to encourage the impatience with which Harris reacted.

"There's more information in the newspapers than in these!" Harris said, shaking the e-mail printouts from Crowe.

That, of course, was false. The newspapers might tell them that the cardinal secretary of state had died and that Cardinal Maguire had suffered a fatal heart attack. If that had been all they had to go on, what would they be permitted to think? Crowe had come through. The two cardinals had been murdered.

"But how?" Harris demanded.

What difference did it make? The two men, and God rest their souls, were dead. The ranks of the enemy were thinning. Besides, something was afoot. Catena was sure of it. Events of this sensational magnitude could not be swept under the rug. At any moment he expected the media to explode. The Sunday Gospels brought the comforting message that the end was drawing near.

It was true that the Fatima messages suggested that after bloody persecution, the Church would know a period of peace and prosperity, having regained Her bearings. Very much like John in the Apocalypse. And then?

It was the bloody scourge that Catena thought might finally be beginning.

Of course, believers were being persecuted all over the globe. It was argued in a book by Robert Royal that there had been more martyrs in the twentieth century than in all previous centuries combined. That was doubtless true. And there was the neo-pagan abomination of abortion, millions of unborn babes murdered every year, a slaughter of the innocents that made King Herod seem an amateur. But the scourge had to strike at the center of the trouble. In his office, he closed the door and stood, thinking of the hope, and dread, of course, that he had known when John Paul II was shot in Saint Peter's Square. It was beginning. But the pope had survived. The assassin was caught and tried and imprisoned. How cloaked in mystery the whole thing had been, but the mystery seemed to enclose a political motive. Bah.

And to think that all along they had known it was coming! Ratzinger's coy remarks to Vittorio Messori in 1985 about the secret Sister Lucia had entrusted to the pope had given no indication that the attempted assassination had been part of it, predicted, prophesied by the Mother of God. And they had gone on as if all was well. The task of the Church was to fulfill the promises of Vatican II, to recover its true spirit! That spirit was killing the Church.

And then five years later came the cynical pretense that the third secret was being made public. There had been photocopies of Sister Lucia's letter, authentic, no doubt, but not the whole letter. Anyone with the least knowledge of Fatima knew that what had been made public could not be all. The time since had been one of unrelieved anguish for Catena. He all but instructed Crowe to steal the original. But the thought of having that document put in his hands filled Catena with fear and trembling. A message from Mary written in the hand of Sister Lucia. To hold that, to read that. It would be like holding in his mortal hands the original of John's Gospel. His messages to Crowe had been accordingly ambiguous, as if he hoped the assistant prefect would make the decision and incur the responsibility.

Tarcisio Bertone's recent book on Sister Lucia did not deceive Catena.

A tap on his door.

Catena straightened, then moved swiftly to his desk and sat. "Come."

Harris shuffled in, wheezing, closing the door behind him, and stood before Catena, his eyes bright.

"It's gone."

"What is gone?"

"The third secret has been removed from the archives."

"You've heard from Crowe!"

Harris sat. The man seemed to be enjoying this. "He is missing, too."

"What do you mean, missing?"

"He has left the country." Harris allowed his voice to drop. "He has flown off to America."

Harris would have liked to parcel out what he had learned, he would have liked to expand on his contacts in the office of Vatican security, but he was too excited for that. Stunned, Catena listened. He felt betrayed. What terrible game was Crowe playing?

Rodriguez had gone to the archives with an authorization from Cardinal Piacere and asked to see the third secret. The box was brought and opened.

"It was empty."

"Did Ratzinger keep it?" A worse thought. "Did he destroy it?"

Harris shook his head. "Oh no. It was returned to the archives."

Harris spelled out what he had learned. Crowe had flown to the States in a private plane owned by a fabulous rich man who could buy anything he wanted.

"Apparently he bought Crowe."

Harris had done research on Ignatius Hannan. He put the results before his superior. Catena read the sheets as if they were a document of Vatican II. Hannan was eccentric, granted, but his interest seemed to be to acquire paintings depicting the mysteries of the rosary. The replica of the grotto of Lourdes that had been erected on the grounds of the man's company was an item that in other circumstances would have charmed Catena. But if Lourdes, then Fatima, and if Fatima . . .

"There is another possibility," Harris said.

Is there anything more corrupting to the human spirit than having surprising information to divulge? Harris was not a better man because of what he had discovered. He was impossible.

"Trepanier," Harris whispered. He had leaned toward Catena to say this, then sat back, awaiting his reaction.

"My God in heaven."

To think it was to believe it. Jean-Jacques Trepanier was in an unsettling way the distorted mirror image of himself, his Fatima magazine and "Our Lady's Crusade" deriving full benefit from its American setting. What seemed zeal in the confraternity seemed fanaticism in Trepanier's efforts. His public and insolent remarks about the Curia, his all but accusation of the pope himself as the chief conspirator, were all the more appalling because they seemed simply to draw out the implications of the convictions that sustained the confraternity. If Catena had imagined himself holding the original of the third secret with fear and trembling, he could imagine Trepanier flourishing it with glee. In his hands, the letter would be a weapon with which to strike down his foes. A means of triumphing over his enemies.

"We must join forces," Harris said.

"Never."

"We must form a united front. How else can we control what that man might do?"

What had seemed a counsel of despair now seemed an instance of prudent caution. Of course. If Trepanier managed to get hold of that document, he did indeed require the moderating influence of the Confraternity of Pius IX.

"But Crowe?" the bishop bleated.

"He is a Judas."

## ❖ VI ❖

### Instead he got drunk.

Hannibald, Vatican correspondent for the largest national Catholic weekly in the States, asked Neal Admirari to a little reception he was giving for Bishop Francis Ascue. Neal couldn't remember the name from the roster of Americans employed in various posts in the Vatican.

"Bishop of Fort Elbow," Hannibald said, as if the identification were not necessary, but he added, "Ohio."

"Ah."

"This is my first real shot at him, and I don't want it to look as if I'm sandbagging him."

It was Hannibald's plan to lure Ascue to a reception with a number of American notables in Rome and then to pounce on him.

"He issues statements," Hannibald said. "Minor encyclicals. But he has never given a one-on-one interview."

"Press conferences?"

"Of course. You think Ferdinand the Bull is good?" This was a reference to the Spaniard who was the spokesman for the Holy See. "Ascue is the master of non-responsiveness."

Meaning apparently that he rejected the premises of questions and discussed other matters he considered relevant.

"What's he doing in Rome?"

"He missed the *ad limina*. He'll see the Holy Father personally."

Ascue had been appointed bishop of his home diocese by John Paul II in what Hannibald called Act III of the Polish papacy. The sort of appointment that would not have been made if only John Paul had had the decency to die, or retire. During the long Babylonian captivity—another of Hannibald's much used phrases—the journalist had lived in agony. The foes of progress held the levers of power, and all one could do was wait in the certainty that the pendulum had to swing the other way with a new pope. And then, as if to prove that there are always worse dreams than those that plague us, Joseph Cardinal Ratzinger was elected pope. Just like that, bingo, without anything like a last-ditch stand on the part of those Hannibald favored.

Since the election, Hannibald had been predicting disaster. The *Panzerkardinal* would not change just because the cassock he now wore was white. There would be some gaffe, some diplomatic indiscretion, perhaps a suppression that would rouse the dormant body of liberal Catholics. Instead, infuriatingly, the new pope seemed to be as popular as the old. He went home to Germany, where most of the sensible ideas rejected by Vatican II had been generated, and they poured into the streets to greet him. It might have been John Paul II and Warsaw. If ever

Hannibald had come near despairing, it was then. If he were a praying man, he would have prayed. Instead he got drunk.

And then, as if his unsaid prayers were answered, the event came, and irony of ironies it came during a later visit to Germany. At Regensburg. Benedict XVI, lecturing at the university, made an allusion to the debates between a Byzantine and a Muslim. By quoting the Byzantine's objection, the pope made it seem that he was voicing his own opinion of Islam. To Hannibald, who had not gone on this papal junket but sat brooding in his Roman tent like Achilles, the first news of the gaffe seemed too good to be true. He had learned not to hope. But the reaction in the Muslim world was explosive. In the weeks that followed, clarifications of what the pope had meant were sought and issued, reactions to such explanations by the most radical of imams. Benedict had already lectured the European Union, chiding it for omitting from its proposed constitution any mention of the fact that Christianity had something to do with the making of Europe. But such clear indications that the man was a conservative had not struck a spark. Now Benedict was revealed as a medieval pope, ready to call a crusade. The difficulty was that the objects of the crusades now occupied Europe.

Benedict had planned a trip to Istanbul. Istanbul! In the wake of the reaction to his Regensburg speech, he was urged to cancel. His life would be in danger. He refused. The trip would go on. Hannibald tried not to formulate the thoughts that came unbidden. Hannibald went on the Istanbul trip as witnesses accompany the condemned to the place of execution.

Benedict had not been assassinated in Istanbul. He had been received civilly and then with warmth. He was a big hit with the patriarch. Hannibald went up the Bosporus on a little cruise and brooded. He almost thought he might become a Muslim, out of spite.

There is a tide in the affairs of men, and Benedict's rolled out once more with the publication of the *complete* third secret of Fatima, the accusation being that the Vatican (i.e., the then Cardinal Ratzinger) had withheld the significant part of it and claimed that the text released was the whole. If nothing else, Hannibald could appreciate the prudence of the suppression.

Look at the storm Regensburg had caused.

What if the Mother of God regarded them as marauding invaders who were destroying Christianity?

Any devotion Hannibald had had to the Blessed Virgin had faded and died under the influence of Vatican II. He understood the Protestant charge of Mariology. What need is there for an ombudsman, or ombudswoman, if Christ is our sole mediator with the Father?

Not that Hannibald found such theological niceties intrinsically important. They would be among the things jettisoned as religious belief moved toward full maturity. As for Marian apparitions, Lourdes, Fatima, allegedly all over the place, please hold Hannibald excused. But for anyone longing for the downfall of Benedict XVI, the third secret of Fatima promised to be a weapon of mass destruction.

Oh, how he looked forward to forcing Bishop Ascue to comment on the present mess! Bertone's book had stirred it all up again.

Neal Admirari found Hannibald's enthusiasm uninfectious.

"What can he say?"

"That's the point! No matter what he says it will be the wrong thing." If QED were a facial expression, it would have been all over Hannibald's face. Neal looked toward the bar set up in a corner of the penthouse apartment overlooking the Forum.

"Gore Vidal once lived here," Hannibald whispered.

"Did you have the place exorcised?"

"Oh, that's good," Hannibald gushed, and went to greet other guests.

Both *Time* and *Newsweek* came, and the *New York Times*, the *Globe*, the *LA Times*. Archbishop Foley was there, as was a baby-faced Dominican in his white habit whose name Neal did not catch. A real doll representing *First Things* made the other women seem a third sex, which might not have been all that misleading. Ascue was a surprise.

Hannibald had made him expect a boy bishop, but Ascue was in his mid fifties, with gray hair and kind but wary eyes.

"I recognized the name," Ascue said when Neal was introduced to Ascue by Hannibald.

"I've been around a long time," he said, but the remark was flattering, not least because he felt Ascue wasn't just saying that.

"*Whither the Priesthood*," Ascue said.

"You read it?"

"A compendium of bad arguments. Was that your point?"

Was Ascue insulting him with praise? Neal had written the book, his only book, in the excited certainty that it would blow the lid off things when it was published. It didn't. It sold five thousand copies. He never wrote another. Who reads books?

"Tell me about Fort Elbow, Bishop."

"Do you want to buy a church?"

Ascue was under pressure to unload church property, consolidate parishes.

"Doesn't getting rid of them make sense?" Neal asked.

"Maybe. If you accept the present situation as final."

"You don't?"

"Hardly."

Hannibald joined them, and others gathered round. Ascue stole his host's thunder. "What do you think of this Fatima business?" Hannibald asked.

Ascue tucked in his chin. "Business?"

"The suppression of the third secret," Hannibald burst out.

"The third secret was released in two thousand. All of it. You must read Cardinal Bertone's book."

"But that begs the question."

"Which question is that?"

Hannibald said in strangled tones, "Whether we can believe what was said in two thousand. Or in two thousand seven."

Ascue laughed. A merry laugh, unforced. "If you disbelieve the Church in two thousand, you must disbelieve Her in two thousand seven. I refer you to Mr. Admirari for the logic of the matter."

Neal found he didn't mind being invoked as an authority on logic. Who would? It also seemed to ally him with Ascue. He listened to the midwestern bishop handle questions that got sharper and sharper by parry and thrust. A dazzling performance. He said as much to Ascue when he got him alone later.

Ascue had a glass of orange juice; Neal, a glass of scotch undiluted by water or ice.

"The press never changes, does it?" Bishop Ascue said.

"How so?"

"Why the hostility and skepticism?"

"To get answers."

"It doesn't work, does it?"

"Not tonight."

Bishop Ascue nodded.

"Maybe I will buy a church," Neal said.

"If I decide to sell any."

Somehow Neal thought he wouldn't. The two of them went down in the elevator together. "You stayed out of it up there," Ascue said.

"I don't like gang bangs."

Whoops. But the bishop either ignored or didn't understand the phrase.

"If you want to talk about it seriously, come around to the Domus Sanctae Marthae. It is a serious matter."

They settled on the day and time. As he watched Ascue go off in a taxi, Neal felt a little leap of hope. Would the bishop of Fort Elbow be the means of realizing his hope for a scoop?

## ✣ VII ✣

### "Gabriel Faust is an art historian."

"Tell him we're engaged," Ray Sinclair said when Laura warned him that her brother John must not be allowed to suspect them.

"Are we engaged, Ray?"

"Paris is worth a Mass."

"Paris wanted Helen of Troy."

Not long before, after they had watched the movie *From Here to Eternity* on DVD, Ray had picked up Lorene's reply to Prewitt when the soldier said that their arrangement was as good as being married. "It's better," Lorene had replied. It became a kind of motto, gathering all the fun and sadness of their relationship into it.

"It's not better," he said now, and it needed no explanation.

She wanted to feel happy, even flattered, but Ray's suggestion had a note of cynicism in it. Would he ever have proposed such a thing if she had not recommended a truce while John was here? And of course she wondered what Nate would say if they went to him and told him they were going to marry. It was her boss's remark about women and Chesterton that came back to her. As a married woman, she would of course no longer want to continue as his administrative assistant. Her place would be in the home; her mission, to have children. As a woman she could not be unaffected by that prospect, but after these exciting years as Nate's administrative assistant, the role of wife and mother seemed a precipitous drop in status.

"What do you say?" Ray had taken her in his arms. She stepped back.

"Ray . . ." she began, but she did not know how to go on. His expression would have stopped her in any case. He had the look of a man who had made a great gamble and not lost. He knew her too well, knew how addictive working for Ignatius Hannan was, but his very knowing made her almost hate him.

"We'll talk about it in better circumstances," he said.

"Wait."

His expression changed. Now she could read him as he had read her. He dreaded that she would say yes, let's, why not? But it was enough to have restored the balance. She put a hand on his arm.

"You're right. We'll talk about it later."

⚜

Did she just imagine that Ray kept out of her way throughout the rest of John's visit? She and her brother had time together while Brendan Crowe gave Nate a crash course in sacred art. They drove to the nursing home to see their mother. Mrs. Burke sat slumped in a wheelchair, her hair just washed and fluffy, and looked at these two strangers who hugged her and called her Mom. John gave her his blessing before they left, and she traced the sign of the cross on her breast. How much did she remember? How much did she know?

"It's so sad," Laura said, tears in her eyes, when they were crossing the parking lot to her car.

"Dante would have had to devise an anteroom for those in Mom's condition, neither living nor dead."

"At least she's spared the fear of dying."

"I suppose," her little brother said.

But what did anyone really know about what went on in the mind of a victim of Alzheimer's?

"It's a pretty posh place," John said.

"Thanks to Ignatius Hannan."

"He's quite a fellow."

"Faint praise." Laura laughed. "John, he's generous as well as acquisitive. He gets what he wants. Father Crowe didn't put up much resistance."

"He did say no."

"I think Nate expected that."

"But you proposed the chief consultant alternative."

"John, I'm his alter ego."

"What's Ray Sinclair's job?"

"Oh, he's money mainly. And general watchdog."

"They were classmates at Boston College?"

"More or less. Nate never graduated of course. They've offered him an honorary degree, but he had heard tales of the theology taught there and took a pass."

They drove in silence. Without having to decide, they went past the house where they had been raised. Laura made a U-turn at the corner and went back, parking in front of the house, and they looked at the scene of their childhood. It seemed as remote as their mother had.

John said, "Coming back makes me realize what an expatriate I am."

"How long can you stay?"

"That depends on Brendan. A few more days at most. He seems to have an apt pupil in Hannan."

"How do you like your digs?"

"It reminds me of the Domus."

The two priests said their Mass in the guest residence, on an improvised altar. Nate apologized for not having thought of asking the architect to include a chapel. This posed a difficulty for Laura. She couldn't receive Communion, of course, being a scarlet woman and all. It didn't help to think of it that way. John made no comment. Perhaps he thought she had received from Father Crowe. Her own mind was so full of her relationship with Ray that she found it hard to believe that John suspected nothing. He was so wonderfully innocent it made her want to cry. It did help that Ray had mentioned marriage. It helped even more when John asked about her and Ray.

"He asked me to marry him."

"And?"

"What do you think, John?"

"Does it matter?"

She looked at him. "Don't you like him?"

❧

When they got back to Empedocles, Zelda Lewis was there. Laura was delighted. It was Ray's fantasy that Zelda would make a good match for Nate.

"Just what he needs, a predatory widow."

"Ray, she is a very nice woman."

Maybe if she kept saying that, she would believe it.

Zelda said, "I've been away for a few days." But she was looking at John when she said it.

"This is my brother John."

"Father," Zelda said grandly, putting out her hand. John took it and turned it over, as if he were going to read her palm.

"And where have you been?" Laura asked.

"Corfu!"

"Corfu?"

"An island off the Italian coast. Heavenly. Do you know it?" she asked John.

"I spent a few hours there once on the way to Greece. Why Corfu?"

"Oh, it was just a spur-of-the-moment thing." But she smiled a great, secretive smile. "And Rome." She lifted her chin. "We were married in Rome."

"Married!" Laura felt an impulse to hug the older woman, so she did. Oh, this was delightful, as all Ray's speculations went up in smoke. Laura hooked one arm into Zelda's and the other through John's and took them off for coffee, where Zelda told them about Gabriel Faust.

"So you married in Rome and honeymooned on Corfu."

Zelda nodded. "We were married in Santa Susanna."

"Ah," John said. "The American church."

"Is it? They made it all so easy."

"But tell us about Gabriel Faust," Laura urged.

"I've known him for years. This was all quite sudden, in a way. But I can see it started long ago. He's an art historian. He catalogued my collection."

"An art historian."

"He made his name in Renaissance art. Italian Renaissance."

Laura's mind was whirling. "What exactly do art historians do? Is he a professor?"

"He was. But he has been an independent consultant for years."

"Not tied down anyplace?"

"He is now," Zelda said.

"Of course."

There were voices in the hallway, and then Nate and Father Crowe and Ray entered the room. Nate suppressed an expression of annoyance at the sight of Zelda.

"Look who's here," Laura trilled. "Mrs. Faust."

"Mrs. Faust." Nate's expression changed, but he came forward warily.

"I assume you missed seeing me at Mass and wondered about it," Zelda said to him. "I thought I owed you an explanation. I ran away and got married."

Nate might have concealed his relieved delight better.

"Gabriel Faust is an art historian," Laura said, planting the seed.

After a time, she slipped away to her office and found Gabriel Faust's web page. His credentials were impressive. Kind of a brooding photograph, but why not? An art historian. And now he lived in the neighborhood.

Laura ran into Heather Adams in the ladies room. "You're back," Heather said.

"Heather, there are some people I want you to meet. Two priests." She put her arm through Heather's. "One of them is my brother John."

# CHAPTER FIVE

✢ I ✢

"We're all priests now."

Jean-Jacques Trepanier had wanted to be a priest from as long ago as he could remember, but he was thirty-five when he finally got ordained. Anyone else would have been discouraged, but adversity had only strengthened Jay's determination. And sometimes it seemed that adversity was all there had been. Of course, his mother had always been there to support his dream.

He had an altar in his room, and his mother made vestments for him, the old-fashioned kind, the only kind she knew. An alb, a cincture, an amice, a stole and maniple, and a bass fiddle chasuble with a magnificent embroidered cross. She let him use the oil and vinegar cruets from the dining room, the ones that were never used anyway, and he had a gold cup for a chalice, and for a paten, a brass disk designed to go under a flowerpot. His first altar missal had been his late father's Saint Andrew's Missal, which had the equivalent of a card deck of memorial cards in its pages, souls of the departed for whom his father always prayed at Mass. His father's card had been added to them by the time his mother handed over the book to Jay with all the solemnity of a liturgical rite.

"I feel I've already fulfilled my obligation," his mother would say proudly after she had acted as his congregation.

She even liked the sermons he preached. His favorite theme was Mary, but then his mother told him she had dedicated her son to the Blessed Mother even before he was born. But if he was encouraged at home, he got no encouragement at the parish school.

Only half the teachers were nuns by that time, and you already needed a scorecard to tell who they were. If anything, they dressed better than the laywomen, but then most of the nuns would themselves be laywomen before many years had passed. It was in third grade that he had first mentioned his vocation to the priesthood. Sister Madeline frowned. "We're all priests now."

He didn't understand, of course. Not then. Later, he would hear all about the priesthood of the laity, which allegedly made the ministerial priesthood redundant. In any case, Jay had learned to keep his counsel with Sister Madeline, though she must have passed the word along, because all the other nuns he had as teachers seemed to single him out for attention. Big, plush Sister Gloria had a way of crushing him against her breasts and running her hands through his hair.

"You have to leave the girls alone," she giggled.

Jay never looked at girls. It was part of his vocation. When he explained this to Sister Gloria, she laughed. "But Jay, by the time you grow up, priests will be allowed to marry."

So he already got a full dose of what Vatican II meant to most nuns before he entered the minor seminary. Later, it seemed a miracle that the place was still open then. Of course, its days were numbered. Jay felt that he had signed on to the crew of the *Titanic*. Father Shipley, the rector—everyone called him Father Fred or sometimes just Fred, and to his face, and he loved it—explained to them that the system they had entered was doomed, thanks to the Council. Ireland Hall had six grades, the four of high school and the first two years of college. Its graduates then went on to the six-year course of the major seminary, two years of philosophy and then four of theology, followed by ordination. All that would be changed. Father Fred told them that the Council had decided that it was unnatural to take boys away from their families at such an early age. Besides, how could any kid know in his early teens what he wanted to do with his life? Father Fred didn't quite say it, but the point was puberty. Until the sexual urge manifested itself, it was nonsense to speak of a life of celibacy, and when it did manifest itself you had to give the alternatives a chance.

"Assuming we stick with celibacy," he added, grinning as Sister Gloria had. Fred had long since left the priesthood and married and became the CEO of a dog food company.

Ireland Hall did shut down, after Jay's junior year, and he had finished at the Jesuit high school where they didn't even teach Latin. His disappointment had impressed Hugh Dormer, S.J., as long as he thought Jay was interested in becoming a classicist. When Jay explained that he wanted to become a priest, Father Dormer said, "Have you been to Mass lately?"

"I go every day, Father."

"You must have noticed it's in English now."

"But it doesn't have to be, does it?"

"Son, we have to acquire the spirit of the Council. The vernacular was voted all but unanimously by the Council fathers."

In those days, anyone who thought the Mass should still be said in Latin, or at least that it was okay for it to be in Latin, was regarded as a schismatic, and not without reason. Lefebvre and his community walked right out of the Church, saying the Church had abandoned them, they hadn't abandoned the Church. There were times in later years when Jay was tempted to join them, but then he got to know about Catena and his crowd and that cured him.

After high school, he wrote to various religious orders, but the common suggestion was that he finish college first and then get in touch. So he enrolled at Saint Thomas Campion.

"Philosophy," he said when his advisor asked him what he wanted to major in.

"You still have to take four courses in philosophy here, whether or not you're a major. Why not choose something else?"

"I still want to major in philosophy."

"How about a double major, philosophy and English?"

He agreed. It was a good thing. At least he learned some English, read a lot, began to write, and started publishing in student magazines. Logic was all right, even if it was all symbolic logic. When he asked about Aristotle he was told that syllogistic is a subset, a minor subset, of formal logic. After that, there was epistemology, in which he learned that the mind is a cookie cutter that creates its own objects; ethics, where every moral problem called for a pro and con treatment that gave you a choice of solutions; and metaphysics, taught by a layman named Boswell who thought Wittgenstein and Heidegger had pretty well put metaphysics out of business. He did find an old Jesuit who agreed to give him directed readings in Scholasticism, but he was a Suarezian who hated Thomas Aquinas. Even so, he let Jay read the enemy.

Jay was on the dean's honor roll every semester, and from junior year he had a column in the student paper, and one of his stories won a national prize, but he had become a pariah. The Jesuits called him Torquemada and Savonarola. Jay had discovered the Ratio Studiorum and argued in column after column that the Jesuits were betraying their own tradition. The four courses of theology were about what you would expect. His only protection was to read and practically memorize the sixteen documents of Vatican II and cite them against the positions urged in class.

"You are the biggest pain in the ass on campus," the dean told him. "Is there anything you like about Campion?"

"Yes, Father. That it only lasts four years."

When he submitted his valedictorian speech, the dean laughed. "No way in the world you're going to give that at commencement."

The runner-up, a girl, gave the valedictory address, a feminist screed the students and faculty and even some of the parents liked. Jay had been in contact with the religious orders that had advised him to finish college first. Now he was told to spend some time in the real world to be sure of what he was doing. But it was because his mother lost her job that Jay spent time in the alleged real world. He might have gone on to graduate work, but they needed the money, so he got a job on a local paper that had a television station. At the station, he wrote scripts for commercials, he wrote the news, he did the weather reports, and then he became a backup news reader. Viewers liked him. There was lots of mail. His television career lasted six years, until his mother fell ill and died within months. She had thought they were poor, but it turned out that there was stock his father had bought, which in the meantime had split and split and amounted to a real pile by the time Jay came into possession of it.

Throughout college, during all the years since, he had gone to Mass every day. The Latin he had learned on his own enabled him to read the office. He found a parish where the Tridentine Mass was said once a month and got to know the pastor, who had overcome the reluctance of the chancery office to have that Mass in Latin. Father Schwartz. He told him he wanted to become a priest. Schwartz groaned.

"The seminary has become a zoo."

"I was at Ireland Hall until it closed down."

"Alienation of Church property, that's what that was. They had no right to sell that property."

Father Schwartz read the *Wanderer* and *Culture Wars* and *First Things* and took morose delectation in the crumbling of the Church and the society he had grown up in.

"We were warned, Jay. The Blessed Mother predicted it all."

He meant Our Lady of Fatima. Schwartz had everything ever written on Fatima, and he lent the books and pamphlets and papers to Jay, who devoured them. Schwartz was right. Unless we prayed the rosary and did penance, terrible afflictions would befall. And they had, as she had said they would. And there was more to come. Jay made the five first Saturdays; he added to the end of every decade of the rosary the prayer Mary had recommended. "Oh Jesus, forgive us. Deliver us from the fires of hell; draw all souls to heaven, especially those in special need." Schwartz might seem an oddity in the diocese, but the Holy Father, John Paul II, agreed with him.

"Lip service," Schwartz said.

"What do you mean?"

He meant that the Holy Father had not, as he had been instructed by Mary to do, dedicated Russia to the Immaculate Heart of Mary. Why not? Politics! Had Jay read the documents of Vatican II? He had. Was there one mention of atheistic communism in any of them? There wasn't. Imagine a Council meeting in the early 1960s that had ignored the most visible threat to the Church and to Christian civilization.

"An opening to the East," Schwartz said contemptuously.

Jay hadn't realized it at the time, but he had just received his mission in life.

"How old are you?" Schwartz asked.

"Twenty-eight."

The pastor frowned. "That's young for a retarded vocation."

He was thinking of Saint John's in Boston and of Holy Apostles Seminary in Cromwell, Connecticut, where older men were trained for the priesthood, widowers, some of them grandfathers. Jay was thirty-one, going on thirty-two, when he was admitted to Holy Apostles. It was wonderful, everything a seminary ought to be. He took remedial courses in philosophy and within a year was asked to teach a course in Thomistic metaphysics while he was pursuing his theological studies. Jay was the star of the place, but the next step was to find a bishop who would ordain him.

For some dioceses, low on priests, Holy Apostles was a godsend. All these men anxious to live the life of the priest. Bishops came and interviewed the seminarians, and many were adopted by bishops before they were ordained subdeacon. The interviews Jay had all began well but led to nothing.

"Don't say everything you think," the rector advised.

But Jay found it impossible not to tell the bishops he spoke with how he regarded the current mess the Church was in or that the only solution was to take Fatima seriously. Nobody disagreed with him. It was his enthusiasm that seemed to bother them. Jay was in his final year and without a bishop when Angelo Orvieto, bishop of a little diocese outside Palermo, visited. Orvieto was a devotee of Fatima; he and Jay got along like a house afire.

"Do you know Italian?" Orvieto asked in Italian.

*"Posso ne legere pero parlare e otra cosa."*

Orvieto smiled. "It will come."

They corresponded. At the end of Jay's fourth year of theology, when his classmates were being ordained for various dioceses, he flew off to Sicily and was ordained by Bishop Orvieto. At the time, he was reconciled to the thought that he would live his priestly life in Italy. Orvieto shook his head.

"No, you must return to the United States." He had before him a thick folder containing Jay's transcripts, student publications, letters of recommendation. "You have worked in the media. You must spread devotion to Fatima by every modern means. In order to do this, you will have to raise money . . ."

And so it had begun. Jay founded his Fatima magazine with his own money; he appeared on EWTN and donations flowed in. He acquired a short-range television signal and branched out. Eventually, he was adopted by a cable service and his program was carried across the country. They had called him Torquemada and Savonarola in college. Now he was the scourge of the hierarchy for their failing to take seriously the warnings of Our Lady. He led pilgrimages to Fatima and gave retreats across America. He established himself outside Manchester, built a state-of-the-art television studio, a building that housed his staff and in which he had his own modest apartment, and he built a chapel. He invited the local bishop to dedicate the chapel and bless the other buildings that made up Fatima Now! The vicar general sent a stuffy letter, describing the demanding schedule of the bishop, and obliquely inquired as to Father Trepanier's clerical status. So Jay flew in Bishop Orvieto for a two-day celebration and the local bishop found time in his busy schedule to attend.

❖

The first donation from Ignatius Hannan caused Mrs. Meany, Jay's secretary, to bring it in and lay it on his desk. She stood in silent awe. Ten thousand dollars. Jay nodded. He was not impressed. Money never impressed him. He never asked for donations; they came unbidden. It was not money that Mary wanted. She wanted our souls. He reminded Mrs. Meany of this.

"Tell it to Mr. Hannan."

"I will."

She was alarmed. "I meant thank him."

"Write a nice note and I'll sign it."

"I am going to get him on the phone."

She did, although it took some time. Hannan was apologetic for the delay. "Not everyone here is acquainted with your work. I am. It helped bring me back to the faith."

Hannan had seen one of the programs Jay had done for Mother Angelica. If some of Hannan's people were unacquainted with what Jay was doing, he in turn had never heard of Empedocles or Ignatius Hannan. He was surprised to find that they were scarcely twenty miles apart.

"You must come see our new chapel," Trepanier said.

"And I'd like to show you the replica of the grotto at Lourdes I've put up here."

For almost a year these two invitations had both stood and neither had been answered.

Through Orvieto, Jay had acquired contacts in Rome. He had been approached by Catena and rebuffed him. When the rumor reached him that the third secret of Fatima had been filched from the Vatican Archives, Jay's first thought was Catena. That very afternoon, a call came from Hannan, urging Jay to come down.

"I have the prefect of the Vatican Archives with me."

"But Cardinal Maguire is dead."

"This is his right-hand man. Father Brendan Crowe."

Jay said he would be delighted to come visit Empedocles, and Father Crowe.


✤ II ✤

"You remind me of Lulu van Ackeren."

Neal Admirari sat at a table in a trattoria in one of the narrow little streets off the Piazza Navona that would never have gotten a license in New York. He said as much to Angela di Piperno.

"Because they allow smoking?" Angela said, exhaling smoke with her head tipped back, making the angle of her eyes as she looked at him even more seductively.

"An observation, not a criticism."

The outside tables were in the street, down the middle of which was a depression through which who knew what filth flowed.

"Tell me about *First Things*."

"The book by Hadley Arkes?"

"I don't get it."

"Richard John Neuhaus stole the title for the magazine, as Hadley often reminds him."

"How long have you been there?"

"I was a summer intern when I was still in college."

"Where?"

"Christendom."

"Where's that?"

"All around you." She smiled. She seemed to have several extra teeth, and large, large eyes, seemingly of the kind Lois Lane had admired in Clark Kent. X-ray eyes. Neal felt he had no secrets from her, and he loved it.

"You remind me of Lulu van Ackeren."

"Who was she?"

That "was" alone would have won his heart. No need to tell

her that Lulu under her unmarried name was writing a column whose syndication had fallen below ten papers. Neal waved Lulu away dismissively.

"And now you're the Rome correspondent?"

"Oh, that's just part-time. I get paid for what they use."

"What are you, independently wealthy?"

"Worse. I'm a student."

She was studying moral theology at Santa Croce, the pontifical university run by Opus Dei. She watched him make a silent inference.

"No," she said. "Not even a supernumerary. But I admire them all to pieces."

"I was a student once," Neal said.

She was supposed to ask where and when, thus establishing his age, thus perhaps convincing her that a man in his fifties was eligible. For the first time since Lulu, Neal felt the marrying urge. For the first time since Lulu, he thought he had met a woman unlike all the others: an error in Lulu's case, but not, he was certain, in Angela's. But she did not take the bait.

"Do you know Endan Farrell?"

"I don't even know what it is."

A laugh, not all the teeth this time. "It's a name. An Irish priest."

"One of your professors?"

"He's a Dominican!"

"No wonder."

Still, she didn't explain. Were Dominicans verboten at Santa Croce?

"He said the most amazing thing about Cardinal Maguire."

"Amaze me."

Angela leaned toward him, bringing along her scent. Her long hair fell forward as if in modest covering. "He said the rumor in Ireland is that he was killed."

Neal remembered his fruitless exchange with Ferdinand the Bull in the Sala di Prenza.

"How do such rumors get started?"

"The undertaker there opened the coffin," Angela said. "There was a huge wound in the chest."

"Endan Farrell, you say?"

"Don't use my name."

"Where will I find him?"

"Where would you expect to find a Dominican?" Angela asked.

Endan Farrell taught philosophy at San Tomasso.

"It used to be called the Angelicum," he added.

"You told them not to use your name?"

Farrell took Neal into the courtyard and lit a cigar. Neal asked him what he taught.

"Epistemology. The last refuge of the scoundrel."

"What is it exactly?"

"Asking about knowing. Does it exist? Is it possible? Can we know? It's like asking out loud whether you're speaking."

"So why bother with it?" Neal asked Farrell.

"Know thine enemy."

"I have an epistemological problem."

Farrell groaned.

"I've been hearing odd rumors about the way Cardinal Maguire died."

"Stabbed in the chest while taking his siesta in his rooftop garden."

"How do you know that?"

"Ah. That's your epistemological problem. I heard the same rumor and I talked to a man who worked with Maguire. Another Irishman. Brendan Crowe."

"He works in the archives?"

"He lives in the Domus Sanctae Marthae."

❧

That was where he had gone to have his interview with Bishop Ascue of Fort Elbow, Ohio, in town to report solo to the pope since he had missed the *ad limina* of midwestern bishops. They had met upstairs, in Ascue's suite—a sitting room, a bedroom, private john, baroque furniture—where Neal was offered mineral water. He took it.

"Every day they leave another bottle." Ascue smiled. "All right. Fatima."

Bishop Ascue said he had spoken with great confidence the other night at Hannibald's reception.

"A priori confidence. How could I believe the Church had lied?"

"That's more or less what you said."

"My confidence is now a posteriori. I have talked with Cardinal Piacere. He worked in the Congregation for the Doctrine of the Faith at the time the secret was made public. Nothing was held back."

"That assurance hasn't convinced some people."

"Father Trepanier? The Confraternity of Pius IX? The Right is as nutty as the Left."

"Which are you?"

*"In medio stat virtus."*

"Isn't that on the Pall Mall package?"

Ascue laughed. "My sister smoked Pall Malls. Actually, there were two Latin mottoes on the package. *Per aspera ad astra.* That's gone. Through difficulties to the stars. The one they kept is *In hoc signo vinces.* Can you imagine? That refers to Constantine and the conversion of the empire. In this sign you will conquer. The sign of the cross. I wonder if they export Pall Malls to the Middle East."

⚜

Ascue just listened when Neal told him he had heard Maguire had been murdered.

"You haven't heard anything like that, have you?"

"Murdered how?"

"Stabbed in the chest."

Ascue shook his head. "It would have to be in the back."

⚜

After the meeting, Neal went downstairs and stopped at the reception desk of the Domus.

"Hello, Donna. Could you tell Father Brendan Crowe I'd like to see him?"

"I could if he were here. He isn't."

"At the office?"

"In the United States."

### ⚜ III ⚜

#### "I have it with me."

"Vincent, I've remarried!" Zelda cried when he got through to her on the phone.

"Congratulations. That's great news."

Was it? Traeger wasn't sure. He was old-fashioned enough to think that widows, if they didn't throw themselves on their husband's funeral pyre, ought to at least live out their days in abnegation and loneliness. Unrealistic, of course, particularly in Zelda's case. Traeger had only become aware of the amount of money she had after Chuck was dead, and at first he thought his departed colleague had made a good thing of undercover work. He wouldn't have been the first. In a crooked world there are no straight lines. But Zelda had laughed away his suggestion.

"Oh, it all came to me from Daddy."

So there she was, a good-looking woman, eligible, independently wealthy, and obviously lonely, as Traeger had often become uneasily aware whenever they got together. In a way it was a relief to have her spoken for. But why hadn't she sent him an invitation? She gave him a breathless account of the wedding in Rome, the time on Corfu.

"I must have been in Rome at the time."

"Oh, Vincent, don't say it. Of course it was a very private ceremony, but oh, if I had only known."

"Did you meet him in Rome?"

"Now, Vincent, it was sudden but not in that way. I have known this man for ages. He is the art historian who catalogued my collection."

"And screwed up your computer?"

"So you do remember."

Zelda obviously didn't want him to think that she had married on a sudden impulse, but at the same time he was to understand how impossibly romantic the whole thing was.

"Gabriel Faust," she answered when he asked her husband's name. "Dr. Gabriel Faust. But what were you doing in Rome?"

"Nothing so interesting as getting married. So what does Dr. Gabriel Faust do?"

She began to whisper. "Nothing is settled yet, but there is a possibility that he will become director of a new foundation being set up by Ignatius Hannan."

"Tell me more."

"That's all there is for now." She was still whispering. "Nothing may come of it. Gabriel hates to be tied down."

It's a small world. Smaller than Zelda knew. Faust was the one who had sold her a Delacroix that was actually hanging in a museum in Cincinnati, Traeger had learned from a man Dortmund put him onto. So he sought and found Gabriel Faust's web page and flicked through the pages of accomplishments and claims to greatness. He went back to the opening page and studied the pensive picture of the art historian. So he had gone back to Dortmund.

"What has art forgery got to do with those murders in the Vatican?"

"Nothing. It's just a little tangent." He thought of telling Dortmund how the widow of their former colleague had been taken, but what the hell. Zelda loved the picture, and the one she had was real enough. He had continued to pursue the tangent, indirectly, calling in a few favors he had accumulated over the years. That is how he learned of Faust's connection with Inagaki. And there the matter might have rested if Zelda hadn't given him the surprising news of her marriage to the shady art historian. That was bad enough, but when she mentioned the possibility that Faust might be taken on by Hannan to run the new foundation, he realized he would have answered Dortmund's question differently. Maybe art forgery was connected with those murders in the Vatican, or would be.

Traeger flew home, drove to Empedocles, and, representing himself for what he was, a computer consultant, got past the guard, a phone call having been made. No doubt they had checked and found that he was indeed a customer. He was greeted by an affable type named Ray Sinclair who offered to show him around before Traeger went off to speak to the technical people. It was in the main building of the enterprise that they ran into Brendan Crowe.

"Hello, Father," Traeger said, advancing on the priest with his hand out.

"You know one another?" Sinclair cried, delighted.

Crowe hesitated before taking Traeger's hand, as if he understood they were enacting a little scenario. No need to make a public fuss of the fact that Crowe had gotten out of Rome just when the third secret of Fatima showed up missing from the archives over which Crowe was now acting director.

"We go way back," Traeger said heartily. "We have catching up to do."

Sinclair seemed happy enough to be relieved of his guide duties and sailed off over the polished marble floor.

"Where can we catch up?" Traeger said to Crowe.

"There's a lovely garden."

It was a lovely garden, filled with dozens of species of flowers whose names Traeger did not know. There was a magnolia tree that wasn't doing well in this climate. Crowe led him to a bench and sat.

"I suppose I shouldn't be surprised that you found me."

"You left a pretty obvious trail."

"Have you solved your problem in Rome?"

"A new one has arisen. But of course you know that. The third secret of Fatima is missing from the archives."

Crowe lit a cigarette, enjoyed it for a moment, and then said, "Yes, I know."

"Where is it?"

Crowe turned to him. "I have it with me."

Traeger sat back. "Can I have one of those?"

Crowe shook a cigarette free and Traeger took it. He had taken to drinking again in Rome, and now he was lighting his first cigarette in years. Crowe had surprised him. He surprised him more by being far more forthcoming than he had ever been before. The cigarette tasted awful, but it gave him something to do while Crowe told him of coming upon the famous document on a bedside table in Cardinal Maguire's suite.

"If that is what the assassin was after, he could have had it easily," Crowe said.

"But you surprised him before he got inside the villa."

"That's true."

"Why didn't you return it to the archives?"

Crowe said, "I think you know why."

"Tell me what I know."

"The assassin must have had inside help. You spoke of a mole. I haven't told you this before, but the Russian ambassador said something to me that suggested he thought the same thing. He asked if I were the one or must he wait for another. The question was put to Jesus by the disciples of John the Baptist."

"He thought you were the mole?" Traeger asked.

"You did, too, didn't you?" Crowe put out the cigarette.

Traeger said, "Chekovsky was interested in the file on the attempted assassination of John Paul II."

"They're connected."

"Through the third secret?"

"Yes. Would you care for another?"

Traeger shook his head. "I remember enjoying smoking."

"It's like running. Painful at first, but it becomes pleasurable."

"You run and smoke, too?"

"Not at the same time."

"You say you have the file with you. Where?"

"In my briefcase," Crowe said. "In my room."

"Why not on the bedside table?"

"I've thought of that. Not that I was particularly worried until you showed up. I will ask Mr. Hannan to put it in a safe place. A safe."

"Here you are!" someone cried.

It was Father John Burke, wearing a cassock. His smile slowly dimmed when he realized he was interrupting. Crowe stood and Traeger did, too.

"They're looking for you," Father Burke said. To Crowe. "The art historian has arrived and Mr. Hannan wants your opinion of him." He looked questioningly at Traeger.

"I'm in the computer business," he said, and to Crowe, "Should I come along?"

"Of course."

Crowe introduced Traeger as a friend from Rome, and Hannan asked him to come along to the conference room.

"Vincent!" Zelda cried when they came in, coming to Traeger and throwing her arms about him. Gabriel Faust watched this with an enigmatic expression. Hannan was delighted that Zelda knew Traeger.

"She's married," he said, sounding almost as relieved by the news as Traeger himself had been.

"This is Gabriel," Zelda said triumphantly, beckoning him forward.

"Hello, Doctor."

"One uses academic titles as sparingly as possible."

"Doctor," Hannan repeated approvingly, and Laura directed his attention to the materials she had put on the table. "Good. That sounds impressive. Let's get started." He pushed the materials toward Crowe. "Everybody seems to know everybody."

"This is Heather Adams," Laura said, indicating the third woman in the room. She smiled serenely and took her seat.

During the next half hour, Traeger decided that Crowe asked questions better than he answered them. Crowe went through Faust's credentials and asked about the various fellowships and commissions he had had.

"And some academic experience as well?"

"More than enough."

Hannan liked that and gave an account of his own truncated college career. Faust seemed unsure that he appreciated the parallel. As the interview continued, Traeger felt like God, knowing so much more about Faust than the others were likely to find out. But when Hannan mentioned the list of paintings that Crowe had made for him, adding that he had been persuaded that he was unlikely to be able to buy them, he asked Faust what he thought of the idea of having copies made. Faust thought a moment before nodding.

"There are computer-made copies now. I wouldn't recommend that. There are artists who can make copies infinitely better than such mechanical ones."

Traeger waited for Faust to mention Inagaki, but he didn't. This turn in the conversation put Traeger at ease. There was seemingly no need to make known to Crowe Faust's experience with the kind of copies he was recommending. He half expected Crowe to show that he somehow knew about Faust and Inagaki, but no allusion was made. It seemed merely a happy conjunction of a credentialed art historian and an art forger with a track record they needn't know about. When the interview was over and Hannan and Sinclair took Faust aside to talk money, Crowe came over to Traeger.

"I'll bring it here now," he said.

Traeger stirred, but Crowe put his hand on his shoulder.

"It will only take a few minutes."

⁂

Laura brought in coffee and she and Heather served it. "Laura tells me you and Father Crowe are saying Mass here," she said when she handed John Burke his cup.

"That's right."

"Would you mind if I attended?"

Struck by her manner, the young priest rose to talk with her. Traeger looked at his watch. The conference between Hannan and Sinclair and Gabriel Faust seemed to be going well. Zelda pretended not to be keeping an eye on the three of them. Ten minutes had gone by and still Crowe had not returned. Traeger interrupted Father Burke.

"Where are you and Father Crowe staying?"

"There is a residence for guests."

"Show me where it is."

Burke seemed surprised by the abruptness of the question. Heather said, "I'll show you."

Traeger followed her along the path, through the garden, past the bench where he and Crowe had talked. The door of the residence building was unlocked. Heather, who had taken out some keys, seemed surprised. They went in.

"Father Crowe was assigned 2B."

The door of 2B was open. Traeger looked in, put out an arm to prevent Heather from coming in, and went to the bed where Father Crowe lay on his back, staring sightlessly at the ceiling. A knife was plunged into his chest.

Heather screamed.

Traeger turned. "Get Laura. Get Sinclair. Just bring them. Don't say why."

She was staring with horror at the body. Then she composed herself and, surprisingly, made the sign of the cross over the body of Brendan Crowe.

The briefcase was on the desk.

It was empty.

✤ PART II ✤

# CHAPTER ONE

✢ I ✢

He vamoosed.

Having sent Heather to spread the alarm and having discovered that Brendan Crowe's briefcase no longer contained Sister Lucia's handwritten account of the secrets of Fatima, Traeger did what both training and inclination prompted him to do. He vamoosed.

The situation was not one in which to become embroiled, not until he had some clearer notion as to what had happened.

He took Crowe's briefcase with him, on impulse, to make sure there wasn't some unzipped zipper that would refute his immediate judgment that the document was lost, and then he left.

When he came into the corridor, he realized that he had registered the layout of the residence building instinctively. If the one who killed Crowe had gone out of the building, it would have been onto the walkway he and Heather had just come along. No, he would have gone away from the main building where there were people who might see him fleeing.

Across the corridor from Crowe's suite was the door of another, and at the end of the corridor were the pale gray doors of an elevator. If an elevator, then a stairway. He ran toward the green exit sign beyond the elevator and pulled open the door.

As it closed behind him, he stood very still. A stairway rose to the next floor, another descended. He looked up, he looked down. Then he began slowly to descend. He came to a metal door, put his hand on the stainless steel knob, and turned it slowly. He pulled. Locked. He turned and went up the stairs in great bounds, on up to the second floor. He came into a corridor like that below with an emergency exit at its end.

He emerged onto a balcony enclosed by a wrought iron railing. The rungs of a ladder were embedded in the walls of the building. He gripped the railing, looking over, and immediately pulled back his hand. It was sticky with blood. So this was the way the killer had escaped. He looked out over the luxuriant mown lawns, toward the road that led to the gate. He dropped the briefcase to the ground and went over the railing, handing himself down the rungs, conscious of his sticky hands, when he heard a car start. He stopped, still six feet above the ground, and turned.

His rental car was disappearing down the road toward gate.

Traeger dropped to the ground and picked up the briefcase. Logic is an inexact science. The move from the known to the unknown is ever mysterious. Traeger was certain that it was the killer who was driving off in the car he had rented, in which he had driven here to Empedocles. The logical thing to do was to continue the pursuit. And now he knew what he was pursuing.

He came around the building, then stepped back when he saw a group running toward the residence hall. John Burke, Hannan, Sinclair, Laura. He gave them time to get inside the residence and then sprinted away toward the administration building. The parking lot was just in front of it. Once he got in among the parked cars, he could select a car and go after the killer. The killer and the missing third secret of Fatima.

But before he got to the parking lot, the doors of the administration building slid open and Heather Adams appeared. She drifted toward him with widened eyes.

"I couldn't go back," she said.

"I understand. Is one of these your car?"

She seemed to have to think before she nodded.

"The killer just escaped in my car. I have to go after him. Give me your keys."

"They're in my purse."

"You're holding your purse."

This surprised her. The girl was still in shock from what she had seen in the residence building. She opened her purse and handed him two keys attached to a medal the size of a silver dollar.

"Saint Christopher," she explained. "You've cut yourself." She was looking at his hand.

"Which car is it?"

She pointed. He ran to the little Toyota and got behind the wheel. When he turned on the motor, he looked back to where Heather still stood. She lifted a hand dreamily, and for a moment Traeger thought she was going to bless him as she had blessed the body of Brendan Crowe.

Getting out of the Empedocles complex did not pose the same problem as getting in. Traeger lifted his hand to the guard and moved right on through, as no doubt the one who had stolen his rental car had done. And then?

⚜

He drove toward Boston because it was where the interstate led. The monotony of driving on the monotonously engineered interstate invited speculation on what had just happened. The thought that Crowe had fled to the States with John Burke in order to escape the questioning Traeger had put him through was not welcome. But when he brushed it aside to concentrate on what he was doing now, he had the sinking feeling that he was heading in the opposite direction of his quarry. North was the porous border of Canada.

Logic be damned, he had allowed an image of the killer to form in his mind, and the face was that of Anatoly. What Traeger needed now was access to the agency and its vast databases. He wanted a check run, an update on what Dortmund had already got for him. He pulled into an oasis and put through a call to Dortmund. His old chief reacted with impatient laughter when Traeger told him, trying to make it sound matter-of-fact, of the missing secret of Fatima.

"What the hell does some message whispered into the ear of a nun seventy-five years ago have to do with anything?" Dortmund asked.

"You'd have to be Catholic to understand."

"I am Catholic!"

Traeger hadn't known this. No reason why he should. "I thought all the Catholics were in the FBI."

"The Irish Catholics."

"A man, a priest, has just been killed for the sake of getting hold of that secret. That makes it important right there."

"A priest?"

"From Rome. He came here . . ." Traeger stopped himself. He hadn't called Dortmund to have a conversation, attractive as that suddenly was.

"Give it to me again," Dortmund said. "All of it. Including what I already know."

Traeger reduced the last several weeks to a crisp paragraph, suitable for framing. He had gone to Rome to see if the assassinations in the Vatican were connected with the report he himself had drawn up on the attempted assassination of John Paul II years before. The Russian ambassador had been pestering Cardinal Maguire to get access to the reports. In the course of the investigation, the third secret of Fatima turned up missing. Several groups and interests regard that secret as the key to modern history. It looked now as if the man who killed two cardinals, a priest, and a basilica guard in the Vatican had been after that third secret. He got it, at the cost of the death of Father Crowe.

"He could have had it easily if he had checked Maguire's bedroom," Traeger added, a little ironic coda.

"Why didn't he?"

"He was surprised and took off."

Dortmund spoke after a moment of silence. "He killed all those people and then panicked because of a witness?"

"He had no idea where the secret was."

Was that true? Had the assassin been informed that the prefect, Cardinal Maguire, had removed the file from the archives?

In any case, when Brendan Crowe found it, he figured it was safer with him than in the archives. When he accepted the invitation to go to Empedocles he had taken the document with him. Dumb? Smart? Who could say? Minutes after he had gone to fetch it from his room in the residence hall, he had turned up dead, the contents of his briefcase missing. Having sent Heather to bring the bad news to the administration building, Traeger had gone on the chase.

"And you think you're chasing Anatoly?"

"It's a possibility." How wan a hope that remark contained.

"Who may have a document you were told was in a brief-case in a residence room in Manchester, New Hampshire?"

"So I want a check run on him, okay? We haven't lost our curiosity about former KGB agents, have we?"

For half a minute, Dortmund's humming was all the answer he got. "Where will you be?"

"I better call you."

"I thought you were the chaser." Dortmund said.

And not the chased? He remembered Rome, where he had become aware that Anatoly was on his trail, but what reason would Anatoly have to trail him now, if he had the document he had already killed so many to get? How much simpler it would be if Anatoly were looking for him. If Anatoly was who he was looking for. If . . . Oh hell.

"Look, old friend and mentor, could we get it about that Crowe was killed for the sake of a facsimile of the secret? An incomplete copy. The real one having been left in the brief-case."

Dortmund was humming again, not in an encouraging way.

"There was an unzipped zipper."

Dortmund stopped humming. "That sounds like one of the proofs for the existence of God we were taught at Georgetown. Whatever is zipped is zipped by another . . ." His voice faded away. "It's a dumb idea but most ideas are. I'll see what I can do."

"I'll be in touch."

"I hope so."

❖

He thought about Dortmund's sign-off while he was in a hotel room in Cambridge.

As soon as he had hit the city limits, he pulled into the lot of a McDonald's and checked the glove compartment. He needed an address to enter in the GPS on the dash. He had told Brendan Crowe that his life might be in danger, because he could recognize the man who had killed the cardinals. In part, that had been to shake Crowe up and make him more cooperative than he was inclined to be. Well, his life had been in danger. Traeger's theory—theory, hell, call it a hunch—was that Crowe had been killed by the same man who had put the knife into Cardinal Maguire's chest.

He lay on the bed and propped himself up on pillows so he could see the Charles River slide majestically by outside his windows. When he had checked into the hotel, he had been carrying the briefcase. Hotels are no longer as curious as they were in the past. Once there were hotel dicks to make sure there was no unauthorized coupling taking place on the premises. Now one was routinely asked at the registration desk how many keys he wanted. And a pretty slim briefcase could count as luggage.

He had only the clothes he was wearing. Or not wearing. The first thing he had done was strip and take a shower, wanting among other things to get that blood off his hands. So he lay in his boxer shorts, staring at the river. Could all great Neptune's ocean wash that blood from off his hands? He told himself he was waiting, giving Dortmund time to scare up what he could on Anatoly. Information alone would be of no help. Traeger was hoping that inquiring about Anatoly would turn up something recent, very recent. Like where the hell he was.

But eating at the edge of his mind was the implication of Dortmund's questions. All Traeger had was Crowe's word that he had brought that document with him from Rome. But if he hadn't, why was he dead?

Well, two cardinals, a priest, and a basilica guard had died in vain in Rome. What was one more pointless murder? Bah. He got out his phone and called his secretary Bea.

"Well, thanks for staying in touch," she said brightly.

Dear God, how good her voice sounded, like a sonar link with normalcy. Once he got through with this assignment, and back in his office . . . But in his present circumstances this was a fantasy not to be indulged.

"You know how it is on vacation, Bea."

"Tell me about it. You know, I'll never get over how clear transatlantic calls are now."

He let it go. "Any calls?"

"Any calls! You've been away weeks and you wonder if there have been any calls?"

"Recent. Yesterday, today."

"Just your old golf partner, Dortmund."

"Dortmund! When?"

"Yesterday. What a clown," Bea added. "He was trying to speak in a foreign accent."

"Didn't fool you, huh?"

"I never forget a voice."

"What did he want?"

"He said he'd call back."

"Tape it when he does," Traeger said, keeping urgency out of his voice.

"Tape it?"

"I can be a joker, too."

Again Bea marveled at the clarity of transatlantic calls thanks to satellites. "When will you be back?"

Back. If only he could just drop everything and go back to his usual life.

"I have one or two things to wind up first, Bea."

"Toodle-oo."

&

That had not been Dortmund, trying to disguise his voice. Anatoly? Who was the pursued? He had half a mind to call back and tell Bea to go on vacation, anywhere, stay away from the office. If Anatoly had the phone number, he would also have the address. He opened his phone, thought for a moment, then closed it. He did not want to alarm Bea, and how could he avoid giving her a reason to go on vacation?

Up until now, this assignment from Dortmund had seemed almost a nostalgia trip, a reminder of how it used to be. The murders in the Vatican, the theft from the archives, meeting Anatoly—none of it had spelled danger, not for him. Suddenly, everything was different.

As long as he was making logical leaps, why not imagine that Anatoly had just driven down the road in that rental car, away from the entrance to Empedocles, then parked and waited. He would have seen Traeger roar by in the little Toyota. Traeger on the chase? Traeger the chased? He didn't like it. He didn't like it at all.

He got off the bed and into his clothes, took Crowe's briefcase, and went down the back stairway to the parking lot to steal a car and get the hell out of there. From among the parked cars, he chose a nondescript Chevy, got it going, and got out of there. He kept his eyes opened and circled the block, checking the mirror. When he was sure he hadn't been followed, he went back to the hotel parking lot for Heather's car. He made a maze of Cambridge and then of Boston, going he wasn't sure where.

❖ II ❖

### "One gets weary of caviar."

Zelda clung to Gabriel Faust after Heather came running in with the news that something had happened to Father Crowe, something terrible. Laura calmed Heather down, got the story, and then she and her brother the priest and Hannan took off, the billionaire flanked by his staff. Gabriel Faust watched them go. Zelda was trembling in his arms. Heather, having brought the news, stood in the atrium of the building where she had found them, turning slowly around as if in search of true north. Gabriel moved toward her, with Zelda still in his arms. They might have been dancing.

Heather stopped turning and stared at them, still in a state of shock.

"What happened? Did he fall? What?"

"Oh, the blood, the blood," Heather keened.

Zelda cried out empathetically in his arms. Gabriel patted her back, wondering what he had gotten into.

The negotiations had gone smoothly, the salary was the fulfillment of one of his mad dreams, they had a deal, Laura would write it up, and now this. Gabriel had the depressing thought that this was going to end like the rest of his high hopes over the past years. Excluding Zelda, of course. She was an unequivocal treasure. In several senses. He dropped his hand and patted her bottom. Heather watched impassively. She turned and walked out of the building.

"The poor girl," Zelda shuddered.

"I think I shocked her, sweetheart."

"How?"

He repeated the pat.

"What would I do without you?" she breathed.

As he held her, he saw Traeger come up through the shrubbery. He talked with Heather, urgently. After a moment, she handed him something, and a moment later he had run off to a car in the parking lot and driven away. Gabriel said nothing to Zelda about this odd little scene, nor to Heather when she drifted back inside.

⚜

That was the little lull before the storm. Hannan was back, hurrying through doors as they slid open. Soon there was a huddle between him and Laura and Sinclair. Hannan wanted the body removed and the whole thing treated as if it had never happened.

Laura said, "Nate, that's crazy. With all due respect. This is murder."

"That's my point," Hannan cried. "What will this do to Empedocles?"

"Nothing," Ray Sinclair said. "Nothing bad," he added.

It took Hannan some minutes before he was persuaded that this was a problem he could not wish away.

"Nate, he's a priest," Sinclair said patiently. "He was working for you."

Hannan thought about that. "God rest his soul," he said absently.

"John gave him absolution," Laura said.

Hannan nodded. He looked at Sinclair. "It could be the work of a competitor."

"Nate, you have no competitors."

It sounded like base flattery, but Faust acknowledged that it was the simple truth. Of course he had learned all he could about Hannan and Empedocles before driving over here with Zelda. He was overwhelmed. The only doubt left was whether Zelda was as buddy-buddy with Hannan as she claimed.

"I wouldn't say buddy-buddy," she said. "Buddy," she added, and smiled, a nice smile, and patted his thigh. "I see him at Mass."

One of the things that Gabriel had learned cuddling with Zelda in one bed or another during what she called their honeymoon was that her remorse over their sporadic affair—what had it been, twice?—had turned her into a church mouse. She had a confessor, a priest named Trepanier, and she had gone to Mass almost every day, doing penance for the fun they had had. But now they were married, and it was like the answer to her prayers. Now it was all right and she found licit sex far more exhilarating than the other kind, among other things because there was no aftermath of remorse. They were only doing what they had promised God they would do when they married in the sacristy of Santa Susanna.

The police were called, inevitably, despite Hannan's initial impulse, along with an ambulance, and then came the people from the crime lab. Meanwhile, they were kept in the conference room by the cop in charge, Purcell, who looked miscast for this murder and awed by talking with Hannan, the legendary tycoon. He explained, deferentially, that he wanted them on call. Gabriel assured Zelda they had no information for the police. All this occurred shortly after the two of them arrived, and whatever had happened had happened in another building where they had never been. He assured Zelda they would be allowed to go soon.

Meanwhile he tried not to feel a certain relief that Brendan Crowe was no longer among the living. He had nothing against the man, of course, how could he, but there had been an edge of skepticism in Crowe's voice when he went over Gabriel's credentials with him.

"How could remaining in the academic world have restricted you?" he had asked.

"Have you ever taught?"

Crowe didn't answer. He noticed that Faust's last NEA had been to study Delacroix.

"That was more or less a lark. One gets weary of caviar, I suppose."

He had to explain that, for God's sake. Renaissance art was the caviar, of course.

"And you returned to it?"

"It's been my life."

"No books?" Faust felt he was being interviewed for a teaching job.

"It has been suggested that I collect my articles."

"Good suggestion," Crowe said, surprisingly. He smiled. "Do forgive the grilling. I was subjected to the same thing."

"Will you be staying?" Gabriel asked.

"Oh, I must get back to Rome."

"Rome." Gabriel sighed. "What do you do there?"

Thank God he hadn't known that Crowe was acting prefect

of the Vatican Library, putting him in charge of books, museums, archives.

"You're just here to grill candidates?"

Crowe did know how to laugh, though he seemed out of practice.

That was the first thing. Gabriel had wondered if he would be working with this humorless priest who went over his dossier as if he were a mendicant. He had thought it necessary to tell Crowe that he had come at his wife's insistence.

"You're not interested in the job?" Crowe asked.

"Yes, I am. Of course. Mr. Hannan makes it all sound quite exciting."

"He is a sanguine man." And Crowe himself was phlegmatic. Those old divisions of character retained their uses. And what was Gabriel Faust?

The director designate of something to be called, improbably, Refuge of Sinners.

"I'll fit right in," Gabriel had said when he heard the name of the new foundation. Only Ray Sinclair laughed.

They had shaken hands all around and then all hell had broken loose. Heather burst in like a messenger in Shakespeare. There was no more Brendan Crowe to make Gabriel uneasy, but he had the awful thought that the deal would not go through now. Had he allowed his doubt to surface? Laura Burke came up to him.

"I'll write up the agreement. You can sign it before they let you go."

Ten minutes later, she was back with the contract. They made a little ceremony of his signing it, in the conference room, Laura and Zelda and Gabriel.

"What a beautiful hand," Laura said.

"Calligraphy is my passion."

"Oh?" Zelda said coyly.

Purcell, when he questioned them, recognized Zelda's name. "Zelda Lewis, until recently," she had said when asked to identify herself. "Now Zelda Faust." It all went smoothly, as he had predicted.

"Was he murdered?" Zelda asked.

"The investigation has just begun," Purcell said. "I don't see any reason to keep the two of you here any longer."

Laura Burke went with them to the car, apologetic. "This

dreadful thing will be occupying us for some time," she said. "Why don't I call you and we can decide when you will begin."

"What happened to Traeger?" Gabriel asked.

"That's what the police want to know."

Gabriel said nothing further, nor did he when, on the drive home, Zelda mentioned that Traeger had been a colleague of her late husband's. In the CIA.

"But I already told you that."

"And that he liked your Delacroix."

## ✣ III ✣

### "Where is Vincent Traeger?"

Father John Burke had difficulty not gagging when he stood over the body of his friend, sprawled on the bed, blood everywhere, and began to give him absolution. *Ego te absolvo*, he began, and then his mind went blank. He could not remember the rest of the formula of absolution. Like an idiot, he then said, blubbered rather, *Salva nos, domine, vigilantes, et custodi nos dormientes, ut vigelemus cum Christo et requiescamus in pace.* The prayer from Compline came readily to his lips even if he had forgotten the formula of absolution. And then the formula came, and he recited it almost lightheartedly, he was so relieved. Afterward, he tormented himself with the thought that his delay might have been the difference between Brendan Crowe alive and Brendan Crowe dead.

The others had held back while he performed his priestly task, but now they surged forward. Laura took Brendan's hand, lifted, sought a pulse. She let it drop. Her finger went to his throat. John looked at his sister. Their eyes met. She shook her head. Then she turned.

"Ray, call the guard shack. Tell them to prevent anyone from leaving. I'll call the police."

"No!" Hannan had cried. "No police."

And so that debate had begun. Ignatius Hannan seemed to want to wish away what had happened to Brendan, his motives incredibly self-regarding. A murder on the grounds of the Empedocles complex posed a business problem, a problem in public relations. Laura took her boss's arm and led him away. John was sure the electronics whiz would lose that argument.

He had been impressed by the calmness and practicality of his sister's reaction. Had it occurred to anyone else that whoever had done this dreadful thing must even then be in full flight? But when the call came back from the gate, the guard said that he had noticed no stranger leaving before Laura's call.

"Where is Vincent Traeger?"

The question was raised more than once during the next half hour after John had covered Brendan's body with a sheet and they had withdrawn to the administration building.

"Who exactly is Vincent Traeger?" Nate Hannan finally asked.

John had one answer. Traeger had been in Rome investigating some troubles within the Vatican. He had discussed them with Brendan.

"What kind of troubles?"

"Does it matter?"

"He is a CIA agent," Zelda said. "At least he was."

"How on earth do you know that?" Hannan asked.

"My husband, my first husband, was with the CIA. He and Traeger were colleagues. And friends."

Gabriel Faust had gone outside for a smoke while this conversation was going on, and John went out to join him. They stood in silence, looking out at the carefully barbered lawns, the clipped shrubbery, the trees. A memory of having a cigarette with Brendan in the basement bar of the Domus came to John and he could not suppress a sob. He looked helplessly at Faust, tears in his eyes.

"He was a good friend," he explained. "I think my best friend."

"I don't think he suffered," Faust said. "I'm sorry. That's a stupid remark."

A moment of silence.

"He knew a lot about Renaissance art," Gabriel said.

"He knew a lot about everything."

Does the intellect retain after death the knowledge it has laboriously acquired over a lifetime? It was the kind of question Brendan liked to discuss. The whole mystery of death struck John as it had not when his father died, or when, visiting his mother, he had realized she did not have long to go. Brendan had been at the height of his powers. The great likelihood was that he would become permanent prefect of the Vatican Library. Suddenly, such things seemed of no importance, trivial. It was an unsettling thought that things he had always known and could recite by rote now took on a significance they had never had before. *We have here no lasting city.* How easy to say, even as one went on living as if there would always be tomorrow. How could he not connect Brendan's violent death with the account he had given of the death of the secretary of state and of Cardinal Maguire? At first John had reacted in disbelief—you never knew when Brendan's unusual sense of humor would come into play. But it became immediately clear that he meant what he said literally. Of course, Brendan had considered him naive, credulous, still awestruck by the fact that he worked in the Vatican. Well, all those things were true. He laid no claim to sophistication, if that meant reacting to several bloody murders with aplomb. And if he hadn't been credulous, wouldn't he have gone on doubting what Brendan was telling him? He prayed to God that he would never become blasé about the privilege of working in such close proximity with the Holy Father.

"Is Vincent Traeger a good friend, too?" Gabriel Faust asked.

"I hardly know him."

"Crowe's friend?"

"Let's just say an acquaintance."

When it became clear that Traeger was nowhere to be found, the significance of his absence became the focus. Purcell, the police detective, wondered why Traeger would have shown up at Empedocles. if he were the comparative stranger Father Burke described.

"You met him in Rome?" Purcell asked, as if he were inquiring about the farside of the moon.

"Brendan—Father Crowe—introduced me to him."

"As?"

John was in a quandary. He knew that Traeger had something to do with the investigation of the murders in the Vatican, murders that were not publicly known to be such. It certainly wasn't his role to speak of those assassinations, particularly since any knowledge he had of them had come through Brendan. And now Zelda Faust said Traeger was a former CIA agent. Had he been sent to eliminate Brendan? Dear God, was the world really as brutal as all that?

"You should talk with Mrs. Faust," he said to Purcell.

"I'll talk with everyone."

Later Laura took him aside. "Of course the police have taken the body to the morgue."

John nodded. He had watched the vehicle carrying the mortal remains of his friend go off down the road to the gate.

"What's to be done when they release the body?" Laura asked.

John could see that his sister considered the decision his. Back to Rome? Most of Brendan's life had been spent there. But what is more insignificant than a mere priest in the vast clerical culture of the Vatican, even one who had been the right-hand man of the prefect of the Vatican Library, a post Brendan himself had been filling on an interim basis?

"Ireland," he said.

"Of course. You'll contact the family?"

"I'll take care of it."

He would contact Brendan's bishop in County Clare. But how in the name of God was he to describe to him what had happened to one of his priests, and one he had scarcely known?

One thing was certain, he himself could not remain in the building where Brendan had been so savagely killed.


❖ IV ❖

"He gave me instruction."


Heather answered as best she could the questions Detective Purcell asked her about the scene she and Traeger had come upon when they got to Brendan Crowe's suite in the Empedocles guest residence. All she had to do was shut her eyes to find that it was imprinted indelibly on her memory. She spoke as if describing the image rather than the reality.

"Why did you go to the guest building?" Purcell asked. His pencil was poised over a little notebook, ready to go into action when answers were given to his questions.

"To show Mr. Traeger the way."

"He asked to go there?"

"Father Crowe had gone there, saying he would be back soon, and the delay bothered Traeger."

"Why?"

"He didn't say."

Heather did not like this. She could see that he was putting an interpretation on her words, perhaps the true one. Traeger had been concerned by Father Crowe's absence, indicating perhaps that he suspected he was in danger. The fact that Traeger was not there to be asked these questions irked Purcell.

"You arrived together?"

"At the guest building? Yes."

"And he entered the suite first?" Purcell went on.

"Yes."

"How long was he alone there?"

"I was at his side."

"You went into the suite, too?"

From the doorway, she had seen the open door of the bedroom beyond the sitting room, the body on the bed, blood. It had drawn her like a magnet.

"What did you do?"

Heather looked at him. She did not want to provide occasion for derision. She said softly, "I blessed him."

Of course Purcell thought she was still in a state of shock, but the shock had lifted soon after she had brought the awful news back to the others and they had run off to the guest building. The Fausts stayed where they were, whispering to one another, and Heather had gone outside. If Purcell had asked when she last saw Traeger, she would have told him of giving the man the keys to her car. But he didn't ask. He assumed that she had last seen Traeger in the suite in the guest building.

She did not regret helping Traeger get away. She liked him, she scarcely knew why. And she understood the desire to flee the awful scene in the guest suite.

❖

John Burke announced that he wanted to move to a rectory in town, a decision that displeased Mr. Hannan.

"You're perfectly safe here, Father."

"That isn't it."

Laura explained the young priest's reluctance to stay in the building where his friend had been so brutally killed. Laura made the arrangements, of course, after consultation with Heather Adams. Was there anything she couldn't do?

"Could you drive John there, Heather?"

"My car is gone."

"What?"

"It's not in the parking lot, Laura."

"For heaven's sake, you should have mentioned that before."

Laura ran off to tell Purcell, and the detective sent out the bulletin through headquarters. Everyone assumed that Traeger had stolen her car.

It was Ray Sinclair who asked how Traeger had gotten to Empedocles in the first place. But Purcell's interest now lay in finding the car in which Traeger had left Empedocles. Traeger's departure was now seen as clearly implicating him in what had happened to Father Crowe.

"Take my car," Laura said to Heather.

"But how will you get home?"

"Ray will take me. The parish is Saint Cyril's, do you know it?"

"Father Krucek."

"It's your parish?"

"Yes."

But there were hours yet before Purcell allowed them to leave. The sun had gone down, but it was not yet evening, and the grounds of Empedocles seemed filled with the competing songs of birds.

"What is Father Krucek like?" Father Burke asked Heather when they finally got under way.

"He gave me instruction."

"You're a convert?"

"Yes, Father."

"Ignatius Hannan has a great influence on you?"

She smiled. Her conversion had nothing to do with Mr. Hannan's excited enthusiasm. Not that she criticized him, but he acted as if he had picked the winning team and had to cheer it on to victory. Nor did she dwell on what she knew of Laura and Ray Sinclair. Almost every prayer she knew was a plea of the sinner, the Our Father, the Hail Mary, the Memorare, maybe all of them, and "sinner" wasn't a pious misdescription of presumably good people. Pray for us sinners meant literally that.

If Laura and Ray were sinners, that did not distinguish them from anyone else. The point was to feel sorrow and resolve to act otherwise.

"How long have you been at Empedocles?" Father Burke seemed to be searching for a conversational opening, but then people often found her difficult to talk to.

"Not as long as Laura."

"What would Hannan do without her?"

"What would any of us do without her?" Heather said.

When they arrived at the Saint Cyril rectory, he wondered if she would introduce him to Father Krucek.

"Good heavens, that isn't necessary. Laura said he's expecting you."

He thanked her and hopped out, perhaps glad that she had not accepted his offer. But how on earth would she have described him to Father Krucek? Laura's brother? The friend of a murdered priest? She wondered if he would tell Father Krucek what had happened to Brendan Crowe.

He might just as well. She turned on the radio and heard of the search for a material witness to a slaying at Empedocles Inc., one of the largest local employers. Heather heard her car described. They gave the license plate number, too, but of course she didn't recognize that. Do people actually remember such things?

When she turned in the drive and started through the wooded lot to her house, she felt that she had been away for ages. The drive dipped before it went behind the house to the garage.

Her car was parked before the closed garage door.

# CHAPTER TWO

## ❖ I ❖

### "They didn't ask."

Traeger heard the car come along the unpaved drive, its running lights flitting through the trees like lightning bugs. Only one car. He watched from a window in the darkened house. He knew that a bulletin had gone out in search of Heather's car. That he had gotten here at all was thanks to the GPS on her dashboard, the main reason he had traded that old Chevy in for it. He fed the address on the registration in the glove compartment into the navigation system and then just followed its directions.

Heather's house seemed the place to go because it did not seem the place to go. If her car was being sought, she had probably told the police who had gone off in it. On the news he was simply an unnamed material witness.

The car stopped behind the house. He was in the kitchen now. The woman at the wheel was Heather Adams. She must have been puzzling over what her car was doing, parked there. If she started to use a cell phone, Traeger would be out the front door and on his way he knew not where.

She got out of the car and stood looking at her house. How unthreatening she looked. Traeger pushed open the door and came outside.

"It's me," he said.

"I can see you."

"Maybe you want to put your car in the garage."

"Why didn't you?"

Not every question has a sensible answer. The remote control on her sun visor opened the door. Traeger had pressed it and watched the door roll up, but driving into the cavernous garage would have seemed like entering a cul-de-sac. He lowered the door and left the car outside. He realized he had been counting on the serene compliance this woman had shown when he asked for the keys of her car.

"Did you tell them I took it?" he asked her.

"They didn't ask."

They stood looking at one another for a moment, and then she turned to the house. "We'd better go in."

When she flicked on the kitchen light, Traeger pulled the cords of the venetian blinds. But suddenly he felt safer than he had for hours.

"I usually have a simple supper," she said. "After I say my prayers."

Traeger had been through the house, wanting to know the various ways to get out quickly if that became necessary, and he had seen the oratory downstairs.

"Go ahead."

"You've been downstairs?" she asked.

"Yes."

Nothing seemed to bother or surprise her. Maybe the sight of Crowe's body had traumatized her, but somehow that didn't seem the explanation.

"You could join me."

From any other beautiful young woman it might have seemed a provocative remark. "Maybe you should first tell me what went on after I left."

"The police seem to think you were responsible for Father Crowe's death."

"You know that isn't true," he said.

She nodded. "But you were concerned about him, weren't you? You thought something had happened to him?"

"Yes."

She waited. When he said nothing, she said, "I'll go downstairs now. You don't mind waiting?"

"Of course not. Are you some kind of nun or what?"

She laughed. "How many kinds are there?"

"I wouldn't know."

"I'm not a nun."

Just a woman who prayed.

He sat in the living room while she was downstairs. It was odd thinking of her down there, praying. Dortmund had surprised him with the information that he was Catholic. Surely there had been some point in their long association when he might have mentioned that. Dortmund must have assumed that Traeger, too, was Catholic, given the Notre Dame degree. Once, on assignment in Australia, the subject had come up and the man he was working with, having learned where Traeger had been to college, said that he was also Catholic. "A retired Catholic," he added with a rueful grin. Traeger was not so much retired as out of practice. The work he had been engaged in did not seem anything God would approve of, however righteous the cause. How long had it been since he had prayed, prayed in the sense that Heather used the term? Oh, there were always quick pleas for help, addressed he supposed to God, most recently when he was getting out of that hotel in Cambridge. Now that he had the police on his track as well as whoever the hell it was that followed him to that hotel, he could use a few real prayers.

Followed him to the hotel. He repeated that thought. Whoever it had been, the person might have seen him in Heather's car, no matter the razzle-dazzle with the Chevy. He did not like the thought that he might have drawn his pursuer to Heather's house. But he was certain, as certain as one could be, that no one could have kept with him on the circuitous route he had taken. It was only when he was out of Boston that he had checked her address and entered it in the GPS.

Traeger got out his phone and called Dortmund again.

"Is that you they're looking for?" Dortmund asked, his tone one of mild rebuke.

"I'm afraid so."

"I won't ask where you are."

Traeger said nothing.

"Unless you have a fax. I could send you what turned up on Anatoly. That seems to be his real name, by the way. We also knew him as George Brandes and by several other names."

"There's no fax here. What did you find?"

"He's KGB. Or was. He seems to be one of the disgruntled ones. If not gruntled." Dortmund chuckled. "Do you read P. G. Wodehouse?"

Dortmund was full of surprises. It was a rhetorical question.

"You say you ran into Anatoly in Rome?" Dortmund asked.

"We had a nice chat. He was tailing me. I think he still is." Silence on the line. "Be careful."

"I may be coming to see you."

"Is that wise?"

"I'll let you know."

"You say Anatoly's in the country?" Dortmund said.

"I think so."

"I could put someone on him."

Traeger thought about it. "I don't think so. But thanks."

He put his phone back in his pocket.

❖

She had come up, and he could hear her in the kitchen. Soon, pleasant smells came from there. Traeger rose and joined her.

"Can I help?" he asked.

"Do you know how to make a salad?"

"No."

She smiled. She prepared a risotto with peas mixed with the rice, and little onions, too, made the salad herself, then set the table.

"Is ice water all right?"

"Of course."

When they were seated, she bowed her head briefly, then looked across the table at him.

"What will you do? Where will you go?"

He didn't answer, because he was eating. He hadn't realized how hungry he was. The risotto was delicious. When he had finished, she got up and gave him more.

"It's good," he told her.

"Because you're hungry." But her pleased smile did not go away.

After they were finished, she suggested tea. Traeger hated tea. "Sounds good."

They stayed in the kitchen, at the table. Traeger had been thinking of his next move.

"Whose car did you come in?" he asked her.

"Laura's."

If he left in that car and then abandoned it, it would be obvious, to Laura at least, that he had taken the car from Heather's. Having exchanged it for her car. For whatever reason, Heather had not volunteered the fact that she had given him the keys to her car and knew that he had driven away in it from Empedocles. She could hardly be expected to say she had no idea what had happened, if her car showed up at her house and the one she had borrowed from Laura was gone. Heather might not volunteer information, but Traeger doubted that she would ever lie. Now he regretted having come here, not only because it was no solution for him, but also because it implicated her.

"I could drive you to where you want to go." She might have been following his thoughts.

He looked at her. She sat up straight in her chair and did not slump. She looked him directly in the eye, and her gaze was as sexless as a child's, but wonderfully benevolent.

"You'd do that?"

"Yes."

"Why?"

"Because I know you're not the one they're after."

"And your car?"

"I'll put it in the garage. I can discover it there in a day or two. Will that be enough?"

"Do you trust everyone?"

"No. There's something I should tell you. Before you sent me back to tell the others, I saw the briefcase on the floor."

"It was empty."

"I think I know what they were after."

The day before, Brendan Crowe had told her he wanted to entrust a file to her, some papers, to be put in the company safe. The papers were in a cardboard envelope; it had a flap and was tied with a ribbon.

"He showed it to you?"

"He gave it to me."

Traeger stared at her. So what kind of game had Crowe been

playing when he went off to his room to get something he had already given to Heather?

Traeger said, "Is it in the company safe?"

"It's downstairs."

He leapt to his feet and went rapidly down to Heather's oratory. There were vigil lights flickering that she must have lit earlier. And then the room was illumined as Heather entered, flipping the light switch. She went to the altar and moved the picture hanging behind it.

"A safe?"

"A tabernacle. I hope that eventually perhaps I can have the Blessed Sacrament reserved here."

But Traeger was interested in the folder she had taken from the recess's repository. She brought it to him.

"What is it?" she asked.

"You didn't look inside?"

"It's in a language I can't read."

Traeger undid the strings, widened the opening, and without taking papers from the file, saw that it was what Crowe had brought from Rome. What he and others had been killed for.

"It's Portuguese."

"Portuguese?"

"Do you know anything of Fatima, Heather?"

"Of course."

"Sister Lucia?"

Her lips parted. She put out her hand and laid it on the file. Traeger had closed it. She picked up the strings and tied them, showing more emotion than Traeger had seen since they came upon the body of Brendan Crowe.

"Why did you bring it here, Heather?"

"Too many people have access to the safe at work."

❖

She drove him to a mall not far from her house. The great sea of parked cars was what he was looking for. He had her pull in and then drive slowly between rows of cars.

"This is fine. Thank you, Heather."

"God bless you."

When had anyone said that to him without his having

sneezed first? The words had meaning as she said them. He got out, stooped, smiled, shut the door, and then turned and went shopping for a car.

## ❖ II ❖

### "Ain't love grand?"

Laura had never had such a day. And never before had she seen Nate Hannan nearly come unglued.

First, there had been the suggestion that they somehow spirit the body of Father Crowe away from Empedocles. As an initial impulsive reaction, okay, but he had to be argued out of it. Nate simply had no recent experience of situations in which he was not in complete control. Second, there had been Nate's insistence that that stranger Vincent Traeger had murdered Brendan Crowe. There was no point in spelling out for him, as Ray had, the difficulties with the explanation. It was an explanation that promised to direct the investigation away from Empedocles, and that was Nate's major concern.

Well, he seemed to have succeeded. Purcell's questioning turned to what any of them knew of Traeger and when Zelda made the extraordinary revelation—revelations, really, first, that her husband, her *first* husband she had clarified while clinging to the enigmatic Gabriel Faust, had been with the CIA and, second, that he had worked with Vincent Traeger—Purcell pursued this eagerly. Perhaps he saw a way of getting the problem off his plate. Laura made a note to herself to avoid meeting a violent death, if it affected the survivors this way.

Eventually, after hours of being questioned, the three of them were alone in Nate's office where something like calm returned.

"I can't believe this happened here," Nate said. "Who would want to kill a priest?"

"Diocletian," Ray suggested, then had to explain it to Nate. The gaps in the great man's knowledge still surprised Laura.

"We're going to have to tighten security around here," Nate said.

"I'll get at it," Laura said. As long as this could be turned

into a soluble problem, Nate would relax. And of course soluble
meant that Laura would take care of it.

"Where's your brother, Laura?"

"Heather took him to a rectory in town."

"Good. Good. I wish we'd thought of that earlier." Earlier,
of course, he had opposed John's going.

"Could Brendan Crowe have been killed off the premises?"
Nate asked. This was a side of Nate's single-mindedness that
was less than attractive.

Finally, they broke up. They got Nate into his car—he
still drove the most modest of Fords, Henry being one of his
heroes—and Laura got into the passenger seat of Ray's car and
heaved a sigh of relief.

"We need a drink," he said.

"At least."

He leaned toward her as he turned the ignition key, and
they bumped foreheads.

"Let's get out of here," she urged.

"My place or yours?"

"Mine."

*"Sed tantum dic verbo."*

And off they went, down the road to the gate. His place, her
place, when would it be theirs?

"What's that mean?"

"What?"

"What you said in Latin. It sounded familiar."

" 'Just say the word.' "

"Where's it from?"

"It's from the Mass. I thought you were Catholic."

She moved toward him on the seat, wanting her shoulder
against his. Wouldn't it be wonderful if they could just be
Catholics together again, no longer half ashamed of their relationship? John had seemed unsurprised when she told him that
Ray had asked her to marry him.

"John could preside," she said softly.

"If you like."

She loved him for knowing immediately what she meant.

❧

At her apartment, she got out the single malt scotch for Ray,
who liked it neat, without ice, to sip as much as to drink. Laura

made a martini for herself. The night had grown surprisingly cool, so she lit the fireplace and they sat with just a single light on. A lovely domestic scene.

"Do you want some nibbles?"

"Later." He puckered his lips and made kissing sounds.

Nate's question earlier was the obvious one. Why would anyone want to kill a priest, specifically Brendan Crowe?

Laura remembered when they had been in Rome, when she had left Ray at the Hotel Columbus and gone to the Vatican to have lunch with John at the Domus Sanctae Marthae where he lived. The man Brendan Crowe had worked for, Cardinal Maguire, had recently died, and Father Crowe was just back from his funeral in Ireland. In Saint Peter's there had been a prolonged pontifical funeral Mass for Rampolla, the secretary of state who also had recently died. When Laura suggested that Vatican City seemed injurious to one's health, John had mentioned the age of the secretary of state. But he clearly hadn't wanted to talk about it. No more had she. But now, sitting in her apartment before the fire with Ray, she remembered that exchange and what seemed to her in retrospect John's eagerness to drop the subject. She would press John on the matter tomorrow.

"You think we're making the right choice with Gabriel Faust?" Ray asked.

"He's got credentials out the gazoo."

"As well as Zelda. I make no mention of gazoos."

She punched his arm. "Ain't love grand?"

"She parades him around like a trophy."

"Brendan Crowe studied his dossier, interviewed him," Laura said. "He said Faust was the real article."

"Well, Crowe certainly came up with the obvious solution to that list of paintings."

Have copies made, copies so perfect they would be as good as the originals. Faust knew all about it, another plus. Nate would have the depictions of the joyful mysteries of the rosary ordered and the new foundation could get under way. It occurred to Laura that she and Ray regarded Nate's determination to add Refuge of Sinners to his accomplishments as a quirk, as if he had suddenly decided to collect antique cars or Civil War mementos.

"Thank God for Heather," Laura said, raising her glass.

Her old classmate had always been serious, it was one of

her charms, but even so, Laura had been surprised by the transformation in Heather. She reported to Ray, but Laura was her superior as well. Why then did she feel like such a kid when she talked to Heather? All the authority that had come along with her success at Empedocles, as Nate's indispensable right hand, seemed to fade away before Heather's manner. How to describe it? She was conscientious, reliable, efficient, and yet somehow otherworldly. She had become a Catholic.

"Heather, I thought you always were."

"Sometimes I think the same." That smile, that smile. If it were anyone else, Laura would feel condescended to, but it was because of Heather's indifference to the usual jockeying and maneuvering in any corporation that, having first doubted it—there were so many ways to maneuver—she now accepted Heather's attitude as the genuine article. And of course Heather and Nate could have intense conversations about their spiritual reading. Well, intense on Nate's part. Once he learned there was a ladder of spiritual perfection, he was intent on the uppermost rung. And Nate could talk to Heather about his plans for Refuge of Sinners. He had actually proposed that Heather run the thing.

"She turned me down," Nate said, another new experience for him.

The foundation would be a corporation separate from Empedocles, nonprofit of course, and Laura and Ray had tried to understand its purpose. Asking Nate was risky, since it led to one of his sermons: not unctuous, more like a business plan.

"Why doesn't he just underwrite Trepanier's organization?" Ray had wondered.

"Because it wouldn't belong to Saint Ignatius."

Well, if Nate had been predictable, he probably would be a computer repairman trying to make ends meet. They had hoped the grotto would satisfy his new interest in the faith of his fathers, but it had been just the beginning.

"I almost wish he had thought of John for the job," Laura said.

"Would he have taken it?"

"No."

"There you are."

It had been Zelda's surprising remark that Traeger had been in the CIA with husband numero uno that cast the events of the day in a new light. Or a new darkness. What she and Ray knew of the CIA didn't amount to much. The agency was often in the news of late, portrayed as a check on if not a rival to the administration. Its critics pointed to the miserable record of the agency in assessing the situations in which they had involved the country. It was something to learn that not even members of Congress were privy to its operations or even knew the extent of its budget, let alone how the money was used. And they had covered themselves with shame in their estimate of Iraq, first in the Gulf War, now in the seemingly endless conflict in which our troops were engaged in the supposedly conquered country. All the talk about weapons of mass destruction had been revealed as so much blather. But it had been based on so-called intelligence. What did all that have to do with what had happened to Brendan Crowe in the guest building at Empedocles? If anything? But the mysterious disappearance of Vincent Traeger made Father Crowe's horrible death seem an event in a game that Purcell and his colleagues were unlikely to understand.

"That gets Purcell off the hook," Ray said. "His relief at the thought is palpable."

"Us, too." She snuggled closer. "Let's talk about us."

"Not in front of the children."

Laura purred. What a lovely thought.

## ❖ III ❖

### "And so to bed."

They went out to dinner, as they usually did, Zelda saying she did not want to spoil their honeymoon by revealing what a lousy cook she was. Honeymoon? What had begun in Corfu had continued nonstop ever since, gaining in intensity after the ceremony in the sacristy of Santa Susanna in Rome. Father Kiernan had been remarkably incurious about Gabriel, apparently assuming that he was as committed a Catholic as Zelda surprisingly was. No, not surprisingly. He remembered her agonies of remorse between bouts in bed after their relationship had altered from expert and client to sexual partners. Calling Zelda from Corfu, more out of boredom than anything, had proved a fateful step.

"Another?" he asked when they had finished their Manhattans.

"Let's." She hunched her shoulders and widened her eyes. But the implied naughtiness of a second preprandial drink was make-believe.

"Tell me about your husband, Zelda."

"You're my husband."

"I had no idea he had been with the CIA."

"He only told me after he retired. Can you believe it?"

"What did you think he did?"

"He said he was a lobbyist. And he was. But it turned out that was more a cover than a job."

"And he worked with Traeger?"

"Gabriel, I am trying to forget about this awful day."

He put his hand on hers. "I thought it had been rather successful."

"Oh, I'm sorry. Of course it has been. And I am so delighted. I'll tell you a secret. I had begun to worry how I could possibly avoid boring you to death. Now you have a wonderful position. What exactly are the arrangements?"

"I thought you'd never ask."

He handed her the memorandum and contract Laura Burke had given him before they left Empedocles. Zelda's plush lips rounded when she read the proposed salary. Gabriel realized how important to him that was. If she had feared the specter of boredom, he had not looked forward to her discovery of how modest his means were. How could he help but feel like a gigolo, particularly the way Zelda displayed him as if he represented some splendid catch? He had insisted on using his credit cards during these past weeks, dreading presenting her with the bills when they came. Now he would have an income beyond anything he had expected. Not even in his optimistic youth would he have imagined such a sinecure.

"I wish I could understand exactly what it is that Ignatius expects you to do."

"He's not too clear on that himself. Fatima is at the heart of it."

Zelda nodded. She knew about Fatima. So did Gabriel, now. He had made a little research project of it when he first got an inkling of what the aim of the new foundation would be.

"But you'll work there in the Empedocles complex?"

"For the nonce, my love. Hannan intends to house the foundation in a new complex."

Attractive, that. Gabriel had appreciated the effortless efficiency of Laura Burke, but the prospect of being under her surveillance was less than exhilarating. Or of Ray Sinclair's for that matter.

Zelda said, "I'm sure those two would be married if Ignatius ever gave them time for it."

"And what of Hannan himself in that regard?"

Zelda inhaled, then adopted her little-girl expression. "I think he had his eye on me. You see what you saved me from."

She could have no idea what she had saved him from.

"He said I could call on Heather as I set things up, Zelda. 'We see eye to eye on these matters.' I am quoting."

"Isn't she a lovely girl?"

Gabriel remembered seeing the lovely girl standing outside the administration building, taking keys from her purse and handing them to Traeger.

"Where does she live?" he asked.

"God knows. She's a recluse, according to Laura."

But Heather's handing her keys to Traeger in order that, as it transpired, he could make his getaway suggested that the two knew one another. If Traeger had been, perhaps still was, CIA, perhaps Heather was as well. Gabriel had spent much of his life in intrigue, but he found such speculation dizzying.

They had their dinner, with a bottle of Barolo, then afterward drove to Zelda's. Her place was fifty miles from Empedocles.

She said, "I suppose we should relocate. To be nearer to your new job."

"I won't mind commuting."

"I would hate to leave this place. The memories . . ."

Did she mean her husband? Apparently not. The reference was to their making love here, in the bad old days.

"Well," Gabriel said. "You know how Pepys ended entries in his diary."

"How?"

"And so to bed."

❖

He drove to Empedocles the following day and talked again with Laura and with Ray Sinclair about the financing of Refuge of Sinners. Gabriel tried to look blasé as Sinclair gave him the figures. There would be a hundred-million-dollar endowment supporting the new foundation. Gabriel had found his salary breathtaking, but this was affluence indeed. Again, he was urged to sit down with Heather for a long talk.

"I can't imagine why," she said. Ash brown hair framed her face, her eyes were like Spanish olives, and her lips seemed to involve more folds and indentations than necessary, like those of Michelangelo's David, but they all enhanced her beauty.

"Is Father Trepanier to be regarded as a competitor or what?" Gabriel asked Heather.

Zelda had told him of the enthusiastic priest whose ministry she supported. Trepanier was practically in the neighborhood, but his operation, Fatima Now!, was largely electronic, a cable channel on which he broadcast twenty-four hours a day, not to mention the worldwide reach of shortwave stations.

"If Mr. Hannan has any criticism of Father Trepanier, it is the tone of his criticism of the Church."

Heather explained. More Fatima. At the heart of Trepanier's efforts was the demand that the Church fulfill the request that the Blessed Mother had made that Russia be dedicated to the Immaculate Heart of Mary.

"Russia?"

In 1917, when the apparitions had taken place at Fatima, mention of Russia—and not the Soviet Union—as the great menace to peace seemed odd, not that the three children would have seen it as such. Had they even known what or where Russia was? Of course, Sister Lucia's latter communication, written under obedience, recalling events at a later date, when she had become a nun, the other two children dead, was the product of a woman whose natural gifts had profited from the education she had subsequently received. There were also accounts of subsequent apparitions when the Blessed Virgin appeared to her alone, but they were not part of the document that had been meant for the pope and that had contained what Sister Lucia called secrets, among them what had come to be called the third secret of Fatima.

"Mr. Hannan has been swayed by those who feel the revelation of that third secret in two thousand was incomplete," Heather told him.

"What does he think was left out?"

"I wonder." Her eyes drifted away, then came back to him. "Isn't it strange how people become fascinated with secrets?"

Heather went on. "There are some who think that in two thousand the Church kept back Our Lady's dismay at Vatican II."

"Is Hannan among them?"

"To a degree. He has his own theory."

"And what is that?"

"That Our Lady warned of the loss of Christendom to Islam."


✣ IV ✣

#### "Any beeping messages?"

Father Krucek was a wry but delightful host.

"If you have any friends who need rooms, I can put them up, too."

John Burke forbore saying that his best friend was dead. The pastor of Saint Cyril's had doubtless buried too many friends and family and parishioners to regard death as any great surprise. Of course, John had told him what had happened to Brendan.

"I'll say a Mass for him."

"Thank you, Father."

Krucek was a monsignor but did not use the title nor indeed wear the red piping he was entitled to on his cassock. He wore his white hair in a crew cut, was seventy-five and thus of retirement age, but he soldiered on as pastor. Once he had had two assistants—"When we still called them that"—but attrition in the ranks of the clergy had long since deprived him of such help. The rectory was large, with accommodations for three priests and a visitor, but now there were only Krucek and Mrs. Krapcinski, the housekeeper and cook whom he called affectionately Mrs. Krap. "My coeval," he added. "She's been here forever. She's worse than a wife."

It was Mrs. Krapcinski's taped voice that was heard on the parish phone, rattling off the hours of Sunday Masses and when confessions were heard, adding that any necessary messages could be recorded after the beep.

"Any beeping messages?" was the pastor's frequently asked question. He asked it now when they came into the dining room, which was redolent with the odor of ethnic fare.

"You'll be the first to know, Father."

They sat and Krucek said the grace in Latin, making no comment when John joined in. The pastor's arthritic hand traced the sign of the cross over their empty plates, and then opened his napkin with a flourish. Mrs. Krapcinski had stood with bowed head during the prayer, then disappeared through the swinging door to her kitchen, to emerge a moment later with a steaming tureen of soup. She filled their bowls, the pastor's first, then John's. It was a delicious chowder, more solid than liquid in state.

The pastor had said his Mass at five, the afternoon Mass a grudging concession to changing times.

"I never concelebrate," he said when John asked if the pastor minded if he said his own Mass. Nor was Communion given under both species at Saint Cyril's. It was not simply that the common cup dared the Lord to prevent the spread of disease. Father Krucek knew the arguments of Reformation times and considered offering the consecrated wine as well as bread to the faithful a betrayal. There were no Eucharistic ministers at Saint Cyril's. The pastor was delighted—if that was not too exuberant a word—to find that John was not a flaming liberal. His brows had lifted and that was all when John mentioned that his assignment was Rome.

"Rome," he said now. "Still a student?"

"I work for Bishop Sanchez Sorrondo in the Office of Pontifical Academies."

"You hear that, Mrs. Krap? He works in the Vatican."

Mrs. Krap was deaf as a post—Krucek's description—but she didn't seem to miss much.

"When I can't hear I'll let you know."

The arrangement was that John would say his Mass in the morning. "We won't make an announcement. People will begin to expect it."

"I will only be with you a few days, Father."

The chowder was followed by pork chops, mashed potatoes, and corn. The bread was delicious, baked by the housekeeper, as was the apple pie that followed. John praised the food, but Mrs. Krap was as phlegmatic as the pastor. She made a little mock curtsy and went through the swinging doors. In his study, Krucek opened a liquor cabinet and asked John what his poison was.

"Whatever you're having, Father."

"Then you'll go to bed sober. I never drink."

"Maybe a little brandy?"

Krucek poured out a generous glass and handed it to John. "I do smoke, however."

"Good." John got out his cigarettes. Krucek unwrapped a cigar and moistened it carefully before lighting it.

"I studied in Louvain myself," Krucek said, the words emerging like smoke rings.

"Did you?"

"Philosophy. I taught in the seminary for years. This is my reward. Captain of the *Titanic*."

"There seemed a good turnout for a weekday Mass."

"The walking wounded. How many young people did you see?"

Somewhat to his surprise, John had noticed Heather among them. Of course she had driven him here from Empedocles, leaving him at the rectory, commending his host, and then, as John had thought, driving off. He mentioned her to Krucek.

"A convert. Extraordinary woman. Most converts come into the Church for the sake of a marriage, and that's a good thing of course, although some of them would become Mormons or Hottentots if that were required. Heather is the other kind."

"How so?"

"What do you know of Edith Stein?"

"Is Heather a philosopher?"

"*Videte ne quis vos decipiat per philosophiam*," Krucek said, adding "Colossians. No, her degree is in business."

John explained how he knew her. At the mention of Ignatius Hannan, Krucek closed his eyes and blew a series of perfect smoke rings. "He's the third kind."

Under prodding, he elaborated. A convert like Heather was a tonic, someone who put a priest on his mettle. He looked at John, "She wants to be a saint. Not that she would put it so baldly. The questions she asked when she came for instruction . . ." His voice trailed off. "When a person like that comes to you, you realize how we've come to take it all for granted. All this hoopla for the last quarter of a century and more, changing this, changing that, until people don't know up from down. Who can blame them for thinking we've jettisoned the whole thing. And then someone like Heather comes and it's as if she is just brushing aside all the nonsense and wants the thing itself. Converts will save the Church, Father. You can quote me."

"And Ignatius Hannan?"

"A Barnum and Bailey Catholic."

John laughed. "My sister is his administrative assistant."

"You understand I don't know the man. I'm not judging him. But he came by once with Heather and wanted to write a check for any amount I named." Krucek grinned. "I said, 'Make it out for a dollar.' And he did." He pulled open his desk drawer and brought out a check. "I kept it as a souvenir."

When the conversation got back to Brendan, John told the pastor that it had apparently been a break-in. That was, if not the whole truth, true. Brendan had gone to his room and apparently surprised the thief.

"What was he after?"

John shrugged. That was what made the thing so pointless. How could anything there have been possibly worth having? The thief might just as well have come snooping through John's suite. Perhaps just the reputation of Empedocles and Ignatius Hannan's known wealth would make a thief think the place was chock-full of gold. But to kill? The Empedocles complex lost a good deal of its taut efficiency after the discovery of the body. It was odd that it was the women who kept their heads. Laura, of course, but Heather, too. On the drive to the rectory Heather told him that she had made the sign of the cross over the body.

"That was all right, wasn't it, Father?"

"Why wouldn't it be? That was exactly the thing to do." He himself, he was afraid, had come too late to be of any good to Brendan's soul.

"And I said a Hail Mary. Now and at the hour of our death. Life is learning how to die."

And now John remembered that she said she'd been told that when she took instruction.

Krucek said, "I was misquoting Plato, as you know."

"I didn't know."

"Philosophizing is learning how to die. Sounds morbid, but try to find a philosopher who isn't fixated on death."

❖

There was a miniature television set in the study. Krucek turned it on for the eight o'clock news. The account of what had happened at Empedocles was so enigmatic it said nothing. The emphasis was on the recovery of the stolen car in which the assailant had fled the grounds. A rental car. There was footage of the replica of the grotto of Lourdes on the grounds of Empedocles. Krucek sighed.

"That's the biggest obstacle for most converts, devotion to Mary."

"Was that true of Heather?"

Krucek shook his head. "She saw the point of it without any difficulty. I just hope Hannan's enthusiasm doesn't affect her. It has to be made clear that devotion to the Mother of God is integral to the economy of salvation. Enthusiasts seem sometimes to forget who Mary is the mother of. She wouldn't like that."

"I notice that your parishioners say the rosary before your Mass begins."

"It's an old custom here. That's probably why we're still in business. Do young priests say the rosary every day, Father?"

John did not want to speak on behalf young priests. He said he himself did.

"Good. One thing I'm willing to bet. These characters who are costing the Church millions? They drifted away from prayer, lost their devotion to Mary. How in God's name could they go on functioning as priests, doing what they were doing?"

It was one of the great mysteries of the day, all the more poignant when delinquent priests were contrasted with a solid pastor like Krucek.

✣ V ✣

"I am fully occupied here, Ignatius."

The information came to Father Jean-Jacques Trepanier from various sources, a bit here, a bit there, and then began to assume a pattern that gave him pause. Something very strange had occurred down the road at the Empedocles complex.

First, there was a break-in, already a bit of a surprise if one credited the stories about the security of the place. Then, a death that became a murder. The victim was a priest! An Irish priest from Rome. Jay went into his office, sat in the chair behind the desk, and turned slowly as if in search of his bearings.

The news that had been coming out of Rome over the past several weeks was equally disturbing. Oh, not in the usual sense, but because of the sudden demise of the secretary of state—an old foe of Jay's who had tried to get him suspended— and also Cardinal Maguire at the Vatican Library. Of course, the Vatican was full of old men, and old men die, and yet there was the persistent suggestion from Jay's principal source that these deaths had not been accidental. His attention was drawn to the young priest Buffoni in the outer office of the secretary of state who had also died that day.

"I hadn't heard that. Died how?"

"He was said to be a diabetic," Harris said.

"Wasn't he?"

"Diabetes is not a fatal disease. And then there's the basilica guard."

Jay had to be wary of his Roman informants, one of whom, Harris, was connected with the Confraternity of Pius IX and seemed not to know of the enmity that had sprung up between Jay and Bishop Catena. Or did know and was trying to send him off on a wild goose chase. An odd phrase, that. Didn't one chase tame geese? More likely when you stop to think of it, since you had them confined in the farmyard. But back to the news from Rome.

The latest was that those deaths had not been accidental and that something was missing from the archives.

"Something?" Careful, careful.

Harris did not care to guess, but of course when one thought . . . The speaker stopped himself. Listening, Jay became more wary still. He was more than willing to expose himself to criticism, even obloquy, in the cause of Our Blessed Lady. The abuse that had been heaped on his head by those who did not want to hear what Mary demanded of them Jay considered a badge of honor. But he was on sure ground when underscoring in season and out the unequivocal demand of the Blessed Virgin that Russia be dedicated to the Immaculate Heart of Mary. Why should so simple a thing be considered a problem?

Of course he caught the drift of what he was being told by Harris, in part because it was he who was being told. The supposed theft from the Vatican Library had something to do with Fatima. One didn't have to be Sherlock Holmes to jump from that to the third secret. But Jay wasn't going to make that jump on the basis of the information he presently had. Besides, he had as much as ceded the third secret to others.

Not that he considered it unimportant. God forbid. Any message from Our Lady was more than important. But arguments about the third secret became technical, seemed to require scholarship, paleography, not to mention a grasp of Portuguese. All that could bewilder the simple faithful. But who could not understand what Our Lady meant when she asked the pope and all the bishops to dedicate Russia to Her Immaculate Heart?

Putting together what had happened down at Empedocles against that Roman background produced puzzling but fascinating results. Thank God for Zelda Lewis.

She had called all aflutter to tell him that she had remarried.

Jay was a little miffed. "Who presided?"

"Oh, it was in Rome. Father Trepanier, I am as surprised as anyone. Imagine, at my age . . ."

He was not good at guessing the ages of women, particularly those like Zelda who could afford to expend large sums to offset the ravages of time. Of course he congratulated her. Of course he would be happy to bless the newlyweds. Zelda had always been generous, but it wasn't a matter of quid pro quo. There was no trace of simony at Fatima Now! Maybe a little rivalry, of a healthy kind. The kind there had been between the apostles. The Confraternity of Pius IX was a distant competitor, if in fact even deserving of the name competitor. Catena had no sense at all of the power and possibility of modern communications. The man still relied on a newsletter! And now Ignatius Hannan had resolved to set up a Marian foundation of some kind. The billionaire seemed unclear just what kind. But he was determined to do something to manifest the return of his faith and his obviously sincere devotion to Mary. He had asked Jay to bless the replica of the grotto at Lourdes when it was completed, and of course he had complied. When, later, Hannan told him of his new great idea and actually advanced the notion that Jay might drop what he was doing and become its director, tact had been required to tell the man no.

"I am fully occupied here, Ignatius."

"We could combine the two operations!"

Jay had looked at Hannan as Jonah had looked at the whale. He would be swallowed up in anything Hannan launched. He was not proud of the resentment he felt at the suggestion, because it was pride, vainglory, as if he were the object of his efforts and not the spread of the message of Fatima. How odd that one's imperfections often prompted the right decision. Imagine if he had succumbed to Hannan's blandishments. He would now be implicated in whatever had gone on at Empedocles.

Yesterday, Zelda and her new husband had stopped by for a blessing on their marriage. Jay had taken them to the chapel, donned alb and stole, lit the candles on the altar, and had them kneel on prie-dieux before him. He was responding to Zelda's descriptions of their breezy nuptials in the sacristy of Santa Susanna. In the old ritual he used he found a perhaps appropriate prayer, one to be said over wives expecting or wanting to expect children. It was in Latin, of course, so there was no need to explain the prayer. Gabriel Faust knew Latin.

"That smile on Zelda's face is not the smile of Sarah, Father."

"I believe Sarah laughed."

"Well, she was older than Zelda. In our case, a smile will do."

"What are you two talking about?" Zelda demanded.

"Boy talk," Faust said, and Jay hadn't liked that at all. For that matter, he didn't much care for Gabriel Faust. But that was before the three of them sat down and had a good talk. Faust, it emerged, was to be the director of Refuge of Sinners.

"Mr. Hannan sees it as complementary to your efforts, Father."

"We must all work together," Zelda cried.

"What on earth happened at Empedocles the other day?" Jay asked.

It turned out that the two of them had been there, Faust to be interviewed for his new position. The mention of two visiting priests came as news to Jay.

"I wonder if I know them."

"They're both from Rome. One is Laura Burke's brother. He works in the Vatican, you know."

"So did the one who was killed," Faust said.

"Killed?"

Zelda told him all about it, emphasizing her reaction to what had happened. Father Trepanier could not imagine what it was like, to be right there when a man was killed, and a priest at that.

"Brendan Crowe," Faust said and pieces of the puzzle flew into a pattern.

Crowe had been the assistant to Cardinal Maguire, and had been appointed acting prefect of the Vatican Library when the cardinal died. His visitors did not see the parallel between the murder at Empedocles and what had happened to Crowe's former superior.

"I wonder what the thief was after," Jay said ruminatively.

They had no idea. But there was more.

The man who was being sought by the police, Vincent Traeger, had been a colleague of Zelda's first husband in the CIA.

"What on earth was he doing there?"

But he was answering the question in his own mind. His informant with connections to the Confraternity of Pius IX had been certain the events in Rome had been somehow connected with the third secret of Fatima. Of course everything was connected to the third secret in the minds of people like Catena. At the moment that did not seem as far-fetched as it usually did. He developed this thought, attributing it to others with inflamed imaginations, not endorsing it himself. Faust was fascinated.

"Tell me about the third secret."

Jay did, putting the matter as succinctly as he could, and feeling as he did and as he had before that the matter was too recondite for easy consumption.

"Cardinal Ratzinger professed to make the whole thing public, in the year two thousand, when he was prefect of the Congregation for the Doctrine of the Faith."

"Professed?"

"There are those who think that the heart of the secret was withheld." He sought to distance himself from such critics, but within he found himself struck by the way near and far events seemed to converge on the secret.

"Why?"

Jay affected a tolerant laugh. "They are certain Our Lady condemned Vatican II."

Faust was more interested in all this than was Zelda. She was looking surreptitiously at her watch. "Gabriel, we have to get on to Empedocles."

They rose and Jay went with them to their car. After he handed Zelda in, Gabriel Faust said, "We have to talk more of this, Father."

"Anytime, anytime."

### ✤ VI ✤

### "They think I did it."

Traeger was letting his beard grow, and he felt a bit like Saddam Hussein when he emerged from his hole in the ground. He was staying in a Red Roof Inn off the interstate that connected Empedocles with Father Trepanier's operation. The pursuit for him continued with the current supposition that he had headed for Canada. It is best for the pursuer to double back on the pursued, to keep him close. Of course, he now had two pursuers, whoever had killed Crowe and the police, local and state. Hence this motel. He had been briefed on Trepanier by Rodriguez when he put through a call to him in Rome. News of Traeger's plight in New Hampshire had not yet got through to Vatican security.

"You've lost another man, Carlos."

He told him about Crowe. No need to spell out for Rodriguez the connection between Crowe's death and Cardinal Maguire's. Carlos wanted all the details, and Traeger gave them, saving the pièce de résistance for last.

"They think I did it."

How pleasant long-distance laughter from the land of sun and wine can be when one is holed up in a cheap motel, the object of a police search and trying to avoid an assassin.

"I left without saying good-bye. They can hardly be blamed for suspecting me."

"Why did you leave?" Rodriguez reasonably asked.

"I went in pursuit of the assailant. He drove off in the car I had rented. I got hold of another and followed him."

"And?"

"We haven't found one another yet."

Rodriguez said, "Of course you'll have help over there."

Carlos meant his associates in the CIA. Traeger had no desire to have the search for Crowe's murderer become a major project of the agency. Dortmund was not answering his phone down on Chesapeake Bay. After talking with Rodriguez, Traeger called Bea to see if Dortmund had tried to reach him there.

"No. Would you like me to put you through to him?"

"Good idea."

He sat listening to the phone ring unanswered for maybe a dozen times.

"He doesn't seem to be there," Bea said.

"You're right. He's not that hard of hearing."

"Anything I can do?"

His problem was that he didn't know who if anyone Dortmund had informed of his mission to the Vatican. If he knew Dortmund, he would have wanted to keep it under his own hat. His criticisms of what had happened to the agency of late were not just theoretical. He told Bea he would be in touch.

"Do you have the number of my cell phone?" he asked her.

"You said I needn't have it."

"That's probably best. À bientôt."

"Hasta la vista."

Bea was not unequivocally proud of her Franco-American background.

Traeger lay on the bed and looked at the ceiling, which was as blank as his mind. He was trying to imagine what he would do if he were in Anatoly's place. Presuming that it was Anatoly who had followed him after he left Empedocles. Too bad they couldn't all just sit down, Anatoly, Dortmund, and himself, to discuss what had gone wrong with the outfits they once had worked for. That was a conversation he had had with Dortmund the last time they were together.

It had been so simple then: the other side the bad guys, your side the good guys. Two superpowers duking it out for global hegemony. Would Anatoly think his side had lost? We are all capitalists now. The Berlin Wall had come down and the USSR had fallen to pieces, literally, with the constituent republics gaining the autonomy that had been merely fictional when all they had been was another vote in the UN for Moscow to cast. All the ethnic differences that had been suppressed now had free expression. We laughed when the Soviets got bogged down in Afghanistan. Now they were fighting Muslims in their old territory.

But who wasn't? In the old days, no one had worried about Muslims. All we had to do was buy oil and let Iran and Iraq shoot the hell out of one another. Palestine kept flaring up, but that seemed local, between them and Israel, and Israel was our ally. The indecisive Gulf War and now the prolonged presence in Iraq, following on 9/11, had changed everything.

"Some planners we had," Dortmund said. "They should have seen it coming."

No need to go into what the agency had done in the Middle East that had contributed to the present situation.

"Once we had the Cold War, nice and neat, you nuke me and I'll nuke you." Dortmund almost sounded wistful.

"MAD."

"Mutual Assured Destruction. Mad in the other sense, too, except that it made sense. It worked." This had been an article in their creed.

"Until our buildup bankrupted the Soviet Union."

"And now we've got guerrilla warfare," Dortmund lamented. "At home and abroad."

The theory behind the Soviet backing of the assassination attempt on John Paul II was that they were mad as hell at the way he encouraged dissent on their side of the Iron Curtain. His visits to Poland had effectively brought down the Communist government. And that was only the beginning.

"So why did they work through the Turks?" Dortmund had asked.

"To throw us off."

"Maybe. Fix me another of these, would you?"

Dortmund was drinking gin and tonic. It was April but chilly, and he seemed to think that drink would encourage spring to put in an appearance. Traeger fixed him another.

❖

Now, lying in the Red Roof Inn, remembering that conversation, remembering all the conversations he'd had with Dortmund, made him even more anxious to talk to his old boss.

He had a pizza brought in for his supper, took a long nap, and at one in the morning got up. There was a pickup in the parking lot he'd had his eye on and this was a good time to borrow it. No need to check out of course. He had surprised the clerk by paying cash; all he saw anymore was credit cards.

"Some of them valid," he added. He had a pivot tooth that looked east when he was facing south.

Traeger's first stop would be his office, where he could get alternative ID and credit cards out of the safe.

The safe was where he wanted to put the file Heather had given him.

The door of his room exited onto a balcony that ran along the front of the building to open stairways at either end. The pickup was there in the lot below. The place was lit up, spots on the motel, the parking lot lined with arc lights. People were whooping it up in a unit Traeger went by, but for the most part the motel was asleep. All lit up but asleep.

The pickup could have used a new muffler. Traeger felt like a mobile Fourth of July getting out of the motel lot. He hit the street and barreled off into the night. When he turned on the lights nothing happened, at first, then they connected. Jeez. He traded the pickup for a Chrysler coupe, which was quieter and faster. Unfortunately, it was nearly out of gas. Traeger looked for another motel. That turned out to be more difficult than he had imagined; he seemed to have gone past a string of them. No signs announced food and lodging ahead. There was notice of a rest area, and he pulled in. A long, swooping entry brought him to the division between roads for trucks and cars. Traeger pulled into a parking spot, cut the motor, and looked at the illumined building before him. Restrooms, free maps, coin-operated food and beverage machines. The restrooms were the draw, even at this hour of the night. Other vehicles pulled in beside him, first on one side, then on the other, and their occupants fled toward the building and relief. Cars had come and gone when one with its headlights switched to high came up the road with a roar and then braked, sending the car into a skid. The driver seemed to lose control, then regained it, but not before hitting a little raised island in the lot. There was a piercing sound as the bottom of the car scraped over the curbing. Once across the island, the car came to a stop. Then slowly it began to move, picking its way to the spot next to Traeger.

The driver's door opened and a man got out, slowly, with an effort. When he was standing, he gave the door a push and nearly lost his balance. The door hadn't closed. He had left the motor running. Traeger watched him reel safely into the building, then got out of the Chrysler, rounded the hood of the Lexus, and threw his bag into the passenger seat. He checked the gas gauge first of all. Three-quarters full. He put the gear in reverse.

"Jim?"

A woman's slurred voice from the backseat.

"Jim, why're we stopped?"

Traeger grabbed his bag, got out of the car, and was up the walkway to the building before the woman in the backseat got into a seated position. Inside, he stood looking at a rack of pamphlets touting things to see in the area. The light in the room was a sickly pallor, and objects that in daytime might seem real enough now looked like props. There was a large map of the state under glass on a low-tilted stand. You are here. A flashing light in the lot. Traeger saw the police cruiser pull up behind the Chrysler, briefly check the license plate, then go on, slowly. It stopped and doused its lights. Two troopers got out.

There were other doors, opposite those he had entered, facing the lot where trucks parked. Think. Think. Since the car was there in the lot, they would assume he was inside. Just then the drunk came out of the restroom, still zipping up.

"Hi, Jim."

He tried a smile, tried to focus on Traeger. "I forget your name."

"You don't know it. A woman in the backseat of your car was calling for you. I see she brought the police."

He opened the door so Jim could see the police cruiser in the lot. He looked at Traeger. "And I'm stinko."

"I have an idea."

Jim liked the idea. They went arm in arm to the Lexus, Jim walking very carefully. Traeger held the passenger door open for him, then went around and got behind the wheel. The trooper who was standing behind them had watched but said nothing. Once more Traeger eased the car into reverse, and this time backed out of the spot.

"Jim?"

"Shut up for a minute."

In a moment they were on the road, up to speed. A grumbling

from the backseat had given way to silence. Jim's relief to be away was replaced gradually with curiosity.

"Say, what about your car?"

"It's back at the rest stop."

"But . . ."

"It's out of gas."

Perhaps Jim sober would not have accepted that explanation.

Traeger exited at the first possibility. Jim protested when Traeger drove into a motel.

"Just let me check to see if I can stay here, okay?"

Comprehension glowed in Jim's eyes. "Take your time."

The older a car the more likely it was to be locked, it seemed. Most cars had a spare set of keys in a magnetic box attached to the chassis below the driver's door. This time Traeger went upscale, selecting a Town Car. When he purred past the entry where he had left Jim and companion, Jim's head was thrown back, his mouth was open, and he was dead asleep. He would be much safer asleep.

Traeger avoided the interstate and took secondary roads to the building in which his computer consulting business was housed and where, in the daytime, Bea was on duty. There were night-lights in the building, and a silence that seemed to lift from the carpeted floors and the pastel walls. He rose in the elevator to the seventh floor and a moment later was letting himself into suite 721.

Now that he was here, now that he had at last pulled back his desk chair, lifted the flap of carpet, and opened the safe, he hesitated. Running around as he had been with the document in his shoulder bag made him feel like a Brink's truck. Brendan Crowe had thought it safe enough in his briefcase in the guest building at Empedocles. He had been wrong. Just as earlier the assumption that being in the Vatican Archives insured safety had been proved wrong. At the very least, his office safe was no more vulnerable than those.

He traded the file containing the third secret of Fatima for a variety of alternate IDs and credit cards. The photograph on the passports showed a beardless face, of course. He put the items in his shoulder bag, patted the Vatican folder, and closed the safe. When he had the mat back in place, he sat in his chair.

Quite a bit had happened since he took Dortmund's call and agreed to come discuss a matter with him.

Since leaving the Red Roof he had been heading toward Dortmund. But now he wondered about the wisdom of that. Better give it some thought. He closed his eyes and an enormous tiredness swept over him. He transferred to the couch. Just forty winks would do it.

❖

"Good morning."

He rose in a single motion and was on his feet, looking around. The voice had come from the intercom. Bea. He crossed to the desk and said hello.

She came in, smiling, efficient, tossing her prematurely gray hair worn defiantly long. "I looked in earlier and was about to call the police. But then they're already on your case."

He nodded.

"You're famous."

She handed him the morning paper.

"Rogue Former CIA Agent Sought in Slaying of Priest in New Hampshire." The story gave an accurate resume of his activities in the agency. Apparently Dortmund had decided to cut him loose, feed him to the fish.

Bea said, "I had no idea I worked for such a celebrity."

Loyalty is a wonderful thing. He would miss it in Dortmund.

"I don't like the beard."

"Neither do I."

"It's why I nearly called the police. Then I saw that the bag was yours. They were here yesterday. I told them I hadn't seen you in weeks."

She was matter-of-fact, unalarmed, if anything, a little amused. She said she'd make coffee and go out for pastry. He nodded. He moved to his desk chair. The fact that they had been here asking about him didn't mean they wouldn't be back. The aroma of coffee from the outer office created the impression that this was just the beginning of another day. Traeger was thinking of other agents who had been discarded over the years, expendable in the light of a higher purpose. What had happened to them? He didn't want to remember.

Bea came closer. "Are you all right, Vince?"

Vince. She almost never called him that. He looked into her concerned eyes and felt a rush of emotion he seemed to have been suppressing for years. He took her in his arms.

"I didn't kill anyone."

"I know that."

She had come closer in his embrace. He was about to say something more, but he checked it. It seemed a temptation. He could not pursue anything with Bea until he had cleared himself, and the only way to do that was to get Anatoly. He let her go, stepping back. Again, that concerned look in her eyes.

"When I get back."

She nodded and said, "Be careful."

# CHAPTER THREE

## ⊹ I ⊹

He looked out over Cefalù.

Monsignor Angelo Orvieto, bishop of Cefalù, just fifty kilometers from Palermo, his native city, was half a year shy of his seventy-fifth birthday and he still had not heard from Rome that his resignation, to become effective on his next birthday, had been accepted. He did not repine. Word would come, either favorable or unfavorable. He could not expect that his little diocese counted for much in the eternal city, however ancient a Christian foundation it was. Cefalù was enjoying a renascence as a target of tourism, its modern beach contrasting with the medieval city, which was of more permanent interest. To the discerning mind, history lay all around one in Sicily: not least, reminders of the coming and eventual going of Islam on the island.

It is a salutary practice of septuagenarians to review their lives and try, while there is yet time, to repair the damage of their errors. Bishop Orvieto, like most of us, had much for which to repent, but any list he was likely to draw up would place at the top the name of Jean-Jacques Trepanier.

The power to ordain is an awesome one, to be able to lay hands on a man's head and pass on to him the priesthood handed down from the apostles. A bishop ordained priests to help him in his ministry, and that is what Orvieto had done over the years, with one exception: Trepanier.

Trepanier had shown him a letter from the priest who had baptized him and had nurtured the young man's vocation, and other letters, more equivocal, particularly those of seminary professors. But what had moved Orvieto beyond the counsels of prudence and good sense was the letter from Trepanier's mother.

Orvieto read it with tears in his eyes. It was written in pencil, on ruled pages torn from a tablet. It might have come from his own mother. The woman described herself as writing on her kitchen table. She recalled the vestments she had sewn for her son when he played at saying Mass as a boy. She prayed that she would live long enough to attend her son's first Mass.

Orvieto had met Trepanier in Connecticut, at Holy Apostles Seminary in Cromwell. Their conversation on the Blessed Virgin had impressed the bishop with the young man's devotion. It seemed wrong that such a man should encounter difficulties in becoming a priest. So Trepanier flew to Palermo via Rome, and Orvieto met him there. He checked over the transcripts of credits, the many years passed as a seminarian. He frowned over the letter that had informed Jean-Jacques that he was too inflexible for the post-conciliar Church. Among the supposedly negative features in Trepanier was his devotion to the Blessed Virgin. If the mother's letter had left any doubt, this would have removed it.

Three months later, in his private chapel, Bishop Orvieto ordained Jean-Jacques Trepanier to the priesthood. Only his vicar general, Sonopazzi, knew the unusual circumstances of the ceremony. The new priest intended to fly home to say his first Mass.

"I will return in two weeks' time." The young man's Italian was already good; he was equipping himself to serve in Sicily.

"Sicily has less need of priests, my son. I want you to function as a kind of missionary in your own country, spreading devotion to Mary."

Orvieto had thought about this. It was not a whimsical decision. Sonopazzi's reaction, eloquent silence, suggested that he not prolong the anomaly by keeping Trepanier in Sicily. The young man was full of zeal. Let him exercise it in his native country.

Once, America had been a long, long distance away, at the end of dreams, as much myth as reality. Now, huge jets dropped onto the island day after day, bringing tourists from around the world, most of them Japanese or Americans. Satellites made all calls local calls. Television brought in the land of Trepanier in primary colors. It also brought in Trepanier.

Sonopazzi, an electronics wizard, had a television set that brought in hundreds of cable programs. One of them was Fatima Now!, Trepanier's program. The title said it all. Trepanier preached devotion to the Mother of God. Orvieto was pleased. His protégé had found his niche. He wrote to congratulate him. That letter was to be invoked over the next few years whenever Trepanier's foes questioned his clerical status. Orvieto received an inquiry from Rome, asking for clarification. Trepanier had become an enfant terrible on a global scale. His attacks on those he described dismissively as Vatican bureaucrats grew more strident. Orvieto began to doubt that his resignation would be accepted. It might seem a reward, and Trepanier had brought him under a cloud.

Only his own deep devotion to the Mother of God would sustain him in his disappointment. From the windows of his residence, he looked out over Cefalù, at the reminders of previous centuries that suggested that the inexorable passage of time had granted them a relative permanence. But beyond was the beach, its littoral crowded with hotels for tourists, the neopaganism of the times, along with a lot of bronzed human flesh, on indecent display. He had reached the end of a decade on his rosary, and now added the prayer suggested by Our Lady at Fatima. *Jesus, forgive us, deliver us from the fires of hell. Draw all souls to you, especially those in greatest need.*

## ✣ II ✣

### Heather kept her counsel.

Heather Adams followed the news and kept her counsel. Had she been right to turn over to Vincent Traeger what Brendan

Crowe had entrusted to her? She trusted Traeger, though she couldn't say why. Most of the things that truly matter elude explanation. Learning that he had been a CIA agent with Zelda's late husband seemed a vindication. His reaction after the discovery of Father Crowe's body seemed to fit that role, and when she had found him in her house and given him supper, it was clear that he saw himself as the pursuer rather than the pursued. He had left Empedocles in order to pursue the one who had killed Brendan Crowe.

And had lost him. And then apparently had been found by him and did indeed become the pursued. By the time he sought refuge with her he was pursued by the police as well. Given his role as an agent, Heather assumed that the police would soon realize their mistake and Traeger's associates would help him in tracking down the killer.

She sat at her kitchen table reading the newspaper story about Traeger. He was portrayed as a demented fanatic who had been harassing Father Crowe in Rome and had apparently followed him to New Hampshire and the Empedocles complex and killed him. His unexplained fanaticism was apparently sufficient as a motive.

Heather put down the paper. She hated newspapers. She hated what was called news. Sometimes she thought she hated the modern world. Not people, of course, but the unexamined premises of their lives. *Vanity of vanities: all is vanity.* A few lines from such a book as the *Imitation* seemed to connect her to the really real world.

Zelda came along with her husband as he settled in to his new job.

Heather said to Gabriel Faust, "You could hire her, you know."

Zelda had reacted with delighted surprise. Her husband simply nodded and stroked his beard. "We'll see."

The fact was that Zelda understood certain aspects of the idea behind Refuge of Sinners better than Gabriel Faust. Not the role of art, of course, he was the expert there, but the spiritual aims of the new foundation. Faust seemed to discuss them as if he were learning a new language. When Fatima came up, he paid close attention.

"I've never been there," he said.

"You should go," Heather suggested.

He looked at her, liking the idea. Zelda liked it even more. Heather left them making plans for their trip.

Laura vetoed Mr. Hannan's suggestion that the couple go in a company plane. She shook her head. "The IRS will be all over you."

"He works for me."

"He is director of Refuge of Sinners."

"I'll buy him a plane."

"You will not."

Laura had to enlist Ray Sinclair to squelch the idea. When he conceded, Mr. Hannan looked at Heather.

"I wish you'd work with Faust."

Heather said nothing. She had already said no, and he had learned that she meant what she said. It wasn't that she was so enamored with her work at Empedocles. She found that she had misgivings about Gabriel Faust that would not go away. When she downloaded for him the material made public by Cardinal Ratzinger in the year 2000, he studied the handwriting of Sister Lucia with an expert eye.

"It looks genuine enough."

"Of course it's genuine," Zelda said.

"Is Sister Lucia at Fatima?"

Heather explained that Lucia was in a Carmelite convent in Spain. And that the Carmelites were an enclosed order.

"Too bad. What did she make of the revelation of the secret?"

Heather let Zelda tell him. Her account was more or less accurate. It did seem a good idea that Zelda should work with her husband at Refuge of Sinners. Meanwhile, Mr. Hannan had asked Duncan Stroik to fly in from South Bend so they could discuss a building site for the new foundation and architectural ideas. In the interim, Faust was temporarily housed in the Empedocles complex.

The various crews from the police department had finished their examination of the scene of the crime, and the fateful suite was ready for occupancy should it be needed. Father Burke had consulted with Father Crowe's cousins in Ireland and the decision had been made to have the burial in New Hampshire. Mr. Hannan got permission for a grave to be dug in the shadow of the grotto and it was there, after the funeral Mass at Saint

Cyril's, that the remains of the slain priest were brought, prayed over, and lowered into the ground. It was a solemn moment. Father Burke's voice had been firm enough when he said a few things about his late friend in the church, but reading the prayers at graveside his voice broke, and for a moment it seemed the tears must come. Beside him, Father Krucek took the book and finished reading the prayer. Father Burke recovered and sprinkled the casket with holy water. The mourners were then asked to do the same, and the sprinkler was handed around. And then all withdrew.

Heather walked to the administration building with the two priests. Laura had arranged for a caterer to provide a breakfast for the group. It was an odd gathering. Only Father Burke had known the deceased well.

"I feel responsible for his death," Mr. Hannan announced.

"Nonsense," Laura said.

"He'd be alive today if I hadn't persuaded him to come over here."

"I did that."

"You know what I mean."

Mr. Hannan wanted to know if he should hire detectives to look into what had happened.

"Nate, the police are already doing that."

"And what have they learned? Nothing."

And now the story about Vincent Traeger had appeared, depicting him as a fanatic and disenchanted former member of the CIA. Mr. Hannan seemed to think that the explanation of Brendan Crowe's death had been found.

Heather kept her counsel still. If anyone knew that Traeger had not killed Father Crowe, it was she. She had been with him when the body was found. His reaction, she realized now, had been professional, and he had prevented her from following him into the bedroom. But she had not been spared the horrible sight. Then Traeger had sent her running back to the main building.

Would the man who had killed Father Crowe—and it was a man who had driven off in Vincent Traeger's rental car—wonder why no mention had been made of the papers he had come for? Would he think he had killed in vain?

⚜

That night, when she arrived at her house, she put the car in the garage. As the door was lowering, the door that led to the house opened and Vincent Traeger said hello.

## ❖ III ❖

### "Yes, we did."

Montreal was both close enough and far enough away, and Anatoly relaxed, feeling that this time he had outwitted Traeger.

In Rome, when Traeger had confronted him after what Anatoly had considered a pretty effective job of tailing, things could have become violent. How oddly friendly they had been, the two of them, both nostalgic for the time when they had been sworn enemies. It had been tempting to tell Traeger about the years of resentment spent in retirement in the south, Odessa mainly, but with a spell in Yalta. He had visited Chekov's house, more than ever a place of pilgrimage. The writer had been taken up during the years of the USSR, a new and elegant edition of the complete works made available, along with the correspondence. Chekov's wonderful account of his visit to the penal colony at Sakhalin had been taken to make the case for the party against the czar. As if Siberia had ceased being Siberia during what was now considered the darkest pages of Russian history. What Anatoly was unable to figure out was Chekov's attitude toward the Orthodox Church.

The official line had been that he was agnostic at best, if not atheistic, but no reader of Chekov could believe that, and now there was no longer any political need to adopt that interpretation. But what was one to substitute for it? Chekov's reading, his fascination with monasteries, the late story "The Bishop"—none of that suggested the party line on Chekov. So he didn't get to church that often, so he didn't fast; the man was an invalid, dying a slow death from consumption. "Anatoly the monk," he had described himself in those last years in Yalta. Tolstoy was another story, mad as a hatter, as the English would say. True religion was to be found in the lives of the peasants. Chekov as a doctor had enough to do with peasants to know better.

Because he had been stationed in Rome, Anatoly had read Solzhenitsyn with dread fascination when he was banned in Russia, hating the man for giving all that ammunition to his country's enemies. Well, the idiot had moved to the West and been thoroughly disillusioned. He had thought he was moving to Christendom. Now he was back in Russia, enjoying the oblivion he deserved.

But it was the internal collapse in the Kremlin, the useful idiot Gorbachev, denouncing the system to which he owed everything, that had drawn Anatoly out of retirement. Not back to the old outfit, of course. From now on he would operate as a freelance. But with lines into altered officialdom. Traeger had his Dortmund; Anatoly had Lev Pakov. And Pakov had offered to engineer the abduction of Dortmund. He had provided the dossier on Traeger's work in the CIA that had been fed to the press to neutralize his adversary. Where could Traeger surface now without finding himself up to his ears in difficulty?

Pointing the finger at Traeger as the hit man who had done away with that priest from Rome had suggested a further possibility.

Pakov listened impatiently while Anatoly spoke of the murders in the Vatican.

"We had nothing to do with that," said Pakov.

"Yes, we did."

If eyes are the mirror of the soul, Pakov had none. When was the last time the man had expressed an emotion? Probably the last time he had felt one. Men now shaved their heads in order to get the effect Pakov had come by naturally. It was hard to believe that hair had ever grown on that muscular globe.

"You?"

"Yes."

Anatoly didn't expect the current equivalent of the Order of Lenin, but Pakov might have commented on the daring and success of the operation.

"What was the point?"

"To get hold of those damnable reports on the attempted assassination of John Paul II. To show we had nothing to do with that."

"You picked an odd way to make the point. Did you get the reports?"

"You know I didn't."

"It is Chekovsky's task to gain control of those."

"Chekovsky!"

"So what's your point? Do you want to try again?"

It was a tempting thought, but if he were inclined to try again he would not let even Pakov know in advance. Things had gone smoothly that day. The basilica guard had been a necessity, his death of no importance. But the secretary of state with his condescending published remarks on the new Russia deserved what he had got. His assistant? Well, he was his assistant. Anatoly's informant had told him the file was with Cardinal Maguire. That was when the plan went awry. He had silenced the cardinal when he heard footsteps coming up the stairs to the rooftop. Escape was imperative. The fact that the events of that day were hushed up by the Vatican convinced Anatoly that even an aborted operation had had its effect. And then had come the crushing blow.

"The file was in his villa."

It might have been a line of poetry. His reaction had not been aesthetic. He stared at the words that were the complete e-mail message. With what intention had they been written? To inform? To express irony? The effect on Anatoly was to enrage him. If there had ever been a time when he might have repeated the operation, it was then.

He had seethed. He had grown careless. That is when Traeger had turned the tables on him, tailing Anatoly, and then confronting him.

He had learned that Traeger and Carlos Rodriguez, the chief of Vatican security, had come to the archives asking for a file.

"Did they get it?"

"What they wanted was not there."

So where had it gone? The Irish priest, Brendan Crowe, was the one who had surprised him on the rooftop of the Vatican Library and spoiled the operation. He was named acting prefect. Anatoly asked himself what the one responsible for the archives would do with a file that was not safe in his archives. Of course Traeger had questioned Crowe. And then Crowe had flown off to America. It could mean anything, or it could have, until Traeger went in pursuit of him. Anatoly followed.

What had happened in the guest residence at Empedocles was a farcical repetition of what had happened in the villa atop the Vatican Library. Anatoly had just entered the suite when he heard footsteps. He concealed himself in the bedroom, but when Crowe shut the hall door he came out and confronted him.

"Where is it?"

"Who are you?" the priest demanded.

Anatoly put the point of his knife on the man's chest. He had not expected resistance from a priest. The priest's arms lifted, and the knife flew free. He pushed Anatoly, who careened toward the bedroom, falling on the bed. How much time before the priest stood over him? He had Anatoly's knife in his hand. He extended it to him, handle toward his hand.

"Take this and get out."

Anatoly had taken it, and this time the point of the knife did not stop on the surface of the priest's chest. Even wounded, he had fought. Finally, weakened like a bleeding bull, he had been unable to fight anymore. Anatoly stood over the body, breathing heavily. And then, my God, once again, footsteps.

It had been a nice touch to flee in the car Traeger had been driving. He had driven half a mile after leaving Empedocles before he pulled over and waited. Sure enough, a car came tearing along the road with Traeger at the wheel. Anatoly had pulled out and followed him.

He would have given the coup de grace in that hotel in Cambridge, but Traeger, the old pro, must instinctively have known he was in danger. And so Anatoly had lost him.

His aim had become to avenge himself on Traeger. This he had done by publicizing Traeger's hitherto secret activities with the CIA. Traeger's presence at Empedocles when the Irish priest had been killed, the fact that he had left the scene, did the rest.

If those murders in the Vatican could also be pinned on Traeger, Anatoly felt that he might be ready to return to Odessa and try retirement again. Meanwhile, he caught his breath in Montreal, keeping an ear out for news from across the porous border.

### ❖ IV ❖

#### "You're avoiding the question."

"John, I'm so sorry that things turned out this way."

He put his arm around Laura's shoulders. No need for any other response. They were in Logan Airport, where he would catch his flight back to Rome, having fended off Ignatius Hannan's persistent offer of a private plane. To travel once that way had been an adventure, but it would not do to make it a habit. Besides, on the flight over he had been able to enjoy the novelty with Brendan.

All departures are sad, at least in part. "I wish I'd gone to see Mom again," John said.

It was her turn not to reply.

She finally said, "We have time for a drink."

He had checked his bag and gotten his seat assignment and there lay ahead the annoyance of security. A drink sounded just right.

When they were settled at a table, drinks ordered, the two of them drawn closer by the conversations around them, the bustle, the constant unintelligible announcements, she leaned toward him. "All right, what do you really think of Ray Sinclair?"

"That you'll be very happy together. Have you set a date?"

She sat back, smiling ruefully. " 'No date has been set for the wedding.' I was always struck by that statement in the announcement of engagements. It makes everything sound so tentative."

"You could marry in Rome."

"In Santa Susanna?"

John laughed. Zelda and her new husband had added a half comic note to recent days.

"John, you do approve of Ray?"

"I approve of everything you do."

"You're avoiding the question."

"I like him. I like him a lot."

Saying it seemed to make it true. The truth was that John didn't know what to make of Ray. There seemed more intensity on Laura's part than on his, and John mildly resented that. He was more impressed than ever with Laura's obvious success. Nothing happened at Empedocles without her imprimatur. Ray seemed to take her for granted.

"Good." She put her hands over his. "Pray for us?"

"I remember you and Mom in every Mass I say."

"And Ray?"

"He's part of the package now."

She sipped her drink. "Nate is a bit overwhelming, isn't he?"

"You seem to have him pretty well under control."

"I'm glad you didn't let him bully you into accepting his offer of a plane."

"How much money does the man have?"

She just lifted her eyes. "You wouldn't believe me if I told you. Not that the amount stays the same. Mainly it just grows."

He wondered if he should repeat Father Krucek's description of Ignatius Hannan as a Barnum and Bailey Catholic. Better not.

"I like Heather."

"Our resident saint."

"She took instruction from Krucek. He thinks the world of her."

"My only fear is that she'll run off to a convent."

"A fate worse than death?"

"I'm thinking of what it would mean to Empedocles."

They finished their drinks and Laura came with him as far as was permitted, then threw her arms around him. He patted her back. "My sister. All departures are sad." There were tears in her eyes when he turned to go.

·❦·

John had never crossed the Atlantic by ship. Now few people do. Once it had been a prolonged adventure, months on the water. That is how their great-grandparents had come from the old country, in steerage. People complained about coach accommodations, but imagine being tossed about for week after week, looking forward to you knew not what. The mystery of families. All those forebears of whom he had no knowledge. Back to his grandparents they knew the names, but little else, and before . . . The thought of all the anonymous generations stretching back to the dawn of time gave a powerful sense of the contingency of life. How easily one link in the chain might not have been formed and he and Laura would not have been even logical possibilities. Now there were just the two of them, and if she did not marry and have children one line would be broken forever.

Napping, trying to ignore the inane films that went on nonstop on screens that seemed to draw the eyes to them, the jangled incoherent memories of his visit succeeded one another in his mind. Krucek. John smiled. Young priests had a way of being condescending toward the previous generation; after all, they had been implicated in the mess that followed the Council. But then there were stalwarts like Krucek.

"You taught philosophy?" he asked the older priest.

"Well, I gave courses in it."

"Such as?"

"The usual seminary fare. The fare that no one was interested in anymore. Worse, I was a Thomist."

"From Louvain?"

"Nowadays you could say from anywhere. It's all dead as the dodo."

"It's coming back," John said.

"The thing itself is as true as it always was. I speak of the reception, or nonreception, of it."

The thought took Krucek back to Heather. "The Church doesn't deserve such converts. But then converts don't deserve the Church."

He meant that conversion was a grace.

"You took your doctorate at Louvain," John said.

"Yes."

"What was your dissertation topic?"

Krucek smiled. "How long it has been since I thought of such things. I wrote on the phenomenology of Edith Stein."

"Ah."

"Louvain is, at least was, a hotbed of phenomenology. The Husserl papers ended up there, thanks to a wily Franciscan. What do you know of Mercier?"

"Not much."

"Ah, the vagaries of reputation. Read David Boileau's life of the man. The same fight is fought over and over. I was there with Whipple and Sokolowski. I suppose you don't know them either."

John laughed. "I feel that I'm flunking an exam."

"Most of the time I feel posthumous."

It had proved more difficult to have a conversation with Heather. In desperation, he asked her what she was reading.

"Thomas à Kempis." She paused. "And Oriana Fallaci."

"What a combination! She's under indictment in Italy for defaming Muslims."

"If what she says is true, why is it defamation?"

"You have to live in Europe to understand."

Well, maybe understanding wasn't the right word. John had

become aware during his visit of the wrangling over Latino immigration in the States, but Europe faced a far more radical problem. Did she know of the Battle of Lepanto?

"I know Chesterton's poem. I can't say that I understand it."

"What if all the battles, all the crusades, are going to be negated simply by flooding Europe with Muslims?" He laughed. "That sounds bigoted."

"No, it sounds like Oriana Fallaci."

# CHAPTER FOUR

## �֍ I �֍

### "I actually fell asleep."

In the garden, under a palm tree, seated on a stone bench with his finger marking his place in his breviary, Bishop Catena succumbed to distraction.

His first reaction to the news of Brendan Crowe's death was that justice had been done, but this was unworthy of him and he pushed the thought away. But there were more unworthy thoughts to come.

Documents were missing from the Vatican Archives, there was no doubt about it. There were too many rumors to that effect; not all of them were consistent, but the net effect was inescapable. Catena was left to contemplate the fact that Sister Lucia's letter, the third secret, had been spirited out of the archives. And by whom better than by Crowe. Who had then flown off to America.

"Trepanier," Harris said.

"But why?"

Harris cleared his throat. "Perhaps he thought he would make more effective use of it."

It was almost refreshing to have it said. Ever since Jean-Jacques Trepanier had burst onto the scene, Catena had felt that the confraternity was threatened. He had been in Europe too long. He had lost the American knack for promotion. For advertisement. The confraternity had become as dusty and irrelevant as the dicasteries it grumbled about. Dear God, imagine what a showman like Trepanier could do with a secret message from the Blessed Virgin Mary.

"And money," Harris added.

Money. Catena stared at Harris, who closed his eyes and nodded, a great Buddha of a man. There were three things that undermined a priestly vocation: sex, drink, and money. Those wholly immune to the lures of two of these seemed almost helpless before the blandishments of the third. The lure of sensual pleasure, mastered and controlled in one form, could spring up in another and overpower a soul. Eternal vigilance, that was the key. As for drink, it was now more or less received opinion that it was more of a disease than a moral fault when a man became the toy of alcohol. But both of these vices, sex and drink, were concrete, of the earth, far more human that the abstract lure of money.

For money is an abstraction and has become ever more so. From pieces and bags of rare metals, shaped, imprinted, and carried about—the coins of previous civilizations were scattered about the world—to paper certificates, to numbers entered in a ledger, we have come to mere digits on a computer monitor. One's money is anywhere and nowhere. Any ATM in the world enabled one to tap into his funds, but where were they? The question no longer made sense. How could anyone be led astray by so ephemeral a thing?

Catena developed these thoughts aloud, with Harris as his audience. They stood and paced the graveled paths of the garden, slowly because of Harris's bulk. They paused to look at the fountain in the center of the garden from which water dripped indecisively rather than flowed, then resumed their walk to the far wall where terra-cotta figures were embedded in the stone.

"Father Burke is back in Rome," Harris said.

Catena had to think. The young priest with whom Crowe had flown off in a private plane. And then the epiphany came.

"No," he said to Harris, as if continuing a previous line of conversation. "Not Trepanier, Ignatius Hannan."

Harris considered the thought and found it good.

"I want you to go talk with Father Burke. It is time for direct approaches," said Catena.

"He is a resident in Domus Sanctae Marthae. Within the walls of the Vatican." Harris, a devout sede vacantist, shuddered.

"You must. This damnable uncertainty must be overcome. Who has the third secret and what do they intend to do with it?"

❧

Harris took a 64 bus to the Vatican, entering and leaving the vehicle with an effort, because of his weight, and stood for a time in the Via della Conciliazione looking at the massive basilica and the circling colonnades that seemed to reach out for him. Harris had been ordained in Saint Peter's, by the pope himself, the real Paul VI, not the imposter with the odd earlobes.

He started off to his left, entered the colonnade, and walked between its huge pillars until he left it and walked with his head down toward the gate manned by two Swiss Guards. They saluted, and one stepped forward and asked for his identification. Harris took the pyx from his inner pocket and displayed it. The guard jumped aside, making the sign of the cross, and Harris passed through. That an empty pyx should have such an effect seemed to him a metaphor of what the Church had become.

As he walked, the great bells of the basilica began to ring twelve, and from near and far in the city other bells chimed in. Harris had never seen the Domus before. John Paul II had it built for resident and visiting prelates, but there were mere priests there as well, and John Burke was one of them. The doors slid open as he approached them, and Harris entered.

"He is at lunch," the woman behind the desk told him. She indicated the closed glass doors.

"I will wait for him."

"Would you like me to show you where the chapel is?"

She took him there and left him. He went toward the wall beyond which the old external wall of the Vatican was visible through the windows. He sat in a chair at the back and looked at the tabernacle and found it impossible to feel that he was in the stronghold of the enemy. The enemy must remain remote and anonymous. In wartime, soldiers fraternized across the lines, their belligerency diminished by the realization that they faced only frightened boys like themselves. He closed his eyes. How tired he felt. He was getting old.

"Father?"

Harris came awake with a start. The young priest put a hand on his shoulder.

"I'm sorry. Were you asking for me? I am John Burke."

"Yes, yes. Do you know, I actually fell asleep."

Something like disappointment showed on the young priest's face. "You're not from Ireland."

He explained what he meant after they left the chapel—when the young priest genuflected Harris heard the sound of his knee hitting the marble floor; he himself settled for a bow—and had gone into the almost deserted dining room. He had thought that perhaps Harris had been sent from Ireland to hear about a priest who had recently died in America.

"Brendan Crowe," Harris said.

"Did you know him?" A lilt of hope.

"Not nearly so well as I would have liked," Harris said carefully. He had the sense of chatting with someone in the opposite trench.

"Have you eaten?"

Harris made a dismissive gesture, but Burke flagged down a little woman busy among the tables.

"Sister, Father hasn't eaten yet. Is it too late?"

A toothy little smile. She could bring some soup and some pasta. Meanwhile, Burke had taken a bottle from the center of the table and poured Harris a glass of wine.

"I hope red is all right."

"I was hungry and you fed me." Harris smiled. He felt that he was being welcomed home.

"Now then," Burke said, having supervised Harris's emptying his soup bowl and making good headway in the pasta. He was refilling Harris's glass. He poured half a glass for himself.

"You mentioned Brendan Crowe," Harris began. "We have heard upsetting rumors that he took a most important file from the archives with him to America."

"What file?"

"We had heard earlier that this important file was missing from the archives."

He seemed genuinely puzzled by these remarks. "You speak of 'we.'"

The moment of truth. Harris had little doubt what would be thought of the Confraternity of Pius IX here, if it was thought of at all. All this hospitality and kindness would doubtless evaporate if he gave a frank answer to the question. Fortunately, they were interrupted by a little priest hardly five feet tall, with wispy, uncut gray hair falling over his ears.

"Father Pouvoir," John Burke said. "Just the man. Father Harris has put some questions to me that I simply cannot answer. I mean to which I do not have the answers. They concern the archives." Burke had stood and now beamed at Harris. "Father Pouvoir works in the archives. I leave you in excellent hands."

"Thank you, Father Burke. Thank you very much." Harris actually raised his glass to the young priest.

Father Pouvoir sat and looked at Harris with pale, lidless eyes.

"It was very unwise of you to come here."

## ✣ II ✣

### A priest in the family!

Remi was the seventh child in a family of thirteen that had scrabbled for a lean existence on a stony little farm located between Montreal and Quebec City. He was a quiet child, unnervingly so, sitting off in a corner seeming to observe the family of which he was a member. Like many children before him, he dreamed that his parents were not his parents, his brothers and sisters not his brothers and sisters. He imagined he was a foundling, brought home and raised as one would take in a lost dog. His silence annoyed his father, who beat him regularly, but then he beat all his children, while his mother wept and prayed that the punishment would soon be over. She might have meant her own.

School had not drawn him from his shell. It was there, noting with wonder that the other children found the lessons difficult, that he realized he didn't. Better to keep it a secret, and he did, striving to keep his performance down to the level of his classmates. It was M. L'Abbé Garnier who discovered that Remi was different. For one thing, he memorized the Latin responses an altar boy must know in an hour, rattling them off as if they were his native tongue. Father Garnier made inquiries at the school. Remi Pouvoir? Average, maybe less. The priest took Remi into his study and poured him a cup of coffee.

"Would you like to learn Latin?"

Remi was wary. Kindness was not something with which he had much acquaintance. After a moment, he nodded.

And so it began. The priest and Remi seemed engaged in a conspiracy. The Pouvoirs need not be told that they had at least one precocious child. Remi learned Latin and then Greek, and Father Garnier could hardly contain his joy when Remi was sight-reading the Iliad before the year was out. He began to talk to Remi of the priesthood.

What he stressed were the studies, the vistas that would be opened up. Where else could a poor boy receive such an education? The seminary was the thing. The Pouvoirs were struck dumb when the pastor went to them.

"Remi?"

"God is calling him to the priesthood," Abbé Garnier said solemnly.

A priest in the family! Suddenly all the difficult years, the poverty and worry, seemed to have a point.

Remi went off to the Petit Seminaire in Quebec and eventually on to the Grand Seminaire. During these years he noticed, as he had in school, that the others had difficulties that he did not. Of course he did not draw attention to this, but neither did he try to mimic them. Effortlessly, he absorbed philosophy and then theology, advancing step-by-step to ordination. When his parents first saw him in his soutane and with the great circular tonsure shaved on the back of his head, they treated him with awe. Remi half expected them to ask him for his blessing. A few years later, he was ordained at twenty-three, a special dispensation having been obtained because of his age. The priesthood continued to be the means, not the end, of his existence. It was study he loved. He was sent off to the Institut Catholique in Paris. Later he was enrolled in the École de Chartes. He spent hours in the Bibliotheque Nationale. It was there that he met Fernand.

Because of Fernand he learned Arabic, which he found easier than Hebrew. For some years he had moved through the streets of the City of Light, going from his residence to class or library, oblivious to all around him. With Fernand he acquired some sense of the lively city in which he lived, but it seemed a terrible waste of time to sit for hours in a café, talking and watching the parade of people go by their table. He spoke little, listened much. At first his French Canadian accent had drawn comment; within a week he was speaking comme il faut, as a

Parisian. Learning seemed the donning of a mask, of a new persona. The real Remi Pouvoir got lost in all the roles he learned to play. Fernand took him to a Masonic lodge. So that was Fernand's persona: the dismantling of Christendom, ridding the world of superstition, leading it, or at least some, the elite, to the worship of the Great Architect. Up until that time, Remi's knowledge of Freemasonry had been derived from *War and Peace* and reading de Maistre. He agreed to be initiated in much the same way as he had agreed to enter the seminary, in order to learn. He missed Fernand when he went back to Cairo.

Ladislaw, a priest from Poland, arrived in the residence where Remi lived in order to study at the École de Chartes. He asked Remi for advice, and Remi found that he enjoyed playing the role of the senior scholar although he was but a few years older than Ladislaw. In those days, it seemed unusual for a Pole to be permitted to study outside his country. Ladislaw did not seem hostile to the Communist government. No wonder. When he spoke of the way the Party had recruited young men to study for the priesthood with an eye to controlling the Church, Remi had the feeling that Ladislaw was talking of himself. The two young men sensed that they were subversives. When Remi, armed with his degree, went on to the Vatican Archives, he kept in touch with Ladislaw, or perhaps vice versa would be more accurate. With the election of John Paul II, Ladislaw came to Rome, hoping to find employment in the Vatican, now that his countryman was in the Chair of Peter. Alas, Ladislaw's connections were no secret to Karol Wojtila; the archives were closed to Ladislaw.

"What will you do?"

Ladislaw was thoughtful. Poland had changed; it was no place he wished to go back to. But where was an unemployed paleographer to find employment? He was taken on by the Goethe Institute in Rome. They had dinner together at least once a week.

## ✣ III ✣

### And so they flew off to Fatima.

Before leaving for Fatima with Zelda, Gabriel Faust set in motion the main thing that had prompted Ignatius Hannan to hire him as director of the Refuge of Sinners Foundation.

Inagaki repeated the name. "Sounds like a prison."

"Far from it, my dear fellow. Indeed quite the opposite. It will free us from the cares that have beset our lives hitherto."

Silence on the line. Faust told himself not to overdo it, but the recent change in his fortune had brought back an ebullience long lying dormant beneath those cares of which he spoke to Inagaki.

"This is what you are to do," he told Inagaki.

He had the list made out by Brendan Crowe on the desk before him. Before he could get to the third item, Inagaki interrupted.

"Do you know where those paintings are?"

"As a matter of fact, I do." Faust read off the cities and museums from the list.

"And the first two are six thousand miles apart."

Gabriel soothed the anxiety of his longtime partner and collaborator. "Your travel expenses will of course be added to your fee, and living expenses while you accomplish your task. And I think we will increase your fee. Say by doubling it."

"You've been drinking."

"No, I have married."

"Married," Inagaki repeated.

"You will recognize her name perhaps. Zelda Lewis."

"Delacroix."

"Exactly."

"Wives cannot testify against husbands," Inagaki observed.

"And how is Mrs. Inagaki?"

"There is no Mrs. Inagaki."

"Well, you will be able to afford her now."

It was a long conversation, one in which the layers of skepticism and wariness had to be peeled away one by one to arrive at the hidden core of Inagaki's mistrustful soul.

"I want it in writing," Inagaki said.

"Of course you want it in writing. And what would you consider an adequate bonus on signing the agreement?"

Magnanimity came easily after the long years of penury. Marriage to Zelda alone, given her wealth, would have more than answered his prayers. He had reached an age when security assumed overweening importance. As a young man, he had survived long, barren stretches because the future remained, and all his hopes and dreams. Alas, experience taught how elusive the objects of hopes and dreams could be. What was wanted was something sure, however modest. No wonder people tailored their lives to the potential of their Social Security checks. When Zelda became Mrs. Gabriel Faust in the sacristy of Santa Susanna in Rome, he had felt the raveled sleeve of care drop away. And now there was the all but bottomless largesse with which Ignatius Hannan had endowed Refuge of Sinners. No longer dependent on her wealth, he discovered in himself new depths of devotion for Zelda.

"Bottomless," he said, slapping her bare behind.

"Oh Gabriel."

Oh Gabriel, indeed. If this be second childhood, play on.

And so they flew off to Fatima. First-class.

⚜

Of late, Gabriel had made a study of Marian shrines, Lourdes first, prompted by the replica of its grotto behind the administration building in the Empedocles complex. The replica retained the rustic air of the original, but Gabriel had studied photographs of the industry that had grown up because of the influx of pilgrims. Not simply the hospitals where putative cures were carefully checked, but the long gauntlet of a street leading to the shrine. A street flanked by shops offering every conceivable kind of religious trinket and souvenir. When they deplaned at Lisbon and had been driven in a hired car to the site of the apparitions, Gabriel was prepared for kitsch.

He was pleasantly surprised.

The car dropped them at the end of the huge plaza across which pilgrims were progressing on their knees toward the church, many of them having rented knee pads to make the penance tolerable. To their left, as they approached the church, was a structure near the tree that had figured in the apparitions.

Inside the church, Zelda knelt, and Gabriel, after only a moment's hesitation, joined her. The semblance of devotion came easily in his present euphoria. He had grown accustomed to accompanying her to Mass, and she had shown no surprise when he had not gone forward to receive Communion. What would be a plausible excuse?

"My first husband was non-Catholic, too," Zelda said.

There was his excuse. But he had told her he was Catholic.

"Of a sort," she reminded him. "I know how people outside the Church can feel somehow in it."

Well, well. "No need to speak of this to Ignatius Hannan," Gabriel said.

"God forbid."

Gabriel Faust crossed himself. He was getting the hang of things.

They saw it all, spending hours wandering about the place, then had their driver take them to the Hotel Cinquentenario. There, of an evening, while Zelda read or pretended to follow the programs on television, Gabriel continued his study of the documents he had downloaded from the web before leaving. In Fatima itself, he was able to buy books that increased his confidence that what had at first presented itself merely as a wild thought might not be so wild at all. But why pursue it?

Even in his recent elation, a fundamental truth had come home to him. With marriage to Zelda, he had passed from a chancy hand-to-mouth existence to affluence. With his appointment as director of Refuge of Sinners, his horizon had expanded exponentially. But what had not come was the thought that he had enough. What can sufficiency mean when it comes to wealth? Already he had begun to sense the oddity of possession. Wealth was invested, stocks rose and fell, there was always the possibility that they might plummet, plunging him and everyone else back into the pit from which he had extricated himself. He wanted more.

And so he pored over the books and printouts on the desk in their hotel room. He got out his pens, and he bought ink and, after a search, some simple school notebooks.

"What are you writing, Gabriel?"

"Just brushing up on my calligraphy, my love."


✤ IV ✤


### "In a safe place."


At first he had used Heather's car, but one day he was pulled over and a cop all leather and metal sauntered up to the window Traeger had opened.

"This your vehicle?" the cop asked.

Traeger got out the registration and handed it to the cop, hoping that this was not going to require drastic measures. The cop wanted his driver's license. He gave him one.

His partner joined them. "The reason we stopped you? This car was reported stolen."

"It was stolen. We got it back."

"That's what I just found out. Sorry." The second officer threw him a salute. The other handed back his license, disappointed. Was their day really that boring? Probably.

From then on he had Heather rent a car for him. When he had come back to her house, he spent a long time explaining to her what was going on.

"Where is the file now?"

"In a safe place."

Unable to get through to Dortmund, he had driven down there, at night, to see what the hell was happening. Every secret he'd had in the agency had been in the papers. If he was being thrown to the wolves, he wanted to hear it direct from Dortmund.

The house was on a spit of land, one of maybe four in all summer places, but Dortmund had lived in his the year round. There was a boat dock but no boat. As far as Traeger knew, Dortmund had never sailed in his life. What is it that makes even landlubbers want to end up by the edge of some body of water? There seemed a nostalgia for a prenatal condition in it.

Traeger approached the house from the sea, coming in a flat-bottom boat powered by a small and noisy engine that he had borrowed from the marina up the shore toward town. He cut the motor when he came in sight of the row of houses. No lights in any of them, but it was two in the morning. He tied up at Dortmund's dock and then crawled toward the house, so far an unopposed landing. Where the hell was Dortmund's dog? He had a big, playful golden retriever named Marvin he seemed to think was a watchdog. Traeger and Marvin were old friends, so where was he?

Traeger stood and saw a fragment of yellow plastic tape fluttering in the wind, caught in the doorway. He pulled it free, and moonlight was enough to tell him it was crime scene tape. He went rapidly around the house, to see if there was any more of it, but that little shred had been all. What crime had taken place here?

As soon as he had let himself in, he knew the house was empty, no Dortmund, no Marvin the golden retriever. He looked around the main room, chiaroscuro in light and shadow. It was here he and Dortmund had talked some months before he had been sent on the mission to Rome. Traeger felt an impulse to report to that empty room. But the tale of his deeds was not one he could take particular pride in. He did tell Dortmund, or the ghost of Dortmund, that as far as he was concerned it came down to Anatoly.

The empty house filled him with a wave of sadness. What was the point of the long crusade he and Dortmund and others had been on for all those years? The older man had preserved a kind of psychic distance from the horrors of the work, and Traeger had tried to emulate this. He looked around at the emptiness. The house seemed to be the tomb of the unknown agent. Who in the hell really cared about what the two of them had done? He shook these bitter thoughts away, with an effort. He would complete what he had set out to do, as a tribute to Dortmund.

It was the murders in the Vatican that had been the basis for Traeger's being sent to Rome. All right. Those murders belonged to Anatoly, so nailing him meant mission accomplished. And now there was the added incentive that Anatoly was making a monkey out of him. Standing in Dortmund's house, Traeger's suspicion that his old boss had thrown him to the wolves disappeared. Dortmund would throw himself to the wolves before he would do that. Here I am, he wanted to say, being sought by the police for a killing Anatoly had done.

And now Dortmund was not in the only place he wanted to be anymore, this house by the sea. A place that had apparently recently been taped off as a crime scene.

Traeger left the boat tied to the dock and walked up the shore to the marina parking lot and his rental car.

The following day the *Washington Post* ran a story attributed to unnamed sources that the rogue ex-agent sought in connection with the murder of a priest in New Hampshire was now suspected of having abducted his former superior, Gillian Dortmund.

Traeger imagined Anatoly grinning at the disinformation he was sowing.

That night he drove again to the building that housed his business and took the elevator up to seven. He unlocked the door and stepped in, and almost immediately wanted to step back.

He covered his face with a handkerchief and moved into the inner office.

Bea sat in his desk chair, which had been wheeled into the center of the room. Duct tape had been used to fasten her arms to those of the chair. Her mouth, too, was taped. Her eyes were full of whatever they had last seen. She had been shot in the forehead.

He looked behind the desk. The flap of carpet was thrown back, the safe gaped open. Empty.

He glanced at Bea as he left. It was a rotten way for a good woman's life to end. The sense of the futility of his work, the feelings he had felt in Dortmund's empty house overcame him. And he remembered those half-formulated thoughts about himself and Bea, of a normal life with her when his task was completed. He wished that he had not learned not to cry.

⚜

On his way back to Heather's he wondered if he was jeopardizing her life as well.

When she came home, she said someone named Carlos Rodriguez had telephoned Empedocles, asking for Traeger.

"I've got to get to Rome," he told her.

"I've never been there."

Heather had a way of responding as if there were two conversations going on at the same time.

She said, "How will you get there?"

He looked at her. She wasn't asking whether or not he would fly, but wondering how he could get on a plane. This took them back to her remark that she had never been to Rome.

The following day she talked to Ignatius Hannan, telling him she wanted to go to Rome. He said he wished she'd brought it up earlier, when he was trying to send John Burke back in a company plane. Heather said she wished so, too. The upshot was that he offered her one of Empedocles' planes. When she told Traeger, she said, "So that is how you'll get to Rome."

✣ V ✣

"If you would steal, you would lie."

The call came on his cell phone, which was unusual, as no one knew the number of his cell phone. Even so, Jay had caller identification, and the area code meant nothing to him. He took the call.

"Father Trepanier."

"Jean-Jacques Trepanier?"

"Who's calling, please?"

"*On peut parler français?*"

"*S'il vous plaît.*"

"*Comme vous savez le soi-disant troisième secret de Fatima a été volé de la bibliothèque du Vatican.*"

Jay said that he had indeed heard of the missing file from the Vatican Library.

"I have it."

There are problems that are the delight of moral theologians. While one may never do evil in order that good might ensue, how is one to construe the case where an innocent life can be saved only by means that, by and large, would be wrong. *"Par exemple,"* Professor Coté would say, his eyes shining with the hope that he could make relativists of them all. "For example, you promise a man that you will not reveal that he has a deadly, communicable venereal disease. He does not tell you and you do not make it a condition of your promise that he will remain celibate. Enter your only lovely daughter announcing that she has agreed to marry the man. Would you keep your promise?" While all around him fellow students were declaring that they would consider themselves absolved of the obligation to keep a secret, Jay alone had held out for the exceptionless character of promise keeping. Debate raged, Jay was attacked from all sides, while Professor Coté looked on, delighted. When the bell rang signifying the end of the class, Jay announced that he had been lying, of course he would break his promise. And why had he lied? It was an agreement he had made with Professor Coté before the class. Coté erupted in fury. No such agreement had been entered into. "Either I am lying when I assert it or when I deny it," Jay had said triumphantly.

Beware of the casuist. That was the main lesson Jay took

away from his study of moral theology. Cases or examples invented for classroom discussion reduce moral decision to a game. He alone had rejected the famous principle of double effect, the usual dodge to get around prohibition of evildoing. I do not intend the death of the unborn child when I remove a cancerous uterus; my intention is to save the life of the mother and not to kill the child, however necessarily connected the two events may be. Again he stood alone against such tomfoolery. Save them both, he had cried.

"That is impossible."

"Nothing is impossible to God."

"A surgeon is not God."

"Precisely my point."

He had not been popular, and he had exulted in his unpopularity. Now, for the first time in his life, and in the real world, he seemed confronted with such a problem.

"How did it come into your possession?" he asked his caller.

"There is no need to go into that."

"If you would steal, you would lie. How do I know it is authentic?"

By asking the question, he had already crossed the line, and he knew it. He was bargaining with a thief but what was at issue was the third secret of Fatima!

"You will know," the man assured him.

"What do you want?"

"Four million dollars."

Jay laughed. "That is absurd."

"Not everyone will think so."

"Wait!" If not everyone, then someone, and Jay knew who that someone was. His mind was darting from thought to thought, from premise to conclusion, but looming behind it all was the face of that someone. "I will need time."

"Twenty-four hours."

The connection was broken. Jay took the cell phone from his ear and stared at it as Adam had stared at the apple from which he had just taken a bite. He closed the instrument and put it in his pocket.

First, he went to the chapel and knelt before a statue representing Our Lady of Fatima, asking what he should do. But he had already made up his mind, and he knew it. He left the chapel, got into his car, and carefully, using both thumbs, punched in the number of Ignatius Hannan.

Laura Burke put him through, despite her initial remark that Mr. Hannan was unavailable. The urgency in his voice convinced her that this call was indeed a matter of life or death. He waited. Life and death represented a contrast that had been brought vividly home to those at Empedocles.

"Hannan."

"This is Father Trepanier. I must see you at once."

"Work it out with Laura, Father. She makes all my appointments."

"She put me through to you. I will say only this." He took a deep breath. "The third secret of Fatima." Another breath. "I have it."

A pardonable anticipation of a future fact.

"That's impossible."

Hannan's matter-of-fact tone brought Jay down to earth. How could he possibly know if his mysterious caller had what he claimed to have? Against his better judgment, he decided that he had to say more if he was to insure the cooperation of Ignatius Hannan. Who else could come up with four million dollars without batting an eye?

As calmly as he could, he told Hannan of the phone call. He reminded him of what they knew of recent events in Rome. No need to emphasize the importance of the third secret itself. With it in hand, they could demonstrate that the so-called revelation of the year 2000 had been only partial.

"You're being had," Hannan said with infuriating calm.

"I am convinced this man has what he claims to have." Hannan's skepticism fed his own sense of certainty.

"He doesn't."

"How can you possibly say that?"

"Because I already have it."

⚜

Jay drove down the interstate in a trance. When one has his eyes tested, he is asked to look directly into a beam of light. Doing so blinds the eye to everything else. Jay drove as if he were heading into such a light. Was it possible that he would soon hold in his hands the little school notebook in which Sister

Lucia had written with her precise and careful hand the message meant for the Holy Father, a message of consummate importance for the Church and the world? Who could regard the revelation of 2000 as conveying such urgency? The whole point of that exercise had seemingly been to marginalize private revelations, to insist that nothing essentially new was in the message. The catechism was more informative of what the Christian needs to know than the document supposedly being made public. They might have been scolding the Blessed Mother for wasting their time. The only way to counter that was to compare what had been released with the message itself. The message Hannan calmly asserted was now in his possession.

At the gate, the guard would not let him through without calling the administration building. Security had been tightened as the result of recent events. Jay was asked to look into a camera.

"It's okay," Laura Burke said, her voice seeming to come from out of thin air. "Welcome, Father Trepanier."

He thanked the camera and proceeded up the drive to the administration building.

❖

How painful to be only a spectator at such an historic moment. In the manner of gawkers, Jay wanted to press through and be among those closest to the table. Gabriel Faust stood behind it.

"We delayed this in order that you might witness it, Father Trepanier," Hannan said.

Now Ray Sinclair stepped aside so Jay could get closer.

Faust began with a lecture! He reminded them of the provenance of the holdings of even the most prestigious museums. Conquerors had carted home works of art, the spoils of war; many items had come into the possession of museums in a manner that would not withstand close scrutiny. Faust cited the Ambrosiana in Milan.

"All this as preface to the fact that I do not intend to discuss how this document came into the possession of Refuge of Sinners. The important thing is that it is here, safe and secure."

"There is no doubt of its authenticity?"

Faust nodded as if to show the relevance of Jay's question. "The leading expert in the field, a friend of mine, as it happens, Miki Inagaki, has subjected it to the most demanding tests." Faust smiled at Jay. "It is authentic."

"And may I examine it?"

Ignatius Hannan took over. "I understand your curiosity, Father."

Curiosity!

"But given all the controversy that has been stirred up by this document, I don't think that any of us has the right to examine it. It is my plan to return it where it belongs, the Vatican Library."

Jay could not believe his ears. Return the rescued lamb to the wolves? That would be insane. Here was the opportunity to settle once and for all the adequacy of the revelation made in 2000 by the then Cardinal Ratzinger, now Benedict XVI. Jay had fallen into the intonations of a television commentator as he spoke, someone on the History Channel, perhaps, stating information his listeners knew perhaps as well as he.

Ignatius Hannan was adamant. He had okayed the purchase of this document in order to return it to the Vatican. There was nothing to discuss.

"I know you understand, Father Trepanier."

"You overestimate me."

Jay watched Gabriel Faust bear the precious notebook away to its temporary resting place in Empedocles' safe. Drinks were served. They seemed to be celebrating the defeat of all his hopes. Sick at heart, he slipped away, but before he left the building, his name was called. He turned. It was Gabriel Faust.

"Could I have a word with you, Father?"

❖ VI ❖

### As he waited, he was thinking.

Anatoly did not make a second call to Jean-Jacques Trepanier. He had picked up the number of the priest's cell phone while sitting outside the entrance to Fatima Now! in the car he had acquired across the border. As they talked, he had been able to watch the priest and he knew he had his fish hooked. If nothing else, Anatoly meant to gain something from this infuriatingly frustrating series of events. He was not one to brood over the lives that had to be taken on the way to the goal. His whole training made that inevitable, neither good nor bad. But to have come this whole bloody way and find that the document he had was not the one he sought tested the slow, sullen patience with which he had practiced his craft over the years.

What he wanted was the documentation on the attempted assassination of John Paul II. He was certain that the investigations would have established that the plot had neither been executed nor drawn up in the Kremlin. It offended his professional sense that such a bungled job should be attributed to the KGB. Imagine an assassin who would become part of such a crowd as that gathered in Saint Peter's Square. Of course Agca had been apprehended immediately. Anatoly knew how he would have carried it off. From the spot where the assassination attempt had been made, Anatoly had often stood looking at the nearby building on the Janiculum hill. The house of the Augustinians was too close, one might as well be in the crowd in the square. No, the perfect position for the assassin would have been on the roof of a building Anatoly learned was the North American College. The concierge was a countryman who had gone over to Rome but welcomed the opportunity to speak Russian. He took Anatoly onto the roof. While they were up there, Lev began patting his pockets. Where were his keys?

Anatoly helped him search. When they gave up, Lev threw up his hands. No matter. There were other sets.

Anatoly left with the keys in his pocket.

It was as if he were demonstrating to himself how that assassination should have been conducted. If ever any accusation had been made publicly, it would have been child's play to show the amateurishness of the attempt.

When he had persuaded the terrified woman in Traeger's office that she would live only if she showed him the safe, he pulled up a patch of carpet behind Traeger's desk and studied the dial. He shot it away and pulled the door up. And there it was, at last. He must have been smiling when he turned. Above her taped mouth, the woman's eyes were wide with terror, looking at the still smoking gun he held. Anatoly had no wish to prolong her agony. He stepped up to her, put the gun to her head, and dispatched her.

And then to find that what he had gotten was the account of private revelations by one of the seers of Fatima!

His fury abated only when he reminded himself that there

were some who wanted this document as much as he wanted
the report of the investigation into the assassination attempt on
John Paul II.

He imagined himself once more entering the Vatican and
confronting whoever was sitting in for the late Brendan Crowe
and proposing an exchange. He smiled at the brazenness of
the idea. He let it go only reluctantly. That would be as stupid
as Acga immersing himself in the crowd in Saint Peter's
Square.

If not a quid pro quo, then money. A huge sum of money.
Money was the answer to most problems, human greed being
what it was. Over the past weeks, he had learned more about
Ignatius Hannan than he had cared to know, but now that
knowledge seemed relevant. But here, too, a direct approach
seemed inadvisable. One did not willingly return to the scene
of a crime. And so he had thought of Jean-Jacques Trepanier.

And Trepanier had taken the bait and gone to the man who
had the kind of money Anatoly demanded. Anatoly followed
him down the interstate, but did not, like Trepanier, enter the
gate of Empedocles. He continued down the road, made a U-turn,
and waited.

As he waited, he was thinking of how the exchange could be
made. The exchange was always the neuralgic point in such
operations. Which is why kidnappers usually came for their
reward only after having killed their hostage. Four million dollars. He smiled at the sum that had come to him as he spoke
with Trepanier. The very amount underwrote the value of what
he had. It was not the money itself that interested him. Oh, a
fantasy of affluence flitted through his mind. He was only human, after all. A Swiss account, a dacha just outside Yalta. He
dismissed the thought. He would be as bored as Chekov there.

What he wanted was vindication, of the organization for
which he had worked, for his country as it had been. He wanted
to show Chekovsky how one went about such things. After that,
the future became vague. It didn't matter. He had lost interest
in the future.

An hour had gone by when Trepanier's car emerged from
the gate of the Empedocles complex. As he followed him, Anatoly punched redial. Trepanier's was the last number he had
called.

"Do you have it?" he asked.

"Do you expect to get your money?"

What did four million dollars look like? "How do you propose that we make the exchange?"

The priest laughed. "Look, I don't know who you are and what kind of stunt you're trying to pull." Ahead of him, Trepanier's car did a slight zigzag in company with his furious tone.

"I have the third secret of Fatima."

"Oh do you? Perhaps it is the fourth. Ignatius Hannan has come into possession of what you so generously offered to sell me."

Anatoly shut off the righteous voice. He glared at the car ahead. He was tempted to stamp on the gas, ram the car, and push the priest with his taunting voice into the ditch. Instead he passed Trepanier, not looking at the man as he went by, but in the rearview mirror he watched the disappearance of one more hope.

Either Hannan had a fraudulent copy or he did. Anatoly was no judge of such matters. He must go to one who was. To Remi Pouvoir.

✣ VII ✣

"That isn't what I meant, Laura."

Heather seemed oddly reluctant to accept Laura's offer to take her to the plane when she set off for Rome, but finally she agreed.

"I hate to put you to any more bother, Laura."

"More?"

"The plane."

"Oh that. It's costing us money just sitting there, Heather."

Heather would know better than she would the money side. In any case, she went by for Heather and was startled to find her waiting with a bearded man who turned out to be Vincent Traeger.

"Oh my God," Laura cried.

"It's all right," Heather said in her calmest voice. "He's coming with me."

Laura looked at the man who was being sought for the murder of Father Crowe, who had recently been described by all the media as an ex-agent out of control, liable to do anything. Had Traeger somehow forced Heather to put him on the Empedocles plane? No wonder Heather had tried to refuse the offer of a ride to the airport. It occurred to Laura that now she herself was in danger.

Heather took her aside while Traeger was putting her luggage in the trunk. "He's none of the things they say, Laura."

"Is he forcing you to do this, Heather?"

Heather actually laughed. "It was my idea."

"And you're sure . . ."

"Laura, he's been staying with me here."

Well, that was a conversation stopper if Laura had ever heard one. Heather with a man in the house? Whatever persuasion Traeger had exercised now took on a different complexion. Laura stepped back, displaying her palms.

"That isn't what I meant, Laura."

And almost despite herself, Laura believed it. Heather still had an otherworldly look. She could probably have a platoon of men in the house and preserve her virtue.

And so she drove them to the airport, went to the private plane terminal, and introduced them to the copilot and pilot, Laurel and Hardy, as Ray referred to them. A special seat had been installed for the pilot, Hardy, who was now checking the flight plan. Laurel came with them into the cabin, to settle them in. It seemed a dirty trick to involve those two in a flight to get a fugitive out of the country.

She waited and watched the plane taxi out and get into line for takeoff. She waited another half hour until she saw it gathering speed as it went down the runway and then lift gracefully into the air. Not so long ago, she and Ray had been flying off to Rome in that very plane, combining business and illicit pleasure. On a mission from Nate. Only she and Nate knew of the mission Heather was being sent on. Laura doubted that Heather would confide in Vincent Traeger.

Driving back to Empedocles, she thought of all the things that had happened since their fateful trip to Rome. More than anything else, she marveled at the ease with which she had accepted Heather's explanation of the presence of Vincent Traeger in her doorway.

*He's been staying with me here.* While the police and no doubt the FBI as well as Traeger's own agency were trying to track down a man described as an out-of-control killer whose skills, once in the service of his country, were now, et cetera, et cetera. Under the flood of coverage it was difficult to resist the thought that, however he had done it, Traeger must be responsible for the death of Brendan Crowe. It had become received opinion at Empedocles. Heather must have heard the talk, the indignation expressed by Nate, the increase in security as a result: heard it all and said nothing. And Laura had accepted Heather's assurance that Traeger was not the man so frantically described in the media.

But her lack of concern in all that increased in direct proportion to her distance from Logan, and by the time she drove through the gate of Empedocles, her mind was full of the problems of the day. Nate's impatient energy was now directed on the new site where Refuge of Sinners would be located. Much of the acreage of the Empedocles complex was still wooded, and the architect found a perfect location not a mile away, through the woods, at the far edge of the property. Nate went with Duncan Stroik, listened, thought about it, checked it with Laura, and then said go ahead.

And of course he meant now. There would be a museum, a chapel, an administration building. For now. Gabriel Faust acted as if decisions were made in this way anywhere else in the world. A strange man. At first he had seemed moody, dim, a bauble Zelda had picked up on her travels, but he had gradually transformed himself into the temperamental expert called upon to explain to the uninitiated the arcana of his trade. The manuscript of the third secret had been a coup.

"How did you learn of it?" Nate asked when Gabriel Faust informed him of the Vatican folder. Of course Laura was present.

"A telephone call," Faust said.

"Some nut?"

"Precisely my reaction. I hung up."

Faust explained, in more detail than was necessary, the care and caution that had led finally to the meeting with the man. At this point, he had brought Nate into the picture. The sequel had been bizarre. Nate made out a cashier's check to the amount of four million dollars, and Gabriel Faust went off alone to keep the rendezvous. It was as elaborate as a kidnapping. Faust had been warned that his life was forfeit if anyone accompanied or followed him. An hour and a half later, he was back at Empedocles, eyes asparkle, clutching the treasure. After its authentication, the announcement was made. Poor Father Trepanier looked as if he would weep for joy.

And now what? Gabriel deferred to Ignatius Hannan on the matter.

"It is stolen property, isn't it?"

"That's a rather stark way of putting it. As I explained, museums are full of things with histories of, shall we say, unusual previous ownership."

"Stolen?"

Faust's shoulders lifted.

"Stolen," declared Nate Hannan. "A message from the Blessed Virgin Mary. That adds sacrilege to the crime."

Faust was unprepared for this. During the announcement of the acquisition, the new director of Refuge of Sinners had been allowed to bask in his triumph. Now he was being faced with something like a scolding.

"Rescued, perhaps."

Laura intervened. "Doctor, have you prepared a release on this matter? Some indication of the contents of the document?"

"I will do so immediately."

"Of course you yourself have read the message," Laura said.

"Of course."

"And the expert you consulted?"

"Inagaki, yes."

"Anyone else?"

A pause, then, "No."

Laura said, "You hesitated."

"I consider my wife my alter ego, not someone else."

"Zelda has read the message?"

"Oh no. No! But we discussed it. As husbands and wives will."

Gabriel went away to prepare the release Laura had mentioned.

"Well?"

Nate looked at her. But Laura had long since learned to discern when he really wanted her advice.

She said, "What do you intend to do?"

"Return it."

❖

Return it unread. Ignatius Hannan had no intention in the world of reading a message from the Blessed Virgin, through Sister Lucia, that had been meant for the eyes of the pope. He had meant it when he had added sacrilege to theft in speaking of how this document had come into his possession. After the announcement, the precious document had gone into the Empedocles safe.

Gabriel Faust brought a statement on the new acquisition. Nate thanked him and had Laura rewrite it.

## ❖ VIII ❖

### He told her about Bea.

When they landed in Rome, Father John Burke met them with a Vatican car. He sat up front with the driver as they took Heather to the Bridgetines near the Campo dei Fiori where she would stay. Then they went on to the Casa del Clero next to the church of San Luigi dei Francesi, where Burke smoothed the way. He came up with him to the little boxlike room with an armoire, a desk, and a bed that looked perhaps two feet wide. Traeger dropped his bag on the bed.

"Thanks, I guess."

"It is pretty austere, isn't it? Laura emphasized something out of the way. What could be more out of the way than a residence for priests?"

Burke assured him that none of his fellow residents would question him or probably show much interest in him at all.

"Temporaries come and go, and the permanent residents hang together. The beard was a good idea."

Well, that cleared that up. Traeger had wondered if Father Burke knew he was sheltering a fugitive. Whatever Laura had told him seemed to have allayed any doubts he'd had. He handed Traeger his card.

"My cell phone is also listed there."

Traeger brought it to his brow in a salute. And then he was alone.

The adjoining bath was almost as large as the room. He put his bag on the floor and lay on the bed. The room had a very high ceiling. Traeger began to compute the square footage, comparing the height of the walls with the width of the room. Turn it on its side, and it wouldn't be so bad.

He was not complaining. At Heather's he had had time to think. He needed more time. The image of Bea, taped in that chair, came and went. The poor, dear woman. During his active years, he had often worried that she might be exposed to danger, but it had never happened. Since his retirement, he had unwisely ceased to worry.

Was Dortmund, too, dead, yet to be discovered, added to the toll Anatoly was taking? But Dortmund had been part of the game, he had survived years of undeclared combat, and he had earned the peace and quiet of his place beside the sea. Now it seemed to Traeger that Dortmund had had some premonition that the two of them were moving back into the target area when he sent Traeger off to Rome.

Well, now he was back in Rome, this time to escape the baying hounds that had been after him in the States. The rogue ex-agent.

"I can't stay here," he had said to Heather when he returned after discovering the body of Bea.

"Of course you can."

"My safe was broken into."

She looked at him. "Is it gone?"

"Yes."

He told her about Bea. The existence of evil did not seem to surprise Heather.

While he was there, she slept on a couch downstairs in her oratory, giving Traeger the master bedroom. That was not the bedroom she used. Across the hall was a smaller bedroom with blue walls, chintzy curtains, pastel pictures, and a fluffy throw rug beside the bed. He assumed that must be her usual bedroom. But down the hall was another bedroom in which there was a single bed, a dresser, and venetian blinds at the windows. On the wall at the foot of the bed was a very large crucifix. On the dresser, a statue of Our Lady of Fatima. A wooden beaded rosary hung from the bedpost.

Grudgingly, Traeger admired Anatoly's skill. Not the murders—any old hand could have done those—but the manipulation of the media. Was he getting help? And from whom? The disappearance of Dortmund made Traeger realize how on his own he was. Maybe it wasn't so far off to call him a rogue ex-agent. He wondered if Carlos Rodriguez would still accept him as an authorized delegate from the old agency. It was time to find out.

He made the call flat on his back, staring at the distant ceiling.

"Carlos. I'm back. Where can we meet?"

"Remember Trastevere?"

"Of course."

"The trattoria next to Sabatini's."

"When?"

"Two?"

"Two."

He hung up. It was not yet noon. Did he dare to fall asleep? The flight over had begun in daytime, against the movement of the sun, gaining five hours as they came. The sun had been setting behind them when they landed in Rome. He closed his eyes.

He walked to Trastevere from the Casa, favoring narrow streets like the Via Monterone, crossed the Vittorio Emanuele, and soon was at the bridge. Central Rome, ancient Rome, is a compact place. He went past the trattoria several times. The outside tables were empty. On his third pass, he went in. Carlos was at a table. Across from him was Dortmund.

"I thought you were dead," Traeger said, taking a seat. For a dizzy moment he had wanted to embrace the old man.

"They killed Marvin." His golden retriever. "Carlos was good enough to offer me sanctuary. Almost literally." Dortmund was housed in an apartment in the Vatican Observatory, within the walls, on a hill behind the basilica.

To Carlos, Traeger said, "I've been snookered."

Carlos ran that through his mental dictionary.

"Screwed."

"Ah."

"Outfoxed and robbed."

He explained the odd itinerary, the stolen Vatican Library

file he had taken until it had been stolen again, from Traeger's safe.

"They got Bea," he said to Dortmund. How easily that was said.

The old man closed his eyes.

"What's new here?" he asked Carlos.

"Aren't we going to eat?"

Both Dortmund and Traeger marveled at Carlos's appetite. How did good news affect him if bad made him so ravenous? Antipasto, minestrone, spaghetti, and then a *coteletta alla Milanese*. Wine? Carlos did away with most of the liter of *vino della casa*. Dortmund had played with his spaghetti, nibbled on bread, and sipped a glass of wine to which he had added mineral water, no crime in Rome. Traeger had what Carlos had. Ordeal by food.

"He's back in Rome," Carlos said, having sat back and scrubbed his face with his napkin.

Traeger waited. Dortmund stopped seeing how many pieces he could reduce a slice of bread to.

"He wants to trade."

"The assassination report?"

Carlos nodded. "Cardinal Piacere refuses. The Holy Father is acting as his own secretary of state, but he has put Piacere in the office."

Traeger said, "I may have a solution."

Traeger had written the agency report that had gone into the Vatican Archives. "It's still on my computer."

Dortmund stirred with disapproval. There had been several instances in recent years of classified materials going out of the agency on the computers of people who should have known better.

"Where is your computer?"

Traeger indicated the shoulder bag he had put beside his chair, keeping one shoe pressed against it as he ate. "So we can make the exchange."

"Are you sure he's got what you want?" Dortmund asked.

"There's only one way to find out," Traeger said.

"First, we'll go where we can print out what's on your hard drive," Carlos said.

Traeger thought of it. "Let's wait until you've made the arrangements."

Carlos looked at him. "You do have it?"

"I have it."

"Show him," Dortmund said.

Traeger got out his computer and a minute later brought up on the screen the report he had written. He scrolled down a few pages. Carlos nodded.

"I'll set it up."

⋇

Back in his room at the Casa, Traeger settled into serious sleep, as if he were making up for weeks of inadequate rest. The end was in sight. Dortmund was safe. Around Traeger's neck was the USB storage device on which there was a copy of his report on the assassination attempt. It was ironic that Anatoly had ended up with the third secret of Fatima and was now eager to exchange it for the report. When you know the contents of a classified document, it no longer has the allure it has for those who do not know.

As he drifted off, he wondered how Heather was doing in the Bridgetine convent. John Burke had offered to show her around Rome.

He slept through the night and when he awoke in the morning was still logy with weariness. Meals were served in the Casa, but Traeger did not avail himself of the refectory. When he went out onto the cobbled street and through a cross street to the Piazza Navona, he became aware of a flurry of excitement around a newspaper kiosk. He approached, saw the headlines, and began to pick up copies of various papers, *Il Tempo*, *Corriere della Sera*, *L'Osservatore Romano*, the *Herald Tribune*. He took the papers across the square to a bar, got an outside table, and ordered coffee. All around him people were reading the story.

Father Jean-Jacques Trepanier had made public the complete text of the third secret of Fatima. Now the portions suppressed in 2000 could be known.

The Blessed Mother had requested prayer and penance, a turning away from sin, a general change of heart in individual persons and in society. The alternative was grim. If her warnings were not heeded, Christian Europe would fall under the scourge of the Mohammedan heresy, with persecution and servitude the lot of those who had ignored her messages.

Trepanier added helpfully that of course the warning had been ignored because it had not been made public. Now the scourge predicted was descending on the continent of Europe. Trepanier wondered if it was too late for a final crusade.

# CHAPTER FIVE

✣ I ✣

The pope was burned in effigy.

The news that the Blessed Virgin Mary had predicted the Muslim occupation of Europe as punishment for sin flashed around the world.

Some were amused, others diverted for a time from ordinary pursuits. Most perhaps would have been unaffected. But an insistent media, countless commentaries, background pieces, and chatter filled the airways, and soon it was impossible to ignore the astonishing revelation. Those whose punishment had been predicted, in the manner of us all when we are guilty, were suffused with a sense of injustice and injured innocence. The supposed instruments of that punishment reacted explosively.

✤

Riots erupted in the Arab world, where the streets were filled with half-crazed crowds, demanding jihad. The fury focused on the pope. Benedict had weathered the storm of protests over his lecture at the University of Regensburg when he had alluded to the debate between a Byzantine and a Muslim. The point had been to underscore that religious faith did not destroy reason, that beliefs could not be in manifest conflict with reason, that members of different faiths could communicate despite their doctrinal differences on the basis of their common possession of reason.

This recherché and subtle argument was not the stuff of street oratory and agitation. That storm had abated largely thanks to the passage of time, and the Holy Father's visit to Istanbul.

Now the rage was renewed and intensified. The pope was burned in effigy in one Arab capital after another. All the mosques of Rome and of the Continent seethed with fury. A march of Muslims began in the Piazza del Popolo and went up the Corso to the great white monument commemorating fallen warriors, gathering members as it went. It turned onto the Vittorio Emanuele and, screaming, shouting, lamenting, praying, too, perhaps, continued across the Tiber. Police cars blocked access to the Via della Conciliazione, but they were simply pushed aside as the marchers surged forward, the sight of the basilica dome eliciting a deep, guttural roar as of anguish.

That Sunday the pope was not allowed to appear at his study window.

In the great square below, the pilgrims who had been gathering for hours in anticipation of the Angelus address at noon were engulfed by the new arrivals as by a tidal wave. *Viva il papa!* banners disappeared, torn from their bearers' hands, trampled on the cobblestones. Others in Arabic replaced them. Christians scampered to safety, leaving the square to the howling mob.

The great bells of the basilica began to toll. Twelve measured strokes. With each stroke the noise in the square diminished until gradually there was silence. Then, with a great swishing sound, most of those in the square turned to the east, dropped on their knees, and lowered their foreheads to the pavement.

A suicide bomber tried unsuccessfully to gain entrance to the basilica. When the metal detector responded in alarm to the corset of explosives she wore, she detonated them. There were fourteen causalities, including the bomber.

At a special emergency session of the European Union, a motion was passed demanding that the Vatican repudiate this alleged heavenly message and apologize to Islam for all present and past outrages against this peaceful world religion.

The Security Council of the United Nations, by unanimous vote, joined its protest to those of the many countries that had been maligned by the so-called third secret of Fatima. The age of religious wars is over. The age of the nation-state is fading. In the new world there will be but one world with no more room for intolerance of any kind.

In Baghdad, twenty-four Christians were stoned to death as they emerged from Mass.

The World Council of Churches begged their Muslim brothers not to confuse Roman idolatry with Christianity. Were not Islam and Christianity two outgrowths of the Abrahamic tradition?

The Episcopalian archbishop of Jasper, Wyoming, thumped her crosier on the floor of the sanctuary as her voice rose in lamentation over this unthinkable insult to our Muslim sisters and brothers. Her brother bishop in New England was driven to the downtown square by his companion and expressed his solidarity with her.

A committee of the American Catholic Theological Society suggested as the topic for its next national meeting "Mary in Islam."

The Major League Baseball schedule was disrupted when Muslim players refused to take the field. The Muslim members of the United States Congress called for sanctions against the Vatican.

At the Vatican a steady stream of long black cars with tinted windows slid through the various gates and their occupants were brought eventually to the acting secretary of state to present the protests of their governments.

Cardinal Piacere received them all with his accustomed grace, listened with bowed head while they read their communications, accepted the documents, offered refreshments, gave no indication that he had been at this for hours, and that hours more still lay ahead. Before the ordeal had begun, he had met with the Holy Father.

"This is nonsense, Piacere." He held a transcript of the Trepanier bombshell. "None of this is in the letter."

"The letter of Sister Lucia, Your Holiness?"

"Yes. Of course."

"I myself have never read the letter, Holiness."

A twinkle appeared in the papal eye. "You do not read the

important documents released by the Congregation for the Doctrine of the Faith?"

He meant the publication of 2000. Piacere made a fluttering gesture with his hands as he nodded. Touché.

"All one need do is put side by side the letter from Sister Lucia and this . . ." For a moment he seemed not to be so much searching for a word, as discarding an inappropriate one. He left it as "this." "The sooner that is done, the better."

"There is a problem, Holiness," Piacere said.

His hands parted, and snow-white eyebrows lifted. "A problem?"

"The letter from Sister Lucia is missing from the archives."

"Missing?"

"Stolen."

The great Bavarian shoulders seemed to slump under the white cape covering them. His fingers moved to his pectoral cross as he realized that the simple and decisive response to the alleged missing portions of the third secret was denied them.

"God help us.

"God and His Holy Mother.

"Amen."

❖

It was like the Holy Father to think that human beings, rational animals, confronted with the same evidence, would come to the same conclusion. Sometimes Piacere thought that the audience the pope envisaged in his mental eye when he prepared an address was a university lecture hall, they the students, he the professor.

The talk he had given at Regensburg was masterful, as a professorial lecture. The reaction could not have surprised the Holy Father more than if, in the old days, a student had stood and attempted to shout down his lecture.

Quite apart from the irrational response, Piacere knew that a cool, documented, measured statement could be drawn up that would indicate that the Holy Father shared many of the assumptions of the alleged new words of Mary.

Had he not met with Oriana Fallaci before the woman died?

Had he not warned the European Union that it must not lose sight of the Christian roots of Europe? Hilaire Belloc had once said that Europe is the faith and the faith is Europe. Taken historically, and Belloc was a historian, the claim made sense. Some version of it clearly made sense to the Holy Father.

Was it intolerance and fanaticism to point out that the number of Arabs immigrating into Europe combined with the falling birthrate of the natives—far below replacement rate, as it had been for half a century—pointed to a Muslim Europe, and not in the distant future? Already the tensions were familiar.

Demands for exemption from such narrow-minded restrictions as monogamy.

Demands for the lifting of the medical prohibition against female circumcision.

Demands that had already been met, however surreptitiously.

Down the Tiber from the Vatican was the huge dome of the largest mosque in Rome, in Europe. More than one imam in Rome had predicted that the time would come when Saint Peter's Basilica, like Santa Sophia long ago in Istanbul, would be converted to the true faith.

A major global crisis was at hand.

### ❖ II ❖

### "What's wrong?"

Carlos had suggested the same restaurant in Trastevere. "It may be safer than the Vatican," he added with a straight face.

Traeger had been waiting outside the door of the Casa when Carlos drove up. Was it fanciful to feel that the very atmosphere of Rome had changed? From the Piazza Navona a few short blocks away a roar of rage rose rhythmically, pulsing through the narrow streets. Visible from where he stood was the central office of the municipal police. Armored cars Traeger had never noticed before were now in evidence, and pedestrians were turned away from their normal passage down the street. He saw the car with VC plates get stopped as it tried to swing into the area before the police station. A moment's delay and it was admitted. Carlos hopped from it and hurried toward Traeger.

"Walking will be quicker, Vincent."

Walking was not easy. Crossing Vittorio Emanuele called

forth the half-forgotten skills of a prep school lineman, and Traeger led interference for Carlos to the far side of the street. They changed their minds and settled for a Chinese restaurant just off the Torre Argentina. The linen-covered tables, the vases of flowers, the exaggerated politeness with which they were welcomed contrasted with the surly scene outside. When they were seated, Carlos asked for hot tea immediately. They would order eventually. Then he said, "The exchange you proposed? We've got to do it."

"Have you made contact with Anatoly?"

Carlos hesitated.

"What's wrong?"

"Think about it. Rome, Europe, the whole damned world, is erupting because of the publication of that new passage from the third letter of Fatima. Anatoly has that letter. Now he wonders if he has any more negotiating power."

"Tell him the revelation was bogus."

Carlos fell silent. "We don't know that. That is, we can't prove it."

Traeger saw the point. Only the document Anatoly had would provide the means of showing that what Trepanier had released was not in it.

"You think that will quiet the mob?"

"Eventually. Eventually." The repetition seemed to convey his doubt. "What else do we have?"

Traeger was wishing he had read the document when he had it. But he had treated it with the respect due a supposed communication from the Mother of Jesus. He remembered a conversation with Heather.

"Are you Catholic?" she asked with her disarming directness.

He looked at her, rejecting possible answers. "Sort of."

"Ah."

"It's been a while."

"Someone described faith as water held in our cupped hands. How easily the fingers can separate and faith drain away."

Is that what had happened to him? Traeger found a certain kind of self-reflection uncomfortable. Maybe everyone does. Well, not Heather. She seemed to thrive on it. Sometimes while staying with her he had joined her in her oratory, sitting just inside while she knelt on her prie-dieu and time became a different dimension. Time measures motion, and what is there to measure when there is only stillness, immobility, silence? He grew used to it. He found himself envying Heather.

"What do you say?" he had asked her.

"Oh, I don't speak. I listen."

Layers of life had covered over any such simplicity Traeger may once have had. Images of operations, duplicity, killings, an endless battle to the death with a great adversary that had surprisingly and, admit it, disappointingly ended.

" 'Not with a bang but a whimper,' " Dortmund had commented.

"Yeah."

So the two of them had gone into a sullen retirement, Traeger to concentrate on the activities that previously had provided merely a cover, Dortmund to his isolated house by the shore of Chesapeake Bay to read the books he had always meant to read and pamper Marvin his golden retriever. No wonder they had responded like old fire horses when Dortmund had been contacted by Vatican security about the murders in the curial palace. He also remembered his surprise when Dortmund said he had always assumed Traeger was Catholic.

"Where else would you learn the opposition of good and evil?"

But how opposed had they been in the lives the two of them had led?

So Traeger had sat in the oratory while Heather prayed and tried to listen. He hadn't heard anything. He could not rid his mind of all the conflicting thoughts and images.

"Go to confession," she said when he told her this.

Confession. To kneel and whisper through the grille all the terrible sins of which he had been guilty? To tell all that to some priest who probably was used to penitents with nothing more weighty on their consciences than impatience, lack of charity, intemperance, maybe from time to time a little sexual dalliance? She seemed to read his mind.

"Father Krucek."

Krucek said the Mass to which Heather went off each morning, returning before Traeger was shaved and showered, hungry for breakfast. One morning he went with her and sat in the pew behind her and watched the once familiar ritual, or at least a reasonable facsimile of it, gone through at the altar. Krucek was like an old soldier who knew the drill and went through it with a briskness immune to doubt. Confessions were heard after the Mass, in the sacristy. Heather turned to Traeger when Krucek made this announcement, before marching out of the sacristy. Traeger felt panic, fear, he actually trembled at the thought of going up the aisle and into the sanctuary. But something of Heather's untroubled certainty communicated itself to him. He rose and went up the aisle and into the sacristy.

Krucek was hanging a chasuble in a closet. He still wore his alb and stole. He looked at Traeger almost impatiently, then nodded toward a kneeler separated from a chair by a screen. When Traeger hesitated, Krucek said, "Come on." He himself settled into the chair. Traeger lowered himself to his knees on the other side of the screen.

He stared at the weblike screen. It was like an optical illusion, convex or concave as you wished. "I don't know how to begin," he began.

"How long has it been?"

"Years."

"We'll make it easy. What sins haven't you committed?"

Traeger couldn't think of any as Krucek ticked them off, as if he were reading a list. Yes, he had done all of those.

"Murder?"

Was this what he had feared? He inhaled. "In the line of duty."

"Military?"

"CIA." He added, as if to mitigate his sins, "I'm retired now."

Krucek expelled air. "Well, I can't just give you a couple Hail Marys to say as a penance, can I?"

Traeger shook his head. Could Krucek see that?

"You're truly sorry for these sins?"

"They didn't seem like sins at the time."

"The killing?"

Again he nodded, but said, "Yes."

"You don't have time, I don't have time, to go into the details. Are you sorry for all the offenses you have committed against Almighty God?"

The question lifted the discussion above this deed and that to what made any deed good or bad. Traeger realized what an influence Heather had been on him, not by anything she said, but by what she was. He wanted to be like that. And Krucek was offering him the first step.

"Yes, Father."

"Okay. This is what I want you to do. Get yourself a rosary. Say it every day. Five decades, I mean. Ask Our Blessed Mother's help to change your life."

Krucek began the formula of absolution after he had recited the act of contrition in unison with Traeger. Traeger turned his head, wanting to hear the Latin words. Krucek's hand raised, and then—whose sins ye shall forgive they are forgiven—he absolved Traeger of his sins.

Krucek remained seated behind the screen until Traeger left the sacristy. Heather looked up when he stopped at her pew. She looked up and, with the smallest smile, rose, and they went home to breakfast.

⋅⋇⋅

Now, sipping hot tea in a Chinese restaurant in Rome, studying the menu, his hunger mounting as he did, Traeger hoped Heather was safe in the Bridgetine convent where she was staying. He couldn't afford to worry about her, not now. Everything depended on his getting together with Anatoly.

"Who's your contact?" he asked Carlos.

Carlos just looked at him. Traeger would have thought less of Carlos if he had told him.

"Can you set it up?"

"God help us if I can't."

⋇ III ⋇

### But moving was on his mind.

Gabriel Faust had given himself occasion to ponder two deep moral truths: greed knows no limits, and hubris is a nemesis to man. He had overreached.

A pardonable pride in his own craftsmanship had led him to imagine that the document he had produced, thanks to his calligraphic skills and a mimicry that in lettering rivaled Inagaki's in oils, was worth the price he put on it. Not least because Trepanier had telephoned him while he was driving to Empedocles for the great disclosure to Hannan that some fraud had offered him what must be a fake for the preposterous sum of four million dollars.

Ignatius Hannan had not blanched at the amount.

"You're certain it is authentic?"

Faust slid across the desk the report Inagaki had made.

"Isn't this the man who is making our paintings?"

"The same."

No explanation is better than a bad one. Faust was beginning to wonder at the much touted shrewdness of Ignatius Hannan. There was no need to instruct him on how to make the money payable in a manner that the seller could accept.

"He will still have to cash it," Hannan said. "No bank will forget such a transaction. Of course they will call to have the check authenticated when it is presented."

Faust thought about that. "It is the risk a thief runs."

Hannan shook his head in disgust. "Imagine trafficking in such a thing." All Hannan's own money had been made cleanly. He wondered how it felt. The check would not be presented as Hannan imagined. The Swiss were far more discreet in these matters. Faust warmed himself at the thought that he was now, unquestionably, a multimillionaire. And if four million, why not more?

"We needn't go through with it," he dared say.

"We are stopping the trafficking, not engaging in it."

Who cannot produce a good reason for what he intends to do in any case?

Trepanier was no Hannan, money-wise, but his operation was wildly successful. How much would the impassioned priest give for a copy of what Ignatius Hannan had paid four million to get?

During the great disclosure, as he made his pedantic presentation, he noticed how effectively Trepanier played his role of the unsuccessful suitor of that secret. Later, he had stopped Trepanier and led him away to his office.

"A great day," he said, settling into his chair. The forged notebook lay before him. Trepanier could not keep his eyes from it.

"You have brought what we agreed to?"

Trepanier patted his breast. There was the crinkle of an envelope in his inside pocket. Faust produced the photocopy he had made of the passage he had added to the secret as it had been made public in 2000.

"Of course you will want to compare the photocopy with the original."

Trepanier did this, leaning over the desk. When he was satisfied, he paused, bent over the forged document, and kissed it reverently. Then they made their exchange, the photocopy for the envelope that Trepanier drew from his pocket. In it was a check made out to Gabriel Faust in the amount of two hundred and fifty thousand dollars.

That was two hundred and fifty thousand that Faust came to regret when Trepanier detonated his public relations bomb. With an expertise that one could only admire, Trepanier managed to get the good news of the supposed Fatima revelation unleashed all but simultaneously in the so-called first world, followed close behind by feverish coverage in the second and the third. Within thirty-six hours, global reaction had taken place, and all hell was breaking loose throughout the Middle East. Muslims in every corner of the earth, and they seemed to be in every corner, rose as one man to protest this attack on their faith. And the bull's-eye of their anger was the Vatican, more specifically, the pope.

The surprise was that Faust was surprised that Trepanier had so quickly and efficiently turned the bogus document into a media event. Gabriel Faust was filled with uneasiness.

It was one thing to hoodwink Ignatius Hannan.

It had been perhaps easier to hoodwink Jean-Jacques Trepanier, his hopes and dreams shaping what he saw beneath his nose. Faust regretted the relatively small sum he had asked when Trepanier bent over the notebook and kissed it.

How could he be surprised that Trepanier, who for years had been grounding his ministry on the claim that the full text of the third secret had been withheld, would not himself withhold what he had come into possession of? Had he been counting on Trepanier's disappointment? Faust might have offered something closer to Trepanier's wishes, some expression of heavenly discontent at the way the requests of Fatima were being met, or not being met, by the Church. But it had seemed wiser to play to Hannan's current fixation on the demographic question and the abandonment by Europe of its traditional Christian identity. It took a bachelor like Hannan to preach passionately the need for reproduction, the imbalance between natives and immigrants in the Old World: the dangerous and seemingly irreversible tipping of the balance.

Faust smiled at this repetition of the onetime lament of the WASP. The immigrants, the Irish, are breeding us out of our birthright. The answer had been birth control, which had encountered a stone wall in all the Christian churches; a stone wall that had crumbled over the years, until the United States had become a great missionary nation, bringing contraception and choice to a benighted world. The immigrant Irish and Germans and Portuguese and Italians and all the rest had eventually been converted to the contraceptive culture, and so, too, the lands of their origin. That, coupled with the toll of total war, had brought about the demise of native Germans, French, Spanish, Italians, willing themselves into extinction. The Scandinavians? Forget it.

Faust had been surprised by Hannan's eloquence. He reminded him of Tom Buchanan in *The Great Gatsby* worrying about the yellow menace.

"Who would have thought the danger lay with the Arabs?" Hannan asked.

"Who indeed?" Ray Sinclair asked, scarcely concealing his sarcasm.

It was clear that Sinclair and Laura Burke were embarrassed by the turn Hannan's great religious conversion had taken. But Faust had seen in this the tack he must take as he labored over the facsimile of Sister Lucia's letter, adding what he was sure would answer to Ignatius Hannan's worst fears.

But Hannan refused even to read the document. All that work, and he might have palmed off a blank book. He treated the document Faust had produced with much the same reverence as Trepanier had, differently expressed of course.

"We must return it to the Vatican."

Here was danger indeed. Imagine the paleographers of the Vatican chortling over the hoax they would be presented with.

Meanwhile, Zelda was more and more eager that they find a house closer to Gabriel's employment.

"I hate the thought of moving," she said.

But moving was on his mind.

He thought of Corfu, and rejected it. That distant isle seemed bound to occur to Zelda.

He thought of Pantelleria.

Ah, Pantelleria. He loved Pantelleria, a little volcanic island off the African coast, reachable from Trapani in western Sicily. It had scarcely more attractions than Juan Fernandez off the coast of Chile where the marooned Selkirk had scrabbled for existence during four years, providing the inspiration for Defoe's Robinson Crusoe. But Pantelleria held the enormous attraction of promising refuge. He smiled. A refuge of sinners. But would he continue to love that lonely island if it became his Elba, his Saint Helena?

✣ IV ✣

"A peek in the poke?"

It was Laura's role to confront Nate with objections and alternatives to his schemes and proposals, but she had never undertaken to second-guess him once he had embarked on a course of action.

The replica of the grotto of Lourdes on the grounds of the Empedocles complex had been a mere bagatelle. Nate could afford it, and the result was, Laura admitted, wonderful, a serene redoubt among the frantic activities of Empedocles. She and Ray sat on a bench facing the shrine after the session in which Gabriel Faust had presented what he had managed to secure for Ignatius Hannan, for Refuge of Sinners, the third secret of Fatima.

"Four million dollars," Ray said thoughtfully.

"It's not the money," Laura said.

"What's the principle, then?"

"What do you really think of Gabriel Faust, Ray?"

"He has a devoted wife."

The nonresponsive answer suggested an attractive tangent, a way of bringing up their own status—"unhappily unmarried," as Ray had recently described it—but Laura was not to be distracted. Perhaps Ray was made uneasy by the same tangent.

He said, "A pig in a poke."

"What does that mean, exactly?"

"A poke is a sack."

"And a pig is a pig."

"You buy it without getting a good look at what you're buying," Ray explained.

"He didn't want to look at it."

The document was now secure in the safe in Nate's office, awaiting transfer to Rome by Heather. Laura said, "You and I could take a peek."

"A peek in the poke?"

"You don't want to."

"You know, I admired Nate's decision. There at last he had it in his hands, the big secret that has caused so much speculation for so many years, including his own, and he backed away from examining it. He didn't have the right. Isn't that what you would do if you thought you had a letter from the Blessed Virgin addressed to someone else?"

"It's from Sister Lucia," Laura said.

But Laura did not say this to diminish what Ray had said. He was right. Nate was right. Get the thing out of here and back to where it belonged.

When she came back from Logan after seeing Heather off, she took Ray aside and told him Traeger was also on the company plane. He reacted with alarm. Of course he imagined that Traeger had somehow forced his way onto the plane in order to fly away from his pursuers. Laura told him what Heather had said.

"He was staying with her?"

"Lower your eyebrows. I thought the same thing. She said no and I felt chided. You know Heather."

"Sometimes I wonder if I know anything or anyone."

"Heather is so transparent she's invisible."

Later, he said, "What is that story of Hemingway's, the nun and the gambler? Or is that Faulkner? I said I no longer know anything. The virgin and the assassin."

"You don't know that, Ray."

"Oh, I'm sure she is."

Laura punched him on the arm.

"Wanna wrestle?"

"We don't have a license."

"Then what are we doing in bed together?"

"What we shouldn't."

And they did, and afterward, for the first time, each of them expressed the remorse they felt. "Let's do it," he said.

"We just did."

"I mean marry."

He meant it, he really did.

"Of course I'll have to pass the blood test," he said.

"You'll have to go to confession is what you'll have to do. What we have to do."

"Will I have to say I'm sorry?"

"Fornication," she mused.

"I'll say I didn't take pleasure in it."

She put a pillow over his face. He freed himself.

"Do you think that maybe Heather and Traeger ever . . ."

She got the pillow back over his face and fell out of bed in the process. She went on to the shower where, all aglow, as if the water were washing her sins away, she sang, not quite in tune, "Get me to the church on time."

❧

But these pleasant plans were interrupted by the bombshell of Trepanier's disclosure of the suppressed third secret.

"Get Faust," Nate said, white with fury.

Ray went away and in ten minutes was back. "He's not here."

"Call Zelda," he said to Laura. "I'll talk to her."

Laura got through to the happy bride and turned the phone over to Nate.

"Zelda," he cried, with delight, and Laura and Ray exchanged a glance.

They listened to the billionaire spend five minutes on trivia with Zelda, minutes that could have been given a more or less distinct calculation of the money they were costing him, and then, "Say, is Gabriel there?"

He listened. His expression changed. But his voice was still sweet when he said, "Zelda, sometimes I think I'll forget my own name."

More schmoozing before he hung up.

He said, "I have just learned that I sent Gabriel Faust to Rome so that he could return the document."

A long silence broken finally by Laura.

"Poor Zelda."

✣ V ✣

## Not Castel Gandolfo.

The Reverend Jean-Jacques Trepanier had arrived at his apotheosis. The dream of crowning achievement had been reached. He had exposed the myrmidons of the Vatican as unreliable custodians of the secrets of Fatima.

The gush of elation that surged through him was slightly abated by the thought that it was difficult to know what he could ever do that would surpass this triumph. Where does a climber go after conquering Mount Everest?

He dismissed such thoughts as unworthy, as distractions and temptations. What he had unleashed upon the world was not about Jean-Jacques Trepanier. If that were all that was at issue, he could confess to a measure of disappointment. But the very surprise of the passage Gabriel Faust had provided him in photocopy seemed a confirmation of its authenticity. Never in a million years had Trepanier imagined that Our Lady had warned of the subjugation of Europe by Islam, a new dark age spelling servitude and persecution. And to think that this had been suppressed when there was still time to storm heaven and pray that the punishment not descend.

He felt no responsibility for the riots and bombings and sacrileges that followed on the release of the suppressed portion of the third secret. The blame for all that must fall on those who had concealed the Blessed Virgin's warning.

That said, he could not look at the television coverage of what was happening, in the Arab world, in the countries of Europe, in Rome itself. Trepanier was appalled at the venom with which the Holy Father was attacked. He himself had always been careful to aim at targets beneath the Chair of Peter itself, to suggest that the pope was the victim of cynical bureaucrats. John Paul II had been too trusting. Benedict XVI was too trusting. If Trepanier felt any sadness it was at the thought of the Holy Father realizing at last how poorly he had been served by those he had trusted.

Calls came from Empedocles. He did not take them. Calls came directly from Ignatius Hannan himself, and still Trepanier did not take them. There was of course some sense of treating Hannan badly. He knew what the man must have paid for that document, whereas he had gotten the nub of the thing for a relatively modest amount. But who could own a message from the Blessed Virgin? Just as poverty and starvation trumped the right of private property, so the demands of heaven put ordinary morality in abeyance. He made a note of that; it could form the basis for his next televised sermon.

In the meantime, he went to the studio, where all scheduled programming was halted while viewers were addressed directly and live by the founder.

*"Haec est dies quam fecit Dominus,"* he began, the text springing to his lips without forethought. But he was accustomed to finding himself inspired whenever he stepped before the camera. Thoughts, insights, connections came to him that he would never have come upon in the privacy of his own mind, so to speak. *"Fides ex auditu!"* That of course was the motto of the station, a reminder that he had begun with radio alone. His personal motto might have been *fides ex loquendo.*

He began with a swift, sure summary of the events of Fatima, of those successive Fridays when the beautiful lady had appeared to Jacinta and Francisco and Lucia. Jacinta and Francisco were in heaven now, beatified, whereas Sister Lucia had lived a very long life, in the course of which she was favored with other visits from the Lady. It was under instruction that she had composed her long account of the apparitions as well as later confidences she had received. These had gone to her bishop, to his superior, and eventually on to Rome, for the eyes of the Holy Father only. These were warnings to the world, made not to frighten but to stave off the punishment that must come if men continued in their sinful ways. It is an old truth, we have it from Paul himself, that no word of Scripture is without its importance, to instruct, to exhort, and so forth, and the same may be said of those words spoken in private revelations. They are all spoken for a definite purpose.

What then are we to make of those who arrogate to themselves the right to prevent the faithful from hearing the message? Who suppress news of the ultimate punishment awaiting if prayer and penance do not define our lives? But that is exactly what happened.

Worse, an effort was made to pretend that the whole had been made public. There was a great media event in 2000, complete with downloadable copies on the Internet and an accompanying theological explanation of Fatima and private revelations generally. Trepanier did not mention now, as he once had, the role Cardinal Ratzinger had played in this. In those days, he had made much of the statements of 2000 and those in the *Ratzinger Report* of 1985.

Then the secret had been called too sensational to reveal. But what was there sensational about the secret supposedly published in its entirety in 2000?

Trepanier would make no direct criticism of the Holy Father. He would leave that to more incendiary groups, no need to mention Catena and the Confraternity of Pius IX.

Now they knew what Our Lady had warned would come. The prayers, the fasting, and the penance that might have turned away the punishment had not been done. Our Lady of Mercy, pray for us.

⁂

He left the studio, waving aside the usual congratulations of the crew, and went on toward his office. As he was passing through the reception hall, his eye was caught by a monitor in the corner. Had he half expected to see himself on the screen? But it was not the scheduled programming of Fatima Now! that was being shown. The monitor had been turned to a commercial station.

Trepanier stopped, stunned at the news. The Holy Father had been removed from the Vatican by helicopter. To an undisclosed location. Not Castel Gandolfo. The Holy Father had insisted that that at least be made clear, lest that lovely town in the Alban Hills also become a target of the howling mob. The pope reportedly said something about not wanting to give the Athenians a chance to sin again against philosophy, an enigmatic remark that kept commentators and pundits occupied, diverting them from speculation about where the pope had been taken.

In Florence, where the baptistery had come under assault by Muslim rioters who were throwing buckets of filth on the engravings on its magnificent doors, a reaction had set in: the populace was rising to protect the culture that gave the city its eminence. Pitched battles were being fought. Trepanier felt his pulse quicken at the thought of Christians in hand-to-hand combat with these raging heretics.

## ✤ VI ✤

### "I don't understand."

John Burke had taken Heather with him when he went to Cardinal Piacere to discuss the package that she had brought with her from the States.

"What is it?" he had asked.

She looked at him for a long time before she answered. As he listened, John felt that he was suddenly swept back into the madness of those days at Empedocles Inc. The secret of Fatima. He looked at the manila envelope she had given him. How in the name of God could that have been taken from the archives, found its way to Ignatius Hannan, and now been brought back by Heather? And even as he asked himself the question, he thought of Brendan. His horrible death had seemed at first only one of those random acts that characterize the modern world, a mindless slaying by a thief surprised at his work. Before John had left, he had of course heard the speculation that Vincent Traeger had been the assassin. And here he was, bearded but recognizable, standing beside Heather on the tarmac after they had descended from the private plane with the logo of Empedocles emblazoned on its tail fin.

On the drive to the Vatican, Heather sat between him and Traeger on the backseat, speaking in her calm voice of what had gone on since his departure.

"They actually thought Vincent had killed Father Crowe." The incredulity in her voice was infectious.

"But how did Mr. Hannan come into possession of this?"

"He bought it."

"From whom?"

"From the one who took it from Vincent's office."

Traeger added to this story, making it more mystifying still. An ex–Soviet agent roaming the country?

"He killed your friend," Traeger said.

"But why?"

"For that."

"My God." The package suddenly seemed heavier than before.

The driver had been given instructions to take them to the Casa del Clero, and once Traeger was settled there, John took Heather on to the Bridgetine convent. It was the following morning that he came by for her, wanting her to accompany him on his visit to Cardinal Piacere. The thought of telling this twisted tale all by himself was not welcome; he wanted Heather there to supply answers to the questions the cardinal would surely ask and to which John himself did not have the answers.

Meanwhile Rome had become a war zone. The main streets of the old city were crowded with men in burnooses and women in burkas. Signs in Arabic and Italian proclaiming that there is no God but Allah were everywhere. At the first outbreak of violence, John had received permission to have Heather transferred to the contemplative community founded by John Paul II, the convent within the walls of the Vatican. A Carmelite welcomed them and Heather stepped back.

"Saint Teresa!" she said.

The nun smiled. "No, Sister Dolores."

"I meant the habit."

"I know, I know." She took Heather's arm and looked at John. "She'll be fine here."

When he came by for her, to take her along on the appointment with Cardinal Piacere, she was radiant.

"What a heavenly place, Father."

"I have said Mass there once or twice."

"Two of them speak English."

"So does Cardinal Piacere," John said, and they started down the road to the office of the acting secretary of state. To their right, higher still, was the observatory, and below them was the building in which John worked, which housed the various pontifical academies. After the tumult of the city, the quiet, the peacefulness was all the more striking.

❖

Bernagni, a priest John knew from the Domus, welcomed them in the outer office and took them right in to the cardinal, muttering about the tightness of the schedule. Piacere rose slightly from his chair, making a little bow to Heather, and asked them to pull chairs up to his.

"So you are the assistant of the famous Ignatius Hannan?"
Cardinal Piacere said to Heather.

"Is he famous? I suppose he is. No, I am not his assistant.
That is Laura, Father Burke's sister."

"And you are a messenger who brings things to Rome?"

"This is my very first visit, Your Eminence." John had told
her the correct form of address.

"You have come in troubled times." Piacere made a gesture
and Bernagni came forward to give him the envelope Heather
had brought. "All because of this."

And then, as John had predicted, the cardinal wanted as
complete an account of the document as Heather could give
him. She made a point of the fact that people had died because of it.

"Father Brendan Crowe," John said.

"And Vincent Traeger's secretary, Beatrice."

Piacere repeated the name with an Italian pronunciation.

"Ah. Be-a-tri-ce. Let us pray that she is with her namesake
in Paradiso." His eyes fell again to the envelope he held. "Yes,
people have died because of this. Many more will, I am afraid.
This is a forgery."

He drew a booklet from the envelope that had been sent to
him, a school notebook, and fluttered its pages.

"It took but a few minutes to determine that this document
is at most a month old. The handwriting is remarkably similar
to that of Sister Lucia, almost identical. Almost—not quite."

John said, "Then all the rioting and attacking of the Church
and the Holy Father is based on . . ."

"A fanciful interpolation to what is in the authentic text."

"Making that public will quiet things down. How soon will
the announcement be made?"

"I have advised against any announcement," Piacere said
softly. "And I will tell you why. First, the claim that this document is a fake, even though accompanied by the written judgment of manuscript experts, would be regarded as a ploy." He
shrugged his shoulders. "Yes, yes, we are well into the age of
suspicion. You can appreciate the paradox: the announcement
that the document that has caused blood to run in the streets is
a fake is accompanied by the expert judgment to that effect.
Fraud and forgery are in the air and they taint the expert judgment as well. But that is not the main reason. The most deci-

sive way to show that this"—again he fluttered the pages he held—"contains an interpolation not to be found in the original and authentic document would be simply to lay them side by side."

"What's wrong with that?" John asked.

"Such a comparison could of course be made now by anyone interested."

"I don't understand."

"All the documentation released in two thousand is still on the web. Nothing at all like this passage that has so stirred our Muslim brothers is to be found there. But, as perhaps you know, suspicion has long been trained on that documentation. There is a certain kind of mind that demands apocalyptic warnings. Doubtless that is why the Apocalypse was made the final book of the New Testament." Piacere smiled. "A book that has been interpreted, reinterpreted, and interpreted again and whose meaning remains elusive. But I digress."

John still did not see the problem. Invite a number of Muslim scholars, let them put the documents side by side and make their own judgment.

Cardinal Piacere's expression was sad. "Because the authentic document is missing from the archives."

Heather sat forward. "I gave it to Vincent Traeger for safekeeping. It was when his office was broken into and Beatrice was killed that it was taken from the safe." Heather pronounced Beatrice *modo italiano* this time.

"And where did you get it, my dear?" Piacere asked.

"From Father Brendan Crowe."

Piacere fell back. "Of course, of course. One of the few men who would have been able to remove the file. He took it to America?"

"I thought I was bringing it back."

He brought his long-fingered hands together. "So you see we have an insoluble problem. God only knows how long this rioting and outrage will continue. It seems to grow more intense every day."

What had happened first in Florence had spread across the Continent, with natives opposing the trashing of churches and museums by the Muslim mobs. In Paris, when the police were called out, a battle broke out between the Muslim and Christian members of the metropolitan police. The divided force was now on different sides of the barricades formed by burning automobiles.

Cardinal Piacere insisted that they have a glass of wine. He wanted Heather to thank Mr. Hannan for his thoughtfulness in wishing to return what he had thought was a document stolen from the archives.

"He paid four million dollars," Heather said.

*"Mamma mia."* He clapped his hands and Bernagni ran in from the outer office. Piacere shooed him away. "No, no, Father, I was simply being emotional." And then to Heather, "To whom did all that money go?"

"I think there was a middleman," Heather said.

Piacere sat thinking, with his eyes closed. After a minute, John feared that he might have fallen asleep from the exertion of his reaction to the news that four million dollars had been paid for a forged document. When he spoke, his eyes were still shut.

"And how is your Vincent Traeger, my dear?"

Heather was not bothered by the possessive pronoun. "He's in Rome. He's grown a beard."

"I should like to see him again. We have met, you know."

"Would you like me to bring him here, Your Eminence?"

"I will get word to him. Thank you, Father Burke."

He rose, they rose, Bernagni appeared, and soon they were on their way back to Heather's convent.

"All this bloodshed over a forged document."

As he often did, John missed Brendan Crowe, but particularly now. Brendan would no doubt have had any number of historical instances of forgeries altering the course of history.

# CHAPTER SIX

## ❖ I ❖

### "Did you tell her it was a fake?"

"Oh my God, he's been kidnapped," Zelda cried when she came to Empedocles for word of her husband.

Zelda had thought that Gabriel Faust was on a mission for Ignatius Hannan, to return the presumed Vatican Archive file to its rightful owner. Laura told her this wasn't the case and was trying to calm her as Nate inched toward the door.

"Nate, you stay here," she said. She was not going to be left alone with a hysterical woman. Hannan was watching Zelda warily as Laura got her into a chair. Ray brought a cup of coffee, which she held in both hands, looking from one face to the other. Written all over her well-preserved, still handsome face was the unasked question: have I lost another husband?

"He bought a fake," Nate said, sitting down himself, but then he had the desk between himself and Zelda. "For four million dollars."

Zelda gasped.

"No one has tried to cash the check yet."

"So far as we know," Ray said, always the life of the party.

"Where is Gabriel?" Zelda wailed.

It was a question everyone in the room wanted answered, for different reasons.

"Have you told the police yet?"

Laura and Ray exchanged glances. Nate had lost millions before, in a sense he did so every day, but not like this. "Find him," he had ordered Ray. "No police. We know how good they are."

Laura took Zelda off to the ladies' room, where there was a cot on which Zelda could lie. Not the best place to play her big scene, the twice-widowed woman, but it got her away from Nate. Zelda had been thinking.

"Vincent Traeger," she said, her voice now under control. "It must be Vincent."

Laura did not ask why, but she got the reason anyway.

"He was jealous of Gabriel. I don't know if you noticed his reaction when Gabriel and I showed up here as man and wife."

"No, I didn't."

"He's the one. We must find him." Zelda sat up. "I know who to call."

Laura eased her back onto the cot. She had brought Zelda's cup of coffee along, but it was no longer hot. Zelda waved it away. "How can I eat or drink?"

She began to weep. She told Laura of their first argument.

"Not argument exactly. We just didn't agree. I suggested he give a painting he had obtained for me to the new foundation. Hang it in his office."

"And he disagreed," Laura said, feeling that she was taking part in a Beckett drama.

A smile drove away the tears. "He said he thought of it as our first real link."

Laura brought her a tissue and Zelda dabbed away the tears. Fifteen minutes later, Laura brought the now calm Zelda back to Nate's office.

"I intend to hire a detective," she announced.

"Work that out with Ray," Nate suggested. It was an order, and Ray now took Zelda off to his office.

"Did you tell her it was a fake?" Hannan asked.

"You mentioned that. She may not have understood."

The cable from John Burke had arrived half an hour before Zelda. The document Heather had brought to the Vatican had been examined. It was a fake. The message that was filling the streets and plazas of the world with rampaging, enraged Muslims was an interpolation.

"Faust said it was authentic," Hannan said.

"He said an expert assured him it was authentic," Laura corrected.

"Inagaki."

"I think you're right."

"I want to talk to him," Hannan said grimly.

Ray was already on that. The notion of hiring a private detective to locate Gabriel Faust had already occurred to him. It was pretty clear that Faust had disappeared, and neither Laura nor Nate could seek consolation in the theory that he had been kidnapped. Only a wife could believe that in the circumstances.

After the cable came, Laura talked with John on the phone and got an account of their meeting with Cardinal Piacere.

"They're sure it's a fake?"

"Laura, he said the experts needed only minutes to determine that."

"How were we to know?" Laura might have been addressing that question to Nate. The truth was that she felt she had let Nate down. And she felt irrationally responsible for the whole sad sequence of events. She had invited John and Brendan Crowe to Empedocles. A thought occurred.

"Father Crowe checked Gabriel Faust's dossier and okayed him."

"So?" John said.

"Gabriel Faust is missing."

Later she would wonder aloud to Ray of a possible previous connection between Brendan Crowe and Faust. How convenient to have a man from the Vatican there to assure Nate Hannan that Gabriel Faust was the kind of expert he needed to run Refuge of Sinners. Where was Faust when Crowe was killed? Had Father Crowe brought the phony document with him? Ray followed this with a wry smile. "Don't ever write a novel," he advised.

"What do you mean missing?" John had asked.

"He's not here. We don't know where he is. His wife doesn't know where he is."

"The Vatican experts did admire the calligraphy of the faked passage."

"John, are you safe there? The news is absolutely horrible. How is Heather?"

"I've put her into a convent of Carmelites."

"Do they make candy?"

John ignored this. "A convent within the walls of the Vatican. She's as safe as I am."

Laura would have liked to find that more reassuring than she did. Laurel and Hardy had returned with the plane in which Heather and Traeger had been flown to Rome, deadheading it back to Logan, as they put it.

"She should come back, John."

"I think she likes it here."

"Heather has the capacity to like wherever she happens to be."

"Oh it's more than that, I think. Traeger came with her," he added.

"I know."

"I got him into a clerical residence. Cardinal Piacere seems to know him."

Ray was right. She would never write a novel. Things should hang together more than they seemed to do.

"It's not the money," Nate said.

"I know."

Nate had plainly been shocked by the thought of buying and selling something like the secret of Fatima. Hence his immediate decision to send the document to Rome. If only Trepanier hadn't broadcast the fake passage, the whole thing would have been settled. They had bought a fake and lost some money, but that would have been that.

"So where is the real document?" Nate asked.

Good question.

"Father Trepanier still won't take my calls."


## ✤ II ✤

### "I make it myself."

Jean-Jacques Trepanier listened with a skeptical smile when Laura Burke and Ray Sinclair told him the judgment of the Vatican experts on the passage he had made public with consequences beyond the scope of imagination. The two minions of Ignatius Hannan had waylaid him as he came from the television studio where he had been informing his viewers that they were now witnessing the heavenly scourge Our Lady had warned of. He was on his way to lunch and he asked them along. At the table, over clam chowder, they had told him what they had come to say.

"Of course they would say that," Trepanier said.

"You don't believe it?"

"My dear woman, what else could they say? Don't you see that half a century of deceit has been exposed? Their duplicity has brought bloody chaos to the world."

"I think you can take credit for that, Father," Ray said.

"I?"

"You broadcast it."

"The truth can never be suppressed forever," Trepanier said.

"Where did you get hold of that passage?" Laura asked.

He should have been prepared for this attempt to blame him for the rioting and outrages being perpetrated throughout so much of the world. Nonetheless, he was surprised. And Laura's question put him in a tight spot. How could he, as the voice accusing the Vatican bureaucracy of mendacity, take refuge in what could have been plausibly described as a mental reservation?

"I bought it."

"Bought it!"

"From Gabriel Faust?" Ray asked.

"Yes."

"But he had already sold it to Ignatius Hannan," Laura said.

"I was content to have a photocopy of the relevant passage."

"Which is fake," Ray said.

"Then why is what it predicted taking place? It is the single topic of the news."

"What would it take to convince you that you bought something fraudulent?"

Again he resented that they had the audacity to blame him. "And what is Gabriel Faust's reaction to this Vatican judgment?"

"He didn't stay around long enough to hear it."

"What do you mean?"

"He vamoosed." The two of them looked at him expectantly. Surely they wouldn't lie about such a thing. If anything, it weakened their case.

"That is neither here nor there," he told them.

They looked at him as liberal seminary professors had looked at him years ago.

"At any rate, now you know," Ray Sinclair said.

"This is very good chowder," Laura said.

"I make it myself."

⚜

When they had gone, he admitted to himself that what they had said made him uneasy. He tried to retain his original reaction that of course Vatican bureaucrats would seek to deny their culpability for keeping such a message to themselves. Hadn't they once pretended to make the third secret public? They had been hoist by their own petard. Convincing as that interpretation was, it no longer satisfied him completely.

The implication of their visit was that Gabriel Faust had been responsible for the passage Trepanier had paid a huge sum for. He got out the photocopy and studied it. He compared it with the pages that had been provided in 2000 when the third secret had supposedly been made public. No expert could deny that the hands were identical. But then the experts would not have been dealing with a photocopy.

It bothered him that the Confraternity of Pius IX was not joining him in condemning the Vatican anew, now that the missing passage was known. How could they fail to see that this development corroborated the charges they had been making for years? If only he could discuss the matter with Bishop Catena. Perhaps they were angry with him for not sharing the explosive news of that missing fragment of the third secret. He considered sending an e-mail. He considered telephoning. He decided that the definitive thing to do would be to go to Rome himself.

This was a thought that filled him with dread. The morose delectation he took in seeing on television those scenes of rioting raging mobs had been possible because of the saving distance between himself and all those crazed demonstrators. The pope himself had been spirited out of Rome. To go there would be like flying into a war zone.

He pondered the possibility of the trip. He prayed about it. In the end, he decided that he would go. Let the Vatican experts try to convince Jean-Jacques Trepanier that he had paid two hundred and fifty thousand dollars for the photocopy of a fake.

After he had made his travel arrangements—there seemed to be no problem in catching a flight to Rome; he was even offered business class gratis—he telephoned Zelda. She answered with an excited yelp.

"Gabriel?"

"This is Father Trepanier, Zelda." The question he had called to ask, not that he thought Laura Burke and Ray Sinclair would lie, seemed answered.

"Is he with you, Father?"

In the circumstances, it was an odd thought that Gabriel Faust should have taken refuge with him. Jay remembered how the just appointed director of Refuge of Sinners had suggested that there should be close cooperation between Fatima Now! and the new foundation. Had Faust been laying the groundwork for a future sale? He brushed the thought away. He told Zelda that her husband was not with him.

The price he paid for his curiosity was to have to listen to her sobbing, incoherent tale of her missing husband. Had she any idea what her husband was being accused of? Apparently not. It was difficult to picture the recent radiant bride as he listened to her, offering it up. He managed to end the conversation by promising to say a Mass for the safe return of Gabriel Faust.

And then he was on his way.

A cleric travels light—the suit he is wearing and in his bag an extra Selma shirt and collar, socks, underwear, toilet articles, his breviary. He left his car in long-term parking and then went on to the terminal and the ordeal of the security check. The only bright spot, though it gave him pause, was the paucity of passengers, once one had moved in a long snaking line toward the band of Keystone Cops who had turned travel into a penitential exercise. Today he was at the barrier in moments. His ticket was examined as well as his passport. Rome? The squat little woman, bulging from her mannish uniform, seemed about to say something, but she waved him on through the metal detector. As usual, his miraculous medal caught the attention of the apparatus. He loosened his collar and brought out the medal. A feral creature gazed at it with suspicion.

"What is it?"

"A miraculous medal."

A blank look. Were there no Catholics left in Boston?

"What does it do?"

Dear God. A sarcastic response was on his lips: It gets me stopped at airport security. But no. He explained that it was a religious medal.

This was followed by hesitation, and then, as if in a concession to tolerance, he was waved through. The man called after him. "I'm Protestant myself."

The episode seemed symbolic of the present state of world affairs. Long ago, in Paris on the Rue de Bac, Our Lady had miraculously produced the medals of which the one he wore was a copy. A heavenly gesture of protection for a fallen world. Now it had become, if not a sign of contradiction, at least an impediment to movement in this vale of tears.

There were two other passengers in business class. The seats behind stretched away, row after row, with here and there the top of a head visible. Was there anyone in first class? He was treated with consummate attention. Perhaps the fey young attendant was Catholic? Apparently not. He addressed Jay as Sir. He was offered a drink before takeoff. Surprising himself, he asked for scotch and water. When it came he sipped it as if it were medicine.

⸎

Thoughts at thirty-eight thousand feet are kaleidoscopic, between sleep and waking. In the first hour, he read his breviary, and when he put it away, he was offered another drink. Why not? Another scotch and water. There was a television set that could be lifted from the arm of his chair. He tried it out of curiosity. A newscast, a montage of rioting, burning, rampaging, in the streets. He turned it off and put it away. To think that he had been accused of being the cause of that. He said his rosary. He slept.

He awoke to a darkened cabin. The couple across the aisle seemed to be sharing a seat. He turned away, looking out the window. A light winked at the end of the wing, beyond which were stars reduced by distance to tiny points of light. Once, they had provided the means of navigation across such oceans as that which lay below. He thought of Zelda's hysterical tale. The man who had sold him a photocopy of the missing fragment of the third secret had, in Sinclair's words, vamoosed. Had he been duped?

He drove the thought away as if it were a temptation against faith itself. He accepted a blanket from the attendant, declined another drink, wrapped himself in the blanket, hugging himself under its warming comfort, and slowly felt his sense of righteousness return.

Leonardo da Vinci was an armed camp, with carabinieri everywhere, but few passengers. He came out into the Italian sunlight and hailed a cab. After only a moment's hesitation, as if he had decided this on his restless flight, he gave the address of the Confraternity of Pius IX.

✣ III ✣

## We are all Semites.

Eugenio Cardinal Piacere had, in his youth, considered a vocation to the Cistercians, but he had entered the diocesan seminary in Bologna, his studies aimed at the secular priesthood. Every Italian schoolboy and schoolgirl read Manzoni, of course, but often that came down to only portions of *I Promessi Sposi*. Piacere's interest had gone deeper. He had read several times the great Milanese author's *La morale cattolica*, most recently in the three-volume critical edition of Romano Amerio. He read Rosmini's *The Five Wounds of the Church*; Rosmini had been with Pius IX before he fled to Gaeta. And of course Dante. The magnificent closing canto of the *Paradiso* had sent him to the writings of Bernard of Clairvaux, and his old dream of a contemplative vocation was reawakened. He made several retreats at a Trappist abbey. He was torn between continuing on the path his feet were on and definitively leaving the world for the monastery. His spiritual director had listened with patience, nodding his head. After a long silence, he said, "It is a temptation."

It was difficult to regard the austere life of a Trappist as a temptation, but Piacere had resolved to be guided by his director, not by what could very well be simply his whims. He continued on the path his feet were on.

Now years later he was a prince of the Church and acting secretary of state and facing the greatest crisis of modern times. From his retreat—the Holy Father was at the Villa Stritch outside the city, but only Piacere and one or two others knew this—he offered his prayers and advice of a rather transcendental kind, not much help in dealing with the string of visitors who besieged his office.

The Holy Father mused about his predecessors who had preached crusades. He remembered Lepanto and the battle of Vienna. Small comfort there. Each man must understand the moment of history he occupies.

"And all because of a fraudulent document," Piacere said sadly.

"The donation of Constantine," murmured the pontiff.

A secure telephone had been installed between Piacere's office and the Villa Stritch. No important decision could be made without the consent of the Holy Father. He did not bother the pope with the importunate demands of Chekovsky.

"Now I see why you have withheld the reports," the Russian ambassador purred.

"And why is that?"

"Obviously they show that the assassination attempt was an initiative of the Turks. If you had made this public, what we are now seeing would have happened earlier."

Piacere had not read the reports in question.

"Releasing them now is your only hope."

"Hope?"

"If you show that these mad Muslims have been attacking you all along, public opinion will be swayed in your favor."

"Interesting."

"And my country will at last be publicly exonerated. It is a matter of justice."

"I cannot authorize their release."

"The city is going up in flames, you are under siege, and you cannot authorize their release?"

"Only the Holy Father can do that."

"Then ask him. Beg him. I will beg him. Get me an appointment with him."

"You know he has left the Vatican."

"And you know where he has gone."

Piacere remembered the late Cardinal Maguire talking about the visits of this tenacious ambassador. Diplomacy is a duplicitous art and provided the means of ending, if on a sour note, the interview. Piacere had not quite promised Chekovsky an answer from the Holy Father.

❖

Carlos Rodriguez expressed hope of obtaining the missing authentic document. Only then could it be made clear that it was a forged message that had ignited the seething animosity of Muslims for the world that Christianity had built.

There was no such enmity between Christians and Jews. The first Christians had all been Jews. If there was a dispute then it was between Jews, those of the old and those of the new dispensation. Pius XI had said it in *Mit brennender Sorge*. We are all Semites. It was otherwise with Islam.

Christian persecution of Jews had been condemned even while it was going on, not efficaciously perhaps, but depriving it of any theological grounds.

The Prophet had proclaimed hegemony over all men, bringing them to heel by the sword if necessary. Jihad. What compromise could there be with such a religion? At Regensburg, the Holy Father had spoken of that ancient quarrel, had like his predecessor invoked the autonomy of reason as well as faith, but reason in the sense he had in mind had no place in Islam.

In the past, the Iberian Peninsula had been a Muslim province, a dark period for the Jews and Christians in that area. Is that what awaited the whole of Europe now? Of more than Europe?

However fraudulent the document that had set off the present conflagration, it had touched on a historic truth. That was why comparing the forgery with the authentic third secret of Fatima held out only a wan hope. But it was the only hope they had. He urged Rodriguez to get it as soon as possible.

"Who has it?" Piacere asked.

"An ex-KGB agent."

"KGB!"

Was Chekovsky playing a game with him? But surely if the ambassador could produce the missing document, he would. What more effective way of securing the release of the reports on the attempted assassination of John Paul II.

When they had publicized the secret in 2000, in the expectation that thereby, once and for all, the wild speculations of people like Jean-Jacques Trepanier and Bishop Catena could be silenced, they had of course been astonished by the reaction.

To be accused of deliberately misleading the faithful in such a matter!

Trepanier refused to accept that the Holy Father had fulfilled the requests of Fatima, and this even in the face of Sister Lucia's own assurances. He wanted the Holy Father to declare from the Chair of Peter that he was dedicating Russia to the Immaculate Heart of Mary. His quarrel seemed to be not with the fact of the dedication—it had been made—but with its mode.

Bishop Catena was what the Americans called another kettle of fish. Vatican II, an ecumenical council, had departed from the traditional teaching of the Church! But such voices had some semblance of a claim.

Piacere had read Romano Amerio's *Iota Unum*. More than once. It was a sober book, written more in sorrow than in anger, the book of a loyal son of the Church. Amerio's analyses were often penetrating and convincing, especially those that bore on what von Balthazar had called the para-council, the interpretations of the spirit of the Council made by some theologians and members of the press. One would not of course go as far as Lefebvre, but even Lefebvre was now getting, posthumously, many of the concessions that he had demanded.

Paul VI, speaking of the post-council, had said that the smoke of Satan had entered into the Catholic Church. Not a remark that the successor of Saint Peter would lightly make. But the tradition of dissent from the magisterium had continued to flourish in the Church, in Germany, in France, in the Netherlands, and derivatively in the United States.

There was little to choose from between the Trepaniers and Catenas and the Hans Kungs.

"Does the man want money?" he had asked Rodriguez.

"That has not come up."

"You might look into that."


## ❖ IV ❖

### "Have you discussed this with Vincent?"

Residents of the Domus Sanctae Marthae no longer regarded the ancient walls of Vatican City as adequate protection from the raging mobs outside. An archbishop had been attacked as he crossed Saint Peter's Square and escaped with his life only when a band of Polish pilgrims had come to his aid. He brought back news of the placards hung on the very doors of Saint Peter's, in Arabic, which he could not read, and of the struggle on the porch of the basilica as crazed zealots tried to tip one of the great statues of the apostles onto the broad staircase below. Prelates particularly were advised to wear secular clothes if they had to venture outside the walls. The guards at the gates had been reinforced. No longer was the Renaissance splendor of the uniforms designed by da Vinci in evidence. Now the guards looked indistinguishable from the armed soldiers one had associated with the Holy Land.

The great question was, if the Vatican is not a haven, what is?

Some spoke of returning to their native countries to wait out the violence, but the news from those countries was scarcely more encouraging than that in Rome itself.

Where else in Rome and its environs was safety to be found?

John Burke knew that the Holy Father had been flown to the Villa Stritch outside the city. It was where he had lived until he was offered rooms in the Domus. When the violence did not subside—as all had hoped it would, with the mob spending its fury and then allowing peace to return—he became more concerned about Heather.

She listened in silence when he proposed that he spirit her away to the Villa Stritch.

"But the sisters will remain?" she asked.

"For now."

"I will stay with them."

Not a mile away was the Colisseum where Christians had been killed for the sport of emperors and the entertainment of the mob. Heather looked like a cinematic version of one of the Christian girls who had waited to be led into the arena.

Equally close was the Marmatine prison in which Peter and Paul had been confined. Both had ended as martyrs for the faith they had helped spread so rapidly throughout the known world.

The whole history of the Church could be read in terms of persecution and martyrdom. Periods of peace seemed anomalous, not the standard.

John persisted. "Heather, I feel responsible for you."

"Have you discussed this with Vincent?"

"I will, if you'd like."

"Please."

The couple seemed devoted to one another, but on a level far above the usual relation of man to woman, though doubtless for different reasons. John found Traeger an enigma. After his sudden disappearance following Brendan's horrible death in the Empedocles compound, John had shared in the general suspicion of the man. But Heather had dispelled such suspicions, he was not quite sure how. Her endorsement of Traeger seemed sufficient. He agreed to talk with Traeger about Heather's possible move to the Villa Stritch.

He telephoned the Casa and asked for Traeger. The phone rang four times before it was answered.

"Yes?"

"You sound half asleep. Look, this is John Burke. I have to see you. Will you be there for the next hour?"

Another sleepy, almost unintelligible yes. Apparently he had disturbed Traeger's nap.

He left the Vatican wearing street clothes, having removed the Roman collar from his Selma shirt and put it in his shoulder bag. The guards at the gate seemed almost hesitant to let him through.

"Is it important, Father?"

"Yes." What is the objective scale of importance?

"Would you like someone to accompany you?"

John looked at the guards. With one of them at his side, he would be more rather than less of a target. He thanked them for the offer and emerged from the gate. To his left was the tunnel leading to the other side of the Tiber, not designed for pedestrians. At the river he looked toward the Vatican and saw the mass of people surging toward the Via della Conciliazione. And heard them, a low animal roar. He turned and walked toward Trastevere.

When he crossed the bridge, he saw the distinctive tower of the great synagogue of Rome, the oldest Jewish quarter in Christendom, where Saint Paul had come to give his fellow Jews the good news. Even as he looked at it, there was a tremendous explosion. Stones, cobbles, pieces of machinery, perhaps pieces of people, rose with eerie slowness into the air, as if trying to escape the explosion. Sirens began to sound when John reached the other side of the river, and he started to move more quickly toward the Torre Argentina. Once there, he hurried through a narrow street, past the L'Eau Vive, a restaurant run by French nuns. On the door was a sign. *Chiuso.* Closed.

Minutes later he was at the Casa. Inside the great arched entrance was a wrought iron gate. He pressed the bell beside it. An unintelligible reply. He stepped close to the speaker.

"Father Burke."

A little ping as the gate was unlocked. He pushed through, stepped to his left, and punched the button for the elevator. On the third floor, he went down a corridor that turned sharply twice and then he was at Traeger's room.

He knocked, looked left and right, and was glad he lived in the Domus and not here. Still, there were priests who had lived here for years, and bishops, Archbishop Miller, now in Vancouver, among them. He knocked again. Then he took the handle, turned it, and found the door unlocked.

"Vincent?"

He must be in the bathroom. That door was closed. John stepped into the room.

The window he faced seemed to light up as the blow struck him, solidly on the head. He made one step forward and then dropped into oblivion.

✤ V ✤

## *Quis custodiet custodes?*

Rodriguez brought Donna Quando with him, and Traeger told them the news of the abduction of Father John Burke. With all the rioting in the streets, the howling and burning and desecration of sacred places, it might have seemed only a small additional outrage. But it didn't. The image of Laura formed in Traeger's mind. All tragedies are personal.

"Just carried him out of here?" Carlos Rodriguez asked.

"The portiere said they went out the gate singing, one man held up by two others. He was more interested in getting the gate locked again."

"After the horse is stolen." Carlos looked at Traeger significantly when he said it.

Donna was looking around the cell-like room in the Casa del Clero. "You've been staying here?"

"We thought it was safe," Carlos said.

"They thought it was me," Traeger told her.

She looked him over with a not-quite smile. "They must have been working with a vague description."

"Let's get out of here," Carlos said. "Bring your things."

Traeger was packed in a minute. "You think they'll be back?"

"I quit thinking a long time ago."

Up a narrow street they found a bar and took an inside table. "How's Dortmund?" Traeger asked.

"We moved him to the Villa Stritch, Vincent. He reads a lot."

"He's making up for lost years. I want to see him."

"Do you know Father Trepanier?" Donna asked.

Traeger looked at her. "Yes."

"He's in Rome. Out by the Anulare, staying with the Confraternity of Pius IX."

Donna had learned this from Father Harris. Now Carlos looked at her.

"Harris came to the Domus," she said. "We had a nice talk. I think he's disenchanted."

"The confraternity has been remarkably silent about recent events."

"They can't decide whether it's good news or bad."

"Not bad enough to be good?"

"I suppose. He came to see Remi Pouvoir."

Now Traeger and Carlos looked at one another. They remembered the wispy little fellow who seemed to blend into the dust of the archives. Traeger remembered that the priest had carried an empty archival box to a table as if it were heavy.

"What do we know about Pouvoir?"

Donna opened the shoulder bag she had placed on her lap. "This is his dossier from the archives." She handed it to Carlos. "I had the cleaning lady let me in his room. It doesn't even look lived in. Of course, he spends all day in the archives, works late."

"We never questioned him," Traeger said to Carlos.

Carlos seemed to be going over in his mind that scene in the archives when they had discovered that the third secret was missing. Pouvoir had seemed just another item in the archives. The invisible man.

"Better late than never." This was meant as an instruction to Donna.

⁂

Carlos drove him to the villa outside the city where Dortmund had been stashed. He was sitting outside, smoking his pipe under a palm tree, the second volume of Shelby Foote's narrative of the Civil War on his lap.

"You look comfortable."

"I miss Marvin."

"Do dogs go to heaven?"

Dortmund frowned. He would never let sentimentality trump theology. He listened as Traeger told him of the abduction of John Burke. The old man winced and fell silent. He looked across the lawn. "When they learn it isn't you, they'll be in touch."

"Who is they?" Traeger asked.

Dortmund tipped his head to one side.

Traeger said, "Anatoly has been working alone."

"No one works alone."

Meaning that someone had been keeping an eye on Anatoly. Well, someone had been keeping an eye on him, too, and on Dortmund.

"*Quis custodiet custodes?*" Dortmund mused. He shook his head. "That doesn't sound right."

"What does it mean?"

"Who will watch the watchers? It's like a daisy chain, just going on and on."

"No unwatched watcher?" Traeger said.

Dortmund groaned. "I'm a bad influence on you."

"Maybe I should stay here."

"You couldn't get in." Dortmund leaned forward. "The pope is staying here."

Donna Quando had lent him her car. Traeger went down the walk to the parking lot, got in, and took out his pulsing cell phone. It was Carlos. The Russians had just delivered the fugitive Vincent Traeger to the American Embassy.

"Is John Burke all right?"

"Fit as a fiddle." A pause. "Is that right?"

"Right as rain."

He could imagine Carlos making note of yet another enigmatic saying.

"Be careful," Traeger said.

❖

It seemed unnecessary advice in a city that was completely out of control. Traeger left Donna's car at the Vatican and walked to the metro. It was still operating. The cars were jammed with people, rocking along beneath the Eternal City, apparently observing a temporary truce. He got out at the Spanish Steps station and walked up the road to the Pincio. On a walkway that was lined with the busts of famous Italians, he sat on a bench by a bust of Thomas Aquinas.

Waiting.

No one works alone. Every watcher is watched. He lit a cigarette and felt suddenly tired. Physically tired. Tired of the goddamn modern world. Someone sat beside him.

"They got the wrong Traeger."

He didn't turn to look at Anatoly. "I heard."

"Can we make an exchange?"

"It's a little late."

"Can you get the report?" The report of the assassination attempt on John Paul II.

"You still want it?"

Anatoly's eyes burned with a mad desire for that document, the document he thought would redeem a lifetime misspent in the service of his country.

"Where?" Traeger asked.

Anatoly thought. "Do you know the North American College?"

"I can find it."

"It's a stone's throw from the Vatican," Anatoly said.

An unhappy choice of expressions in the circumstances.

"I just knock on the door?" Traeger asked.

"The portiere's name is Lev. He will bring you to me."

"Where?"

"I'll be on the roof." He stood up. "No funny business."

"I work alone."

Anatoly went away up the path, cut across the lawn, then was gone.

The custodian's name is Lev. *Quis custodiet custodes?*

❖ PART III ❖

# CHAPTER ONE

❖ I ❖

"Is he up there?"

Traeger outlined the plan for Dortmund and watched his old chief's frown deepen. Exchanges with the enemy were always dangerous. Traeger knew that, which was why he had come to Dortmund, now well ensconced in the Villa Stritch.

"Are things quieting down?" he asked when Traeger showed up.

"Far from it. You're not keeping up with the news?"

Dortmund smiled. "No, thank God."

Was peace of mind a function of ignorance? Not to know that the global madness that had followed on the publication by Trepanier of a fake passage in the third secret of Fatima seemed to be increasing permitted Dortmund to sit on his little balcony reading Jane Austen and enjoying the view of the magnificent grounds. This is where the pope had sought refuge, but Traeger was sure that the pope was kept apprised of how things were going in the city, which doubtless was why he was still here.

Traeger explained. "The sooner I get the authentic document, the sooner we stand a chance of placating the Muslims and ending the burning and looting."

Dortmund had come unwillingly out of the eighteenth century of his novel. He had closed the book on his finger, but was obviously eager to open it again and immerse himself in the doings of the Bennet family.

"You'll be alone?" Dortmund said after he heard the plan.

"So will he."

"Let's hope so."

"He wants that report on the assassination attempt on John Paul II as much as the Vatican wants the authentic secret back."

"Then he can't be working alone."

"I think he is."

Dortmund shrugged. "Are you?"

"What do you mean?"

"Vincent, whoever blew your cover had a hostile intent."

Traeger had tried to believe that somehow it was Anatoly who was responsible for the publicity that had made his departure on the Empedocles plane with Heather seem like the last flight out of Casablanca. But that meant that either Anatoly had an accomplice in the agency or access to the KGB file on Traeger. Which in turn meant that Anatoly was not working alone. But there was more danger on the streets of Rome than there could possibly be on the roof of the North American College.

Rodriguez had taken Traeger to a nearby building that housed the Augustinians, from the roof of which they could study the North American College. Traeger brought it all closer with the binoculars Rodriguez handed him, checking the doorway that gave entrance to the roof, moving the glasses along the low ledge bordering it. There were chairs and tables scattered about. Students must go up there to relax, for the view. There was no one on the roof at the time.

Rodriguez drew his attention to other buildings higher up the hill from the college.

"You'll be in view at all times."

"No," Traeger said. "I gave my word."

"That you would come alone. And so you shall."

"The man is a pro, Carlos. The first thing he would have done is make just such a survey as this. He would know if I'm not alone."

Reluctantly, Rodriguez agreed that he would not have men on those nearby buildings. Traeger wished that he could believe him.

He had printed out the assassination report that had been on the hard drive of his laptop all along. The pre-edited report, from which Dortmund had excised all indications of their own involvement in those long-ago events before he turned it in. It was in exchange for that report that Anatoly would turn over the authentic third secret of Fatima.

"Wednesday," Anatoly had said on Monday.

"Wednesday."

"I will meet you on the roof."

"What time?"

"Three."

"Okay."

"Three in the morning."

Traeger smiled. Anatoly was a pro. The college would be asleep; it would be too dark for observers to monitor the exchange from nearby buildings.

"I'll be there."

On Tuesday at two in the afternoon Traeger's cell phone vibrated.

"Yes?"

"Now." It was the voice of Anatoly.

The connection was broken. The Three Little Pigs. Anatoly wanted to meet a day earlier than agreed. Traeger approved. Now he need not worry that Rodriguez would have people watching over the exchange.

Taken literally, "now" meant the time Anatoly had called. But Traeger had to get from the Casa del Clero to the North American College, a fair distance in the best of conditions, but now, with the city still erupting, public transportation shut down, and the whine of sirens as fire trucks tried to control conflagrations, it was like crossing a battlefield during a major operation. He could only hope Anatoly took into consideration the difficulties he faced.

He took a circuitous route, avoiding the Piazza Navona, crossing the Vittorio Emanuele through a crowd of demonstrators, cutting through the Campo dei Fiori to the river. The North American College was across the Tiber, and the bridge was jammed with abandoned cars, charred ruins that had gone up in flames on the first day of the riots. Traeger picked his way among them. In the backseat of one half-intact vehicle, a couple snuggled, love among the ruins.

On the far side, Traeger took out his cell phone and pressed buttons as he walked. The hope that he would find the number from which Anatoly had called recorded on his phone so he could tell him he was coming was rewarded. He punched and listened through a dozen rings, moving swiftly as he did.

"Pronto."

"Anatoly?" Traeger asked.

"Eh?"

Traeger hung up. He had not reached Anatoly's cell phone. A public phone? Were they still working? Thanks to satellites, communication through cell phones was the one sure way left during this tumultuous upheaval.

Lev, the portiere, was apparently expecting him. He was an unshaven man whose eyes would not meet Traeger's. He let Traeger in without a word and pointed him to the stairway.

"Is he up there?"

Lev shrugged.

By the time Traeger got up the final staircase and was facing the door to the roof he was huffing and puffing. He paused to catch his breath. He was not as young as he used to be, no doubt of that. But who was? He pushed the door open and went out onto the roof. Immediately his eyes were drawn to the great dome of Saint Peter's to his left. It was so close that he felt that he could reach out and touch it. He looked around the roof, but there was no sign of Anatoly. Traeger crossed to the ledge and sat. Anatoly must have watched him enter the building and would be waiting to make sure he was really alone.

Traeger shook a cigarette from his package and lit up. A low animal roar lifted from the streets below. He could not see Saint Peter's Square but knew that, as it had been for days, it was filled with an angry chanting crowd. They had been calling for the pope to show himself at the window, as he did for the Angelus on Sundays. What would they do if they knew that the pope was not in the Vatican?

He finished his cigarette, checked his watch, and waited. Half an hour went by, and still he waited. Had something gone wrong? When he moved his arm, he could feel the printout in his inner pocket. He looked at the buildings higher up on the hill. Would Anatoly have observed him come onto the roof from a vantage point up there before coming to join him?

After an hour and two more cigarettes, impatience grew. And then he felt the vibration of his phone.

"Yes?"

"Later." Anatoly.

"Later than what?"

No reply.

"When?"

But the connection was broken. He returned the cell phone to his pocket and went angrily to the doorway. Going down all those stairs was easier than coming up them, but he was now in a foul mood. When he got to the ground floor, there was no sign of Lev. Seminarians were moving up and down the hallway.

He tried to see the exchange through Anatoly's eyes. Anatoly would know the value of the document he had, how desperately it was wanted by the Vatican. How tempting it would be to overpower him, repossess their stolen property, to hell with any exchange. Grudgingly, he approved of Anatoly's caution.

Since he was so close, he decided to visit Heather.

✣ II ✣

*Sub specie aeternitatis.*

Heather Adams was told by Father John Burke that Laura had called, anxious about her. She wanted to send a plane to bring Heather home.

"Has Vincent contacted you, Father?"

"No."

"I wouldn't want to just go off and leave him."

The difficulty lay in knowing how long Traeger meant to stay in Rome. Returning to the States presented difficulties for him, of course. After all, he had been a hunted man when they flew off together in the Empedocles plane. The truth was that Heather was looking for an excuse to prolong her stay.

At the convent, she followed the routine of the nuns, the office in chapel, Mass, periods of silence, but also the usual housekeeping chores, laundry, keeping everything spotless. For several hours in the afternoon, they sat in the common room, sewing, painting, reading, the happy babble a contrast to the bracketing silences. How innocent they all seemed, how untouched by the world. Did they realize what was going on just outside the Vatican walls, in Rome, in cities throughout the world? In college, Heather had seen a performance of Bernanos's *Dialogues of the Carmelites*, set in a convent during the time when the French Revolution turned bloodiest and the decision was made to stamp out religion. All those nuns were eventually guillotined and Heather remembered the singing as they mounted the scaffold, going out of sight of the audience, the number of voices diminishing until there was only one singer. Then silence. What a dreadful thought that these happy, holy women faced a similar fate.

The seed of Heather's conversion had been planted by that play.

In the convent, the point of life was brought into brilliant focus. Our few years on earth are given us so that we might prepare for eternity. Yet most lives are passed in distraction, in busyness, in fretting and worrying about things of only passing importance. It is as if most lives are lived in order to obscure the point of it all, to become forgetful that all our joys and sorrows here must end in death. Once, in a philosophy class, the professor had asked them what they thought of death. As little as possible, would have been the honest answer. And then he had asked whether, in the light of all the advances in medicine, they thought a cure for death would be forthcoming. Most of the students had thought so! As if mortality were a flaw that could be remedied by medicine. Postponed, surely, and made more tolerable, but eradicated? And Heather realized that she, too, had some such thought, insofar as she thought of it at all. These cheerful nuns with whom she was staying lived their lives *sub specie aeternitatis*. Once, she might have thought it morbid to have the constant reminder that this is a vale of tears, that we are meant for something incredibly greater, union with God himself. Heather came to dread the thought that she must eventually leave this community and go back to her old life. She thought of her oratory and it seemed such a poor substitute for the routine of the convent.

Was that a temptation? She scarcely dared think that she had a vocation to the religious life. Her job at Empedocles awaited her, with all the time-consuming tasks that made up her day.

In the convent library she found a book, *Fatima in Lucia's Own Words*, the memoirs of the surviving seer of Fatima, after she had become a nun, a Carmelite. Interleafed with the printed pages were facsimiles of the original document, in Sister Lucia's handwriting. Reading the book, Heather realized how weird it was that the handwritten document recounting the so-called secrets of Fatima had ended up in Empedocles, brought there by Father Brendan Crowe. It must have been to get possession of that document that the man who had broken into the guest residence had killed the Irish priest, and then, surprised, fled without the thing he had come for. Heather had taken it home for safekeeping in her oratory and later gave it to Vincent Traeger. He had put it in the safe in his office. His secretary had been murdered, the safe broken into, and the document stolen. Where was it now?

Most horrifying of all was the forged document that Gabriel Faust had bought with millions of dollars of Mr. Hannan's money and that Father Trepanier had made public, using it as a weapon in his strange crusade. As a result, the world had erupted in such a way that Heather was reminded of the madness that had swirled around the Paris convent that provided the scene for *Dialogues of the Carmelites*.

Later that day, in chapel, the Mother Superior had come to Heather and whispered that she had a visitor. Heather left the chapel with reluctance. The Mother Superior had asked her earlier to speak to a reporter who wanted to do a story on the convent, Angela di Piperno. Heather could see that the young woman regarded the contemplative life the nuns led with fascinated dread.

"Are you a postulant?" she asked Heather.

"Good heavens, no. I'm just a guest."

"Tell me about yourself."

The young woman's question had so surprised Heather that she obliged.

Now Vincent Traeger was waiting for her in the visiting parlor.

"You've shaved off your beard."

"It looked too much like a disguise, Heather. Father Burke tells me that his sister Laura thinks you should get out of here and go home."

"Will you go, too?"

He paused. "There is something I have to do first."

"The third secret?"

"Yes."

"I can wait."

He thought about it. "You're safe here, in any case."

Vincent told her that he had made arrangements to exchange a report he had written for the authentic document.

"You know who has it?" Heather asked.

"He contacted me."

"Who is it?"

He looked away, as if trying to think of a way to say it. "A killer. A former Soviet agent."

"A killer."

He nodded. "He killed Father Crowe, for one. Beatrice, my secretary, for another."

"Good Lord. Vincent, you must be careful!"

"I am dealing with a careful man."

"What on earth does he want that document for?"

"It is what I have that he wants. We will trade."

"And then we can go home?"

"Things should settle down once it can be shown that the passage Father Trepanier made public is a forgery."

He did not sound very hopeful of that result, at least as an immediate consequence of allowing representatives of those who had been enraged by what Father Trepanier had made public to compare it with the original document.

"When will you make the exchange?" she asked.

"I'm waiting to hear."

"God bless you, Vincent."

He seemed startled by the sentiment. Heather was a bit surprised herself that she had uttered it. It was a phrase that lost its meaning by repetition, like "good-bye." She had some inkling of how Vincent had spent his life, from their conversations while she was putting him up in her house. Was the man he was to meet his counterpart? Had Vincent, too, killed?

She went with him to the door and watched him go down the pathway toward the basilica. One had no sense in Saint Peter's Square that the Vatican was indeed a hill, one of the seven hills of Rome, but within the walls the steep paths, the long ascent from the Domus Sanctae Marthae, made that inescapable.

Heather remained outside, using her cell phone to call Laura. It was still morning in New Hampshire.

"Is it as bad as it seems on television, Heather?" Laura asked.

"They've put me in a convent inside the Vatican where all is peace and quiet."

"Heather, Mr. Hannan is very anxious about you. He feels responsible for letting you go there."

"He mustn't worry, Laura. I am perfectly all right."

"And Vincent Traeger?"

"He just left here."

"Don't tell me he's staying in the convent, too?"

"Hardly."

There were voices in the background. Laura talked away from the phone. Then she said, "Mr. Hannan wants to speak to you."

And then she heard the authoritative voice of Ignatius Hannan. "Heather, I want you back here."

"In just a little while."

"What's the delay?" he demanded.

She decided that she could tell him something of what Vincent had told her. There was silence in New Hampshire, as he seemed to be digesting this.

"I'm coming over," he said.

"Do you think that's wise?"

"It wasn't wise to send you there. Of course I had no idea what was about to happen. And I feel responsible for that."

"You're not responsible."

Now he was talking away from the phone. When he was back, he said, "We'll be on our way in hours."

"We?"

"Laura and I. Probably Ray as well. See you soon."

Heather put away her phone and went back inside, intent on enjoying what was left of her stay.

### ❖ III ❖

### "A busman's holiday."

Chekovsky stood before a painting by Paul Klee with his head tipped to one side as if sunk in aesthetic meditation. The man beside him studied the museum catalog.

"Childish," Chekovsky grunted.

"Not quite."

Chekovsky considered the response, a small smile on his lips. Ambiguous. Not quite as good or not quite as bad, take your pick. He moved slowly past other paintings that seemed intended to frustrate one's expectations of art. Perhaps that was a definition of modernity.

In the brightly lit cafeteria, he sat at a little circular table with a marble top and wrought iron legs, facing a wall that was a mirror. In a residence, such a mirror would have the function of increasing the apparent size of a room. Here its function was more difficult to discern. Given the setting, the Borghese Gardens just beyond, a windowed wall would have made more sense.

But it was because of the mirror that Chekovsky liked the cafeteria as a meeting place. His contact came into the museum restaurant, still holding the catalog, and came clattering among the tables toward him. Not that he joined him. He took the table next to Chekovsky's, the backs of their chairs not quite touching.

"A busman's holiday." Chekovsky had spent his earliest years as a diplomat in the consulate in Birmingham, Alabama. It had always been his practice, wherever he was assigned, to move beyond competence in the native tongue into the richer colloquial world.

"Meaning?"

But before Chekovsky could give himself the pleasure of a pedantic explanation, Remi Pouvoir was interrupted by the waiter who posed for himself in the mirror. The waiter turned his head to one side, then the other; he shifted his feet. Ignoring Pouvoir, he also took his order. He glided to Chekovsky.

*"Signore?"*

*"Cappucio."*

*"Bé."*

Pouvoir had ordered tea and made a ceremony out of pouring it, squeezing lemon into the brew, and adding several packets of sugar. He tasted it with a connoisseur's expression. The verdict seemed to be that it was passable. And then he reported.

Chekovsky felt a bit like the waiter while he listened, posing in the mirror, trying out expressions, not missing a word. Were such precautions necessary anymore? They were when one was dealing with a maverick like Anatoly. The man was a throwback, an anachronism. God knows what he might do. What possible use could that assassination report be to an idiot like that?

"Traeger has it?"

"There will be an exchange," Remi Pouvoir said, as if addressing his raised cup.

Chekovsky already knew this, from Lev. A plurality of sources was an elementary precaution. What Lev did not know was when the exchange would take place. There had been a trial meeting, with Traeger showing up at the North American College and cooling his heels on the rooftop for an hour before answering his cell phone and leaving. Did Anatoly suspect that the rooftop was under observation? The cryptic phone message had been picked up. "Later." There would have been no need for Lev to lock the rooftop door once the two men met.

"Traeger got the report from Rodriguez?"

Pouvoir reflected on this, in the mirror. His shoulders moved. "Presumably."

"The report is no longer in the archives?"

"No."

So the exchange would be of two stolen documents. Traeger would obtain the famous third secret, and Anatoly would have the assassination report he lusted for. The former agent's quixotic purpose was to prove that the KGB had nothing to do with the attempted assassination of John Paul II. What would he do when he learned that was not true? Well, he would not have the report long enough to study it.

"You would have saved all concerned a good deal of trouble if you had delivered it to me." Chekovsky tried not to sound petulant.

In this lovely setting, high above the Piazza del Popolo, the dome of Saint Peter's visible in the hazy distance, it was possible to ignore the angry mobs raging through the streets of the city below. Pouvoir had assured him that the passage made public by Jean-Jacques Trepanier was a fake. A fake so obvious only a fool would have been taken in by it. But it was the message, the longed-for message from heaven, that explained the credulity of Trepanier. What he and others had been agitating to see was apparently the foretelling of what was now going on in the streets of Rome, Paris, and Baghdad, the jihad now seeming to have the sanction of the Mother of God's prophecy.

"I thought he was one of yours," Remi Pouvoir said.

"No longer."

"You might have told me."

Pouvoir had provided the information Anatoly had needed in order to move like a scythe through the Apostolic Palace, slaying cardinals as he went. The rampage had been pure terror, without rational purpose. And the bloodbath had been hushed up by the Vatican, making it even more purposeless. As purposeless as his chiding Remi Pouvoir and being chided in return.

When Chekovsky had been importuning Cardinal Maguire, seeking the release to his government of everything in the archives concerning the assassination attempt, he had not yet known that Pouvoir was their man within the walls. For decades he had been dormant, unused, an insurance policy against they knew not what. It had been so easy to imagine that such a mole, forgotten for so long, would have lost the youthful zeal that had made him apt for so prolonged and uneventful an assignment. The breakup of the USSR could have been taken to write finis to any loyalty he was supposed to have. For a time, Chekovsky had thought Brendan Crowe might be the mole.

He almost missed now those sophistic exchanges with Maguire and Crowe. However frustrating, they had taken place on the far side of events, when gaining possession of that assassination file had seemed a diplomatic possibility. Oh, how he had dreamt of feeding it all to the flames once he had it. Whether or not his personal fears were borne out by the reports.

Chekovsky licked the cream of the cappuccino from his lips, then patted them with the absurdly small paper napkin. The waiter approached, watching himself in the mirror, and dropped the *conto* on the table. He dealt another to Pouvoir, with a flick of the wrist. The waiter was an ass, and doubly so because of the mirror. Chekovsky pushed back his chair. It made an unnerving screech. He did not rise.

The fat little priest who had taken a table near the entrance seemed to be making a point of not noticing Chekovsky. Or was it Pouvoir he pretended not to notice? The ambassador glanced at Pouvoir's reflection. Of course it had occurred to him that the little archivist had turned double agent, working with Rodriguez and Vatican security. Whatever his own anxiety to get and destroy those assassination reports, the anxiety of the Vatican to get back its Fatima file had a more global importance. Did they seriously think that they could call in the imams and pore over the documents, the false and the authentic, and then the rioting in the streets would stop? Well, Chekovsky thought with smug satisfaction, he would gain possession of both files.

"What would they give for it?" he asked Pouvoir.

"What you want."

"But that is gone."

"I think Rodriguez will be able to find it."

Of course. Chekovsky rose then, ignoring himself in the mirror. Avoirdupois had once been a sign of eminence in the Soviet diplomatic corps. Chekovsky had been affected against his will by all the nonsense in the West about obesity.

He paid his bill, ignoring the fat little priest by the entrance. He felt a fleeting camaraderie with the overweight cleric as he went out the door and moved at a dignified pace toward his waiting car.

## ✢ IV ✢

### "To what end?"

When Jean-Jacques Trepanier showed Bishop Catena the photocopy for which he had paid so large a sum, the older man had studied it closely. He got out a book and compared the handwriting with a facsimile of Sister Lucia's.

"They are indistinguishable," he murmured. He looked up at Trepanier. "The handwriting, not the Portuguese."

"How so?"

"Would she have used *'desagravar'*?"

"As a matter of fact, she does."

As had been the case whenever he met with Catena, there was initial verbal sparring as each tried to establish his primacy in the matters that concerned them both. Jay would not sit still for the suggestion that he was anything but an expert on what Lucia had written. Hadn't he learned Portuguese in order to read her in the original? Catena was now studying Trepanier as he had the photocopy.

"And who is Gabriel Faust?" Catena asked.

Trepanier told Catena what he knew of the art historian. "He seems to have disappeared," he added at the end.

"With his ill-gotten gains."

But Trepanier had no desire to dwell on what a dupe he had been. He had not come to Rome to be patronized by Catena. He told his old adversary of Vincent Traeger.

"I think he is working for Ignatius Hannan," Trepanier said.

"To what end?"

Trepanier gave Catena a little word picture of the eccentric electronics billionaire who had regained his faith and was determined to put his vast wealth at the service of his beliefs. Catena nodded with approval when he told him of the replica of the grotto of Lourdes on the grounds of Empedocles Inc. He told him of Hannan's plans for Refuge of Sinners.

"He had hired Gabriel Faust as director." It even sounded sarcastic.

"And he has disappeared?"

Trepanier stirred in his chair. "With Hannan's millions and my money."

"You might have persuaded Mr. Hannan to support your efforts."

"He proposed that I join my efforts to his!"

Catena's smile did not become him. Trepanier sat forward. It was important that he join forces with the confraternity. Catena had connections in Rome, in the Vatican. Surely he must see the unprecedented opportunity they had.

"Opportunity?"

Trepanier spelled it out for him. The document they had sought to have released in its entirety was still theirs for the getting. Didn't Catena understand the significance of what he had told him? Anatoly, the mysterious Russian, had the Fatima file. It was, one might say, in the public domain, no longer in the control of those in the Vatican with a vested interest in keeping the third secret a secret. There was of course no need to convince Catena that the supposed publishing of the third secret by Ratzinger in 2000 had been a ploy to damp down the continuing interest in what had not been made public.

"This faked message is a mere diversion. I can almost believe that it was engineered to discredit . . ." Jay was about to say "me" but stopped himself in time, saying instead "those of us with the interests of the Blessed Virgin at heart."

Catena's brows lifted and the corners of his mouth went down. "Causing global chaos in the process?"

"Oh, they would have hoped for a quick exposure . . ." Of course Catena had a point. It had eaten deeply into Trepanier's self-esteem that he had been taken in by such an interloper as Gabriel Faust. Had the art historian any notion of what that message could bring about? It helped, some, to deflect his own sense of guilt onto the flown Faust.

"The third secret was intended for the People of God," he said to Catena.

"Via the pope."

"But the pope was to make it known in nineteen sixty! The Vatican has lost its right to Sister Lucia's document. We have to get hold of it."

Catena had been subdued by the rioting, the sacrileges, the threats against the Church, no doubt of that, but under the effect of Trepanier's enthusiasm some of the old fire was rekindled.

"No one will believe anything the Vatican says anyway," Trepanier assured him.

As Catena's old self took hold, Trepanier suggested that he bring in Father Harris.

"I have told you everything he has told me." Catena sounded piqued.

"But I want to discuss what we must do."

⁂

Catena sent for him and ten minutes later Harris shuffled in. He wore the kind of sandals once favored by Franciscans, but this was because of the condition of his feet, supporting all that weight. Harris seemed a most improbable contact with friends in the Vatican, but perhaps that was in his favor. Harris eased himself into a chair, expelling air as he did so. His hands moved from the arms of his chair to meet on the vast expanse of his belly.

"Tell me about Remi Pouvoir," Trepanier urged.

Harris looked at Catena, who nodded.

Harris had become acquainted with Pouvoir while he was

working in the Vatican on Our Lady of La Salette. The apparitions at La Salette had not captured the wide attention that Lourdes and later Fatima had, largely because of the Church's efforts to discredit the caustic criticism of the hierarchy that the seer attributed to Our Lady of La Salette. Leon Bloy had had a great devotion to La Salette, and he had transferred it to his godson, the eventually world-famous Catholic philosopher Jacques Maritain.

"Maritain wrote a book on La Salette," Harris said.

"He did?" Trepanier asked this dubiously. He knew of no such title by Maritain.

"It was never published. While he was working on it, the Vatican put an embargo on discussions of Our Lady of La Salette. Maritain tried to get around the ban. During World War I he actually came to Rome, talked with the pope and others."

"And?"

"He never published the book."

"Converts can be so docile," Trepanier said. "What became of the manuscript?"

"It is at Kolbsheim where most of Maritain's papers and letters are. He and his wife are both buried there." Harris sighed. "I visited there."

"And saw the manuscript?"

"Yes."

Harris was not allowed to make notes as he studied what Maritain had written, but he did keep a diary, writing up what he remembered at night in his room. Remi Pouvoir had been fascinated when Harris returned with the tale. It was the beginning of their friendship.

"And Fatima," Trepanier said. "What does Pouvoir think of Fatima?"

"He told me he had read the third secret."

Trepanier leaned expectantly toward Harris. "What did he say?"

"Oh, he is a very discreet man."

"Didn't you ask him whether what was made public in two thousand was the whole story?"

"Yes."

"Well, what did he say?" Trepanier asked excitedly.

"He just smiled."

"And what did you take that to mean?"

Harris inhaled and exhaled. He made breathing seem an Olympic event. "What you take it to mean."

Harris then reviewed what he had learned of the former CIA agent, Vincent Traeger.

"I've met him," Trepanier said.

"In Rome?"

"No, no. In New Hampshire. He was flown here in one of Ignatius Hannan's planes."

Harris said, "He intends to exchange the CIA report on the attempted assassination of John Paul II for the Fatima file."

"How did you learn this?"

"Chekovsky, the Russian ambassador to Italy, told Pouvoir."

"Why would he do that?" Trepanier asked.

Harris thought for a moment. "People tell Remi things. Chekovsky actually suggested to Remi that he remove that file, the one on the assassination, and turn it over to Chekovsky."

"And he refused?"

"That file also seems to be missing from the archives."

"Good. Good." Trepanier looked brightly around. "That underscores how unreliable a custodian the Vatican is."

Harris grew uneasy. "We must not criticize Remi Pouvoir."

"Tell me about the plans for the exchange."

It seemed simple enough. Two men would meet on the rooftop of the North American College, exchange files, and go their separate ways. Except that one of those men was a rogue agent currently being sought in the United States.

"And the other is a murderer," Trepanier said.

"A murderer!"

"It is my guess that he is the one who broke into the guest residence hall at Empedocles and killed Father Brendan Crowe when he was surprised. No doubt that is when he came into possession of the Vatican file."

Harris nodded. "Remi is certain that Brendan Crowe removed the Fatima file from the archives."

"And flew off with it to Ignatius Hannan," Trepanier said. "Perhaps he meant to extort money from Hannan as Gabriel Faust did."

"So what can we do?" Catena asked.

Trepanier stood and smiled at the two men. "Your Excellency, I thank you for your hospitality. I think I shall take up residence elsewhere."

Harris and Catena waited.

"I will ask for one of the guest rooms at the North American College."

✧ V ✧

### "Our own streets are full."

The ambassadors to Italy from Syria, Iran, and Saudi Arabia arrived at the Vatican in the cars Cardinal Piacere had sent for them, the better to keep secret their acceptance of his invitation. The cars avoided the great streets, which were still in the control of the mob, a mob that would have erupted even more at the thought of these ambassadors accepting an invitation from the acting secretary of state of the Vatican. The cars slipped along the streets of the Borgo Pio and darted through Saint Anne's Gate, waved in by the alerted Swiss Guards. Cardinal Piacere had come down to meet them, as a conciliating gesture.

Protocol ruled as the four men bowed to one another. Piacere pointed to the door that was opened wide for these important guests. Small talk sufficed as they rose in the elevator. Father Ladislaw, who was filling in for Bernagni, ushered them into a room where brocade chairs were arranged as if for a seminar.

"I am grateful to you all for coming," Cardinal Piacere began, when they were seated stiffly before him.

"There must be no announcement of this visit," Syria said. There seemed to be real fear in his voice.

"Our discussion is covered by the most solemn and profound promise of total secrecy."

The ambassador from Saudi Arabia nodded. Of course this solemn promise had been a condition of their acceptance. But it seemed best to make it a formal premise of their meeting. It occurred to Piacere that these men were as terrified of the mobs surging through the streets as he himself was. It was nonsense to imagine that the rioters were somehow the instruments of these diplomats. The reverse would have been more accurate.

Piacere joined his hands as if in prayer. "Let me begin by

reminding you that the document that has caused all the trouble is, without any doubt, a forgery and a fake."

"Repudiate it!" The demand was in polyphony, several of his visitors speaking at once.

"You will have read the Holy Father's statement."

The pope had actually issued two statements, both of them, alas, characteristically cerebral. In his own name, Piacere had repudiated the forged document, saying it was an outrage to imagine that heaven wished a new crusade against the Muslim world. As he wrote the statement, Piacere tried not to think of Saint Bernard of Clairvaux, who in the twelfth century had urged on the crusaders.

"That is not enough, Your Eminence. Careful statements are not enough. The pope must apologize to the people of Islam. He must expose the one who forged that document. There must be punishment."

"Condign punishment," said Saudi Arabia smoothly. Piacere had never before seen him in anything other than the flowing robes and distinctive headdress of the ruling family, of which he was one of the numerous members. In his Western-style dress he might have been Omar Sharif. "I believe there are still oubliettes in the Castel Sant'Angelo."

Piacere listened carefully. Ladislaw took notes surreptitiously. The secretary of state said that he fully understood the desire that those who had contrived this crisis should receive fitting punishment.

"Contrived?" Syria said.

"As I have said, the inflammatory document is a fake."

"But does it not express the true sentiments of the Church toward Islam?"

Syria picked up his attaché case, placed it on his knees, and snapped it open. He drew out a sheaf of papers and began to read, his voice becoming falsetto with rage.

"Who wrote that?" Piacere asked.

"Oriana Fallaci." Syria made the name sound like a sexual aberration.

Piacere opened his hands. "My friend, Oriana Fallaci was not a Catholic. She called herself an atheist."

"A Catholic atheist."

"That is a contradiction in terms."

"Why did the pope receive her in a private audience?" Iran wanted to know.

Piacere had not expected this. At the time, he had thought the Holy Father's gesture of compassion a fitting one. But what must it have seemed to these men?

"She was dying," he said. "It was an act of compassion."

"Is it customary for popes to give a last blessing to atheists? And to such an atheist?"

From that, Syria turned to the pope's lecture at Regensburg in Germany. In it he had cited a Byzantine critic of Islam and the Arab world had erupted. It seemed a foretaste of what was happening now.

And then there was the Holy Father's insistence that the constitution of the European Union stress the essential role that Christianity had played in the formation of Europe. "This was a direct attack on the millions of Muslims now living in Europe, Your Eminence."

"The Holy Father's point was a historical one."

"Then why did he not speak of the great role Islam played in Spain?"

As the discussion continued, Piacere found himself surprised by his surprise that he was being confronted with an indictment of the Church, a bill of particulars against Catholicism. The forged message had proved to be merely an occasion that brought out all these scarcely suppressed resentments. In the manner of diplomats, he remained calm, noted what was said, and managed to avoid any reply that would compromise the Holy See. Eventually, gently, he went on the offensive.

"Gentlemen, it would be helpful if your governments would condemn the rioting and burning and sacrileges that are going on."

"Our own streets are full," cried one.

"Of course there has been no encouragement of these actions," said another.

"They are understandable, however unfortunate," the third remarked.

"Could you propose to your governments that they contrast this rioting with the peaceful faith of Islam?" As a boy, Piacere would have crossed his fingers when making such a remark.

Syria exploded. "You are blaming what has happened on us?"

"Of course not."

"Do you think that these people are enraged because of something we have done?"

"Would you like me to issue a statement that the Church does not blame responsible Muslims for what is happening?" Piacere asked.

They wanted nothing of the kind. They wanted an apology of the most abject sort. They wanted an admission that the Catholic Church had been an enemy of Islam for centuries and the instigator of crusades, the invasion and occupation of Arab lands in the name of the cross.

Piacere's suggestion that they have tea was indignantly refused. They had not come here to be placated in so meaningless a fashion.

"Let me tell you what the Holy Father wishes," Piacere said.

The three fell silent.

"The Holy Father would like your governments or your religious leaders or both to name a committee of Islamic scholars to come and study the true and authentic Fatima document. They will see that there is no similarity at all with this outrageous forgery."

"In order to exonerate the Holy See?" Syria asked.

"In order to see the truth of the matter."

Disdainful as they were of this proposal, they did not reject it out of hand. Clearly, they had no better proposal to put an end to the riots and demonstrations that were wracking their own countries as much as those of Europe. But the most he could get from them was agreement that they would bring the matter before their governments.

Piacere let Father Ladislaw take them down to their cars. Before they left, he thanked them for coming.

"That must not become known!"

"I have given you my word."

On Syria's lips seemed to tremble a litany of instances when Islam had regretted taking the word of Christians.

And then they were gone. Piacere went into his inner office and knelt on the prie-dieu there and invoked the aid of Our Lord and His Blessed Mother. And he had a very specific request. May we regain possession of the Fatima file so that scholars, if they were appointed, would have something to scrutinize.

## ❖ VI ❖

### "Didn't Saint Peter carry a sword?"

Joseph Ratzinger, when he first came to Rome as prefect of the Congregation for the Doctrine of the Faith, remarked that his new staff was smaller than that he had had as archbishop of Munich. Bureaucratically speaking, he had taken a demotion. It continued to be a feature of the Curia that the dicasteries were run, and run reasonably well, by a very small number of men. Compared to their secular counterparts, if such there were, they were risibly understaffed. The same thing could be said of Vatican security.

Presidents and prime ministers had special cadres of protective police, on duty twenty-four hours a day, forever on the alert for some maniacal attempt to harm the public person they were pledged to protect. There was no greater target for such madness than the pope. Would anyone believe how minimal the protection afforded him was? How few there were to keep harm from him?

"I have asked Father DiNoia to find me all the scriptural passages alluding to Our Lord's bodyguard."

That had been the pontiff's humorous response to the most recent suggestion that Carlos Rodriguez be allowed to bring his handful somewhat closer in number and firepower to the Secret Service that protected the American president.

DiNoia had suggested John 8:59, when the Pharisees took up stones to throw at Jesus but he walked through them unscathed.

*"Jesus autem abscondit se et exivit de templo,"* came the Bavarian murmur.

The problem was that the Vicar of Christ on earth did not have similar power to become invisible and thus elude his enemies.

❖

After the slaying of the previous secretary of state and his assistant, as well as of Cardinal Maguire, Carlos Rodriguez felt that he had a heaven-sent argument for enlarging his staff. How easily on that occasion the assassin could have surprised the pope at his desk. The matter was taken under advisement—small or large bureaucracies have the same modus operandi—but in the meantime Carlos was authorized to seek help from the wider world. Hence the call to Traeger.

Once, the civil arm could be counted on to supplement the small Vatican security contingent, but in those days the ornamental and largely symbolic Swiss Guards, always thought of as garbed in their Renaissance uniforms, seemed proportional to the danger. No matter that popes in the past had been kidnapped, chased from Rome, and, in the early centuries, martyred one after another. In a world of superpowers the little postage-stamp state of Vatican City had itself seemed an anachronism, a remnant of the papal states and papal armies and all the mix of secular and religious that had so incensed Dante. Within the walls, the attitude toward security had continued to be otherworldly.

"Fatalistic," Traeger had said, when he was briefed by Rodriguez.

"Providential," Carlos had replied.

"Didn't Saint Peter carry a sword?"

"He was told to put it away."

Summoning Traeger to Rome had turned out to be a mixed blessing. On the one hand, Carlos had favorable memories of the efficiency with which the agent had conducted his investigation into the assassination attempt on John Paul II. Of the various reports submitted to the Vatican by different investigative agencies, the American had been most circumstantial. And accusative. A Turk may have pulled the trigger and later stuck to his story that he had been acting alone, but Traeger had detected the Soviet hand manipulating the strings. The principal puppeteer had been Chekovsky, then in Moscow, now Russian ambassador to Italy. No wonder the man was concerned that the reports be turned over to him.

"Russia must not be tarnished with the misdeeds of the Soviet Union," Chekovsky had said unctuously during one of his efforts to have those reports in the archives released to him. Rodriguez had been told this by the late Brendan Crowe.

Crowe, Donna Quando had reported, surprisingly had contacts with the Confraternity of Pius IX. Her listening post at the

Domus had proved to be a fruitful source of information that seemed to bear on security, and her employment there kept her off Rodriguez's modest budget. The confraternity carried on a constant attack on the Vatican, but it was rhetorical, of words, not sticks and stones. Nonetheless, the fact that Crowe, the right-hand man of Cardinal Maguire, had been seen chatting on the parapet of the Castel Sant'Angelo with Catena and the corpulent Harris gave food for thought.

The thought was further fed when Crowe went off without fanfare to the United States where he was murdered in the residence for guests at Empedocles Inc. That episode had also sent Traeger on the run. He had been spirited out of the country on the plane that brought Heather Adams to Rome, her mission to turn over the forged message that had caused such turmoil in a world that seemed defined by the confrontation of a militant Islam and a wishy-washy Christendom. The gates of hell might never prevail against the Church, but that was no guarantee that Europe would not be colonized and turned into caliphates from the Channel to the Caucasus. The island of Vatican City had survived in a rising secularizing sea. How would it fare if surrounded by Islam?

Rodriguez had told Traeger's amazing story of the itinerary of the missing third secret of Fatima to Cardinal Piacere, but as yet had not committed it to writing. Imagine Crowe flying off to America with that file, being murdered when he had surprised the man come to steal it who then fled without the file, a file Heather had taken home, and then she had given shelter to the pursued Traeger, who took the file and stored it in his office safe in the mistaken hope that it would be secure there. His secretary had paid the price of his mistake on that score. All this had brought them to the point where Traeger was negotiating with the madman who had the third secret, offering to trade his report on the assassination attempt on John Paul II for the third secret of Fatima.

"Of course," Cardinal Piacere had said, when Rodriguez sought authorization for the exchange. "I am counting on the retrieval of that file."

The problem was that Rodriguez felt reduced to the role of spectator in the matter. Traeger and the madman he was dealing with would call the shots.

But Rodriguez meant to take his role of spectator seriously.

He stood now with Donna Quando on the roof of the Vatican Library. In the square below them, temporary shelters had been set up by the angry protestors. Banners with a strange device fluttered from the twin fountains in which children were disporting themselves. Wisps of smoke rose from the fires on which the squatters prepared their meals. But Rodriguez was checking from this site the visibility of the North American College. It was visible enough, the building, but from this vantage point the roof could not be seen.

Donna Quando had an alternative. Father Ladislaw's apartment was higher up the Janiculum hill.

"He lives up there?"

"Rather comfortably," Donna said.

It seemed an odd location for an assistant of the secretary of state, if only because it was outside Vatican City.

"That is not his address in the Vatican directory," Rodriguez said. "How did you hear of it?"

"Remi Pouvoir mentioned it."

"But will he let us use it?"

"I will make him an offer he can't refuse."

Rodriguez looked shocked. Had he added a Mata Hari to his force? But it was not concupiscence that Donna had in mind.

"I will tell him that we will ignore the fact that he has been leaking things to the press."

# Chapter Two

## ❖ I ❖

### He read around in Marcus Aurelius.

Neal Admirari had not thought he was being sent to a war zone when he accepted the Rome assignment. Like others of his generation, he had lived his working life with an eye to retirement. It wasn't that he didn't think he still had a lot of miles in him, but work had always seemed merely a means toward that future hyped by the insurance companies, a graying couple sunning themselves in Florida, sustained by their wise investments. Once, Lulu van Ackeren would have shared the yacht in which he floated about on an imaginary Gulf of Mexico. That, alas, was not to be. Meanwhile, the thought of vegetating in Rome while the rest of the world burned was not without its attractions. He remembered the trattorie and ristoranti, he remembered the sun, he remembered the women and the promissory hum that seemed to pervade the eternal city. Where better to approach the evening of his career, if not his life?

At first, there had been some semblance of that imagined existence. Several days a week, he drifted from his office in a building across the Tiber from the Palace of Justice to the Sala Di Prenza, picked up the press releases, schmoozed his new colleagues, and kept in touch with Donna Quando. She had been an invaluable source for the story he had written on the murders in Vatican City, which had been edited beyond recognition before it appeared in print. Once, his professional ego would have been wounded by that, but something like a philosophical mood seemed to be descending upon him. There was little integrity or the hunger and thirst for truth among the current representatives of the media. Neal sometimes thought of himself as a dinosaur, representative of a better time. He read around in Marcus Aurelius and went up to the Capitolio to study the old Stoic emperor on horseback, a mounted pagan in a post-Christian city. He glanced at the truncated printed version of his story and tossed the magazine into a trash can.

Subsequent events had piqued the curiosity of his editors, however. What in God's name was happening in Rome? With the appearance of the hitherto suppressed third secret of Fatima, the city had become a war zone. Admirari had pursued in a desultory fashion, more out of habit than passion, his acquaintance with Angela di Piperno and had been introduced to her editor, Richard John Neuhaus. The former Lutheran pastor, now a priest of the archdiocese of New York, seemed to have easy access to all the nerve points in the Vatican. Neal had not liked playing the role of tyro being instructed by the knowledgeable, wired-in cleric. He was not unhappy to learn that Neuhaus had left the city.

"Interesting fellow," he said to Angela.

"He didn't like you either."

"What did he say?"

She smiled. "You wouldn't want to hear."

"You're right."

Her reticence seemed flirty—I know something you don't know, so try and get it out of me—and feigned indifference seemed the best way to find out what the editor of *First Things* thought of him.

"Read 'The Public Square' if you want to know," Angela suggested.

This was the extended section at the back of each issue of the magazine where the editor opined on a bewildering number of topics with the ease of someone in the know.

"He's a little jealous of Father Fessio," Angela said.

Joseph Fessio was the founder of Ignatius Press and now provost of Tom Monahan's new university in Naples, Florida: Ave Maria. Ignatius Press had a corner on the English versions of Ratzinger's writings. Fessio had been a student of Ratzinger's, had kept up the acquaintance over the years, and now, according to Angela, was *persona muchissima grata* in the Vatican, accorded face-to-face chats with his old professor, now pope, whenever the lanky Jesuit popped into Rome.

"Did you read it?" Angela asked. They were in his office on the bank of the Tiber. Her reference was to the "Public Square" pages in the most recent issue of *First Things*.

"Not yet." He had glanced at the section, but the opening sentence about how Luce was currently dimly represented in Rome by a veteran of the mainstream media had been enough. No doubt Neuhaus had gone on to spell out the meaning of *luce*.

"I've met the most amazing person," Angela said, then stopped.

"Is that all?"

"I thought I'd tell you over lunch."

"Good idea."

In the interest of safety, he drove them out of the city, along the Via Cassia Antica, to a rustic ristorante where their table was under a trellis crawling with vines.

The amazing person Angela had met was Heather Adams. "They've stashed her in the convent inside the Vatican walls."

"Stashed her?" Neal said.

"She works for Ignatius Hannan." Angela paused. Neal nodded and went on sipping his wine, indicating that he knew the electronics tycoon.

Angela alternated between a glass of mineral water and the pricey Barolo that Neal had ordered, as if mixing wine and water would temper her excitement. Well, it was an exciting story, if true.

"True! Heather is the most innocent and honest person I've ever met."

This innocent and honest person had told Angela of the grisly goings-on at Empedocles Inc., the murder of Brendan Crowe ("He worked with Cardinal Maguire!"), her being entrusted with the third secret and taking it to her house where she turned it over to a CIA agent, Vincent Traeger.

"The rogue former agent," Neal murmured. This was the standard way of referring to the fugitive Traeger.

The secret was then stolen from Traeger's office safe, his secretary murdered, and the rogue former agent had flown to

Rome with Heather, who had been commissioned to turn over the bogus document that had set the world aflame.

"The authentic third secret's still missing?" Neal asked.

"Traeger hopes to get it from the man who stole it."

"And murder his secretary?"

Angela sat back. "I know, I know. It sounds like a bad movie starring Tom Hanks. If anyone other than Heather had told me all this I would have been skeptical, too."

These revelations spoiled Neal's lunch. It was one thing to be condescended to by Richard John Neuhaus, but to be scooped by a girl just out of college was worse.

"That pretty much matches what I've learned," he lied.

"From whom?"

He looked wise and, with one of his typing fingers, bisected his lips, ruby with Barolo.

"Neal, would you have told me what I've told you if you had known it and I hadn't?"

"Well, it's hardly a story for *First Things*."

It said something about his character that he managed to get back his appetite when the *saltimbocca alla romana* came. He ordered another bottle of Barolo, too, as if he had something to celebrate.

"You're going to have to drink that yourself," Angela said.

She had gotten a little tipsy. What a lovely thing she was. In another world, in the world he had inhabited when he was younger, Neal might have tried to benefit from her slightly impaired sobriety. In the present world, he did a fair imitation of an American journalist in Rome enjoying a sumptuous repast on his expense account, entertaining a young colleague with highlights from his past. He made the mistake of mentioning Lulu van Ackeren and Angela perked up.

"As she then was. Her married name is Martinelli."

"She broke your heart." There was soft concern in Angela's voice.

Who was being affected by the Barolo, this chit of a girl or Luce's current dim light in Rome?

"It was mutual," he said, and let it go at that.

⁂

In town, she asked to be dropped at a metro station. "I wouldn't advise that, Angela. Take a cab."

"Maybe I will."

"Do."

He put his car in the underground garage beneath his office building and walked to the Vatican, trying to look like a neutral as he hurried through the hostile crowds. At the gate, the Swiss Guards wouldn't let him through, but he persuaded them to call Donna Quando. Whatever she told them got him inside the Vatican.

She was waiting for him outside the Domus Sanctae Marthae. They crossed the cobbles to a little park and sat on a bench where, when the breeze freshened, they were lightly sprinkled with spray from the gurgling fountain. Neal gave her a quick version of what he had just heard from Angela di Piperno.

"Who told you that?" Donna asked.

"Not you, my dear. I thought we were friends."

She lay her lacquer-tipped fingers on his sleeve. "It's all true."

She told him of the exchange that Traeger was arranging and that she and Rodriguez would be monitoring it from a building higher up the Janiculum.

"I want to be there, Donna."

She thought about it. "Will you behave?"

"Only if provoked."

## ✣ II ✣

### "Oh, do get us in there."

Nate spent the first several hours of the flight in the front cabin with Laurel and Hardy, on a little jump seat. Laura busied herself in the galley, readying a meal—all prepared, just pop things into the microwave—while Ray sat, contemplatively sipping single malt scotch and looking down at the clouds. The trip had been set up on the spur of the moment, but what trips with Nate were not? Nate was convinced that what was going on in Rome could only benefit from his presence, and his general track record made that seem less presumptuous than it might have. Laura had put through a call to her brother John from the airport before takeoff.

"Things are a mess here, Laura."

"That's why we're coming. How is Heather?"

"Happy as a lark."

Get thee to a nunnery? Who knew? Maybe that was Heather's destiny, although Laura had been surprised when she found that Heather had been giving asylum to Vincent Traeger. Heather's hiding him had removed any smidgeon of doubt Laura might have had about Traeger's responsibility for what had happened to Brendan Crowe. Heather's protective attitude had, at least momentarily, suggested something more.

"Where will you stay?" John had wanted to know.

"The Hilton?" Laura said.

"Better not. That was one of the first targets of the rioters, I don't know why. I'll get you into the Villa Stritch."

"Where you used to live?"

"A secret, Laura. The pope is there now."

"Oh, do get us in there."

After the call, Laura said to Ray, "We may be staying with the pope."

"I thought he'd got out of there."

"Out of the Vatican. He's still in Rome."

"He might consider Avignon," Ray said wryly.

"Ho ho."

With everything ready to go in the galley, she took a seat next to Ray.

"This is great scotch. Want to try it?"

"Maybe later."

He passed her his glass. She took it and sipped. It confirmed her belief that scotch was a man's drink.

When Nate joined them, he just shook his head at the suggestion of a drink. It was the first chance Laura had had to tell him of the Villa Stritch. It was only when she added that the pope was there that he reacted.

"I want to meet him."

"We'll see."

"I want his blessing on Refuge of Sinners, Laura."

"I told John you'd like an audience." And so she had, weeks ago.

"Good. Good."

She went on to tell him of Traeger's thus far unsuccessful efforts to retrieve the third secret of Fatima file.

"I hope he's careful," Nate said. "The man who has it killed for it."

"More than once. Traeger has something the man wants more."

Nate had been involved in enough business negotiations to realize that many things could go wrong with even the most carefully planned deal. A quid pro quo could look pretty good until one began to think of getting the quid without giving up the quo. But what would that assassin want with the third secret of Fatima?

"Did you ask about Heather?" Nate asked.

"She's fine."

"She can fly back with us."

Laura fed Laurel and Hardy first, and then the three of them settled down to their meal.

"There ought to be some wine back there," Nate said.

"Red or white?"

"Not for me." He was on some kind of ascetic kick but wouldn't talk about it. He had found a spiritual director at Saint Anselm's, a Father Fortin, in whom he was well pleased. So pleased, he had talked with the abbot about assigning Fortin to Empedocles as resident chaplain.

"He said the college would fall apart without him."

"Father Fortin said that?"

Nate frowned. "No. The abbot."

After the meal, they dimmed the lights. Nate kept the light over his seat on so he could read *The Soul of the Apostolate*. Laura cranked back her seat and closed her eyes. Who would have thought when she went to work for Ignatius Hannan that she would get swept up in a one-man religious revival? She and Ray were celibate for the nonce, their form of wedding preparation. Nate had not seemed surprised when they told him their plans.

"You'll have to find your successor, Laura."

"Are you firing me?"

"But you'll be resigning."

"Marriage and resignation go together like a horse and carriage," Ray said.

❖

The weather got choppy as they approached the Continent. Nate went forward again and Ray dozed, thanks to the single malt scotch. The sun had been coming to meet them throughout the flight, and it was a clear bright morning as they came down the coast of Italy. They landed at Ciampino and John was there to meet them.

"We all set at the Villa Stritch?" Laura asked.

"All set."

As they drove to the villa, John said, "Traeger was there when I left, talking with a man named Dortmund."

"Who's Dortmund?"

"A former colleague, apparently."

✢ III ✢

"No one is more ruthless than a zealot."

"I still have the floor plans you drew for me," Anatoly said, increasing Remi Pouvoir's surprise at finding him at his elbow in the Vatican Archives.

"How did you get in here?" the little priest asked.

"I just followed your directions."

Pouvoir looked left and right, beyond Anatoly, then took his arm and drew him off behind a row of cabinets. "What you are looking for isn't here," he hissed.

"You're sure?"

"Of course I'm sure." Pouvoir thought. "I can show you where the reports should be."

"And I will trust that you are telling me the truth."

Fear is a remarkable aid to honest reactions. He could almost see the thoughts sliding through the little priest's mind. This was the man who had killed the secretary of state, Buffoni his aide, and then Cardinal Maguire. What restraint could be expected of a man with that kind of bloody record? Anatoly recalled the almost eager complicity with which Pouvoir had drawn up the floor plans and given him directions. Had he imagined that Anatoly would burn those sheets after they had served their purpose?

"I know the reports are not here. I have arranged to get them."

Pouvoir nodded. "I know, I know. You will make the exchange at the risk of your life."

"Explain."

Pouvoir's mood of eager complicity was back.

"First of all, there is Rodriguez and his people. They will have an excellent vantage point to the proceedings."

"And you think they will try to take me out?"

"There are others," Pouvoir said.

Others from the CIA were in Rome, their mission to apprehend Traeger. "He is wanted for a murder committed in the States."

Anatoly smiled. He took pride in the way he had neutralized Traeger after they had played their cat and mouse game in New Hampshire. Of course the pursuit of Traeger would continue once they knew he had escaped to Rome. But that meant Traeger was at risk, not him.

"You could be a target of opportunity." But Pouvoir simply said it, laying no stress on it. "The Confraternity of Pius IX will give anything to get hold of the third secret of Fatima." He peered at Anatoly. "You have it?"

"I have it."

Pouvoir stepped back to study Anatoly. The little archivist's fear was waning. He and Anatoly were allies, were they not? Had he not awaited him through the years, and helped when his help was asked? Of course, Pouvoir had thought he was acting in an official capacity, that Chekovsky had run out of patience pursuing the reports in a diplomatic way and had decided on direct action. Anatoly had encouraged that inference; it had got him the floor plans, the incriminating floor plans, as Pouvoir must now realize they were.

"And Chekovsky?"

Pouvoir was surprised. "You would know more about that than I."

He let it go. "What about the confraternity?"

"I know their minds. They would not consider the use of force in taking that file from you as a breach of morality. No one is more ruthless than a zealot. Jean-Jacques Trepanier has come to join forces with Catena. He is a greater zealot than any of them. Think. You have stolen a message from the Mother of God. What moral prohibitions could protect you?"

"They know where the exchange is to take place?" Anatoly did not like this.

"They have heard." He passed a thin hand over his sunken cheek. "There could be others there as well, I think. The electronics billionaire Ignatius Hannan has come to Rome with his staff."

Anatoly was not surprised that the proposed exchange should have drawn such attention. One of the reasons for drawing Traeger to the rooftop on what he did not realize was a trial run was to give the planned exchange a chance to be more widely known. There were too many people too deeply interested to expect that it could have been kept secret. He didn't want it to be a secret. He wanted many rival and competing interests to be represented there. Traeger he trusted. He doubted that Traeger had divulged the plan for the exchange. Obviously Anatoly had not been the only one to observe him come onto the rooftop of the North American College. If no one else, Rodriguez would have kept himself informed of what Traeger was doing.

But it was not from such people that he felt danger would come. Chekovsky's interest in the reports of the assassination attempt on John Paul II had been too intense, too persistent, to be merely a diplomatic interest, the activity of a man representing his country. His country! With that animal Putin in charge of the government. The others Pouvoir mentioned were interested in the document he was willing to exchange. Only he and Chekovsky seemed interested in what he would receive for it. No, if there was to be danger for him, it would come from Chekovsky.

"I appreciate your help," he said to Pouvoir. "As always."

"Is that why you came here?"

"In part. But also to remind you of your helpfulness in drawing up those floor plans."

"Then you will know your way out."

"First, another favor. Where is the apartment Rodriguez will use for observation?"

Pouvoir told him. "I don't think he would harm you."

"You might want to tell them to be on the alert this afternoon."

❖

Anatoly moved easily through the angry mobs that thronged the streets. They would consider him one of them. Perhaps he was. He crossed the Tiber, sat on a ledge, and telephoned Traeger.

"Two thirty."

"Tomorrow morning?"

"This afternoon. Come alone."

## ✤ IV ✤

### "It's a priest."

Neal Admirari had just settled himself for forty winks when Donna Quando called.

"H hour approaches."

He actually had to think before he understood. "When?"

"I'll meet you in the penthouse apartment." She gave him Ladislaw's address.

"I'm on my way."

And on the way, unbidden thoughts came. The realization that the gap between his age and Angela's precluded any of the dalliance that, for better or worse, characterized his professional life, invited speculation about Donna. There was no impediment of that sort with her, but that seemed a remote premise for anything amorous. Was he wrong to think that she enjoyed his company? It had been a pleasant surprise when he first met his contact in the Vatican. He had kept that first appointment with the fear that he would be meeting some nunnish lady who would see him as simply a conduit for favorable publicity. But the meeting had been like a date.

"What's a nice girl like you doing working in the Vatican?" Neal had asked the second time they met, outside the Vatican.

"Who said I'm a nice girl?"

"I just did."

Her smile formed slowly, revealing a lovely row of teeth, one at a time. "You even look like a journalist."

"It's the lighting here," he said.

"Here" was Ambrogio's in the Borgo Pio. Cats slithered around among the tables, and birds perched, defying the cats as they swooped in for fallen crumbs. A carafe of the house red was on the table before them, better than he expected, and they were doing justice to it. She sat across from him with the air of a woman who had the afternoon before her. When they exchanged phone numbers and e-mail addresses, to facilitate their arrangement, there seemed to be more than business involved.

"What's Mr. Quando do?"

"The same thing Mrs. Admirari does."

"There is no Mrs. Admirari."

"I know."

Well, well. But it had turned out to be just a get-acquainted meeting. He decided that she was simply the kind of woman who could not help being a woman. She reminded him of Lulu van Ackeren, of unhappy memory. Well, not entirely unhappy. The trouble with Lulu was that there had been a Mr. van Ackeren, something he only learned when he had proposed. They lay side by side while Lulu told him the sad story. She had been turned down for an annulment. She might have been providing him with a way to get off the hook. He had been devastated. As soon as he had gone to bed with Lulu, he regretted it. She was not, he told himself, that kind of girl. He was eager to make an honest woman of her. Instead, he had got the story of her first marriage, still undissolved in the mind of the Church.

They tried to think of ways around the problem. They both knew priests who would be delighted to defy the Church's marriage laws. Lulu knew a canon lawyer who told her she could grant herself an annulment. He sounded like a Muslim. I divorce you, I divorce you, I divorce you. But neither of them could bring themselves to be such scofflaws. At the time Neal had been writing for the *NCR*, and so had she, except in her case the *R* stood for *Register* and in his for *Reporter*. God knows orthodoxy was not part of his job description there. His stories had echoed the angry dissent from official Church teaching. But in his heart of hearts he was the Catholic boy his parents had raised. So he and Lulu were stymied. Their love withered on the bough, flaring up from time to time, but each time bringing them to their insoluble problem. And then Lulu had solved it by marrying Martinelli.

"Sad," Donna said, when eventually he told her all this. But she was smiling as she said it. "Is that what you call a line?"

He was hurt. Of course she was right. Lulu might very well be the way past Donna's defenses. Maybe hers was a delayed reaction. Maybe this invitation to the penthouse allegedly to observe from on high the exchange to take place on the roof of the North American College was at least partially a ploy.

And so with a light heart he entered the building, found there was no elevator, and climbed what seemed ten thousand stairs to the penthouse. He had called from below. She was waiting in the open doorway. All business.

"Come."

She led him across the room to where open windows gave onto a balcony. He started out and she stopped him.

"No, no. Not yet. We don't want to scare them away."

He stepped back.

"I have two thirty," Donna said. "What do you have?"

He pushed back his sleeve. "The same."

And then a bell sounded.

She looked at him, he looked at her, they both checked their cell phones. The second time they realized it was the doorbell.

"Would you see who it is?"

Neal went to the door, looked through the peephole, and turned. "It's a priest."

"A priest?"

She came across the room and pulled open the door.

He was tall, taller than the cassock he wore. When Donna opened the door, he pushed it in, shut it behind him, and said, "You're coming with me."

He was holding a gun.

❖ V ❖

### He toppled backward into the yielding air.

Dortmund tossed *Sense and Sensibility* onto the little metal table beside his lawn chair under the trees on the grounds of the Villa Stritch. He had just ordered Traeger to call off the exchange with Anatoly and Traeger had refused.

"With all respect, you're not my boss any longer."

"I'm not anyone's boss! I thought you considered me a friend."

Traeger nodded. A tender moment. But he intended to keep his appointment with Anatoly. He explained to Dortmund that, bleak a hope as it was, getting possession of the missing third secret was the Vatican's only possible way of lifting the siege.

"It won't work, Vincent."

"What else is there?"

Dortmund reached for Jane Austen, then withdrew his hand. He looked as if he wished he had a basin of water in which to wash it and his other.

"Everyone knows of the planned exchange," he said.

"I know."

"Vincent, the two of you will provide target practice for a number of competing forces."

Traeger knew that. At first, Anatoly had seemed the great danger. The disenchanted former KGB agent was determined to expose the role Chekovsky had played in the assassination attempt on John Paul II. When he had asked Traeger if the now ambassador of Russia had been involved in that plot, Traeger had looked him in the eyes and said nothing. There are many ways to respond to a question. Anatoly saw in this some vindication of his life, pursuing a logic Traeger could not follow. What he did understand was the sense his old foe had that the world had passed him by, moved into another and madder phase that rendered the lives they had both led absurd. To what end all the killings and subverting and maneuvering with an adversary for domination in a black-and-white world? The world had become gray. The world was colorless. Mindless mobs took to the street, no longer the convenient dupes of higher purposes, but possessed of religious zeal. It was one thing to risk one's life for what one considered a great cause, but what can you make of people who voluntarily blow themselves up in crowds, fly airplanes into high-rise buildings, and are willing pawns of a heaven promised to the terrorist zealot?

Anatoly would see their meeting on the roof of the North American College as a Götterdämmerung, the twilight of all their former gods. It would be in a way his manner of making a bomb of himself. In that scenario, Traeger was merely a supernumerary, expendable. He had known that.

But he also knew that what Dortmund said was true. How had the exchange become so widely known? Heather had known of it. Piacere knew because Rodriguez would have told him. And the agency knew. Dortmund had been approached at the Villa Stritch by three clean-shaven and cold-eyed men who had thought Dortmund had been kidnapped and was being held prisoner, somehow the victim of Traeger.

"They want you," Dortmund said.

"When this is over, I'll turn myself in. There's no case against me."

"But will you live to stand trial?"

He was accused of murdering Brendan Crowe. More painfully, he was accused of murdering Bea!

Like Anatoly, he was on his own. Then the call came and he headed for the rendezvous.

❖

Lev was in his little windowed gatehouse. Traeger looked a question and received his answer with a glance. He entered the building.

The doors of the chapel were open and the sound of organ music swelled and then the seminarians began coming out, two by two, wearing cassocks and surplices, the music making them seem on parade. Traeger pressed against the wall and they went by him. There seemed to be hundreds of the young men. And then they were gone, dispersed, to their rooms, wherever. Traeger continued down the hall to the elevator and soon was rising toward his meeting with Anatoly.

On the top floor, he went up a half flight of steps to the closed door to the roof. He grasped the knob and pulled it open. After the dimness of the building, the sunlight momentarily blinded him. A great ball already settling west. At the far end of the roof were three figures, a man and woman and a priest. What were they doing here? Something must have gone wrong.

He turned to go, but the priest hurried toward him. "Wait!"

The priest was Anatoly. And he held a gun.

"Come meet our witnesses. Do you have it?"

"Do you?"

Anatoly reached beneath the buttons of his soutane and produced a large envelope.

"Come."

"You shouldn't be here," Traeger said to Donna Quando when he got to her.

"We were forced to come here," the man cried. "I am a member of the press. This is outrageous."

Anatoly looked at him with contempt. Neal Admirari then identified himself as Rome correspondent for *Time*.

❖

The noon Mass at the North American College was a pontifical of sorts, of the newer sort, said by a visiting bishop, but Trepanier in cassock and surplice among the seminarians and student priests in the facing choir stalls that filled the nave of the chapel in the North American College offered up the pain he felt at what had been done to the liturgy since Vatican II. The best that could be said for it was that the Mass was valid and licit—he had no sympathy for those who condemned the Novus Ordo as a breach with tradition as decisive as had been the alteration of the ordination ceremony by the Anglican Church. But finally, mercifully, it was over, and Trepanier joined the procession that filed from the chapel. The sight of Traeger pressed against the wall as they went by made his heart leap. How easily he might not have noticed the man.

Trepanier dropped out of the procession when it turned off toward the refectory, letting the files of clerics go by him while he looked intently toward the corridor from which they had turned. He saw Traeger hurry away, as if he had been freed from the procession by a kind of Crack the Whip. Trepanier scampered back the way he had come and rounded the corner just in time to see Traeger enter the elevator.

As he watched the numbers above the door light one after the other, he sent up a prayer of thanksgiving for the inspiration that had led him to seek a room here at the North American College. At the time, it had been proximity to the Vatican that commended the switch from the guest room at the Confraternity of Pius IX. He was certain that he had been sent here to witness the repossession of the third secret of Fatima! He was on a mission.

The elevator stopped at the top floor, the very floor on which Trepanier's room was. Rather than wait for it to descend, he took the staircase. After two flights, he regretted this decision, but to alter it would have taken more time, so he pressed on.

When he emerged onto the top floor, he stopped. He listened. Nothing. He stepped forward and saw nothing but an empty corridor. Perplexed as to what to do now, he began to walk. That was when he noticed the door with "Roof" on it. With a certitude that defied all logic, he knew that that was where Traeger had gone.

He pulled the door open and went up another short flight, at the top of which was another door. His breath was coming in short, excited gasps. He could feel the proximity of Sister Lucia's document. He opened the door only wide enough to slip through. At the sight of the people Traeger had joined, he took up his vigil behind a table on which a collapsed umbrella gave him some concealment and a good view of the proceedings now under way.

❖

Anatoly held up the envelope. "This is the famous third secret of Fatima, missing from the Vatican Archives. I am exchanging it with Agent Traeger for the report on the attempted assassination of Pope John Paul II." The words might have been rehearsed. Anatoly spoke them loudly, as if others might be listening.

"Where did you get that?" Neal Admirari asked.

"Neal," Donna Quando said. "Please shut up."

The ceremony proceeded with great formality. Traeger extended his envelope, Anatoly extended his. Each grasped the other's with his free hand. It might have been a drill by a rifle squad. The two men stepped back, each in possession of what he had come for.

That was when Traeger felt the pain in his shoulder. He spun away from Anatoly, who turned toward where the shot had come from, holding his useless pistol. Then Anatoly began to run toward the doorway. Other shots were ripping into the stone floor of the roof, sending shards in all directions. The shots were following Anatoly.

❖

Suddenly a soutaned figure sprang from behind a table, pushing it aside as he did so, and fairly flew across the roof toward the wounded Traeger. It was Trepanier, and he had eyes only for the envelope Traeger still held, the document he had longed to see for years, the object of all his hopes and fears. He picked up speed as he neared Traeger, who saw him coming. Just as Trepanier lunged for the envelope, the wounded Traeger stumbled to one side. The priest's momentum carried him on. He had turned and was facing them when he hit the ledge bordering the roof. It caught him behind the knees. His hands flew up, a look of terror took possession of his face, and then he toppled backward into the yielding air.

The sound of his dying scream was audible despite the noise of an approaching chopper.

⸎

Anatoly got to the door and through it without being hit and found Lev waiting for him. He pulled the roof door shut and began ripping off the cassock while hanging on to the envelope he had gotten from Traeger.

"Get me out of here."

"Follow me," Lev said.

They clambered down the flight of stairs and ran past the elevator, down a narrow corridor to a service elevator. Lev did not get in.

"It will take you to the basement. You can leave from there."

The doors closed on Lev, and Anatoly descended. It was all he could do not to tear open the envelope. He felt triumphant. Soon all would be clear. He would be vindicated.

The elevator lurched slowly down. When it reached the basement, the doors slid open. Two men were waiting. Anatoly walked into their fire as he emerged from the elevator. As he fell, one of the gunmen grabbed the envelope and the two of them hurried off, leaving the dying Anatoly on the basement floor. The last thing he saw on earth was all his hopes disappearing out a door to the parking lot.

⸎

The white chopper lifted from the Vatican heliport, flew low behind the dome of Saint Peter's so as not to be seen by the mob in the square in front of the basilica, and within minutes reached the roof of the North American College, where it settled in a great rush of the wind it created, which sent buckets and chairs and tables and other loose objects scattering about the rooftop. Neal Admirari watched from where he lay, pressed against the ledge of the building. Some feet from him, Donna was tending to the wounded Traeger.

The great rotor continued to turn after the cab doors opened. Carlos Rodriguez hopped out and ran to Traeger.

"Did you get it?" he asked.

Traeger handed him the envelope he had received from Anatoly.

The rooftop door opened and three men burst through it,

coming across the roof. Two were armed; the other was flapping his credentials at Rodriguez.

"U.S. Government," he called.

Rodriquez glanced at the credentials while the other two converged on Traeger.

"Vincent Traeger, you're under arrest," one of them said.

The other said, for Rodriguez's benefit, "We have an extradition order."

"Where are you taking him?" Donna demanded.

"Now? To the American Embassy."

She turned to Rodriguez. "Lodge a protest immediately."

Neal Admirari, on his feet, approached the group, looking warily at the spinning rotor.

"Press," he announced. "Neal Admirari of *Time* magazine. Could I see the extradition order?"

"Just drop by the embassy."

Rodriguez stepped forward. "I'm taking this man to the infirmary. He's wounded, but then I suppose you know all about that."

Donna urged Traeger toward the chopper. The three men considered what to do.

"What infirmary?" one of them asked.

"In the Vatican."

Traeger managed to get into the chopper, with Donna's help. His arm felt useless and he was losing blood.

"Come on, Neal," Donna called. "Get in."

The reporter looked at the machine, at the rotor, at the cab. He shook his head.

"I'll walk."

# EPILOGUE

Was it too late?

In the weeks that followed, a militant mood swept over the countries of Europe and a belated effort was made to control those immigrants who had swarmed onto the Continent and become intent on altering it to their imported beliefs. Concessions had been made. Craven concessions. Rulers and populace, their own faith and morals all but gone, had been intimidated by these newcomers with their fierce demands who condemned the societies into which they had come.

But the rioting and burning and pillaging and iconoclastic assault on churches and statues and images so familiar they had become invisible had at last stirred some semblance of the spirit that sent Don Juan of Austria into the Battle of Lepanto and had animated the defenders of Vienna against invading Islam.

An eager willingness to interpret the Crusades as a Christian assault on Islam was replaced by the memory of the Islamic invasions of Europe. It was now clear that the enemy was within.

As if their raison d'être was at last made clear, armed forces swept the marauders from the streets and squares of Europe. Laws were abrogated, immigrants expelled from the Continent by the boatload from Mediterranean ports.

The date of Oriana Fallaci's death was declared a national holiday in country after country.

Our Lady of Fatima may not have predicted this ultimate conflict, but the Catholic atheist had.

The European Union was dissolved.

The euro became obsolete. Once more colorful lire, pesetas, marks, and francs were restored as currency in and between reinvigorated nations.

Sheepishly, at first women and children, but then men, too, in increasing numbers, returned to the faith of their fathers. Cynics spoke of a new puritanism when pornography was banned and abortion made illegal.

In Jerusalem, Israelis and Palestinians, representatives of two aggrieved peoples, abandoned by their erstwhile supporters, sat down, and at last brought the seemingly interminable peace process to a conclusion tolerable to both.

The governments of the Middle East protested the treatment of their returning coreligionists and introduced resolution after resolution in the General Assembly of the United Nations. Nothing came of them. The West had grown weary of being instructed in morals by governments who sponsored terrorism and jihad. When bloody civil war broke out between various Islamic factions in their countries, these delegates, accused of infidelity, one by one resigned and sought asylum in New York. They were refused and flown back to the tender mercies of their countrymen.

Was it too late? Could the spine of Europe, of the West, stiffen sufficiently to carry the counterrevolution through to the end?

❖

The pope returned to Vatican City. As before, he could look out on the square before the Basilica of Saint Peter filled with pilgrims and penitents and peaceful tourists. When the Vicar of Christ on earth raised his hand in blessing, the blessing went forth far beyond those before him. It went out, in the phrase *urbi et orbi*, to the city and to the world.

Laws and armies and force were nothing without trust and belief in Almighty God and the intercession of his Blessed Mother. The struggle, as always, was with principalities and powers. The Holy Father's learned Angelus messages, applauded when given, later studied and understood by some, provided the only fitting rationale for the legal and social reforms that were under way.

❧

Dortmund, before returning to his cottage on Chesapeake Bay, came by the Vatican infirmary to say good-bye to Traeger.

"You're lucky to be alive," he said, taking a chair by Traeger's bed.

"Who isn't?"

"You may be right."

"I'm told they're dropping the charges against me," Traeger said.

"Who brought them?"

"Some rogue prosecutor."

A chuckle from Dortmund was equivalent to a guffaw from anyone else.

"Come see me when you get back, Vincent."

After Dortmund left, Traeger wished that the thought of going home was more attractive. Poor Bea was gone, brutally killed by Anatoly, one more notch on his assassin's weapon. There would be no more victims. Rodriguez told him of the discovery of Anatoly's body at the back entrance of the North American College.

"No clues," he added.

"Did he still have the report I gave him?"

"No, he didn't."

"There's your clue, Carlos."

❧

Chekovsky simply nodded distractedly when the report was brought to him.

"Just leave it. I'll look at it when I have time."

When his aide left, closing the door, Chekovsky snatched up the envelope and brought out the sheaf it contained. He glanced at the first page, shuffled the others, then threw them on the desk. All he had gotten was a printout of a preliminary report, not that which had been contained in the Vatican Archives. But what he had made him more determined to get what he did not have. He had to know whether the mention of Chekovsky in this preliminary report had survived into the final one.

He shredded the document before leaving the embassy, taking the resulting confetti home to his apartment, where he burnt it in his fireplace. Burning paper creates a clean smell and little smoke.

⚜

"I congratulate your Eminence on the recovery of the sacred document," Chekovsky said to Cardinal Piacere when he met with the acting secretary of state some days later.

"An almost miraculous recovery. I understand we are indebted to you, Excellency."

"To me?" Chekovsky said.

"The man Anatoly was working for you, was he not?"

A denial would deprive him of the cardinal's surprising gratitude, but an affirmation could lead he knew not where.

"The Holy See can always count on the cooperation of my country."

"Russia seems to have been spared the chaos other countries have suffered."

"Thank God," Chekovsky said. When in Rome . . .

"And His Blessed Mother. She seems to have a special concern for Russia."

"She has always been held in veneration by us."

"A converted Russia could lead to an extended era of peace."

"Converted to Rome?"

Piacere smiled and steepled his fingers. "Union would not mean the end of Orthodoxy, that beautiful liturgy, that long tradition. Have you read Vladimir Soloviev?"

"Not as yet," Chekovsky said carefully. "Your Eminence, I would like to renew an old request."

"The reports on the attempted assassination of John Paul II?"

"How can you keep so many things in your mind! But yes, I mean the reports."

"They, too, were stolen, Your Excellency."

"Your Eminence, who on earth would want them?"

"Who indeed? But I am informed by one of our senior archivists, Remi Pouvoir, that they have been returned. Another miracle perhaps."

"So my request has an object?" Chekovsky said, as calmly as he could.

"The Holy Father has agreed that all these reports should be turned over to you. With one proviso." He unsteepled his hands and lay them side by side on the desk. "They must all be destroyed."

"Of that, Your Eminence, you may be absolutely certain. I will oversee their destruction myself. When may I have them?"

"At once. When you leave, Father Ladislaw will take you to Father Pouvoir and the transfer can be made."

❧

Zelda Lewis Faust insisted on sponsoring a reception after the ceremony and Laura could find no charitable way of refusing. Her brother John was flown in to say the nuptial Mass and witness the exchange of vows between Laura and Ray Sinclair. Nate Hannan gave away the bride, leading her down the aisle to the waiting groom. During the ceremony, Zelda wept audibly, a wife who had lost two husbands, at least one of them permanently, perhaps both. Nate Hannan had hired an investigator, a man named Wallenstein, who came with the highest of recommendations, to find Gabriel Faust. One of the objects of the quest was to restore Faust to the bosom of his wife.

❧

From his hotel room overlooking the harbor at Pantelleria, Gabriel Faust watched a small craft fighting the current to gain entrance. After almost an hour it succeeded, slipping through the narrow opening into the calm waters within. It seemed a metaphor of his own situation.

But peace and security are cloying. After years of struggle, sailing in choppy waters, it was an equivocal blessing to be in port at last. He missed the excitement of uncertainty, he missed the pull of an unknown future. He missed Zelda.

Inactivity brought on unwelcome bouts of thinking, against which he had no defense. His new wealth, however questionably acquired, existed in Zurich databases. The check he had gotten from Trepanier had gone swiftly into another account and now underwrote the only credit card he used. Barring the logical possibility of a general and absolute collapse of the Western economy, he had not a worry in the world.

There was little opportunity for dissolute living on Pantelleria. The women were either ugly, chaste, or married. There were no brothels. The bars closed at ten o'clock! He missed Zelda.

Without a worry in the world, he worried. Moth and rust might not consume, nor thief break in and steal, but all that money gave him only a fragile sense of security. Did it really matter that he was rich? Once, wealth would have meant mobility, at least. Now he did not dare venture from Pantelleria. No one would dream he was here. If only Zelda were with him.

He missed her inconsequential chatter. He missed her vacant, receptive smile when he talked to her. He missed her warm, plush body against his own.

And he missed an audience. He felt like a magician who had performed the ultimate trick—in darkness. To an empty theater. He longed to confide in someone what a coup he had brought off. Not just any ear would do, of course. Only Zelda's, really, would serve.

At night, after the hotel bar closed and he returned to his room and the solitary continuance of his drinking, he explored ways of bringing Zelda to this island. All of them involved unacceptable risks.

❖

"Doctor Faust?"

The man who had sat beside Gabriel on the bench overlooking the slips in which boats bobbed rhythmically to the gentle movement of the water looked out on that nautical scene when he spoke. Gabriel did not recognize him.

"Have we met?" he asked.

"At last."

Gabriel studied the man's profile, which looked like a fist. His hat, all wrong for this climate, was pushed back and sweat lay damp upon his brow.

"Wallenstein." Still looking out at the harbor, he thrust a hand at Gabriel. Gabriel took it.

"American?"

"Whoever isn't wants to be nowadays. Of course you know why I'm here."

"Tell me."

"Ignatius Hannan."

"Ah. What made you come here?" Faust asked with a sinking heart.

"Of all places? I had an interesting conversation with Miki Inagaki."

*Et tu, Brute?* But what, apart from a prosperous business relationship, friendship of a sort, and honor among thieves, did Inagaki owe him?

Wallenstein sighed. "Ah, the power of money. It can buy anything."

"I wouldn't know."

"Ho ho, Doctor Faust, let me put a problem to you."

Wallenstein's problem was, in effect, whose money he should take. He could of course, having located Gabriel Faust, bill Ignatius Hannan for having done so. On the other hand . . .

"I should think fifty-fifty would leave us both content," Wallenstein said.

"You could take half my money and still turn me in."

Wallenstein turned his sad, pouched eyes on Gabriel. "To what end?"

"To get Hannan's money as well as half of mine."

Wallenstein's eyes seemed to go up and down like cherries in a slot machine. "That's true."

Would he have thought of it if Gabriel had not mentioned it? The next day, after Gabriel had instructed the bank in Zurich, Wallenstein returned with the local constabulary. Gabriel was under arrest. He would be flown back to the United States to face his accuser.

⁂

In the Carmel of Philadelphia, a new member was being received into the community. For the occasion, she was adorned as a bride, all in white, with a bridal veil, advancing down the aisle to accept her mystical spouse. The bishop on his throne in the sanctuary awaited her. Off to the right, behind a grille, was the community the candidate soon would join.

Traeger sat in a back pew watching Heather Adams go up the aisle. She might have been walking away from him, like the ending of *The Third Man.* Nonsense, of course. There had never been anything between them. He tried to think of her as his sister, and almost succeeded.

❖

The governments of France, Germany, Italy, and Spain brought a joint action suit against Fatima Now! The charge was inciting the violence that was only now subsiding in their countries. Ignatius Hannan asked his lawyers to represent the organization of the late Jean-Jacques Trepanier. In the event, the plaintiffs were awarded a sum equal to the assets of Fatima Now! Even the buildings and land had to be sold. *Sic transit gloria mundi.* The judgment gave even Ignatius Hannan pause.

He had not been granted a private audience with the Holy Father, either at the Villa Stritch or after the pontiff returned to Vatican City. Later, thanks to an assist from Cardinal Piacere and the invocation of Kevin Flannery, S.J., John Burke intervening, Hannan was included in a group of fifty, each of whom received a rosary and a papal benediction. Hannan settled an enormous amount on the Pontifical Academy of Saint Thomas Aquinas.

"PASTA," Father Burke said.

"I've eaten," said Ignatius Hannan.

❖

In the Hotel Columbus on the Via della Conciliazione, Mr. and Mrs. Raymond Sinclair snuggled in a narrow bed.

"Returned to the scene of the crime," Ray whispered in Laura's ear.

"It's no longer a crime."

"It's better."

❖

In the Sala di Prenza, Ferdinand the Bull parried the weak thrusts of the representatives of the media credentialed to the Holy See.

"Ask a question," Angela di Piperno urged Neal Admirari.

"What's the point?"

The recent unpleasantness that had wracked the cities of Europe and the Middle East, which had made Rome itself, including the Vatican City, a war zone, was dismissed as a mere bagatelle.

"Like the Reformation," Neal grumbled.

"Can I buy you a drink?" Angela asked, when the charade was over.

"After I buy you one."

They drove out to the rustic ristorante on the Via Cassia Antica.

"Our place," Angela said, fluttering her lashes prettily.

Neal patted her hand. She was only a quarter of a century younger than he was.

"Do you ever see Donna Quando?" Angela asked, sipping a glass of white wine.

"Only by daylight."

"Good."

He touched the rim of his glass to hers.

**Don't miss the page-turning suspense, intriguing characters, and unstoppable action that keep readers coming back for more from these bestselling authors...**

Tom Clancy
Robin Cook
Patricia Cornwell
Clive Cussler
Dean Koontz
J.D. Robb
John Sandford

**Your favorite thrillers and suspense novels come from Berkley.**

**penguin.com**